"What's it about?" Ron Joffe focused on the big article his editor was pitching him.

"Have you ever heard of a delicatessen called Bloom's?" she asked.

What New Yorker hadn't? He shopped at Bloom's regularly. It was a terrific store. It sold more bagels than Broadway sold tickets to shows—and Bloom's bagels probably got better reviews, too. He'd bought his own significant share of those bagels over the years.

But still...*Bloom's?* What the hell would he write about a deli?

"Bloom's isn't just a deli," she went on. "It's a huge business. One year ago Ben Bloom, the president of the company, died. I want you to get past the food and write about the business. One year after Ben Bloom's death, how is Bloom's doing? Are their finances shaky now that Ben Bloom is gone? There's your story, Joffe. A business story about food. You're just the one to write it."

He disagreed, but disagreeing with her wasn't something a *Gotham* staffer—even an esteemed weekly columnist—did out loud.

"Okay," he said. With a forced smile he backed out of her office. Backing out was a joke among his colleagues. Someone had once dubbed his editor the *Gotham* Goddess, and someone else had said it was bad luck to turn one's back on a goddess, so they all remained facing her when they left her office. Ron wasn't superstitious, but he knew better than to tempt fate.

Oddly enough, though, as he retraced his steps to his own office, contemplating his new assignment, he couldn't shake the eerie notion that his editor had just given his fate a karmic realignment. *Bloom's.* A fabulous deli, the death of the head honcho, family intrigue involving the granddaughter with the amazing eyes who'd replaced him. Food, money, heirs, power. Tradition. Schmaltz.

His nonexistent fancy was definitely turning.

Also by JUDITH ARNOLD

HEART ON THE LINE
LOOKING FOR LAURA

JUDITH ARNOLD

LOVE IN
Bloom's

MIRA®

ISBN 0-7783-2114-2

LOVE IN BLOOM'S

www.MIRABooks.com

Printed in U.S.A.

To Carolyn, the best sister in the universe

ACKNOWLEDGMENTS

Enormous thanks to my agent, Charles Schlessiger,
for sharing his dreams with me, literally.
Thanks also to my editor, Beverley Sotolov, and the
entire MIRA staff for their support and encouragement.
Finally, thanks to my parents, my husband, my sons,
my aunts, uncles, cousins, in-laws, nieces and
nephews and grandparents, for teaching me
the meaning of family.

Prologue

It wasn't Ron Joffe's kind of story. But he was a professional, and *Gotham Magazine* paid him a generous salary—a significant portion of which he'd spent in Bloom's over the years. So what the hell. He'd poke around and see if he could stir something up. Maybe he'd buy a few snacks and include them in his expense account as research costs.

Bloom's—the ultimate delicatessen, a hallowed New York institution, a tourist mecca, practically a landmark—in trouble? Yeah, there could be a story here. A New York story, just the sort of scoop *Gotham*'s readers would devour as greedily as they devoured their Bloom's bagels smeared with Bloom's cream cheese and crowned with Bloom's smoked salmon.

Standing outside the store, which occupied half an Upper Broadway block, he shielded his eyes against the glare of April sunshine and scrutinized the clutter in the showcase windows: an abundance, a glut, a veritable cornucopia of kosher-style cuisine. Bloom's marketed not just food but memories, nostalgia, the myth of Eastern European Jewish immigrants back in the olden days, preparing similar food for their loved ones.

Of course, most of those immigrants couldn't have afforded the kind of food sold at Bloom's. But the people shopping in Bloom's today believed they were buying what their grandmothers might have served their families fresh off the boat. And those people shopped and shopped and shopped. In the five minutes he'd been staring at the window, at least a dozen people had gone into the store, well-dressed, well-heeled Manhattanites with money to burn.

Three more customers entered in the time it took him to turn his back on the window and saunter down the sidewalk and around the corner to the entry of the Bloom Building, a large apartment tower built above the store. On its third floor were Bloom's business offices.

His appointment was with Deirdre Morrissey, but he hoped to talk to some of the third-floor offices' other occupants: Jay Bloom, Myron Finkel, and of course Julia Bloom, who was allegedly responsible for the store's current state, whatever that might be. The person he'd *really* like to talk to was Ida Bloom, the Queen Mother of the company. Rumor had it that Ida Bloom was terrifying.

Ron loved scary people, especially scary women. They got his blood pumping and his brain firing. His own grandmother used to petrify him. She'd been short—under five feet tall—and she'd had a voice like a crow's, dark and nasal, and fingers like claws. "Ronnie, get over here this minute!" she'd caw, and he'd want to crawl under her bed in her stuffy, tiny apartment in the Bronx. But he'd always come when she called him, and listen as she screeched about his transgressions: "You left these dirt smudges all over my clean towels. What'sa matter with you? Are you an idiot? You're supposed to wash your hands thoroughly. You know what that means, Ronnie? *Thoroughly.* Now I'm going to have to do another load of laundry."

For years, the word *thoroughly* had caused a chill to ripple down his spine. He was older now, though. He could handle the word *thoroughly*—and he could handle terrifying women. He was ready for Ida Bloom.

He didn't think he'd get a crack at her. His research informed him she'd recently kissed her eighty-eighth birthday goodbye. If her relatives were smart, they probably kept her as far from the business as possible.

He entered the building, pressed the button for the elevator and got in. For some reason, he had hoped it would smell the way Bloom's smelled: crusty, oniony, like some fantasy grandmother's kitchen. It smelled of lemon air freshener. He tried not to wrinkle his nose.

Out at the third floor. He found himself in a wide hallway with a few chairs and couches, lamps, Marc Chagall prints in cheap frames on the walls—a reception area, except it was a little too long and narrow. He patted his jacket to make sure his notepad and pen were tucked into the inner pocket, patted another pocket to make sure he had his tape recorder, then strode down the hall in search of Deirdre Morrissey's office. According to his research, Deirdre had been Ben Bloom's assistant when he was alive and running the place. Assistants like her often knew more than anyone else about what was going on.

He located her office door and rapped on it. The door swung inward, and he found himself standing eye-to-eye with a red-haired amazon. She was nearly six feet tall and had a bony face, her freckled skin stretched taut over acute cheekbones. Her teeth reminded him of Bugs Bunny's.

"Hi, I'm Ron Joffe from *Gotham Magazine,*" he introduced himself, producing a business card and handing it to her.

"Oh…" She glanced at her watch. He glanced at his. He was three minutes early. "Let me just run some papers next door, and then we'll talk," she promised him.

He stepped out of her way, and she left her office. He realized she wasn't quite an amazon after all; her feet were crammed into shoes with three-inch heels. She seemed too old to be wearing such uncomfortable-looking shoes. Not that she was *old*—he'd place her in her mid-forties at most. But women that age, at least the sensible, competent ones, tended to be smart enough to recognize the relationship between pain-free shoes and a mellow temperament.

He watched her half swagger, half stagger toward the door at the end of the hallway. She opened it and said, "Julia, you're going to need these forms."

Peeking past Deirdre, Ron caught a glimpse of a woman seated at a large desk in the center of the office. A pale complexion, straight black hair that fell an inch or two past her shoulders, coral-tinged lips and large, dark eyes. Soulful eyes. Eyes glinting with resentment and impatience and maybe a bit of fear. Eyes that could wreak havoc with a man's psyche—to say nothing of his libido.

Ron Joffe prided himself on being intelligent, deliberative, not the sort of guy who got sidetracked by a pair of beautiful eyes. But suddenly he found he didn't want to talk to Deirdre Morrissey.

He didn't want to talk to anyone but Julia Bloom.

1

One month earlier

For the chance to eat brunch at Grandma Ida's home, Julia would put up with just about anything—including Grandma Ida.

She stepped out of the elevator on the top floor of the Bloom Building. The family owned the Upper West Side building and earned a tidy fortune off the rentals, but Grandma Ida had a schizophrenic way of dealing with her success. She loved money, loved power, loved being whatever the Jewish female equivalent of *capo di tutti capi* was, but when asked she would say, with tremulous humility, that she simply "lived above the store." Which she did—twenty-five stories above the store. Julia's mother and Aunt Martha both resided in the Bloom Building, too, but on the twenty-fourth floor. Julia's mother considered it proof of her independence that she wasn't on the same floor as Grandma Ida, but Grandma Ida seldom passed up the opportunity to remind her: "Don't forget, Sondra—you're living under my roof."

"Under your floor," Julia's mother would mutter. Fortunately, Grandma Ida's hearing was beginning to go, and muttered comments generally didn't register on her.

If necessary, Julia would mutter during her brunch with Grandma Ida. If necessary, she would shout. She'd been lured here with a promise of food—real food, rich, flavorful, fresh-from-Bloom's food—and while she didn't know the reason for the invitation, she didn't care. She was going to *eat*. She'd even worn slacks with an elastic waistband, just in case.

It wasn't that she never ate. She did, when she had time. But she hardly ever ate Bloom's food. Bloom's food was merchandise. It was something you sold, not something you enjoyed— at least, not if you were a Bloom. For as long as Julia could remember, breakfast in her family had consisted of Cheerios or doughnuts. Warm, chewy bagels, Nova smoked salmon sliced tissue-thin, herrings in artery-clogging cream sauce—these were profit centers, not comestibles.

Ah, but today… Today they were her dream come true. Today, as Grandma Ida's guest for brunch, Julia was going to indulge, gorge, test the limits of her elastic waistband.

She pressed the doorbell beside her grandmother's door. Within seconds, Lyndon swung it open, blasting the hallway with the aromas of hot coffee and warm bread. Julia's mouth went damp.

God, she loved good food.

"Hello, sweetheart." Lyndon greeted her, ritualistically kissing the air next to her cheeks. Tall and slender, with walnut-hued skin and elegant braids framing his smile-wide face, Lyndon had more flair than anyone in the Bloom family. He dressed with a stylishness that bordered on affectation, and he tolerated Grandma Ida with a patience that bordered on saintliness. Julia didn't know how much Grandma Ida paid him, but it had to be a lot.

"Come on in," he said, waving her inside. "Your grandmother's waiting for you."

"I'm not late, am I?" Julia joined him in the foyer and un-wound the red cashmere scarf she'd wrapped around her neck and shoulders in a feeble attempt at panache.

Lyndon took the scarf from her, shook it smooth and grinned. "You're not late. She's just waiting."

Julia lowered her voice to a whisper. "Do you know why she asked me to come?"

"She's your grandmother. Does she have to have a reason?"

"She always has a reason. What kind of mood is she in?"

"Barometric pressure's holding steady. Go on in and say hello to her. She's already in the dining room, having coffee. Shall I get you a cup?"

"Get me a two-gallon jug," Julia requested, then gave Lyndon a brave smile and marched down the hall to the formal dining room.

Grandma Ida's apartment screamed prewar. The rooms were majestic in proportion, with high, molded ceilings and tall windows that welcomed in a flood of brilliant morning sunshine. The nine-foot ceilings always made Julia feel even shorter than she was. Barefoot, she stood five foot five using her best balance-a-book-on-her-head posture—and she was the tallest female in her family.

She'd augmented her stature today by wearing ankle-high leather boots with two-inch heels. She liked to have added height when she was summoned to Grandma Ida's. It made her feel a little less intimidated.

She found the Bloom family matriarch seated at the head of the formal dining table. The furniture, like the architecture, was prewar: heavy, dark pieces, a hutch sparkling with a display of pink Depression glass, dour curtains of burgundy velvet framing parchment-yellow shades on the windows. The rug beneath the mahogany table featured a busy, multicolored pattern. As a child Julia had loved that rug, because it camouflaged all the crumbs she inevitably dropped during the course of a meal.

Grandma Ida seemed prewar to Julia, too—as well she was. Her short, wavy hair was an unnatural black, as solid as an ink spill. Surely she could afford the services of a more skilled hair colorist, but she insisted on patronizing the same salon she'd been going to since Bloom's first introduced nonkosher products back in the sixties. "Bella knows what to do with hair," Grandma Ida insisted. As far as Julia could see, Bella knew what to do with hair the way Itzhak Perlman knew what to do with an electric guitar. He might have a general idea, might be able to get a few interesting sounds out of it, but you wouldn't want to pay money to hear him play.

Beneath her strange black hair, Grandma Ida was blessed with an unusually wrinkle-free face—and unlike her hair, her complexion had not been artificially tampered with. She had a smattering of creases, and a deep line rose from the bridge of her narrow nose like an exclamation point, but her skin lacked the crepey texture one would expect of an eighty-eight-year-old woman who had worked hard, endured much and consumed more than her share of stale doughnuts over the years. She was petite and her fingers had developed a few arthritic knobs at the joints, but her brown eyes remained clear and her jaw was steady. And her tongue was sharp.

"Julia. It's about time," she barked, as Julia circled the table. She tilted her head at a regal angle to accept Julia's kiss. "Lyndon had to put the microwave on time-cook."

"I did not," Lyndon called in from the kitchen. "I'll start the eggs as soon as I get some coffee for Julia."

"She can get her own coffee," Grandma Ida retorted. "Start the eggs." She leveled her gaze at Julia and pointed to the chair at her right. "Sit."

Julia sighed and forced a smile. "Let me pour myself a cup of coffee, and then I'll sit."

"Sit now. Lyndon can get you your coffee later," Grandma Ida said, contradicting herself.

She sipped her coffee, which smelled to Julia like a narcoleptic's idea of nirvana. Julia filled her lungs with the fragrance and tried to imagine the taste on her tongue.

Her grandmother glowered. Julia sank into the high-backed

chair, resentful and anxious. Had she done something wrong? Breached some invisible line? Or was Grandma Ida going to spend the morning castigating her for someone else's sins, or perhaps just firing salvos at the world at large?

"How are you?" Julia asked, disguising her uneasiness behind an ingratiating tone. She tried not to let Grandma Ida cow her. She was an adult, after all, mature, responsible, as on top of her life as any twenty-eight-year-old who worked sixty-hour weeks doing all the stuff her boss didn't want to do, while he claimed the glory and the big bucks, and spent her spare hours alternately worrying about her family and trying not to get sucked into their nonsense. She'd earned the right not to be rattled by her grandmother.

But Grandma Ida always managed to rattle her anyway. For all her grandmother's scowling, her scolding, her testiness and her chronic dyspepsia, Julia still loved her, and because she did, she couldn't develop an immunity to the old woman.

"How am I?" Grandma Ida echoed. "How should I be? One whole year since I buried my son. That's how I am."

Well, yes. It had been one whole year since Julia had buried her father, and Julia's mother had buried her husband. Grandma Ida didn't get to claim first prize in the grief competition. They'd all been devastated by Ben Bloom's untimely death. They'd all spent a year mourning, coping, healing. If Grandma Ida had demanded Julia's presence in order to wallow in sadness…well, the food had better be extremely good, that was all.

"What's that on your mouth?" Grandma Ida asked, apparently willing to abandon her bereavement for the time being.

"My mouth?" Julia frowned. She hadn't eaten anything yet, hadn't even had a sip of that freshly brewed and tantalizingly fragrant coffee, so she couldn't have food residue on her lips. "A tinted lip gloss?" she guessed. She'd slicked some on before leaving her apartment.

"Tinted lip gloss." Grandma Ida's frown deepened.

"Mom says it protects the lips from getting sunburned."

"Sunburned lips. I never heard from such a thing."

Several retorts filled Julia's mouth, but she exercised restraint and only said, "I'm going to get my coffee, Grandma.
I'll be right back." She shoved away from the table and stalked
into the kitchen before her grandmother could order her back
to her chair.

The kitchen was big enough to accommodate a small breakfast table, which meant it was enormous by Manhattan standards. The appliances were full-size and the counters were
lined with kitchen gadgets too old to have come from Bloom's,
which hadn't added a kitchenware department until the early
eighties. An antiquated popcorn maker, a hand-held mixer and
one of those little scales that dieters were supposed to use to
measure their portions cluttered the available space. Why her
grandmother needed that scale was beyond Julia. The woman
was definitely not fat.

The kitchen smelled so good Julia didn't want to leave. Her
gaze fell on a wicker basket filled with poppy-seed bagels, and
it took all her willpower not to grab one and slather it with scal-
lion-flavored cream cheese from the tub beside the basket—or
better yet, to grab a few bagels, escape from the apartment, and
devour them in the elevator on her way downstairs to freedom.

But more than granddaughterly respect kept her from fleeing. Lyndon stood at the stove, stirring a pan full of scrambled
eggs and lox. Merely looking at that glorious mass of pink-
flecked yellow curds made Julia's knees go soft.

"Lyndon," she murmured, then emitted a sigh of longing.
"Lox and eggs."

"Your grandmother specifically requested them. She knows
how much you love them. You ought to treat her nicely."

"I do treat her nicely. But lox and eggs…" She leaned over
the pan and let the rising scent fill her nostrils. "Nobody makes
them as good as you. Marry me, Lyndon."

He grinned. "I would, honey, except you're the wrong color
and the wrong sex, and if you were the right sex we'd have to
elope to Vermont. Coffee's in that cranky old percolator. Why
don't you buy your grandma a Mr. Coffee?"

"My mother did. Grandma Ida made her return it. She said she knew the markup on that item and would rather sell it to a stranger than have it sitting idle in her kitchen. You know her. She *likes* the cranky old percolator."

"*She* doesn't have to clean it," he grumbled. "I do, and I hate it. Buy *me* a Mr. Coffee."

"Only if you marry me," Julia bargained, grabbing a teaspoon and dipping it into the scrambled eggs.

Lyndon slapped her hand away before she could pry loose a piece of lox. "Wait till it's cooked. I got the coffee from downstairs, and the hell with the markup. It's that Kenyan roast. I like it—good ol' African coffee. Maybe it'll put a curl in your grandma's hair."

"Her hair is hopeless," Julia whispered, finding the mug Lyndon had set out for her and filling it with coffee. "Thanks. Really—I'm serious about that marriage proposal. I'd even let you mess around behind my back if you'd only keep me in lox and eggs."

"You're too easy, Julia. Gotta raise your standards." He spooned the pan's contents onto a porcelain platter, and Julia's spirits lifted. The eggs were done, neither too dry nor too wet. That meant she'd be eating soon. She'd eat until there was no longer a trace of tinted lip gloss on her. She'd eat until she was drunk on the marvelous food, drugged by it. Warm, fresh bagels, lox and eggs and...oh, was that a plate of rugelach, glistening with honey, on the table? Her heart thumped.

She carried the basket of bagels and her mug back into the dining room. Lyndon followed her, conveying the rest of the food on a tray. Grandma Ida's expression changed almost imperceptibly, a flicker of approval brightening her eyes as Lyndon set the heavy serving plates down on the table.

"The bagels are already sliced," he informed Grandma Ida. "The cream cheese is softened. Let me refill your cup, and then you two can have your little chat."

Those two ominous words—*little chat*—tempered Julia's ecstasy. Food this good didn't come free. Grandma Ida was going to make Julia pay.

She didn't care. She'd feast, and then she'd settle up.

She scooped a small mountain of eggs onto her plate, took a bagel and smeared cream cheese on its warm surfaces. The thick china was a dull white, the silver bulky and ugly. Grandma Ida had been using the same table settings for as long as Julia could remember. They'd been her mother's, she'd told Julia— and someday, if Julia was very, very good, they'd be hers. If ever Julia had had an incentive not to be good, that was it.

The stout plates and silverware didn't bother her today. For a brunch this spectacular, she'd eat off paper, out of the pan, on the floor. The eggs were divine, the coffee heavenly. The bagel's crust resisted her teeth for a moment and then yielded, warm and thick in contrast to the cool, smooth icing of the cream cheese.

"That's it," she said with a swoony sigh. "I'm never eating doughnuts again."

"You're too thin," Grandma Ida criticized. "What do you eat?"

"For breakfast? Doughnuts."

"And for lunch?"

"I usually don't have time for lunch," she admitted. "I try to make up for it at dinner."

"With that boy? That blond boy? The lawyer. What does he make you eat?"

Julia stifled a chuckle. In her blissful gastronomic state, she couldn't take offense at her grandmother's apparent dislike of her current boyfriend. Julia wasn't sure *she* liked him, either, so it wasn't worth arguing about. "He doesn't make me eat anything. If we go out for dinner, we choose a place together. If not, I go home and eat whatever is in my refrigerator. Or I'll pick up something on my way. If Bloom's were on my way, I'd pick up stuff here."

"You'd be one of those *meshugena* ladies in the fancy suits and the sneakers."

"They aren't *meshuge,* Grandma."

"You don't wear sneakers with a fancy suit."

"They only wear the sneakers going to and from work. When they get to their offices, they change into real shoes."

"It's crazy. Sneakers with a suit like that. And all of them picking up 'heat-n-eat' dinners on their way home. They should be home making a proper meal for their families, not crowding Bloom's looking for food."

"The store makes lots of money with those prepared meals," Julia reminded her.

"Thank God for that. *Meshugena,*" Grandma Ida clucked, shaking her head. "So you eat what?"

"Nothing as good as this," Julia swore, then shoveled more eggs into her mouth.

Her grandmother ate, as well. Not as enthusiastically, not as voraciously, but she held her own. Even at her advanced age, she had most of her original teeth, and chewy bagels couldn't defeat her.

"This is wonderful," Julia finally said, leaning back in her chair and feeling a contented ache in her belly. "Thank you." She knew the little chat was imminent, but she figured a show of gratitude might make it go more smoothly.

Her grandmother drained the last of her coffee and dabbed her mouth with a napkin. Then she settled herself in her chair and glared at Julia, her eyes dark and focused as if she were seeing not Julia but her own soon-to-be-revealed purpose.

"It's been a year," she began.

"I know." A year since Julia's father had died. She no longer felt that squeeze of emotion in her guts, in her lungs, no longer felt the pinch in the bridge of her nose, releasing tears. Her father had been what he was, but she'd loved him, they all had, and he shouldn't have had to die of food poisoning while on a trip to St. Petersburg to meet with his sturgeon supplier. For months Julia had been haunted by images of him suffering in some foreign hotel room, and Russian doctors at the hospital babbling in their guttural, Slavic language above his wracked body, inserting tubes into him, attempting to jump-start his heart... And all because he'd tasted some tainted sturgeon.

"So, we mourn for a year and then it's over," Grandma Ida said.

"It's never really over, Grandma."

"In terms of God, it's over. A year passes, you unveil the stone—and then you go on."

"All right. Fine." Julia wasn't going to argue.

"So here I am, an old lady, and the son who ran Bloom's is gone a year. Your father was president of the store, Julia. This I don't have to tell you."

Julia warily took a sip of her coffee. It had cooled down, but she sensed now would not be the best time to head into the kitchen for a hot refill.

"Bloom's needs a president. For a year, now, it's been without. But we must go on."

Julia nodded her agreement. Grandma Ida was going to tell her she was putting Uncle Jay in charge. Julia expected it. Even her mother expected it, although the thought enraged her. Julia's mother had worked hand in hand with her father all these years. She knew the business as well as Uncle Jay did, and she was more disciplined and diligent than he was. She deserved to be named president. But Grandma Ida was going to favor her surviving son over her widowed daughter-in-law, and she was going to ask Julia to break the news to her mother. That was the reason for the brunch.

She relaxed slightly. Her mother had already suspected Grandma Ida would do something like this. She'd thrown several anticipatory fits about it. Once the decision was handed down, she'd likely throw several more fits—and then she'd get back to work overseeing the store's inventory, because she had nothing better to do.

"I want you to take over," Grandma Ida said.

Julia choked on a mouthful of tepid coffee. "Take over what?"

"Bloom's. I'm naming you president."

"What?" The word came out a squeak.

"You are going to be president," Grandma Ida said, as if the question was already resolved.

"Grandma." She stretched her spine back into balance-a-book posture and met her grandmother's rigid gaze. "I can't be president. I've already got a job."

"Some job." Her grandmother sniffed dismissively.

"I'm a lawyer, Grandma."

"Well, hoo-ha. I'm supposed to be impressed?"

"As a matter of fact, yes! I spent three long years in law school, remember? And passed the bar exam on my first try."

"And now you work in a big hoo-ha firm with that blond boy, and what do you do? Do you send murderers to prison? Do you defend the innocent? Do you go to Washington and tell Congress to write new laws to protect *faygalas* like our Lyndon?"

Unfortunately, Julia's legal training didn't lend itself to fiery litigation, noble Constitutional defenses or battles to protect *faygalas*. She worked in a firm that could only be called "hoo-ha," a huge legal factory where she and the other associates toiled long hours researching cases for their bosses, the partners. The work was tedious, it was frustrating and at times it was distasteful. But it wasn't retail merchandising in a world-class deli, and it wasn't under Grandma Ida's control. It wasn't Bloom's. It was a place where Julia could just be Julia, far from the universe in which she'd grown up.

"I like my job," she said.

"Your job has no meaning. It's not family."

"That's one thing I like about it," she muttered.

Grandma Ida's hearing was operational today. "So, you don't want to work with family. So, fine. You're president—you could fire them all."

"Fire Mom and Uncle Jay? They're the only ones who know how to run the place."

"We've got staff. We've got Myron, the accountant. And your father's secretary, the Irish one, Deirdre. They know how to keep things running."

"This is what I went to law school for? To run a glorified delicatessen?"

"You're the smartest one in the family," her grandmother explained. "All that schooling, that law—it makes you smart, am I right?"

"My mother's smart."

"Your mother doesn't even have the nose God gave her."

This was true. Julia's mother had celebrated her sweet-sixteenth birthday by subjecting her nose to surgical improvement. But Julia had never known her mother with any other nose. The nose she had was all right—somewhat impersonal, perhaps, but adequate. And it had no bearing on her ability to run Bloom's, which she'd been doing rather efficiently for the past year.

"What about Uncle Jay? He's got his own nose," Julia pointed out.

"He's my son, God knows, but he spends all his time doing that computer stuff. And he married that Wendy. Not a smart man, my son Jay."

Julia had to agree with Grandma Ida. Wendy, dubbed The Bimbette by Julia's family because she was too cute to be a mere bimbo, offered proof that Uncle Jay was lacking a certain degree of maturity. Or sensibility. Or gravitas. His first wife, Aunt Martha, had enough gravitas to send most men diving head-first into the nearest perky bosom. Perhaps Jay's greatest flaw was that he was so predictable—or that his current wife's bosom was so amazingly perky.

But some of the computer stuff he did for the store was useful. "Grandma, Uncle Jay has worked for Bloom's all his life. So has my mother—"

"Not *all* her life," Grandma Ida quibbled. "She was a wife, a mother. She did other things. Fund-raising, volunteer work."

Julia refrained from pointing out that most of the work she did for Bloom's was volunteer, too, since she didn't get paid. She'd fought Julia's father about it, but he'd explained that it wouldn't be fair for her to be paid a salary separate from his, because then his branch of the family would be taking more of the store's profits than his brother's branch. Julia's mother had replied that they deserved more because they were both working for the store, while Aunt Martha—Uncle Jay's wife back then—was contributing nothing to the store but her personality, "and she's got the personality of a dried mushroom," her mother had concluded with a flourish.

Julia's father had given himself raises to cover his wife's contributions to the store. This had resulted in a very nice household income, but it hadn't addressed Sondra Bloom's real concern, which was that she was working and not getting paid. Once he died, the store finally put her on the payroll. She got *his* salary. Never her own, though.

If Julia became president, that would change.

Not that she was going to become president.

"My point is," she explained to Grandma Ida, "they've both worked for Bloom's. I never have—other than a few summer jobs running a cash register. I have no idea how to manage a retail store. I don't know the products we sell. I couldn't begin to tell you the difference between Turkish olives and Greek olives."

"Turkish cost more," her grandmother informed her, as if it were that simple.

"I mean, why *me?* Why not Susie?"

"Your sister?" Grandma Ida's lips imploded, as if she'd just sucked hard on a lemon. "She's got that thing on her leg, that tattoo."

Julia would admit Susie's tattoo had been a foolish move, but that didn't make her any less suited to run Bloom's. Nobody could be less suited to run it than Julia. "How about Adam?"

"He's still in college. You think he should drop out and run the store?"

No, of course not. But Julia didn't think *she* should run the store, either. "Or Jay's kids. Neil and Rick. They're both out of school. Neil already runs his own business—"

Grandma Ida made a contemptuous flapping gesture with

her hand. The thick gold bangle around her wrist glinted in the sunlight. A while back, Lyndon had mentioned to her that some people believed copper bracelets eased the symptoms of arthritis, so she'd taken to wearing bangles. Fourteen-karat gold ones, though. "If copper is good, gold must be better," she'd reasoned.

"Neil is a bum," she proclaimed. "He lives like a *shaygetz*."

"What's not Jewish about chartering sailboats in the Florida Keys?"

"Everything," she snapped. "And Ricky? He's always asking me for money. I'm going to trust him with the store?" She shook her head and laughed sadly, an eerie cackling sound. "I've thought about it, Julia, and you're the one. You'll become the president. You're smart, you're responsible and you remind me of me."

Julia knew her grandmother intended this as a sincere compliment, but she couldn't help being insulted. She might be smart and responsible, but she wasn't bossy. She wasn't manipulative. She never acted illogically, and she would never let Bella near her hair.

And until a minute ago, she hadn't known that the only difference between the Turkish olives and the Greek olives sold at Bloom's was the price.

"Grandma…" She sighed and prayed that her expression looked sympathetic. "It's not that I don't love Bloom's. I do. That's why I wouldn't want you to entrust it to me. I respect the place enough to know that you need someone with more expertise in the president's office, overseeing everything. You need someone who understands the business—"

"What are we talking about, 'business'? It's a delicatessen. You think I understood the business when I married Isaac, may he rest, and we turned this place into what it is today? You learn. You get some flour on your face, some cheese in your hair, a little kugel under your nails—and you're an expert."

"I don't want kugel under my nails."

"So you'll sit in your father's office and push papers around, like he did. He made Bloom's a very successful outfit. A brand-name, he used to say. Chartered buses from Jersey, regulars from Brooklyn, tourists from Europe—they all come to Bloom's. We ship mail orders around the world. And you'll do even better." She folded her hands in front of her, as if sealing her pronouncement with a prayer. "I'll be talking to the lawyers, a bunch of *gonifs,* but it has to be done. You'll make me proud, Julia."

Julia didn't know what to say. If she spoke her mind, Grandma Ida would be hurt. Or angry. Better to keep silent, to say goodbye, to leave the apartment and go somewhere where she could digest everything she'd just taken in.

One thing she knew: it was going to be much easier to digest the lox and eggs than her grandmother's decision.

2

Eddie was a Snickers.

Susie and her roommates knew a little about sex, but they knew a lot about chocolate. So they'd taken to rating men in terms they understood. Encounters that didn't go far were "Hershey's Kisses." Young guys were "Junior Mints." Under-endowed guys were "Baby Ruths." Rich guys were "Paydays," even though Anna insisted that Paydays contained no chocolate. Guys who specialized in foreplay were "Butterfingers." Guys who specialized in oral sex were "Charleston Chews." Guys who came too quickly were "Milky Ways." Guys who indiscriminately screwed around with airheads were "Tootsie Rolls." Caitlin recently mentioned "Three Musketeers" in reference to a long, hot night that had begun at a party for a visiting hockey team from Canada, but Susie had chosen not to ask her for details.

"Snickers" seemed to peg Eddie pretty accurately. He was robust and cheerful, satisfying in a comfortable if not particularly breathtaking way. Susie genuinely liked him, but she had no fear that love might sneak into the situation and throw everything out of whack. She and Eddie were compatible, they laughed a lot when they were together, and although his husky build sometimes squashed her when he was on top, it made him wonderfully cozy to cuddle up with afterward. His chest was nicely upholstered, his body always warm. Sleeping with him was a pleasant way to pass the dark hours.

A cell phone was chirping. "Is that mine?" Eddie asked sleepily.

"No." She eased out of the curve of his arm and sat up. "It sounds like mine."

"Sounds like mine, too. They all sound alike."

"I'm pretty sure it's mine." She shoved back the wool blanket and the musty top sheet and reached for her camisole and panties, which lay on the floor right beside the bed. She yanked the burgundy cotton knit over her head and wriggled it into place, then slid the matching panties on and swung her legs over the edge of the mattress. The cell phone chirped again as she strode across Eddie's small, cluttered bedroom for her bag.

By the time she'd reached the black leather hobo-style bag, she knew it was her phone. It twittered up from the depths of the bag like a trapped bird. She loosened the drawstring, dug out the phone and flipped it open. "Hello?"

"Susie? It's Julia. We've got a disaster."

"Huh?"

"Susie. It's one o'clock. Why do you sound like you just woke up?"

Susie ran a hand through her hair and gazed across the shadowed room at Eddie, who had closed his eyes and drifted back to sleep. Her watch lay with her earrings on the splintery orange crate that served as his nightstand, and the only other clock in the room was on his VCR, which she couldn't see from where she was standing. To glimpse its digits, she'd have to return to the bed, but she didn't want to disturb Eddie while he dozed.

She'd accept Julia's claim that it was indeed one o'clock. Big deal. Why shouldn't she sleep late? She'd worked past midnight last night, and then she and Eddie had gone out to an all-night movie house to see *Outside Providence,* and then they'd gone to a café for lattes and returned to his place and done the Snickers thing until the caffeine from the lattes finally wore off.

So, yeah, one o'clock seemed about the right time to be waking up. It was Sunday, after all. People were allowed to sleep late on Sunday.

"What do you mean, *we* have a disaster?" she asked. Julia never had disasters. She was too organized, too in control. She was a lawyer, for God's sake, well dressed, well groomed, the sort of role model chronically held up to her younger sister as an example of the right way to manage one's life.

The word *disaster* must have reached Eddie's ears. He blinked awake and stared at her, not an easy thing to do without lifting his head off the pillow. His neck was crooked at such an odd angle it almost seemed dislocated, and his thinning red hair splayed across the pillowcase like cobwebs.

"I can't talk about it on the phone," Julia said. "Can you come to the store?"

A store disaster? What? Had the refrigerator cases lost power and now the place was reeking of rotting cheese? Had one of the ovens exploded and sent pulverized knishes flying through the Upper West Side sky? "What kind of disaster?" she pressed Julia. "Are there injuries?"

"Not yet. I might have to strangle Grandma Ida."

"Oh, that sounds like fun." Her worry abating, she sent Eddie a reassuring smile. He nodded, rolled over and sank back to sleep. "Why do I have to come all the way uptown so you can talk to me?" she asked.

"Because you're my sister and you love me, and you don't want me to go to jail for murdering our grandmother. So you'd better get up here and restrain me."

"Can you restrain yourself for an hour? I'm not dressed yet."

"It's one o'clock, Susie!"

"Thanks for reminding me. I'll see you in an hour. Where will you be?"

"In the olive section. Did you know the only difference between Greek olives and Turkish olives is that Turkish olives cost more?"

If Julia was babbling about the price of imported olives, she must be really upset. "I'll try to get there in less than an hour," Susie promised, then turned off her phone and stuffed it back into her bag. "Eddie, I've got to go."

"Yeah, okay," he said, his voice muffled by the blanket. "Everything okay?"

"Everything's fine." She searched the room until she located the long black skirt and the loose-knit black sweater she'd worn last night. She liked wearing black, but she especially liked wearing it over colorful underwear. It was her little secret, her deception, her taunt. *Aha!* her apparel said. *I am wearing all black like a typical downtown girl and you think you know who and what I am. But you can't pin me down so easily. Underneath this black attire lurks flamboyant lingerie.* Not that burgundy was the most flamboyant color, but Susie also had orange, turquoise, pea-green and siren-red panties, polka-dot, striped and jungle-print bras, and a complete wardrobe of camisoles and chemises because she was flat chested and they fit her better than the bras.

Once dressed, she made her way into Eddie's bathroom, which had a suspicious smell, part citrus and part mildew. Lacking her own toothbrush, she had to borrow his, which was icky but better than not brushing her teeth at all. The mirror above the sink was missing large patches of silver, but enough remained to reflect her groggy face back at her. Her cheeks were mottled, her eyes glazed. Her hair didn't look too bad, at least. She'd gotten a really good cut last week, chin length, the ends ruler straight. A few fluffs with her fingertips and she looked salon fresh from the eyebrows up.

She left the bathroom, gathered her jewelry from the crate and crossed back to her purse. Wedging her feet into her clogs, she called to Eddie, "Gotta go." She spotted her black denim jacket draped over the back of a chair and put it on.

"Yeah, I'll see you," he mumbled without opening his eyes. If she were in love with him, she would be insulted.

Someday, she thought as she clomped down the stairs to the front door of his building and exited onto the sun-washed pavement of Avenue B, she'd like to find someone a little better than a Snickers bar. A Swiss truffle, perhaps. A hand-dipped strawberry. A slab of homemade cream-cheese fudge riddled with pecans. Not that she was ready to settle down, not that she would *ever* be ready to settle down—but a little gourmet chocolate, something a touch less sweet, a touch deeper and more complex… Chocolate liqueur, perhaps. Chocolate-covered halvah. Perugina. A girl could dream.

The train was fairly crowded for a weekend afternoon in March. In another month, a day this sunny would inspire hordes of New Yorkers to travel uptown to hang out in Central Park. But today wasn't quite a hanging-out-in-Central-Park day. The air still held a chilly bite. Winter stood at the open door, on its way out but loitering on the porch as if it had one final bit of gossip to share before it departed for good.

At Grand Central Station, Susie took the cross-town shuttle, then hopped onto another uptown train. She could understand why Julia lived on the Upper West Side, even if it was their old neighborhood and way too close to Mom and Grandma Ida. Julia was living an uptown life—nylons, manicures, DKNY ensembles and Body Shop facial cleansers. In a way Susie felt sorry for her sister. Julia was trying so hard not to live their mother's life—yet there she was, slowly, inevitably evolving into their mother.

Whenever the tracks curved, the train's metal wheels shrieked in protest. Even though there were plenty of empty seats, Susie chose to stand, balanced against one of the vertical poles. Her muscles were a little stiff, especially in her shoulders and her thighs. Eddie had just a bit too much heft. He was always coming into Nico's and ordering a slice of pizza—so he could see Susie, he claimed, but honestly, he didn't have to order a jumbo slice of Sicilian with everything if all he wanted was to see her. Ten pounds, fifteen at most—lay off the pizza, add a little exercise, and he could lose the weight without suffering inordinately. If she ever believed she had a relationship with Eddie, something real, something that implied a future, she'd get him organized into a proper regimen.

He'd appreciate it, too, wouldn't he, she thought with a sarcastic snort. "Gee, Susie, I'm so glad you love me enough to turn into a shrew, nagging me not to eat that extra-big slice with the works."

The train whined as it rolled into the Seventy-Second Street station. Susie was the first one out the door. Eddie faded from her mind as she focused on her more immediate situation. What disaster could have arisen that would make Julia want to murder Grandma Ida?

Actually, Susie could think of lots of possibilities. Grandma Ida bugged the hell out of her. She didn't favor murder as a way to resolve problems, but if Grandma Ida were removed from her life, Susie wouldn't have to spend so much time and energy dreading her.

All right. She didn't exactly *dread* Grandma Ida. She just…resented her. Grandma Ida had never left any doubt that she considered Julia a vastly superior specimen of granddaughterhood. She'd always criticized Susie. As a child, when Susie sat at Grandma Ida's imposing dining room table for a Passover seder and Grandpa Isaac would drone on and on in what sounded more like gibberish than Hebrew, she'd get bored and swing her feet under her chair, and Grandma Ida would humiliate her by interrupting the gibberish to announce, "Susie, stop kicking."

Julia never kicked.

But being scolded for kicking wasn't the worst of it. When Susie had gotten B-pluses in school, Grandma Ida had called her an underachiever. When Susie had set the table, Grandma Ida had chided her for not folding the napkins symmetrically.

When Susie had run up and down the hall, Grandma Ida had yelled at her for making too much noise and failing to act lady-like. When Susie had drawn pictures to hang on the refrigerator, Grandma Ida had pointed out all the flaws: "This bush has blue leaves on it. Why did you put blue there? Leaves are green."

Susie had always believed leaves could be blue. She'd believed buttons could be soldiers and a sewing box could be used to stage an imaginary war. She'd believed that a cookie before supper did not necessarily spoil a person's appetite. She still believed that writing poetry was a higher calling than marketing bagels and lox to yuppies.

"Poetry?" Grandma Ida would sniff. "You can't eat poetry, can you?"

So if there was going to be a homicide involving Grandma Ida today, Susie definitely wanted to be there to witness it.

A few blocks north of the subway station, she spotted the Bloom Building. Above the broad ground-floor display windows chaotically crammed with what appeared to be at least one of every single product in the store's inventory, a banner sign circled the building with Bloom's-Bloom's-Bloom's painted in white letters against a dark-brown background. The repeated names sloped upward, each *B* at the bottom of the sign and each *s* banging against the top edge. For some reason, the effect made Susie think of the Rockettes, a line of dancers all leaning back and kicking high.

She knew the store. It had changed over the course of her life, but so had she. She wasn't the three-year-old she used to be, chasing her big sister along the aisles, her flailing hands swiping at boxes of crackers and delicately balanced pyramids of sardine tins. Bloom's had grown up, too. Sometime in the eighties, the linoleum floors had been replaced by hardwood floors that looked simultaneously more rustic and more elegant. Varnished oak shelves had appeared where once uninspired metal shelving had stood. The second floor had been reborn as a kitchenware center, walls hung with copper-bottom pots and cast-iron skillets, displays jammed with potato peelers, apple corers, egg slicers and rice steamers, counters crammed with bread makers, yogurt makers, pasta makers, melon-ball makers, ice-cream makers and any other kind of maker a person might want in her kitchen.

So much stuff. It boggled Susie's mind that her family had been able to accumulate a significant fortune by selling people four different kinds of specialized cheese slicers when any old knife would get the job done.

Or corkscrews. These had been articles of great fascination to her as a teenager, when sneaking the occasional bottle of wine with her friends had been considered the ultimate triumph. Bloom's sold about a dozen different kinds of wine bottle openers, from the basic portable corkscrew model to hundred-dollar gadgets. Susie used to fantasize about owning a wine bottle opener—any style would do—but of course she couldn't ask her father to bring one home from the store for her. Nor could she purchase one herself. In those days, all the clerks had known the boss's daughters, which meant they'd also known Susie was years below the drinking age and had no legitimate use for a corkscrew.

She could legally drink wine now, and she owned a simple corkscrew with "Nico's" etched into it, from the pizza place. As for all the other kitchen gizmos sold at Bloom's, well, she and her roommates didn't do that much cooking. Their kitchen wasn't much bigger than the average shower stall; they couldn't all fit into it at the same time. They went through a lot of coffee and tea, and the refrigerator was usually full of bottled water, clementines, leftover sushi and Caitlin's nail polish, which she claimed lasted longer if it was kept cold. Susie got free dinners at Nico's, and other than that, she lived on cereal, yogurt and fresh fruit. Most of the meals she knew how to cook weren't worth eating, at least not the way she cooked them.

Entering Bloom's, she acknowledged that if she lived uptown, she'd stock her fridge with gourmet cheeses. Bloom's was a study in indulgence run amok. Only the sort of people who

needed four different kinds of cheese slicers would demand
seven different kinds of extra-sharp cheddar, imported from up-
state New York, Vermont, Wisconsin, England, Ireland, Canada
and Australia. Australian cheddar cheese, she thought with a
faint shudder. A big hand-printed sign announced that the
Australian cheddar cheese was priced at a special discount.
Susie wasn't surprised.

She wandered farther into the store. The Sunday-afternoon
crowd included lots of tourists—people from the outer bor-
oughs and New Jersey for whom Bloom's was worth a special
trip to Manhattan. They carried canvas totes with "Bloom's"
stenciled onto the cloth, the word angled just like on the sign
outside. People actually bought these totes and used them
whenever they made the pilgrimage to Bloom's, as if the tote
marked them as cognoscenti.

Real cognoscenti lugged their Bloom's purchases home in
free plastic bags.

The store might have changed, but its aromas were the same
as she remembered from her childhood. The cheese section
smelled dense and earthy. The coffee section smelled dark and
rousing. The bread section smelled the best—rich and crusty.

She was nearing the bakery department when she spotted
Julia's bright-red pashmina scarf. Julia had spent way too much
money on that thing. Susie had told her she knew a guy on
Houston Street who sold pashmina scarves for less than half of
what Bloomingdale's charged, but Julia preferred to be ripped
off by fancy department stores. "Who is this man on Houston
Street?" she'd asked indignantly. "How do you know he's not
selling stolen merchandise?"

"I take his word for it," Susie had said.

"And how do you know it's really pashmina? It could be just
regular cashmere."

"If a person can't tell the difference, why pay more for it?"

Julia had shaken her head, as if gravely dismayed by her sister's lack of class.

The scarf *was* pretty, a vivid clutch of color underlining Julia's pale face. She was always pale, so Susie didn't take her chalky complexion as a sign of disaster. And her hands didn't seem to have any blood on them, so Grandma Ida was probably still alive.

Susie worked her way around a trio of overweight women braying to one another about the nuances of virgin olive oil and extra-virgin olive oil in heavy Bronx accents. She almost paused to listen. She'd always wondered how a thing could be *extra* virgin. Either it was virgin or it wasn't, it seemed to her. Being extra virgin was like being a little pregnant.

But she continued on to her sister, who looked, if not apoplectic, deeply concerned. She was studying a rack of small olive oil bottles as if searching for the meaning of extra virgin. Susie sidled up to her and tapped her shoulder. "Hi."

Julia flinched, spun around and relaxed. "Look at this." She pointed to a slender bottle featuring a painfully tasteful label. "Fifty-nine dollars for this."

"Fifty-nine dollars?" Susie squinted at the bottle. Olive oil. Six ounces. Extra virgin. "Why would anyone pay fifty-nine dollars for that? One salad and it's gone."

"I think you use it a teaspoon at a time."

"For that price, it ought to be in a crystal bottle with a stopper, so you can dab it behind your ears. Lucky I found you here. I thought we were supposed to meet by the olives, not the olive oil."

"It was even more crowded by the olives. It's too crowded here, too. Let's go to the stairs."

"If this disaster isn't the sort of thing you can discuss in a crowded place, maybe we ought to leave. Everywhere is crowded at Bloom's."

"That's because Bloom's is such a successful store," Julia said, then winced.

Susie scowled. The fact that Bloom's was a successful store shouldn't fill her sister with angst. The success of the store enabled their mother—and Grandma Ida and Uncle Jay—to enjoy a very affluent lifestyle. This was a good thing.

"Let's just go to the stairs," Julia said in answer to Susie's un-voiced question.

Susie turned in the direction of the stairway—and felt her heart seize. *Godiva.* That man behind the bagel counter was definitely Godiva—dark chocolate, maybe spiked with hazel-nuts—or no, filled with marzipan. Deserving a wrapper of pure gold.

"Who's that?" she whispered.

Julia followed her gaze and shrugged. "How the hell should I know?"

"He's gorgeous."

"He's a bagel guy," Julia remarked, sounding not conde-scending but simply matter-of-fact.

"I'm in love."

"You're insane."

Susie was *not* insane. The fellow counting bagels into a bag for a woman in a sari was gourmet chocolate. He was tall, and lanky, with dark-blond hair pulled back into a neat ponytail, a long face, a forceful nose and chin, and green eyes so round his lids didn't seem able to open all the way. They drooped slightly, giving him a deliciously sleepy look. His smile was sleepy, too. Lazy. Dangerous.

She wanted to eat him up.

"Come on, we've got to talk." Julia clamped her hand around Susie's elbow and tried to steer her away from the bagel counter, toward the stairs. Susie tossed a look over her shoulder, but he didn't notice. He was busy with his bagels.

It occurred to Susie that, much as she wanted to eat him up, she wanted even more just to eat. Julia had sounded panicked enough on the phone that Susie hadn't stopped to grab a bite before leaving Eddie's apartment. She hadn't consumed any-thing since that latte at around three o'clock that morning. She was famished.

"I never had any breakfast today," she said.

"It's too late for breakfast."

"I never had any lunch, either. I've got to get something to eat, and then we'll talk." At Julia's impatient frown, Susie added, "I bet you've eaten breakfast *and* lunch."

Julia looked sheepish. "Brunch at Grandma Ida's. Lyndon made lox and eggs."

Susie felt a stab of jealousy. Lyndon's lox and eggs qualified as five-star cuisine. "You ate that, and you're going to make me starve to death, and I'm supposed to help you with your disaster?"

Julia conceded with a sigh. "Fine. Go get something to eat, and then meet me at the stairs."

Susie hurried over to the bagel counter. Godiva was busy wrapping a wire tie around a plastic bag filled with bagels and grinning at the lady in the sari.

Susie sidled up behind the woman. Another, older, clerk working the bagel counter was available to help her, but Susie could survive another few minutes without food for the opportunity to talk to Godiva. When the older one tried to catch her eye and beckon her over, she pretended to be fascinated with the marble ryes stacked on a shelf beside the bagel bins.

At last the sari-wrapped woman departed. Susie leaped forward and planted herself in front of the man. "Hi," she said.

His smile was slow and effortless. "Hi."

No "Can I help you?" No "What do you want?" Just a husky-voiced "Hi."

Her stomach rumbled hollowly. "I'd like a bagel," she said.

His smile didn't change. His eyes were as much gray as green, she realized now that she was close to him. "Okay," he drawled.

"What flavor do you recommend?" she asked, gesturing at the variety of bagels. Raisin. Whole wheat. Cranberry. Pumpernickel. Pesto? Who in their right mind would want to eat a pesto-flavored bagel?

Godiva gave her a thorough perusal, his gaze lingering at her mouth, at her unspectacular chest and lower, in the vicinity of her navel. "Egg."

"Egg sounds great." She watched as he plucked a square of wax paper from a box and used it to lift an egg bagel from the bin. His fingers were long and thin, surprisingly graceful. As he handed it to her, his smile grew warmer. "Why did you pick egg?" she asked.

"Because you've got a nubile look about you."

Nubile. What kind of bagel counter-man knew the word *nubile?*

Definitely, she was in love. "I can't remember the last time I ate a Bloom's bagel," she told him. "Are they any good?"

"They're awful," he whispered, his eyes glinting with the kind of mischief that made Susie giddy with lust. "People just pretend to like them. It's the biggest scam in town. You want some cream cheese to go with that?"

"No, I'll take it straight up."

"Pay for it before you eat it," he warned, as she lifted it to her mouth. He gestured toward the cashiers at their posts along the front window.

She sighed at his dismissal of her. He'd made his sale; he didn't need to flirt anymore.

Okay. She'd go pay for her bagel and eat it and get some nourishment out of this encounter. Obviously, her nubility failed to leave him in a state of abject passion. Several customers had formed a line behind her—and he probably found one or two of them even more nubile.

"Thanks," she mumbled, then spun away and stalked to the cashier.

She could have told the woman there that she was Susie Bloom, of *the* Blooms, and then she wouldn't have to pay for the bagel. Assuming the cashier believed her. She'd probably ask for two forms of identification, and then she'd fuss and shout across the line of cashiers, "Look who's here! It's one of *the* Blooms!" And then Susie would have to smile and be charming, and she wasn't in the mood to smile and be charming after Godiva had sent her packing.

And it wasn't as if she couldn't afford the eighty-five cents.

She paid, took a bite of her bagel and shook herself out of her Godiva fantasy. Christ, what was wrong with her? Not much more than an hour ago, she'd been in Eddie's bed. She must be some kind of slut, yearning for a total stranger with droopy eyelids.

No, she wasn't really a slut. Just a chocoholic.

She found Julia waiting halfway up the stairs on the landing, perhaps the only place in the store that wasn't full of chattering, browsing customers. Susie took another bite of her bagel and glanced around. They were surrounded by wall clocks in a variety of colors, offered at a variety of prices. To have so many clocks staring at her was like being trapped in a Salvador Dali painting.

"So, what's this disaster?" she asked, feeling a little better now that she had some food inside her.

"Grandma Ida wants to name me president of Bloom's."

"She wants to name Mom president? That sounds about right to me."

"Not Mom. *Me.*"

"You?" Susie guffawed. Her sister could no more run Bloom's than Bart Simpson could run the Vatican. And her sister wouldn't *want* to run Bloom's. She was a lawyer. Lawyers didn't sell lox. Fifty-nine-dollar bottles of olive oil, maybe, but not lox and latkes and round slabs of stuffed derma. "Why the hell would Grandma Ida do something like that?"

"Because she's Grandma Ida," Julia explained, twirling a finger nervously through the fringe of her scarf. "Because she's crazy. Because she's pissed at Uncle Jay and she can't bring herself to turn the place over to someone who isn't a blood relation."

"Why is she pissed at Uncle Jay?"

"Because he married The Bimbette and he spends too much time doing Internet stuff."

"The Web site is pretty cool. It's got all these great pictures of gift baskets overflowing with bread and phallic-looking salami and big green apples." Every now and then, when she was Web surfing, she liked to visit the Bloom's site, just to get in touch with her roots.

"Grandma Ida doesn't understand the Internet, so as far as she's concerned it's useless."

"And this president thing can only go to a blood relative?"

"That's why she won't give it to Mom."

"That's ridiculous." Susie tore off a small chunk of bagel and popped it in her mouth. "Why you? How come she didn't name *me* the president?"

"You've got a tattoo," Julia told her.

Grandma Ida was clearly exercising great wisdom. Uncle Jay had married The Bimbette, so he was out. Susie had a little butterfly inked into her skin above her left anklebone, so she was out. Mom had spent thirty years married to Dad, but she carried no Bloom blood in her veins, so she was out. "It should have gone to Mom," Susie said.

"I know. I feel sick about this. I don't want it. Mom does want it. Grandma Ida has managed to screw us both."

"So why don't you kill her? I'll be your character witness during the trial. I'll testify you were driven to it. I'll say you acted in self-defense."

"Thanks," Julia grumbled. "I knew I could count on you."

"What does Mom have to say about all this?"

"She doesn't know yet. Grandma Ida asked me to come for brunch, and then she laid this on me."

"Yeah, but she laid lox and eggs on you, too," Susie reminded her. There was a limit to how sorry she could feel for Julia, given the quality of Lyndon's cooking.

"She said she's going to talk to her lawyers next week. We've got to do something."

"What can we do? She owns the damn company."

"And if she wants it to stay solvent," Julia said, "she'll name Mom the president, because Mom ran the damn company with Dad for years, and she's been practically running it all by herself since he died."

"Well, you'd better tell Mom. She's going to shit a brick."

"What do you mean, *I'd* better tell Mom? We're going to tell her together."

"Why do I have to be there? You're the president."

"I can't tell her alone. You see what I mean? I can't become president of Bloom's. A president would have to have the guts to give people bad news. I don't."

"You're a lawyer. You give people bad news all the time, and charge them hundreds of dollars an hour for it."

Julia ignored her remark. "What I thought was, if Mom is home now, we can go upstairs and tell her. The three of us can come up with a plan."

"What if she's not home?" Susie asked hopefully. She really didn't want to have to go upstairs and deliver such lousy news to her mother. There would likely be a scene, and Susie hated scenes—at least, she hated scenes involving her family. Scenes involving strangers she found kind of fascinating.

Julia hauled her cell phone from her purse. "I'll call her, and if she's home I'll tell her we're coming up."

Susie nibbled on her bagel and issued a silent prayer that her mother wouldn't answer. God must not have been paying attention, because in the time it took her to swallow, Julia. was saying, "Mom! You're home! Wonderful!"

Wonderful, Susie thought grimly. *Just wonderful.*

3

Jay Bloom steered his BMW Z3 coupe down the ramp to the garage beneath his East Sixty-Third Street apartment building. A few degrees warmer and he might have put down the convertible top. But while it was a bit too chilly for top-down driving, it hadn't been too chilly for golf.

He adored golf. A nice Jewish boy, born and reared in the heart of Manhattan, and he'd fallen deliriously in love with this *goyishe* suburban sport. Until four years ago, he'd never even swung a club, except for miniature golf with the boys on family vacation trips to Point Pleasant, New Jersey. But then his attorney had invited him out to Great Neck one Sunday for a round of golf, "to celebrate your divorce being finalized." Jay had definitely been ready to celebrate, so he'd accepted the invitation.

He'd been dazzled by the beautiful setting, all those gorgeous rolling lawns, the meticulously groomed trees and ponds and sand traps, the discreet paths and white fencing. For a city dweller, being surrounded by such lush greenery was a treat, and Jay always responded to visual appeal, whether in a location, a car, a woman or a Web page layout. But even more than the splendid scenery of the golf course, what Jay loved was swinging a club, feeling the muscles expand and contract in his shoulders and along his spine, the shift of balance in his hips, the liberating sweep of his arms and that fat, satisfying *thwack* as his club hit the ball.

Athletics had always come easily to him. It didn't surprise him that by the eighteenth hole of his divorce celebration he was able to drive the ball three-hundred-plus feet with consistency, any more than it had surprised him eight years ago when he'd tried squash for the first time and wound up beating the photographer, a fellow fifteen years Jay's junior, who shot the layouts of gift baskets and braided bread that appeared in the Bloom's catalogs. Or twelve years ago, when Jay had strapped on a pair of skis for the first time at Hunter Mountain and by the end of the day had figured out how to use his edges to make clean turns.

These skills came naturally to him. He didn't know why. He wasn't a jock.

But now he was a member of the Emerald View Country Club out on the island, and the owner of a magnificent set of titanium golf clubs for which Wendy had bought little socks with breakfast pastries embroidered on them: a bagel, a croissant, a muffin, a doughnut, a Danish— "They reminded me of Bloom's," she'd explained. And on the first sunny Sunday in March, Jay had spent the day out at Emerald View with Stuart, being the suburban golfer.

If his mother knew he spent his Sundays golfing on Long Island, she'd hold it against him. She was a tightly clenched woman with a lot of what Martha, his first wife, would call "issues." After Ben died last year, the old lady had become even more tightly clenched and issued.

He wasn't finding fault that she'd grown crankier since Ben's death. He had two sons; he couldn't begin to imagine what it would be like to lose one of them. He missed Ben, too. He'd grieved, he'd mourned, he'd sat shivah at his mother's house for the week, wearing a cheap black necktie with a symbolic rip in it. It was terrible that Ben had died. It stank. Tragic. Awful.

But life went on, and not playing golf wasn't going to bring Ben back.

He waved to the garage attendant on his way to his reserved space. He had to pay extra for the privilege of parking his own car, but he considered the expense more than worth it. With his own parking space, he never had to wait for one of the attendants to shuffle the cars around, jiggling this one here and that one there in order to free up a car buried in the back. The reserved spaces were right in the front, just past the gate, and Jay could come and go at will. He liked that.

In fact, he liked a lot about his life right now: his pretty wife, his seven handicap, the tiger-purr of the Z3's highly tuned engine and the fact that the year of mourning was finally over. Now even Ida might be ready to accept that life went on.

Life wasn't the only thing that went on, either, he thought as he climbed out of the car, pulled his clubs from the trunk and wiped an errant fingerprint from the chrome latch with the knitted sleeve of his jacket. Bloom's also went on.

He had been more or less running the business single-handedly all year. Oh, sure, Sondra butted in every now and then, meddling and carping and muttering, "Ben always did it *this* way. Ben reconciled the inventory lists using *that* format," as if Jay didn't know computers better than she did. But he had essentially run the show, and now that a year was up, Ida was going to have to name him president.

He'd never fill Ben's shoes, of course. Younger brothers never got to fill their older brothers' shoes, never got to be the Number One Son, never served as first in line to the throne…but when older brothers passed on, younger brothers moved up. It was simply the way of things. He'd understood it when Ben was alive, and he understood it now.

On the seventh day of shivah after Ben had died, Myron Finkel, Ida's accountant since forever, had asked her about who was going to become the company's president now. Ida had peered up from her stool—she'd gotten a sudden surge of religion with the death of her firstborn, and had insisted that the immediate family sit on low stools instead of the comfortable upholstered sofas and chairs in her spacious living room—and said, "For a year I'll be in mourning. When that year is up I'll make decisions."

The year was up now, and the decision would be made. Jay would be the president of Bloom's.

It was going to feel good. To take on the office, the power, the prestige... Oh, yeah. It was going to be sweet. Sweeter than cruising the Z3 down the winding, tree-lined driveway of Emerald View with the first hints of new grass dotting the fairways as winter thawed away. Sweeter than sinking a driver into a ball and watching it soar in a perfect arc through a weekend-blue sky and land on the green. Sweeter than telling Sondra to go *shtup* herself, because he was going to be doing things his way from now on.

Very sweet.

He could hardly wait.

Stepping out of the elevator, Julia saw Aunt Martha emerging from her apartment. She would have dived back into the elevator and slapped the Door Close button, but Susie was right behind her, blocking the way, and by the time Susie realized that Aunt Martha was out there and that escaping back into the elevator would be a prudent move, Aunt Martha had spotted them.

"Girls," she said in a growl that seemed to seep through a bed of gravel in her throat. Martha was tall, with a football-shaped head—a narrow forehead and chin widening into her cheekbones—and eighteen inches of gray-streaked brown hair rippled down her back like yarn with kinks in it. She wore a dowdy skirt, thick, ribbed stockings and Birkenstock sandals. She'd wrapped around her an outer garment that looked like a wool blanket with armholes cut into it, and she carried a canvas tote bag stenciled with the women's power symbol. Earrings that resembled the contents of a man's trouser pocket—clusters of coins and lint—dangled from her ears. She looked as though she were heading to the nearest bazaar to haggle over the price of a camel.

"Hi, Aunt Martha," Julia said politely. Susie echoed the words half a beat behind her.

"Going to visit your mother?"

"Yes," Susie said, carefully avoiding eye contact with Julia. Where else would they be going? The only people they knew on the twenty-fourth floor of the Bloom Building were their mother and Aunt Martha, who had refused to give up the apartment when Uncle Jay divorced her. Allowing her to remain in their seven-room residence in the Bloom Building had been quite a sacrifice for him, but he'd consoled himself by buying a place just as big on the East Side and setting his new wife, Wendy, loose inside it. Wendy had decorated the entire place in Laura Ashley, a huge change from Aunt Martha's decor, which tended toward terra-cotta and burlap.

"Where are you off to?" Julia asked, since Aunt Martha was trying so hard to be affable, something she had to put a real effort into.

"A poetry reading at the Women's Center," Aunt Martha told them. "Sharnay Clingan is reading. Perhaps you've heard of her?"

"Sharnay Clingan" sounded like a character from a cheesy science-fiction movie. "No," Julia said, "but I'm sure she's good."

"She has her strengths, one of them being a marvelous sense of diction. Well, I'd best be off. I don't want to get there late. You girls really should stop by the Women's Center sometimes. Your generational cohort seems to think it's unnecessary to be feminists, but it's more important than ever. The fight has not yet been won."

"We're feminists," Susie cheerfully assured her.

"Then, come to the Women's Center. You'll like it."

Julia thought she'd like it about as much as she liked doing her income tax, but she didn't say so. She also thought that if her aunt was such a committed feminist, she ought to call her nieces "women" instead of "girls." "Thanks for the invitation, Aunt Martha," she mumbled, starting down the hall to her mother's apartment.

"Give Sondra my best," Aunt Martha ordered them before stepping into the elevator and disappearing.

"Her best isn't very good," Susie whispered, as if afraid the elevator door would slide back open and Aunt Martha would overhear the insult.

"She hangs out with people named Sharnay Clingan. What do you expect?"

"Did she always give us the willies?" Susie asked, falling into step next to Julia. "Or is it just recently? I can't remember."

"She always gave us the willies."

They'd reached their mother's door and Julia pressed the doorbell. She wasn't worried about Aunt Martha overhearing anything they might have to say. Grandma Ida, one floor above, was the one who worried her.

Grandma Ida wouldn't hear them. The floors were thick. And anyway, Julia wasn't going to say anything Grandma Ida didn't already know.

Her mother swung open the door and beamed. "What a wonderful surprise! There I was, just sitting around this afternoon, doing the *Times* crossword puzzle and feeling lonesome, when all of a sudden my sweethearts telephone me from downstairs and say they're coming up! It's a mother's dream come true!" She wrapped one arm around each of them and stepped back, simultaneously hugging them and pulling them into the foyer. They momentarily got jammed in the doorway, and then Susie moved forward while Julia moved backward, and they wiggled through without breaking free of their mother's double embrace.

Sondra Bloom kissed each of them, then released them, took a step back and beamed at them. Julia contemplated how lucky she was to have been born to this woman instead of, for instance, Aunt Martha. Not that her mother was perfect. She could be abrasive, temperamental and melodramatic. She could damn with faint praise—and often did. And her rhinoplastic nose was too small for her face. Grandma Ida was right about that.

But she never dressed as if she were on her way to the bazaar to buy a camel. She wore flowing slacks and long sweaters that hid her age-widened hips, sensible flat suede loafers from Land's End and a discreetly sumptuous tennis bracelet around her left wrist. Her hair framed her face in a tidy chestnut-hued page-boy, and she always layered her mouth with a subtle lipstick—to protect her lips against sunburn.

She also still wore her wedding band, which Julia considered touching, even though it would likely scare away potential suitors. If asked, Sondra would probably claim she wasn't ready for suitors yet. Julia could respect that. She only hoped her mother would change her mind eventually. Sondra Bloom was still a vibrant woman, and if her entire life revolved around her children, every time Julia looked up her mother would be orbiting her like a nosy, hyperactive satellite.

"Susie, look at you! New haircut, right? It's perfect. Let me see." Rather than walking around Susie, Sondra lifted Susie's hand and spun her like a music-box ballerina. "It's perfect. Isn't it perfect, Julia?"

She'd said "perfect" enough times to suggest she hated Susie's haircut. "It looks great," Julia said, pulling off her coat.

"You're just glowing, Susie. The haircut really brings something out in your face."

"She's in love," Julia interjected, pulling Susie's denim jacket down her arms and carrying both coats to the closet. "With the bagel guy downstairs," she added.

"I'm not in love with him," Susie argued. "He picked out a very nice bagel for me, though."

"So, you've eaten? Are you girls hungry? I'm sure I've got something…" She wandered down the hall to the kitchen, mumbling about what edibles she might have in stock.

"I'm always hungry," Susie called after her, then shot Julia a hostile look. "I'm not in love with the bagel guy," she said. "All I ever said was, he's cute."

"Yeah, sure. I was standing right next to you, Susie. I heard you hyperventilating."

"That wasn't love. That was lust. Too bad you don't know the difference."

Susie's taunt irked Julia. It also irked her that she was hanging up Susie's coat as well as her own. But if she didn't hang it up, Susie would just toss it on the leather settee beside the mail table in the spacious foyer, and that would have irked their mother. The poor woman was going to be irked enough once Julia told her why they'd come. She didn't need to be irked about uncloseted jackets, too.

"What is she going to feed us?" Susie asked, waiting while Julia shut the closet door, as if by doing so she was helping. "More bagels, do you think?"

"Carrot sticks, probably." Sondra was usually on a diet. The Blooms had been blessed with vigorous metabolisms. Even if they did eat their merchandise, they wouldn't get fat. But Sondra was a Bloom only by marriage, and she'd inherited the Feldman physique, which was unfortunately susceptible to such forces as childbirth, age, gravity and caloric consumption.

Susie wrinkled her nose and strolled down the hall with Julia. Although their mother's apartment had a floor plan identical to Grandma Ida's, it didn't feel at all prewar. The walls were assorted shades of white, the furniture streamlined and modern and the artwork abstract, giving the rooms a chilly atmosphere. Sondra always claimed it was less an aesthetic choice than a practical one: modern furniture was easier to keep clean. "None of those little nooks and curlicues," she explained. "None of those ornately carved feet to collect dust." She had a woman who came in once a week to clean—it used to be twice a week when their father was alive, because he'd insisted on a high degree of tidiness in his residence. But the apartment was so big that their mother probably went weeks without entering some of the rooms. The place managed to stay neat—especially when Julia made sure Susie's jacket was properly put away.

In the kitchen, Sondra set out Ziploc bags of cut fresh vegetables and a tub of dill-and-sour-cream dip. "Is this from downstairs?" Susie asked, examining the tub.

Sondra shook her head. "Their dips are too expensive."

"You don't have to pay for them," Julia reminded her.

"If I take one, it comes out of the profits."

"The store makes a nice profit, Mom," Susie argued. "If anyone ought to know that, it's you."

"And do you know why the store makes a nice profit?" Sondra swirled a stalk of celery through the dip. "Because the Blooms don't go filching inventory, that's why. Because the merchandise is there for retail purposes. We sell it. That's how we make a nice profit."

Julia glanced at Susie and found her glancing back. "You'd better tell her," Susie said.

Julia would have kicked Susie if they'd been seated at the table where her mother wouldn't have been able to see the foot movement. But they were standing, leaning side by side against the polished granite counter, while their mother pulled a chunk of cheddar cheese—no doubt some cheap store-brand from the supermarket down the street, not from the international collection at Bloom's—out of the refrigerator and placed it on her marble cutting board.

"Tell me what?" she asked, her dark-eyed gaze traveling from one daughter to the other.

"That cheese looks great," Susie said brightly, lifting the silver knife and slicing into it.

Sondra zeroed in on Julia. "Tell me what?"

"I had brunch at Grandma Ida's this morning," Julia said.

"Which is why Susie's eating and you're not. What did Lyndon make?"

"Lox and scrambled eggs. I asked him to marry me."

"He's not your type, sweetie."

"He's a great cook."

"If cooking was necessary for the success of a marriage, your father and I wouldn't have stayed married for thirty years."

This was true. Neither of them had excelled in the culinary arts. On and off over the years, her mother had hired a cook. She'd also often resorted to prepared dinners for the family—from the supermarket down the street, not from Bloom's.

Then again, cooking or no, Julia sometimes wondered how her parents had managed to stay married for thirty years. Julia had loved her father, but Ben Bloom hadn't been an easy man. The store had consumed him. He'd had moods, often acting as if the fate of every last roll of liverwurst and Jordan Almond rested on his weary but all-important shoulders. He'd missed dinner more nights than not—maybe because he couldn't stand Sondra's cooking—and frequently worked on weekends. He'd never seemed as "at home" in this apartment as he had downstairs in his corner office on the third floor, directly above the kitchenware department.

But Julia had always known he loved her. He loved Susie, too, and Adam—although he hadn't been around enough for Adam. He hadn't made himself available to do all that father-son stuff, like taking him to Central Park and teaching him how to throw a baseball. Adam had learned baseball from Uncle Jay and the cousins, and Julia sensed that he still resented their father for failing to teach him the techniques necessary to throw a curve and a sinker. It didn't matter how often Julia reassured him that he was better off learning such things from Uncle Jay, who unlike their father was a natural athlete and who was always eager to abandon his office for a few hours of catch in the park with the boys.

Sondra pulled three tumblers from an overhead cabinet and placed them on the counter. "So," she said as she swung open the refrigerator door again and reached for a lidded plastic pitcher of iced tea, "what did Grandma Ida invite you to brunch for?"

"She said she intends to name me president of Bloom's."

Sondra straightened, set the iced tea on the counter and

smiled hesitantly, as if certain she'd misheard. "She intends to do what?"

"Name me president of Bloom's," Julia enunciated.

Sondra issued a dramatic gasp. Her dark eyes narrowed. So did her lips, compressing into a pinched pink circle. She reached into another cabinet and pulled out a bottle of scotch. After pouring a generous slosh of it into one of the glasses, she crossed to the dinette table, sank onto one of the leather-and-chrome chairs and took a long slurp. "This is a joke, right?"

"No joke," Julia said.

"This is serious? Grandma Ida told you she's naming you president?"

"Yes."

"Of Bloom's?"

"I'm afraid so."

"She doesn't want me to be president," Susie said cheerfully, pouring an inch of scotch into each of the other glasses and handing one to Julia. "Apparently, I was disqualified because of my tattoo."

"It's an embarrassment, that tattoo," Sondra remarked. She sprang out of her chair, yanked a box of Cheese Nips from a shelf, settled back into her chair and scooped a fistful of the crackers out of the box. "Don't forget, your Grandfather Isaac came over to this country in, what, 'thirty-eight? Just steps ahead of the storm troopers. A Jew with a tattoo makes some people think of concentration camp survivors."

"I don't believe the Jews in the concentration camps got butterflies tattooed onto their ankles," Susie argued.

"That's not the point. The point is, you wanted a tattoo and you got one. Don't expect your grandma to approve. But you…" She turned her gaze to Julia. Her lips had taken on a slightly orange coloration from the Cheese Nips. "You're a lawyer! You've got a wonderful career! What the hell is Ida up to? What is wrong with that woman?"

Julia thought "wonderful career" might be a bit of an overstatement, but other than that, she agreed with her mother's sentiments. She didn't agree with her choice of beverage, however. She didn't drink hard liquor; it tasted too much like liquor. But to dump her scotch into the sink would look like a condemnation of her mother's and sister's choice, so she gingerly took a sip of the stuff and tried not to grimace.

"I have worked my fingers to the bone for that store!" Sondra ranted. "I learned the business from your father. Who was I? Just his wife. But I learned. First I helped him with typing. Then with the books. Then with decisions. I was the one who said we should be selling gourmet flours. I was the force behind our coffee corner—and look at what a profit center that's turned into. Years before Starbuck's took over the world, I was telling your father that Bloom's needed to get out front with gourmet coffees. Was I right?"

She stared at Julia and Susie long enough for them to realize this wasn't a rhetorical question. "Yes," Susie said, while Julia murmured, "Absolutely."

"And that crazy woman thinks my daughter should be the next president? I run the damn place! I know the job better than *she* does, the great Mrs. Ida Bloom, the Grand Pooh-bah herself! Does she hate me that much?"

"She said you weren't a Bloom by blood," Julia explained in a gentle voice. It was a terrible reason, but that was what Grandma Ida had said. "Also, she doesn't like your nose."

"I don't like her nose, either!" Her mother pounded her fist on the table, causing her glass to tremble. "What is her problem?" She placed the Cheese Nips box on the table, stood, paced, frowned. "You know what? Maybe she's senile. She's eighty-eight. Maybe her brain is beginning to go. More than beginning. Maybe she's deep into Alzheimer's territory, and we just never noticed."

"She doesn't have Alzheimer's, Mom," Julia argued. If Grandma Ida was demented, her dementia had nothing to do with her age. She'd been ornery and unreasonable for as long as Julia could remember.

"So…she hates me that much," her mother muttered. "She

hates me so much she'd refuse to let me run the store I'm already running. Girls, never get married. I don't mean that," she hastily corrected. "Of course get married, have babies, make me a grandma. But just remember—you get married and you wind up with a mother-in-law. Maybe you should both marry orphans."

"I'll do my best," Susie offered, downing another robust sip of scotch.

"And Jay? Why didn't she pick him? She doesn't like his nose, either?"

"She said he spends too much time on the computer."

"The computer business is the only worthwhile thing he's ever done for the store," Sondra retorted. "The woman is senile. Completely *meshuge*. So, okay. Jay spends too much time on the computer and I've got a nose. And Susie's got a tattoo. Did she have equally good reasons for disqualifying everybody else?"

Julia sighed. She felt uncomfortable rehashing her post-brunch conversation with Grandma Ida. Enduring the discussion once had been unpleasant enough. "Adam's too young. Neil lives in Florida. Rick's always broke. It would be crazy putting *any* of us in charge. None of us knows thing one about how to run a place like Bloom's."

"*I* know thing one," her mother asserted. "Also things two, three, four and a hundred. I should have been named president. Ida knows it. She just hates me."

"I don't think she hates you, Mom—"

"She hates me," Sondra said decisively. She stopped pacing, flopped back into her chair and took a swallow of scotch. "So, what are you going to do?"

What Julia *wasn't* going to do was take over the presidency. She'd endured nearly her entire life surrounded by Bloom's. Her parents had worked at the store, she'd spent her after-school hours at the store, and on those occasions when they'd all come upstairs together for a late supper, her parents had spent the entire meal talking about the store. Over reheated macaroni-and-cheese or pan-fried burgers, they'd debated the markup on multigrain bread, the menus of heat-n-eat meals, the efficiency of the catering service, the decision to expand into housewares. Julia still remembered a virulent fight that had lasted several days over whether to pipe background music into the store. Sondra had put in time at the library reading studies claiming that shoppers spent more money in stores with piped-in music, but Julia's father hadn't cared. "We've never had music in Bloom's," he'd said. "Bloom's isn't a goddamn elevator, okay? It isn't a dentist's office."

Julia had lived Bloom's from the moment of her birth until the day she'd left for Wellesley nine-and-a-half years ago. She had no intention of living Bloom's as an adult.

She wanted her mother to be the president. Sondra deserved it. She'd earned it. The size of her nose was irrelevant; for the sake of the store itself, for the solvency of its future, for the legacy of yet-to-be-born generations of Blooms, Sondra ought to be the one at the helm.

"You need a plan," Susie commented. She swirled a vivid green slice of bell pepper through the dip and popped it into her mouth.

"What are you talking about?" Julia asked.

"A plan so Mom can get to be president."

"You have any ideas?"

Susie gave her a grin broad enough that Julia would have blamed its excessiveness on the scotch if Susie had consumed more. "Here's what I think," she said. "Julia, you tell Grandma Ida you'll be the president. Then you act as kind of a dummy president. Mom does the actual job and you keep your job at Griffin, McDougal."

"That's a stupid idea," Julia said, although for some reason it didn't seem quite stupid enough.

"How long would we have to play this game?" Sondra asked. "How long would we have to pretend Julia's the president?"

"How long do you think Grandma Ida's going to live?" Susie asked. With a remorseful cringe, she added, "I'm not saying we should start hoping for her to die or anything. I'm just

saying, how much attention is she really going to give to all this?
She hardly ever goes to the third floor. She doesn't visit the offices much. How often, Mom? Maybe once or twice a month?
On those days, Julia will have just stepped out of the office. Or
she's got an appointment with the vinegar dealer. Or she's at a
sour cream tasting."

"I'm not going to a sour cream tasting," Julia protested.

Susie gave her an impatient look. "Of course you're not.
You're over at Griffin, McDougal, running up billable hours.
Grandma Ida doesn't have to know that."

"Uncle Jay'll figure it out. He'll tell her."

"Uncle Jay doesn't pay enough attention to figure anything
out. And if he does…well, maybe sometimes you'll have to stop
in at the store and act like you're in charge. You could bring
your files with you and work in Dad's old office, couldn't you?"

"What if Uncle Jay asks me a question about something and
I don't know the answer?"

"Tell him you haven't mastered the job yet. Tell him to
check with Mom in the meantime. Eventually, Grandma Ida is
going to…well, do whatever she's going to do eventually. And
then, as president, you can name Mom your successor."

"What a brilliant idea," Sondra said.

Julia took a quick, biting sip of scotch and tried not to
wince. The idea was miles from brilliant, but it still didn't
sound stupid enough. She needed it to sound stupid. She
needed it to sound so stupid she could laugh about it, and then
tell Sondra and Susie that it was the stupidest idea she'd ever
heard.

She eyed the bottle of Dewar's sitting innocently next to the
bags of raw vegetables. It was two-thirds full. There wasn't
enough scotch in it to make this idea sound as stupid as Julia
needed it to sound.

She didn't want to be the president of Bloom's. Not even
the dummy president. Not even a fake, fool-Grandma-Ida,
grease-the-skids-for-Mom president.

"It's a brilliant idea," Sondra gushed, gliding across the room and gathering Susie into a smothering hug. She relaxed her hold on Susie only enough to reach out and snag Julia, who was drawn tight against the two women she was closest to in the whole world. Three bosoms smashed together at the center of the circle of Sondra Bloom's arms. "It's an absolutely brilliant idea. Let's do it. *Mazel tov* to Julia, the new president of Bloom's."

Shit, Julia thought, as her mother hugged her tighter. Like Sondra's hug, the idea wrapped around her and squeezed. And she couldn't see a way to escape.

4

Ron Joffe leaned back in his chair. The spring in the hinge had gone a bit flabby, so he had to do this carefully or he'd wind up flopping over backward and banging his head on the industrial-strength carpet that blanketed the floors of *Gotham Magazine*'s headquarters, a block from Union Square. The right corner of his desk was occupied by his computer, which filled his office with a white-noise purr. The monitor displayed the text of next week's column. He ought to skim it one final time, but he didn't want to. He'd gone over it often enough to recognize the configurations of the letters and the patterns of the paragraph breaks.

The column was fine. It was great. It was done, finished, history.

He enjoyed being *Gotham*'s financial columnist. It beat having to wear a necktie to work. Journalism had been his first love, anyway—the business degree had come later. Having a weekly gig at New York City's top-circulation magazine suited him the way a career in finance never would. Journalism and business—the perfect marriage.

Shifting his attention from the computer screen, he stared at the framed print of a lion hanging on the wall across from his desk and felt a keen identity with the animal, its muscles taut and bristling with energy beneath its tawny skin. The lion was one of eight large photographs of animals that decorated his office. Some days he was partial to the photo of two pandas. They looked so sweet and cuddly and child-like. Other days he was partial to the photo of the lion, which looked the exact opposite of sweet and cuddly and childlike.

Today was a lion day. Energy burned under his skin, making him want to prowl.

He groaned. What was wrong with him? Why did he feel so restless? Why were his thoughts skewing toward romance, images of first loves and perfect marriages? He knew that old saw about how in the spring a man's fancy turned to thoughts of love, but in the spring his fancy usually turned to thoughts of the Yankees—if he even had a fancy, which he sincerely hoped he didn't.

He was not suffering from spring fever. Lions never suffered from spring fever, did they?

Actually, he wasn't sure about that. It was possible they mated in the spring. Or maybe spring was when they gave birth to their cubs. He knew squat about wild animals, with the possible exception of urban cockroaches, a species he'd had some experience with over the years.

Cockroaches. Ha. A man with a fancy didn't think about cockroaches. This must prove he didn't have a fancy.

The thought failed to soothe him.

He hit the combination of buttons on his keyboard that would send his column to his boss, and shoved out of his chair. He tried prowling for a minute but it didn't satisfy him. Maybe if he had four legs, if he could prowl on clawed and padded paws instead of scuffed and battered sneakers, if he could prowl through an African savannah or an Asian jungle, or wherever it was that real lions prowled, the exercise might have a more therapeutic effect. At least he had a great head of hair, he thought, sending the lion poster a defiant glare. Mr. Pussycat there might have more of an eighties Bon Jovi coif, but Ron's hair wasn't chopped liver.

Why was he thinking about chopped liver?

Maybe he was hungry.

He left his office, resolved to go downstairs and buy himself something edible. Preferably something that included meat, given his leonine mood. He'd go find a hot dog vendor and pounce with a roar.

He slowed his gait as he neared Kim Pinsky's office at the far end of the hall. Not that he felt he had to sneak past her, but if she saw him leave, she'd want to know where he was going and why. She was like a mother, only worse—too young, too smart and too hard to bullshit.

His slowing was a bad move, though. It allowed his shadow to slide through her doorway. "Joffe?" Her voice wafted out to him, a deceptively gentle soprano.

Sighing, he followed his shadow into her office. She sat at her desk, blond and mercilessly gorgeous, the antithesis of a hard-boiled editor in appearance if not attitude. "Where are you going?" she asked.

"Out for lunch."

"It's ten-fifteen."

"A very early lunch."

Her smile didn't reassure him. "Where's your column?"

He was relieved to be able to say "Probably sitting in your e-mail In-box right this very minute."

"And?"

"And I'm hungry," he said.

She flicked a long, golden lock of hair behind her ear with her hand. Her hair was better than his. So were her claws, perfectly filed and painted a metallic copper.

"You're hungry for a challenge," she told him.

"Actually, I was thinking along the lines of a couple of hot dogs."

Her teeth were also better than his, too even and white to be natural. He was pretty sure she regularly subjected them to professional bleaching. He was also pretty sure she'd had cheek implants at some point. She was a Californian by birth, after all.

"I have an idea for a bigger article," she said. "Maybe a cover story, if you think you can handle it."

He straightened, even though he knew she was manipulating him. She was blond and he was a man. Of course she could manipulate him. "I can handle it."

"It's about food," she said. "A very New York piece. A new challenge, Ron. Something to get your juices flowing."

If she were single and he had a fancy, his juices might start flowing just from the velvet texture of her voice. But she was married—to a high-priced lawyer, in fact—and bitchy. And Californian. And his boss. All in all, not his type.

So he focused on the big article she was pitching him. "What's it about?"

"You're familiar with Bloom's?"

What New Yorker wasn't? He shopped at Bloom's regularly. It was a terrific store. It sold more bagels than Broadway sold tickets to shows—and Bloom's bagels probably got better reviews, too. He'd bought his own significant share of those bagels over the years.

But still… *Bloom's?* What the hell would he write about a deli? "Just because I'm hungry doesn't mean I'm a food expert," he argued.

"Obviously. If you were a food expert, you'd stay away from hot dogs. Do you have any idea what goes into them?"

"Not knowing is part of the fun," he said.

"Bloom's isn't just a deli. It's a huge business. One year ago, Ben Bloom, the president of the company died. I want you to get past the food and write about the business. One year after Ben Bloom's death, how is Bloom's doing? Are their finances shaky now that Ben Bloom is gone? There's your story, Joffe. A business story about food. You're just the one to write it."

He disagreed, but disagreeing with Kim was something a *Gotham* staffer—even an esteemed weekly columnist—didn't do out loud. "Okay," he said, realizing he wasn't that hungry after all. Or else perhaps this assignment had taken his appetite away.

With a forced smile, he backed out of Kim's office. One of his colleagues had once dubbed her the *Gotham* Goddess, and someone else had said it was bad luck to turn one's back on a goddess, so they all remained facing her when they left her office. Ron wasn't particularly superstitious, but he knew better than to tempt fate.

Oddly enough, though, as he retraced his steps to his office, contemplating his new assignment, he couldn't shake the eerie notion that Kim had just given his fate a karmic realignment. *Bloom's.* A fabulous deli, the death of the head honcho, family intrigue. Food, money, heirs, power. Tradition. Schmaltz.

His nonexistent fancy was definitely turning.

Susie sat cross-legged on a chair near the front window of Nico's, the whiteboard on the table in front of her and a marker clenched in her hand. The last poem she'd written had been up for nearly two months. It was time for her to compose a new one.

She stared at the streaky white surface for a moment, doodled a couple of round red tomatoes in the bottom-right corner of the board and tried not to think about the poetry-writing techniques she'd learned at Bennington. College professors knew how to coach students to write the sort of poetry that got good grades. Nico wanted the sort of poetry that would entice people into the restaurant to buy pizza and pasta and pitchers of beer.

The window poetry had been her idea. She didn't mind waiting on tables—she wasn't crazy about it, but it paid her third of the rent for the crowded little walk-up on East First Street that she shared with Anna and Caitlin. However, she had artistic inclinations. After working at Nico's for a few weeks, she'd asked Nico to let her redesign the pizzeria's window. He'd put her off for a while, but finally he'd given her permission. She'd arranged some of her old stuffed animals around a toy table in the window and put a big fake pizza on the table. She'd tied a bib around the neck of Mr. Beanie, her stuffed elephant, taped a plastic fork to the paw of Aussie the koala and a wedged piece of a bread stick into the bill of Inga the stuffed duck, and she'd set before them glasses filled with water darkened with red food coloring to look like Chianti.

Then she'd written a poem that would have earned her at best a C-minus in Sadie Rathbun's advanced poetry writing seminar at Bennington:

> Pizza isn't matzo.
> What it is is lotsa
> Crust and sauce and toppings and cheese.
> So come on in, PLEASE!

Not only had many people come in and ordered pizza, but they'd all commented on the charming window display and the poem. Nico had decided that Susie must be some sort of genius, and he'd asked her to change the window display every few months.

Her new display entailed a poster that showed a pizza broken up like a pie chart, with different-size wedges. A two-thirds-of-the-pie wedge was labeled "Percentage of New Yorkers who can't resist Nico's pizza." A ninety-degree wedge was labeled "Percentage of people who prefer sex to Nico's pizza." A very narrow wedge was labeled "Percentage of people who, if stranded on a desert island, would rather have a good book than a slice of Nico's pizza."

Nico loved the pie chart, but he wanted a poem, too. "The customers expect it," he explained to her—even though this grand tradition was little more than a year old. "They want the poem. Gotta give 'em what they want."

She studied the blank surface of the board, wishing words would magically materialize on it. Magic failed, and the board remained blank.

"Okay," she whispered, then forced herself to write:

I gave my love a pizza;
In return he gave his heart.
He carries the taste of pizza
In his soul when we're apart.
And when he's far away from me,
Nico's brings him back.
The pizzas I give him are the ultimate
Aphrodisiac.

Not her best. At the moment, pizzas didn't seem like aphrodisiacs to her. Bagels, on the other hand...

No, she wasn't going to think about the guy selling bagels at Bloom's. Not for the next ten minutes. She'd already been thinking about him too much, and for no good reason. Who was he, anyway? Some clerk who'd given her an egg bagel—and reminded her to pay for it, as if she were a potential shoplifter. And he'd called her "nubile," which, when she considered it, had a kind of iffy feel to it.

She reread her poem, decided it would do and set the whiteboard on its easel in the window. Through the glass, she saw a familiar-looking man pausing to read it. She waved at him, and he smiled and nodded, then steered his attention back to the poem.

She closed her marker and carried it across the small dining room to the counter. The tables were empty. Her shift ran from three to eleven today, and the place wouldn't start filling up until closer to five, when hungry customers began drifting in after work. She could visit a little with her cousin Rick if he came in.

He did, moving in his shambling way across the checkerboard floor tiles to the counter. "Hey, Cous'," he greeted her, tossing his unkempt black hair back from his face with a jerk of his head.

"Hey, Rick."

"New poem?"

She nodded. "What do you think of it?"

"I think any poem that has the word *aphrodisiac* in it is okay." He leaned on the counter and gave her an ingratiating smile. "Would your boss kill you if I had a cola on the house?"

"No, he wouldn't kill me. He'd just ask me to pay the buck-fifty," she said, her smile growing a little stiff. Rick was always trying to mooch food off her.

She didn't know why he never had any money. Well, yes, she did: because he never worked. He usually had a supposed deal in the offing, some project about to happen, but until the deal or project reached fruition—which was about as likely to occur as the earth colliding with the moon—he subsisted on hand-outs. Uncle Jay usually came through for him. So did Aunt Martha. One advantage of having divorced parents was that you could hit them both up for money and neither had to know you'd already hit the other one up.

Still, Susie liked Rick. They were the same age, second-born kids, arty types, downtowners. He lived in a flat in TriBeCa that he couldn't possibly afford without assistance from Uncle Jay, and he sporadically took classes at NYU's film school. He saw himself as the next darling of the independent film world. At least he would be, if he ever managed to make a movie.

"If I staggered in here dying of thirst, so parched my skin was turning to dust like Oklahoma in the thirties, you'd still make me pay for a cola," he said. "Is that what you're trying to tell me?"

She had to laugh. That was the thing with Rick: he made her laugh, and that made her give in. "I'll treat you, but first you've got to tell me what you *really* thought of my poem."

"If you're treating me, I *really* thought your poem was a work of brilliance. It resonated, Suze. It rocked."

She was laughing harder. Her cousin was going to get his

cola. And Nico probably wouldn't make her pay for it, anyway. He was back in the kitchen, prepping for the dinner surge. He'd never even have to know about the cola. She'd tell him she'd taken it for herself.

And he wasn't paying her extra for the front windows. The least he owed her was a cold drink.

She decided her resonant, rocking poem was worthy of two drinks. After filling two plastic tumblers with cola from the machine and poking straws into them, she emerged from behind the counter and led Rick to a table. He unzipped his hooded sweatshirt and slouched into a chair. His pants were fashionably baggy, and he wore ratty-looking Teva sandals with no socks.

"Aren't your feet cold?" she asked as she settled into the chair across from him.

"I never get cold feet," he joked. He sucked a length of cola through his straw and sighed. "Ahh. A marvelous vintage. Playful yet serious, with a profound sparkle and a note of butterscotch."

Susie laughed again. "So, how's your latest project coming?"

"Don't ask." He took another drink, then reconsidered that pessimistic response. "I've got some actors interested in the script, but none of them has a big enough name to bring in money. You know, this city is crawling with excellent actors nobody's ever heard of."

"And they're all waiters," Susie pointed out. "I'm the only waiter in the entire city who isn't an actress."

"You're a poet. Speaking of which, I came here because I've got a deal for you. There's going to be a poetry slam at this club down the street from me. No entry fee, and there's a two-hundred-dred-fifty-dollar prize. You could get rich."

"Not if I keep paying for your drinks."

"It'll be fun, even if you don't win. Lots of people, wine, words and meter and all that crap, you know?"

She wondered whether the Bloom's bagel man ever attended poetry slams. That was an absurd thought—and it had snuck up on her before her ten minutes of not-thinking-about-him was over. God, she hadn't been infatuated like this since her adolescence, and back then, it was usually over rock musicians or TV stars, not men who put bagels into plastic bags at Bloom's.

"You could bring some friends along. You still seeing that big dude with the red hair?"

Susie opened her mouth, closed it, then took a sip of her cola. *Was* she still seeing Eddie? It wasn't as if they were going together. They didn't phone each other on a daily basis. She didn't know what he did on those nights he wasn't with her, and she didn't want to know.

And now, when her brain had been hijacked by the bagel man… Shit. If only Grandma Ida had picked *her* to be president of Bloom's, she could work with him every day. She could find out his name, so she wouldn't have to keep thinking of him as Godiva. She could be his boss. She could give him a huge promotion, one that would entail his abandoning the bagel counter for her third-floor office. He could bring bagels with him when he moved up. They could eat bagels together, maybe share them, take turns smearing them with cream cheese, lick the excess cheese off each other's fingers…

And then she'd get sued for sexual harassment. Because there was no way she'd be able to have him working in her office, tempting her for eight hours a day, and not act on that temptation. After all, what would be the point of having him there with her if she wasn't going to *do* anything?

"Um, hello? Did I lose you?" Rick asked.

Susie gave her head a sharp shake and concentrated on her cousin's face. His hair was as long as hers, but not well cut. A brown fuzz blurred his chin—his feeble attempt at a goatee. His eyebrows were thicker than his beard.

But he had a sweet face. He had Grandma Ida's narrow nose and the Bloom physique, lean and low maintenance. Around his neck he wore a lens on a leather cord, his one major affectation. The beard was a minor affectation as far as she was concerned.

"I'm still here," she assured him. "Just thinking."

"About what?"

About how, thanks to her ingenuity, her mother and sister were going to be able to outmaneuver Grandma Ida. About how it would be really cool if Rick could make a movie someday, and the whole family could go to the premiere, and afterward they could have a party catered by Bloom's. About how if her father were still alive, he would think that was a dumb idea, because he'd always been like *his* mother, considering pursuits such as filmmaking and writing poetry frivolous. About how if she were Rick, she'd make a movie about Grandma Ida. It would be a horror flick.

About how she hadn't yet answered Rick's question about Eddie. "That big dude with the red hair? No," she said. "I don't think I'm seeing him."

"So, you wanna bring someone else to the poetry slam? Bring your roommates. I like them."

"If you sleep with either of them, I'll kill you," she warned.

"I'm not gonna sleep with them," he promised. "But just for the record, why would you kill me?"

"It would be incestuous." Besides, she would have to listen to Caitlin or Anna describe her cousin in terms of chocolate, something she'd prefer to avoid. Much as she loved Rick, she dreaded to think of how he'd emerge from the chocolate test. Would he be a Mr. Goodbar? Malt balls? Every time she saw him afterward, would she have to think, Anna said he was a Milk Dud? It would just be too weird.

Rick cupped his hands over his mouth and spoke, making his voice sound as if he were addressing her from a distance on a two-way radio crackling with static. "I'm losing you...come in, Suze, come in....Hello? Are you out there? Captain, I think we've lost her."

"I'm here," she snapped. His teasing was beginning to wear on her. She'd given him a free cola—he ought to treat her kindly. Hadn't he ever been in love?

Not that she was in love. Nothing like it. Just a silly, giddy crush on a man with bedroom eyes and the devil in his smile. Devil's food cake.

If Rick didn't like it…well, he could give her back his free cola.

Mine, Sondra thought, standing in the center of Ben's office. *This should be mine.*

She still remembered the day, more than fifteen years ago, when Isaac had retired as president of Bloom's. He'd remained a co-CEO with Ida—their idea of corporate hierarchy was imaginative, to say the least—but the years had played hard on him and he'd decided he no longer had the stamina or interest to continue running the store on a day-to-day basis. It was time, he'd said, to let Ben take over.

Sondra had always been fond of Isaac. He'd been a gentle fellow, somewhat cowed by Ida. To this day, the old witch probably still believed he'd married her as a way of breaking into the food retail business, when Sondra was certain he'd married her only because he loved her.

What food retail business, anyway? When Isaac had arrived in America, Ida's parents were selling knishes from a pushcart on Broadway. If Isaac had been hoping to marry money, he could have chosen better.

But he'd taken over their pushcart, then moved the operation into a tiny storefront. He'd asked Ida to manage the books, while he managed the inventory, cooking and selling and kibitzing with customers, putting in long days even on *shabbat,* building the company pickle by pickle. More than good product, it had taken social skills, and Isaac had had social skills in abundance—unlike Ida, who'd wisely remained in the back office with her Burroughs machine and her ledger books.

Bloom's had bloomed. It had expanded into an adjacent storefront on one side, and then an adjacent storefront on the other, widening until it took up the entire ground floor of the building. It expanded down into the basement, which was used partly as a storage area and partly as a kitchen. Then it expanded up, taking over the second floor for offices. And up again to the third floor, so the second floor could be used for kitchenware. Eventually the family had taken ownership of the entire building.

Even as he'd prepared to retire from his empire, Isaac Bloom had seemed little altered by his success. He'd still called Sondra "sweetheart," and his first question to her had always been, "You taking good care of my *boychik?*" That was all he'd ever cared about—that she took good care of Ben. It was Ida who cared about everything else, who would never be able to open her heart to Sondra no matter how well she took care of Ben.

Sondra had done her best to make Ben happy, but nothing she could do for him would have made him as happy as his mother had the day she'd told him "Your father is retiring and you will take over." A more thoughtful woman might have *asked* rather than *told* him, but Ben didn't mind. He'd wanted to be president of Bloom's.

The office hadn't changed much from its Depression-era atmosphere when Ben had moved into it. Sondra still remembered the slight shudder she'd experienced as she'd entered the musty, gloomy room with its filmy windows overlooking Broadway and the side street, and the bulky, homely furnishings—file cabinets an indeterminate brownish-taupe shade, a coat tree that looked like a prop from a high school production of a Kaufman and Hart play, the squeaky swivel chair on four wheels that weren't quite level, and the desk, a massive, scratched block of old wood stained with cigarette burns, water rings and spilled ink.

Sondra had immediately set to work redecorating the office for Ben. She'd bought a simple teak desk that had looked ultramodern when it was new and retained its stylish flair even today, a brown leather chair on five wheels that all touched the floor at the same time, a couch of matching brown leather, attractive teak file cabinets and vertical blinds for the windows. Ida had shrieked over the money spent on the new decor, but for God's sake, the woman shrieked every time the price of postage stamps went up a penny.

Well, Sondra shrieked every time the postal rates went up, too. But that was different. *Everybody* shrieked about that.

The one thing Ben had refused to let her do was remove his father's desk from the office. It occupied one corner of the room, locked and empty, with only a potted plant standing on it—another addition of Sondra's. Since plants supposedly exhaled oxygen, she'd felt it important that Ben have one in his office so he could breathe more efficiently while he worked.

"Oh, yes," she whispered to the spirit of Isaac Bloom, which hovered somewhere in the vicinity of the old desk. "I took good care of your *boychik.*"

And now he was gone, a whole year, because she hadn't been in St. Petersburg to take care of him when he'd eaten that kaflooey sturgeon.

He was gone, and this office should be Sondra's.

All right, so it was going to be Julia's. Susie's plan was cocka-mamie, but it just might work. And it would keep that bastard Jay from taking over and running the company into the ground, a genuine risk given that the store's earnings had dropped since Ben's death. Jay was exactly like his father—except without the brains, the discipline, the ambition or the diligence. No way could he run Bloom's, unless he had someone else doing the actual work.

The only someone who fit that profile was Sondra, and she'd be damned if she was going to do the actual work while Jay got to sit in this office, pretending he was the boss.

So she and Julia would manage this charade. It could work. It *would* work. Sondra was so proud of her daughters, one for concocting this scheme and the other for becoming president of Bloom's. A daughter of hers, president of Bloom's... It made her chest swell like a balloon at the Macy's Thanksgiving Day parade, even though Julia didn't know her ass from her elbow when it came to running a business.

Well, she wasn't going to be running Bloom's. Sondra was. And if Ida ever found out...

Let the old bag find out, Sondra thought with a huff. Let her find out it had been Sondra all along, Sondra nudging Ben when he needed a nudge, Sondra keeping Jay out of Ben's hair, Sondra monitoring which coffees sold better, charting the growth in popularity of decaf, pushing to get a nice selection of herbal teas on the shelves. It was Sondra who had kept things running smoothly on the home front so Ben could stay focused on Bloom's. Sondra who had enrolled the kids at Dalton and checked their homework and taken them to Dr. Schwartz for their shots and strep tests. Sondra who had made sure they had nice friends and didn't stay out all night. Did Ben's offspring ever get head lice? Half the city's schoolchildren were infected with head lice at one time or another, but did Julia, Susie or Adam show up with a single louse?

Sondra had made sure they didn't.

She'd done *everything*. She ought to be president of the goddamn world. For thirty years she'd been Ben's wife, his assistant, his valet, his housekeeper, his bookkeeper, his polestar—and she still didn't have a title or a salary, for all the hard work she did. The company had been paying her a nice sum each month since Ben's death, but that little worm of an accountant, Myron Finkel, had explained that this was because Ida wanted Sondra to keep receiving Ben's salary. *Ben's.* Even when he was dead it was still his.

She wanted her own salary. She wanted her own title. She wanted her own corner office.

She wanted *this* office. She'd been the one to put the plant on that old desk, to fill the room with healthy air. Now it was her turn to breathe.

Thank God for her daughters. They'd make sure she got her turn.

Heath filled Julia's doorway. She hadn't recalled leaving her door open, but maybe she had. She was working too hard; she could barely remember her own name, let alone whether she'd left her door open.

Her office at Griffin, McDougal was slightly larger than a

coffin and about as lively. A couple of bookshelves protruded from brackets screwed to the wall behind her desk, and it had taken her several months to get used to bowing her head when she rose from her desk so she wouldn't bang her skull against the lower one. The wall across from her used to have a Mostly Mozart poster tacked to it, but Daniella, the persnickety office manager, had told Julia that posters were against the rules. "This isn't a college dormitory." She'd sniffed. "If you want to decorate your office, get a properly framed picture and run it by me."

Julia hadn't had a chance to purchase a "properly framed picture." So the wall facing her desk featured only four thumbtack holes marking the corners of a poster-size rectangle.

She hated this office.

"I brought sushi," Heath announced grandly.

She also hated sushi. But she managed a smile for him, which was all the encouragement he needed to enter her office and drop a clear plastic tray on top of the mountainous stack of folders on her desk.

"I don't have time for lunch," she warned him.

"Sure you do." He dragged over the tiny room's other chair and flopped down into it. With his snowy blond hair, his long legs and his easy grace, he had a way of making every room he entered his own. When she'd first met him, his presumptuousness dazzled her.

Right now, she didn't have time for it. She had all those folders to go through—and a few formidable folders at home, sent to her by Grandma Ida's lawyers. In those folders were documents proclaiming her the new president of Bloom's, inventory lists and budget printouts. Every time she walked past the package the lawyers had sent her, she swore she could hear it ticking like a bomb.

Nobody at Griffin, McDougal knew about her title at Bloom's. She couldn't tell anyone, because then they'd assume she was planning to quit the firm. And she wasn't. Even being trapped inside this minuscule office with a plastic platter of raw fish and a man boasting an attitude of entitlement so encompassing he made Donald Trump seem humble was better than joining the family business.

Heath was handsome, at least. He had elegant features, and he dressed in Armani and he was going to make partner within a year. Everybody knew it.

Maybe her life would be simpler if she loved him.

But how could she love someone who brought her raw fish? Smoked she could have handled. Smoked salmon, orange and oily and sliced for a bagel, or cut into scrambled eggs...

"I'm not hungry," she told Heath. Staring at those suspicious cylinders of gray and white made her even less hungry. Belatedly, she realized she might have sounded rude, so she added, "Thanks for bringing this, but really, I'm going to work through lunch today."

"What are you working so hard for? Tell me the truth, Jules—" he liked giving everyone uninvited nicknames; she assumed it was some sort of strange WASP custom "—is there anything in any one of those folders that can't wait fifteen minutes?"

"No. But if you add up everything in all the folders, the answer becomes yes."

"But I'm free now. So we can eat this sushi together. It's good stuff—not from the place on Madison Avenue. You remember, the one where Mindy Hawthorne was eating *ika* and she saw a roach scamper across the table?"

Julia knew she shouldn't ask, but she couldn't help herself. *"Ika?"*

"Raw squid, Jules. You haven't been paying attention."

He'd been trying to teach her about sushi for a long time. And he was right—she hadn't been paying attention. She was paying attention now, though, and the combination of raw squid and cockroaches convinced her she'd just as soon skip lunch.

"I'm really not hungry," she murmured.

He pried the lid off the tray, handed her a set of chopsticks wrapped in a tube of paper and pulled another set of chopsticks off the tray for himself. "Here I am, trying to broaden your horizons, and you say you're not hungry."

"It's the truth." She gestured toward the tray. "Go ahead, eat. It's all yours."

He used the chopsticks to pluck a chunk of something— squid, perhaps, or eel, or some other disgusting specimen of sea life that would never, ever be sold at Bloom's as long as she was president—and popped the morsel into his mouth. He chewed, swallowed and issued a satisfied sigh.

"This isn't because of your father, is it?" he asked.

"What?" Her state of mental overload? Her growing pile of folders, which she couldn't catch up on because she couldn't bring any of them home to work on, since she had all those materials about Bloom's to read? Her anger at herself over her inability to ignore those materials and let her mother run the store?

"Your aversion to raw fish. Just because your father died from eating bad fish doesn't mean this is bad."

"I hated sushi before my father died," she assured him.

He popped another blob of fish into his mouth and munched enthusiastically. "Are you free tomorrow night?"

"What's tomorrow night?"

"Friday," he enunciated, as if addressing an idiot. "I thought maybe we could go out for dinner, catch a movie, pretend we're a couple."

She smiled noncommittally.

"We've been enjoying each other's company for six months now. I've even met your grandmother. When are you going to sleep with me, Jules?"

She sighed to keep herself from answering "Never." She didn't know if she'd ever sleep with him. What she knew was that she wasn't in love with him, and for some reason that meant a lot to her.

Much as she adored Susie, much as she conceded that they had exactly the same brown eyes, the same narrow Bloom nose and the same hair, straight and thick and nearly black, she sometimes wondered whether they'd sprung from different gene pools. Susie seemed to have no qualms about sleeping with men she didn't love. And damn it, she *enjoyed* herself when she slept with them. She truly got a kick out of sex. Julia had slept with a grand total of three men in her life, and she hadn't gotten anything out of it at all.

She'd been madly in love with the first boy she'd slept with, in college, and she'd been so eager to keep him happy in the relationship that she hadn't wanted to upset him by saying that the sex just didn't feel as good to her as it seemed to feel to him. After they'd broken up, she'd had a fling with a fellow she'd met during a summer internship, just to prove she wasn't hung up on her first lover. That relationship hadn't worked out so well, either. Her third big affair had been in law school, and that time she'd tried, hesitantly and with great embarrassment, to suggest things he might do to make the experience more pleasurable for her. His response had been "Don't you trust me?"

Trust had never been the problem. Orgasms had.

She'd decided she wasn't going to venture down that path again until she met a man who knew the difference between trust and orgasms. So far, Heath had done nothing to convince her he was that man.

"Please don't pressure me about this, Heath." She wished her voice didn't have a begging little whine in it.

"We're adults."

"I know how old we are," she said. "I just don't feel right about sleeping with you."

"I always thought Jewish women were earthy. You know, loose."

"Is that what they taught you in Sunday School? That Jewish women are loose?"

"Actually—" he ate another piece of sushi "—the only woman who got any airplay was Mary. Look, Julia—I like you. I think you like me. I think you're beautiful. I think we'd be very good in bed together. I know for a fact that *I'd* be very good. That's a joke," he added before she could object. "I think the world wouldn't come to an end if we did this. I think we'd have fun, and I think fun is a good thing. How about you? Do you think fun is a good thing?"

She sighed again. She really did like Heath, even though he was an obnoxious twit. "I don't know what fun is these days. My life is swamped right now. I've got too much on my mind."

"Sex could take your mind off all those things that are on your mind."

"Maybe it could." She smiled wearily and shook her head. "I've got to figure out what I'm doing before I do anything with you. I'm sorry, Heath, but that's just the way it is."

He shrugged and polished off the last of the sushi. If sex meant all that much to him, he would be pressuring her. Or abandoning her.

Maybe he didn't mind her refusing him because he was sleeping with other women. Julia found the possibility oddly comforting.

She simply couldn't imagine herself lying under him while he had fun and was very good, and thinking about anything other than Bloom's and all those papers the lawyers had sent her. No matter what tricks she and her mother pulled, no matter how successfully they maneuvered the situation, how effectively they bamboozled Grandma Ida, how well they deceived Uncle Jay…

She was the president of Bloom's. Even sex with Heath wasn't going to change that.

5

Julia's cell phone bleated.

Because she was buried in the stacks of the firm's law library, the phone sounded louder than usual. Because she knew the call would concern her family, it sounded louder still. Only members of her family would phone her on her cell phone rather than her office phone while she was at work—and calls from her family always seemed to ring very loudly.

She glanced around and saw no one in her vicinity. Balancing a leather-bound tome of legal precedents in her left hand, she used her right hand to pull her cell phone from the pocket of her blazer and flip it open. "Hello?" she whispered. Even though no one was nearby, her surroundings demanded a hushed tone.

"Julia, it's Mom. You've got to get over here right away."

Julia sighed. The book felt like a boulder in her hand. Six hundred seventy-four pages of case law in alimony judgments could weigh a lot. She slid the volume onto an empty space on one of the shelves. "I'm working," she reminded her mother.

"Your grandmother is on the loose. She just stopped in, said Lyndon was taking her for a walk around the block, and after she got her airing she would be back to see how things were going. You've got to be at the store when she gets back, Julia. You're the president."

She'd been the president for a whole week, and so far she'd managed to avoid the store. She'd grown quite fond of that aspect of the job: not having to do it.

"I can't just drop everything and run over there," she argued. "I've got a job to do here, too."

"What am I supposed to tell your grandmother? You're in an all-day meeting with a herring vendor?"

Julia sighed again. "All right," she conceded. "I'll get over there as fast as I can."

"What do you want me to tell Ida if she gets back here before you arrive?"

"Tell her I'm on my way. Tell her I still have things to take care of at Griffin, McDougal. Whatever you do, *don't* tell her I'm in a meeting with a herring vendor." Merely thinking about such a thing made her want to take a shower.

But for her mother's sake, she would schlep across town and show her face on the third floor of the Bloom Building. She stashed her phone, lugged the alimony volume back to its proper shelf so the librarian wouldn't have to waste a day looking for it when it turned up missing and then hurried down the spiral stairs to the floor where her office was located. Griffin, McDougal occupied three floors of a steel-and-glass box on Park Avenue. The building's elevators stopped at all three floors, but internal stairways also connected the floors, and they were faster than the elevator.

She ducked into her office to grab her briefcase and the files on her desk, then stopped by Francine's desk on her way out. "Family crisis," she said. "I've got to run. I'll call in later to let you know how things are going."

Her usually cheerful secretary bit her lip in a show of concern. "It's not sturgeon again, is it?"

"This time it's herring," Julia confided before darting out the door.

The day was a good ten degrees warmer than that fateful morning a week and a half ago, when she'd traveled to the Bloom Building and learned about the future Grandma Ida had planned for her. Today was beautiful, sunny and full of spring-time—no wonder Grandma Ida had gone out for a walk with Lyndon. Julia could imagine her grandmother with her hand hooked through Lyndon's arm, the two of them moving along Broadway in a pace that was a cross between stately and halt-ing. For her age, Grandma Ida was in terrific shape, but the last time Julia had gone for a walk with her, it had taken them nearly an hour to circumnavigate the block. Of course, that was at least partly because Grandma Ida had had to stop to check out the other store windows in the neighborhood, critique the other pedestrians and complain about a yappy little dog someone was walking, the rudeness of certain drivers and the utter unfash-ionability of those ladies who wore sneakers with their busi-ness suits.

Julia waved at an approaching cab, but it zipped past her. The second cab she spotted stopped for her, and she dove in and gave the driver the address. As he pulled into the uptown flow, she sank back against the cracked upholstery and let out a long breath.

She didn't want to be the president of Bloom's. She couldn't imagine why she'd let her mother and Susie talk her into this. She just couldn't do it. Griffin, McDougal needed her.

Right. They needed her to look up a bunch of figures an office temp could look up just as easily. That looking up fig-ures made her feel needed was the most pathetic aspect of her entire situation.

She wasn't saving the world. She wasn't fighting for justice, defending the innocent and prosecuting the guilty. She was try-ing to help her boss put together an argument for why his mul-timillionaire client shouldn't have to pay the woman he'd been married to for twenty years a penny more than three thousand dollars a month in alimony.

The scumbag *should* pay her more. His wife had put up with him for those twenty years, and after meeting him Julia was aware of what an enormous sacrifice that must have been. But he was the one paying Griffin, McDougal—paying them big, paying them more than he wanted to pay his ex-wife—and Julia's job was to protect his assets.

Her other job was to convince her grandmother she was running Bloom's.

The cabbie was listening to loud sitar music on his radio. The nasal whine of it made her skull vibrate. She didn't want to be here. She didn't want to be tearing across town in this cab with monotonous ragas reverberating in the air. She didn't want to save a sleazy multimillionaire cheapskate a few bucks a month in alimony, and she didn't want to do anything that could be mentioned in the same sentence with the word *herring*.

She couldn't be in two places at once. She wasn't a magician, she wasn't a superwoman—and Aunt Martha notwithstanding, she wasn't even sure she was a feminist. Let Susie be president of Bloom's. She was the one who'd concocted this scheme. She was obviously a genius, even if she did have a tattoo. Let her run the damn store. Let her do Julia's job at Griffin, McDougal, too, if she was so damn smart.

Julia had built up a nice head of steam by the time she'd paid the cabbie an obscene amount for having transported her less than three miles. Climbing out of the cab, she straightened her spine, adjusted the shoulder strap of her briefcase, and lifted her chin, doing what she could to project height and dignity. She was going to tell them all the truth. She was going to say this deception was absurd and refuse to be a part of it anymore.

But then what would happen to her mother? And Uncle Jay? And Grandma Ida? And Bloom's? Not only would Julia be jeopardizing the entire family legacy, but everyone—including Susie—would be royally pissed at her.

Julia supposed she could continue the pretense for a little while. She wasn't going to wait for Grandma Ida to die—that was a really morbid aspect of the plan—but in time things might settle down. Sondra would gradually take over more of the president's job, and Grandma Ida would be so pleased by the way the store was running that she wouldn't delve too deeply into who was actually running it. And Uncle Jay…well, maybe he could get a raise and a fancy new title. Director of outside sales and service. Chief mail order and Internet executive. Something impressive. Something that would make The Bimbette swoon, honored beyond words to be married to a powerful chief-director-hotshot like Uncle Jay.

Julia paused before entering the store. The cluttered windows always made her breath catch, but not exactly in a positive way. The overwhelming array of *stuff*—bottles of herbed vinegar, stacked boxes of crackers, wooden crates of tea bags, flourishes of radicchio and parsley, wedges of low-fat Jarlsburg, cylindrical tins of butter cookies and humble paper bags of biscotti, cinnamon sticks, olives from Greece, Turkey and who knew where else, braided cloves of garlic and braided loaves of bread—gave her heartburn. Maybe they ought to have a roll of antacids on display in the window, too.

She entered the store, avoiding eye contact with any of the employees—as if they'd have a clue that she was their president—and climbed the stairs to the kitchenware floor. In the early afternoon lull, the aisles weren't too crowded, and she found herself studying the merchandise with a curiosity she'd never felt before. Why was the store selling table fans? What did that have to do with food? Why did they have such a limited selection of salt and pepper shakers? Wouldn't salt and pepper shakers be a relatively cheap item to keep in stock? Couldn't they carry some whimsical designs? Most of the salt and pepper shakers for sale here resembled the boring shakers found on the tables in greasy-spoon diners.

She reached the staff-only door at the rear of the kitchenware department, used her key to unlock it and took the private stairs to the third floor. A kind of calm ruled on this floor, due mostly to the absence of clutter. A hall wide enough to double as a reception area was lined with offices, many of which had their doors open so people could scream back and forth to one another without leaving their desks. "Who stole my Seder-in-a-Box layouts?" Uncle Jay hollered from the depths of his office.

"Nobody stole them." Julia's mother's voice emerged through another open doorway. "Besides which, isn't it a little late to be promoting the Seder-in-a-Box?"

"The Seder catalogs are already out, Sondra." Jay's disembodied voice slithered through the hall. "What am I, an idiot?"

"You want me to answer that?" Sondra's voice shot back.

"I need the Seder-in-a-Box photos to load onto the Web site. Believe it or not, some people order their seders at the last minute. That's what we have a Web site for."

"I thought we had a Web site to keep you busy," Sondra muttered. Julia could hear her—and she hoped Uncle Jay couldn't.

She stepped into her mother's office, which was separated from her father's old office by a narrow room occupied by Deirdre, her father's tall, svelte secretary. Julia had always been fascinated by Deirdre, partly because of her height, her freckles and her intriguing overbite, and partly because the woman seemed so utterly competent. When Julia was a child, doing her homework or crayoning pictures in a coloring book on Grandpa Isaac's old desk in her father's office, all her father would have to do was shout "Deirdre!" through his open door, and the woman would instantly materialize, holding whatever papers he needed, supplying whatever information he was looking for, assuring him that she'd taken care of anything he could possibly have wanted taken care of. Julia was in awe of her.

She entered her mother's office. "What's a Seder-in-a-Box?" she asked.

Her mother spun in her swivel chair and leaped to her feet. "You're here!" Excitement and relief energized her muted voice. "Go to Dad's office. I'll be right there."

Sondra seemed agitated enough that Julia decided not to argue. She could get her questions answered later; for now, she should position herself in her father's office—which was actu-

ally her office now. And maybe, while she was waiting for her
mother to join her and explain Bloom's from A to Z, she could
get a little work done on those alimony files.

With a nod, she left her mother, tiptoed past Deirdre's office
and entered the corner office. The vertical blinds were adjusted
to let in as much natural light as possible, and in the stripes of
sunlight Julia could see specks of dust dancing in the air. The
carpet was nearly bald in spots—her childhood memories of
this office had included a carpet as thick and soft as plush velvet, but that had been years ago. To be sure, she'd remembered
everything as being bigger than it actually was. Her father's desk
was smaller than her desk at Griffin, McDougal, and her grandfather's idle desk in the corner looked old and forlorn, the var-
nish eroded and the top surface slightly warped. Tiny cracks
laced the leather of the sofa, and the chair behind the desk
seemed to list to starboard.

So much for the exalted position of president. Maybe
Grandma Ida had named Julia president because she didn't
want any of her other loved ones to have to work in this seedy,
dreary room.

Julia crossed to her grandfather's old desk and fingered the
limp leaves of the coleus wilting in a pot on one corner. The
poor plant looked as if it hadn't had a drink since New Year's
Eve. If she were her father, she'd turn around and find Deirdre
filling the doorway, holding a watering can.

But she wasn't her father, and when she turned, no one
stood in her doorway. She returned to her father's desk, set her
briefcase on it and settled into the chair. It was too big for her.
Her feet barely touched the floor.

"A Seder-in-a-Box," her mother said, waltzing into the office and carrying an ominous-looking computer printout of a
multipage spreadsheet, "is an arrangement of traditional *Pesach*
dishes that we pack into a box and ship to customers. The box
includes some of that matzo we import from Israel, jars of
chicken soup with homemade matzo balls, a tub of fresh-
ground horseradish, *charoseth,* gefilte fish, macaroons, parsley—

everything but the roast shank and the hard-boiled eggs. It was a big seller last year."

Instant seder, Julia thought. Add eggs and stir. It sounded peculiar to her—but what did she know? She was only the president.

"So, your uncle Jay puts pictures of the different seder arrangements we offer—different sizes, some with wine and some without—on the Web site. People order it. It makes him feel like a big *macher*, contributing something worthwhile to the company."

"How many sales do we get over the Internet?" Julia asked.

"That's not for you to worry about." She pulled Julia's briefcase off the desk and hid it in the well, accidentally setting it on Julia's left foot and nearly crushing her big toe. Then she spread the computer printout across the dusty blotter. "This is what you're working on, okay? It's an inventory list."

"I'd really rather hear more about the Web site," Julia said, wiggling her toe inside her shoe to make sure it wasn't broken.

"When your grandmother comes in here, you should be *doing* something, not learning about the Web site. Okay? This is easy. You just look this over, see what we've got a lot of and what we should be ordering more of. You'll notice the coffee continues to show a lot of activity, no thanks to your uncle Jay, the schmuck. Let him worry about the Web site. It keeps him busy. You all set? Are you hungry?"

Julia glanced at her watch. She hadn't squeezed in any lunch before her mother had summoned her. She ought to be starving.

"I've got half a sandwich in my office, if you want it. Tuna on whole wheat."

A cornucopia of gourmet noshes downstairs, and her mother was offering her a tuna sandwich. She'd rather remain hungry. "I'm fine," she said.

"Okay, then. Get to work."

Before Julia could respond, her mother was gone.

She directed her attention to the printout on the desk. She

supposed that as president she ought to know which products were selling and which weren't. It was as good an introduction to Bloom's as anything.

But she didn't want to think about how well the Gouda and Havarti and Feta sold—an asterisk next to the Havarti noted that offering free samples of the cheese had increased sales significantly. She didn't want to read statistics on egg noodles and Red Bliss potato salad—or on bagels, the data for which filled three complete pages.

She wanted to figure out whether her mother and Uncle Jay truly hated each other, and if so, how much, and whether by attempting to fill her father's too-large chair she had somehow positioned herself at the center of a tug-of-war. She also wanted to figure out exactly why Grandma Ida had bestowed upon her the dubious honor of taking her father's place.

All in all this seemed a lot more complicated than hammering out an alimony agreement.

She was here. At last. The goddamn president of the company.

Jay hunched over his computer and simmered. He hated feeling this way—about his niece, no less. He'd never had a negative thought about Julia before. Well, maybe one, when she was graduating from fancy-schmancy Wellesley while his own brilliant son was dropping out of the University of Miami after spending two years amid the palm trees and fraternities, consuming vast quantities of beer and scant quantities of knowledge. Neil was smart—he was running his own sailboat charter business, wasn't he?—but Julia had always been the golden girl, the straight-A wunderkind. And here she was, the golden-girl straight-A wunderkind again. President of Bloom's. He wanted to shove her face in.

Of course he loved her. She was his brother's daughter. Sweet Julia, always the best-behaved child at the family gatherings, always polite and thoughtful and eager to please.

He still couldn't believe his mother had done this—not just

to him but to his family, his sons. It ate at him. It hurt going down, like a bone in a piece of carp, scraping his throat, churning in his stomach. It pained him that his mother had phoned him a week ago Monday and announced this news as if it were nothing more significant than the weather report. "I tried you earlier," she'd said, "but your wife—" she always referred to Wendy as "your wife" "—told me you were playing some *goyishe* game at a club, I don't remember what. Paddleball?"

"Racquetball," he'd told her.

"Paddle, racquet—I'm supposed to know the difference?"

"It doesn't matter, Mom. I'm home now. How are you doing?"

"I'm all right, considering. I wanted to let you know Julia is going to be president of Bloom's."

"Julia who?" he'd asked stupidly. It just hadn't occurred to him that Ida could be referring to his pipsqueak niece.

"What do you mean, Julia who? How many Julias do you know? Ben's Julia. You think I'd give Bloom's a president who wasn't a Bloom?"

"I'm a Bloom," he'd said even more stupidly.

"So you understand how important it is to keep the company in the family. Julia will do a good job, such a smart girl. She reminds me of me."

Jay had wondered whether being likened to Ida Bloom could possibly be a compliment. "She's a *child,* Mom."

"She's twenty-eight years old. You know how old I was when your father and I opened Bloom's?"

"Twenty-eight," he'd guessed.

"Twenty-three. And before that I helped with the knish cart."

"You were a regular child prodigy," Jay had grunted under his breath. Out loud, he'd said, "She's never even worked at the store."

"She was a cashier."

"A couple of summers in high school. You know what I mean, Mom. She's never put in time on the third floor. She doesn't know how we do things."

"That's why I'm telling you. I want you to help her out, teach her what she needs to know. She's a hard worker. She'll learn."

He'd understood what his mother was insinuating: she didn't think he was a hard worker. Well, damn it, who said you had to be at your desk 24/7? Where was it written that working hard was more important than working smart? Jay got his work done. He just didn't act like a drudge about it.

And for that, he was being dethroned by his own niece.

The only thing that made it tolerable was that she was never there. The lady with the big title and the corner office was a no-show. If she remained AWOL awhile longer, he'd be able to go to his mother and point out her mistake in having entrusted the family business to a child who couldn't even seem to find her way to the third floor. He'd explain to Ida that somehow the place was running just fine without Julia—because *he* was there, making sure things got done.

And that bitch Sondra wouldn't be able to take any credit for the fact that things were getting done, because to take credit would mean belittling her own daughter. So he'd get all the credit, and his mother would come to what few senses she had, and she'd make Jay the president, the way she should have right from the start.

But now that plan wasn't going to happen, because Julia was here. Damn it.

He hit the Save button on his computer and rolled away from the desk. He was the only person on the third floor smart enough to have laid down a slab of Plexiglas under his chair so it could roll smoothly. He was the only one with a halogen lamp on a dimmer switch, so he could make his office as bright or as dim as he wanted. He was the only one with a pen stand from the Levenger's catalog—high-class writing equipment, not the schlocky pens Sondra bought by the gross. He was forward-thinking, creative. Exactly what Bloom's needed to grow in the new century.

And that little ninny—his beloved niece—was his boss? Not in this lifetime.

He shoved back his hair, which was as thick as a teenager's if maybe a little grayer. Wendy liked the gray. She said it made him look mature. He looked a hell of a lot more mature than Julia, that was for sure.

Quick strides carried him from his own office past Myron's, past Sondra's and Deirdre's, to the end of the hall. He peered through the door and found Julia at her father's desk, squinting at a stack of inventory printouts.

Jay exerted himself to look nonthreatening. "Julia, honey! Hi!"

She spun around and smiled hesitantly at him. "Hi, Uncle Jay."

"Nice of you to drop by." Sarcastic, but he didn't give a shit.

Her smile changed, warming with apology and love and endearing helplessness, and he felt ashamed of himself for resenting her.

"Oh, Uncle Jay, I've wanted to get started here sooner, but I've been so busy trying to smooth the transition at my other job. I couldn't just bolt from Griffin, McDougal. These things take time."

Of course those things took time, especially when you were a big shot at a law firm. His own sons could have taken over the presidency on ten minutes' notice. Well, Rick could, anyway. All he did was wander around Lower Manhattan, grubbing for financial backing for his movie and framing shots in his mind. Neil—it might have taken a full day for him to pack up and fly to New York. They weren't attorneys like Julia. They had nothing better to occupy their time.

But she *did* have something better, which made it all the crazier that she was here. This job should go to someone who could take it over full time, full force, full commitment. Like his sons. Like him.

"So, what are you doing?"

"Mom told me to review these lists to see what's selling well and what's selling slowly."

"You don't need to study that." More accurately, she shouldn't *have* to study it. She should know it by now.

"All these statistics are really confusing." She sighed and shook her head, then smiled hopefully at him. "Actually, what I really wanted to find out was about the Seder-in-a-Box. That sounds like such a bizarre idea."

"It's not bizarre. We're doing well with it." Sales had been a little slow, he had to admit, but as Passover drew closer he was sure they'd skyrocket. The concept was ingenious: pull off the lid and pull out a seder. The deluxe box even came with *yarmulkes* and a CD of Passover songs.

His idea. For that alone, he should have been rewarded with the presidency. He knew the boxes would sell. And the beauty part was there was no languishing inventory. An order came in, a box could be assembled in an hour or two and out it went.

"I would think," she said slowly, "that families like the labor of preparing a seder. Even the most rushed, modern family— if they're going to have a seder, they view it as a chance to touch base with the rituals of their ancestors, don't you think? They like doing things the old way."

"I think most people like doing things the easy way," he retorted. Little smart-ass, trying to undercut his concept.

She must have sensed his resentment. Her smile grew even less certain.

"Well, it's a very creative idea."

"I'm a very creative man." *And I should be sitting at that desk,* he almost added. "You know, it takes a lot of creativity to keep a place like Bloom's moving forward. You don't want to stagnate in this market. You have no idea what this market is all about. But one thing it's about is not stagnating." People went to business school for years to learn the sort of wisdom he'd been born with. He could run the entire Bloom's enterprise with what he knew instinctively. Hell, he could probably run the city.

And here he was, answering to a niece who didn't know her *tuchis* from her elbow about how to run a deli in the new millennium. It was outrageous.

Julia eyed him quizzically. He took a deep breath and forced a smile. "I don't know if you'll ever learn everything you need to know," he said, deliberately refusing to offer comfort or encouragement. "I've been working here forever, and I know Bloom's the way I know my own name." That didn't sound right, but he forged ahead anyway. "It's in my blood, Julia. If it's not in your blood, I don't know how you're going to get the job done."

Her smile remained, but her eyes sharpened, dark and shiny like black olives.

"I'll do my best," she promised.

Her best would never be as good as his mediocre. Damn it, *this should be his.* "Well, I guess you'd better get back to those inventory lists," he said, satisfied that he'd undermined her enough for now.

He turned and crossed the threshold in time to see his mother emerge from the elevator, her hand resting firmly on the forearm of her…what the hell was Lyndon, anyway? Her cook? Her valet? Her companion? Her boyfriend? With his angular smile and all those little braids sticking out from his scalp, his body clothed in a silk turtleneck and slim, pleated trousers, he looked like one of those painfully sharp fashion models in *GQ.* "Your grandmother's here," Jay alerted Julia, adding silently, *impress her the way you just impressed me, and you'll be out of this office in no time.*

"Jay," Ida greeted him, her brow dipping in a frown that emphasized the creases in it. "How is our new president doing?"

"She's doing swell," he assured her. *Go ahead. Ask your little pet if she's figured out our inventory yet. Ask her if she's doing anything to earn her fat salary and her office. And her title. Ask her if she knows one-hundredth of what I know about Bloom's.*

"You just keep helping her until she has the job down," Ida said—a blunt command.

He watched as his mother and her chic black buddy vanished into the president's office. Then he turned and entered his own office. He didn't want to be there. The hell with the Web site. If his own mother could stab him in the back, why should he stick around, working his ass off until she returned to stab him in the chest?

He switched off his computer, grabbed his suede jacket from the hanger on the back of his door and left the office. It was two o'clock in the afternoon, and he'd already accomplished everything on his calendar. As for the Web site, he could get the pictures scanned in tomorrow.

He ought to have Rick come uptown and scan in the pictures. That would let Ida know that Julia wasn't the only wonderful grandchild she had. Rick knew computers, and he had such a strong visual sense. He could probably come up with a way to animate the Seder-in-a-Boxes on the screen. He could make them dance the goddamn *hora*.

Jay took the elevator downstairs and exited the back door into the narrow alley behind the building where he parked his car. He pulled off the canvas cover and circled the car to inspect it for signs of vandalism—even though the likelihood was pretty small that anyone would wander down this alley just to scratch his BMW, when there were so many other scratchable cars parked conveniently on the street. Satisfied that his vehicle had survived the day unscathed, he got in, revved the engine a few times and backed out of the alley.

The traffic was wretched, but that was no surprise. The roads were straight, the lights supposedly staggered, and the pedestrians knew how to dodge cars as well as he knew how to dodge pedestrians. He cruised through the park and made it home in fifteen minutes. As always, his precious parking space was waiting for him in the underground garage. Worth every goddamn dollar, he thought as he got out of the car and locked it.

He hoped Wendy wasn't home. He just wanted silence and a generous glass of single malt. He wanted to drink and think, figure out a way to make this whole Bloom's fiasco work out for him.

He had rights. He had needs. He had a mother's unspoken promise to her son. Julia Bloom didn't belong in that office.

Or maybe *he* didn't belong. They wanted to hand the family franchise over to Julia? Fine. Let him open his own competing deli. Jay's. Jay's Gourmet. Jay's Gourmet Emporium. Yeah.

It would be a lot of work, he pondered as the elevator carried him upstairs. A hell of a lot of work. He could delegate, though. He could hire good people. Maybe he could even hire Deirdre. Not that idiot accountant Myron, who probably still added on his fingers.

He could do the whole thing on-line. Skip Manhattan's exorbitant rentals, set up a warehouse in Jersey and do everything mail order, through catalogs and the Web. Not just Seder-in-a-Box but Succoth-in-a-Box. Rosh-Hoshanna-in-a-Box. Shabbat-in-a-Box. Yom-Kippur-in-a-Box—and he could ship an empty box!

A great idea, but it wouldn't prove how indispensable he was to Bloom's. If he could just show them how much they needed him; if he could just get through to his mother that Julia couldn't spread the mayonnaise, let alone cut the mustard, as the president; if he could make sure his mother found out that her beloved granddaughter wasn't even on the third floor most days… If he could convince her that the only reason the enterprise hadn't collapsed like one of those dynamited buildings imploding was that *he,* Jay, the son of Ida and Isaac, was holding everything together, making everything work.

He could almost hear his mother's voice, weak with age and relief, as she said, "Jay, I was wrong about you. You're a better man than your brother ever was. Please—I beg you—take over the store."

He was actually smiling as he entered the apartment. He didn't even mind that Wendy was there, reading a magazine on the couch and wearing the silk kimono he'd purchased through a Web site that sold Japanese stuff. What he liked about the kimono was that it was held shut only by a sash. One simple knot was all that stood between him and her lush body.

"You're home!" she said, tossing aside her magazine and

leaping to her feet. Her face still amazed him, the way it always glowed. She was thirty-three but didn't have a single wrinkle, because she never scowled, never worried, never thought too hard, never did anything to crease that flawless skin.

He was feeling better. Much better. He'd prove how indispensable he was to Bloom's and wind up on top, exactly where he was supposed to be.

And in the meantime, he thought as Wendy pranced across the airy living room, her arms outstretched and her smile welcoming, he'd open the knot of that sash.

6

In the olden days, a room like this would have been blue with smoke.

Susie didn't like cigarette smoke. It smelled harsh and bitter and made her eyes sting. Yet something had been lost in the city's transition to smoke-free. Something atmospheric. Something to do with consistency. She'd be willing to bet more people got sick from the scarcity of sunlight, which was blocked by the city's multitude of tall buildings, than by secondhand smoke, but no one was passing any laws to knock down the skyscrapers and open up the sky.

A poetry slam in a TriBeCa basement club ought to have smoke. This poetry slam had everything else: bad lighting; lousy acoustics; uncomfortable chairs crowded around small, wobbly tables; enough unbathed participants to make her think cigarettes would have smelled appetizing in comparison; cheap beer and the kind of wine that caused migraines. Susie found herself wondering why she had even come.

She was sharing a spindly table with Anna, Rick and a buddy of his named Ross. Ross was skinny, with long, curly hair and cheeks pitted with acne scars. Susie imagined he would be a Raisinette; there was a kind of desiccated quality to him. She suspected Rick had brought him along to distract Susie so she wouldn't interfere if he made a play for Anna. But she knew he and Anna were all wrong for each other. He was interested in Anna only because she was Susie's roommate, and maybe because her grandparents were from Taiwan, which made her exotic in his eyes even though Anna had been born and bred in Brooklyn.

Some guy on the stage—a platform not much bigger than an unabridged dictionary—was wailing an inane poem into a mike that distorted more than amplified his voice. Smoke would not have irritated Susie's sinuses as much as his poem did. The entire verse consisted of a list of words that rhymed with *fuck*. At first they'd been pretty pedestrian—*duck, luck, stuck*—but then the poet had gotten more elaborate—*moonstruck, hockey puck, nunchuk, Alma Gluck*.

"So," Rick was saying to Anna, "there'd be a great part for someone like you in my movie."

"I don't act," Anna informed him.

"Everybody acts. Susie's going to go stand on that stage and do a poem tonight. That's acting."

"No, it's not," Susie argued. "It's standing on a stage and doing a poem."

"Ross acts, too," Rick continued.

"I act," Ross confirmed with a nod.

Susie suppressed a snort of disbelief. She'd bet real money that the only acting Ross did was on the telephone with his mother, when he told her he was eating well and getting enough sleep. He "acted" the way Rick made movies.

She wondered why she was in such a sour mood. Rick had told her about this slam because he thought she'd enjoy it and because it came with a nice money prize. He'd been doing her a favor, even if the only reason he'd done it was so she would bring Anna or Caitlin along with her. His attraction to her roommates wasn't exactly breaking news. Whenever he was horny and between girlfriends, he made plans with Susie that would include one of her roommates. He'd never had any luck with either of them, but for some reason he wouldn't stop trying.

Anna or no Anna, Susie shouldn't be so churlish. She'd gotten the night off from Nico's, decked herself out in her favorite black denim overalls with a slim-fitting black turtleneck underneath, wolfed down a cup of yogurt for dinner and was now sipping some of that migraine-vintage wine with friends. Even inane poetry was better than no poetry.

She felt as if she'd been suffering from PMS for the past two weeks. She felt as if the sun had dropped ten degrees in temperature at its core, and she was at the catastrophically icy end of the chain reaction that change had caused. She felt as if the world's supply of Prozac had run out—and she was the world.

Caitlin had suggested she was reacting to the one-year anniversary of her father's death. She didn't think that was it. Jews had that death-anniversary thing worked out pretty well: you mourned for the year, you unveiled the headstone and said some prayers—and then you moved on. Sure, you were allowed pangs and twinges and bouts of tears, but no fixation with calendar dates and tragic anniversaries.

Frankly, Susie didn't suffer too many teary bouts. She missed her father, but not that much. He hadn't been so strong a presence in her life that his absence would be keenly felt. He'd been a phantom, floating in and out of the apartment, floating in and out of his office when she'd visited the third floor. Julia used to do her homework in his office, but Susie would do hers—when she did it—in their mother's office a few doors down. If she'd done it in her father's office, he would have gotten on her case to make sure she was actually doing it.

The only thing he'd ever been really interested in was Bloom's. Every conversation with him had revolved around the store; every family occasion had been scheduled with respect

to the store's demands. When something fabulous happened—
like the day Susie had won the eighth-grade poetry contest—
the family had celebrated with a babka from Bloom's.

Sure, she missed him. She had to tread carefully around the
hole his death had left, so she wouldn't accidentally fall into it.
But that didn't explain why she'd been in such a pissy mood
for the past two weeks.

She didn't need an explanation. She knew the cause of
her funk.

The slam's emcee, a stocky fellow in ostentatious striped
pants and a too-tight T-shirt, took the mike and said, "Our next
contestant is Susie Bloom. Susie, come on here and see how
your, er…*luck* goes." Shooting the "fuck" poet a sly, sleazy grin,
he searched the room for Susie.

"Go for it, Suze," Anna said, nudging her out of her chair.

"Knock 'em dead, Cous'," Rick added.

Inhaling deeply, Susie rose from her chair and wove through
the crowd to the tiny stage. The emcee gave her a big, Den-
tyne-smelling grin and nudged the mike at her.

"Let's put them together for Susie Bloom," he urged the
crowd, a few of whom obeyed him, clapping with jaded listless-
ness.

She'd written her poem nearly two weeks ago, just as this
mood had begun to infect her. She'd fussed with the poem since
then, revised, reshaped—but now it was too late to make any
more improvements. She'd memorized it, and she'd give her
recitation her best effort—and maybe there would be some
prize money for her when she was done with it.

She adjusted the mike downward to accommodate her
height, nodded at the crowd and began.

Round
Endless, round, rolling roll
Round, round, hollow hole
Surrounded by roundness.
Eat. Chew. Devour.

Nubile circle.
The bagel you gave me.
I taste it still.

Her poem was shorter than most, but it said what it needed to say, and like a bagel, it required nothing extra. It existed unto itself.

A paean to the bagel man.

She couldn't believe two whole weeks had elapsed and she remained obsessed by him. He wasn't a downtown kind of guy. He didn't dwell in her environs. She knew nothing about his background, his education level—his use of the word *nubile* might have been simply a fluke. She didn't even know his name.

Yet she'd been mooning over him, moaning over him. One five-minute exchange at the bagel counter, and she was possessed.

"That was great!" Rick gushed once she'd made her way back to their table amid the ragged percussion of applause, finger snapping, table pounding and foot stomping.

"It wasn't great," she retorted, wondering why Rick was so enthusiastic. He must want something. Anna, probably.

"It was fine," Anna said, flipping her waist-length black hair back over her shoulder to reveal the six silver studs in her left ear. "Why are you putting yourself down?"

"I'm not putting myself down. I'm being realistic." She glared at Ross, exasperated that he wasn't the bagel man. "What did you think? Great or not great?"

"I like the way it ended on the word *still,*" he said. "*Still,* you know? That's cool."

It wasn't cool. Nothing was cool. Nothing would ever be cool until she could at the very least find out the bagel man's name. Once she could put a name to him, he'd become a person to her. Not an idol, not an object of fantasy, but a human being, blood and bone and flesh. And sleepy, sexy eyes.

If his name was Engelhoffer Pigeontoe, it could change things.

Well, her sister was the friggin' president of Bloom's. If anyone could find out the name of an employee, surely the president could. Susie would ask Julia. Not their mother, who would want to know why Susie was asking, and who, if Engelhoffer Pigeontoe or Studman Godiva or Billy Bialy or whatever turned out not to be Jewish would make a big deal about it, as if Susie was planning to pledge her troth and whelp a litter of young ones with him. She didn't want to marry him, for God's sake. She just wanted to be in love with him for a while.

Julia would understand that. Tomorrow, Susie would telephone her and ask her to find out the guy's name. If Julia was over at her law office, she could look him up in the personnel files the next time she showed her face at Bloom's. How big could the bagel staff be? If there were ten names, Susie would simply choose the name that came closest to Studman Godiva.

She had a plan, and that made her feel infinitely better. She smiled at her companions, said, "*Still* is definitely cool," then turned in her seat, careful to avoid smashing her knees against Anna's chair, and listened to the new poet at the microphone as he recited a poem on the subject of convection ovens, in perfect iambic pentameter.

Julia's boss wanted a summary of all the alimony decisions handed down by Superior Court Judge Marcus DelBianco over the past six years. Julia's mother wanted her to decide which flavors of canned macaroons to carry—"The rocky road macaroons sold very well last year, but the banana ones just died on the shelf, go figure"—and sign the order forms so there would be something official with her signature on it. Grandma Ida wanted her to arrive a half hour early for the family seder, "so we can talk." Heath wanted her to sleep with him. And Susie wanted the names of all the men who worked in the bagel department—"or specifically, that one man. You know which one I mean."

Julia's bathroom sink was full of hair.

"I can't do this," she said to her reflection in the mirror above the sink. "I am stressed. My hair is falling out."

She wasn't sleeping well. She wasn't eating well. She took a bite of the cinnamon doughnut she'd brought into the bathroom to munch on while she fixed her hair. She couldn't see her scalp, but the hair in the sink looked dire, black strands slithering into the drain as if she'd already gone down feet first and those strands of hair were all that was left of her.

"That's it," she muttered, pulling back the hair from her temples and fastening the locks at the back of her head with a tortoiseshell clip. "My life is going down the drain. *I'm* going down the drain. I'm drowning."

She took another bite of the doughnut. It tasted like raw flour with a tang of cinnamon.

"Like I give a rat's ass about macaroons. Like I give a rat's ass about Marcus DelBianco. Like I'm going to ask Deirdre to pull out the personnel files for me so I can figure out the name of this jerk Susie's panting over. Like I want to figure out why the numbers from the bagel department don't add up. Like I want to spend a half hour talking to Grandma Ida before everyone else arrives at her seder." Given the other crises clamoring for her attention, sleeping with Heath almost sounded palatable.

Why couldn't she be like Susie? Why couldn't she just get a swooning crush on a guy, have wild and sweaty sex with him, and then move on? Why couldn't she not have to be working sixty hours a week at Griffin, McDougal and another twenty-five hours a week trying to psyche out the macaroon-buying habits of the typical Bloom's customer? Susie didn't realize how lucky she was.

Grandma Ida's seder would be next week. Passover used to be one of Julia's favorite holidays—right up there with Thanksgiving because they both involved eating—but she wasn't looking forward to it this year. Maybe she could skip the "next year in the Holy Land" part of the ceremony and just pop over to the Holy Land this year, putting a good eight thousand miles between her and her family. She wondered if she could order a Seder-in-a-Box from Jerusalem.

Maybe she'd bring Heath with her. They could have sex in the Holy Land. She didn't expect she'd enjoy it much, but it would be one less item on her to-do list.

She didn't want the life she was living right now. She didn't want sex with Heath. She didn't even want the doughnut she was forcing down her throat, swallowing several times with each bite. She wanted moist lox and eggs, and a toasted bagel on the side, and a rugele. And a cup of fresh-brewed Kenyan coffee. And a lover she could love. Was that really asking so much?

Apparently, it was. With a heavy sigh, she tossed the remainder of her doughnut into the garbage pail, dabbed some tinted gloss on her lips and left the bathroom. Griffin, McDougal awaited—along with everyone else. And since Julia was a good girl, she'd try to satisfy them all.

Well, probably not Heath.

Ron Joffe didn't need sensory aids when he was writing his weekly City Business column. But for a story about Bloom's, he did. Not just gustatory aids—although he was certain that devouring some Bloom's delicacies would put him in the mood for this assignment—but visual aids. Specifically, pictures of the players.

He found a photo of the Bloom brothers, the late Ben and still-alive Jay, in a spread about smoked fish published in the *Journal of the American Delicatessen Association,* a professional organization he suspected very few people outside the delicatessen industry knew about. Good-looking men, both of them, beaming above a platter of sable. Both Blooms had full heads of dark, well-styled hair, brown eyes, sharp noses and smug grins. Ben wore a suit and tie, while Jay sported a blazer and a shirt open at the collar. What did that tell Ron? That older brothers dressed more conservatively than younger brothers?

He learned a lot more about Ben Bloom from his obituary in the *New York Times,* two columns of text accompanied by a posed studio portrait. The son of immigrants who'd started the business selling knishes from a pushcart, he'd graduated from Columbia, married Sondra Feldman and built the company into a "major force in the delicatessen world." Christ. Who would want to be a major force in the delicatessen world? That was like having the biggest house in Newfoundland. Some people might actually care about such a prestigious designation—probably the same people who subscribed to the *Journal of the American Delicatessen Association*.

Moving on, Ron did an Internet search of Bloom's current president, Ben's daughter Julia. She was listed in the Wellesley College Alumnae Directory, and he immediately pictured her father's face feminized and attached to a female body in a prissy high-necked white dress. Or maybe in one of those clingy, stretchy, body-hugging minidresses that seemed to have been designed for no other purpose than to cause men to get erections in public. Did Wellesley women dress for sex? He wouldn't know; he didn't have any Wellesley women among his circle of acquaintances.

Before Wellesley, Julia Bloom had attended Dalton. The exclusive prep school was just a subway ride away.

The lion on the wall across from his desk gave him a feral look: *It's springtime. Go prowl.*

Fortunately, Kim Pinsky wasn't in her office, so Ron was able to leave the building without justifying himself to her. Out on Union Square, he wove through the mid-morning crowd to the subway station and caught an uptown train. Swaying and jostling as he clung to one of the center poles, he contemplated what he expected to learn about Bloom's from a visit to Dalton. Not much. But at least he was out and prowling.

He needed something. Something different, something new. The Bloom's article was a start, but he needed more. A challenge. A mystery to solve. Sex.

Well, that last item was a given. He wasn't involved with anyone at the moment—by his own choice, he reminded himself. He'd had something nice going over the winter, but she'd wanted marriage and what they'd had going wasn't *that* nice, so he'd suggested that she find herself a more nuptially inclined man. She'd been willing to wait for him to come around, though. In fact, she'd been so convinced she could persuade him to marry her within a year that she'd offered a fifty-dollar wager on it.

He'd refused the bet. What was he going to do—continue to see her for the next year and then break her heart by telling her he didn't want to marry her, and oh, by the way, could she please pay him the fifty bucks she owed him?

So he was alone, and it was spring, and he had to write an article about a Dalton and Wellesley alumna who was currently running a "major force in the delicatessen world." Did schools like Dalton and Wellesley view Julia Bloom with pride, or were they embarrassed to have a graduate of their elite programs managing a deli?

The receptionist in the main office at Dalton specialized in supercilious frowns, but she gave him a few yearbooks to look through. He found Julia Bloom in the third one. In her senior photo she had straight black hair that fell well past her shoulders and features like her father's, only downsized: a sharp nose, an angular chin, lips etched into a slight pout and dark eyes that seemed to take up half her face. She looked younger than eighteen in the photo, but pretty.

He thumbed through the book, searching for other photos of her. He found a candid shot of her sprawled out in a window seat with a book open on her knees and a dreamy look in those caramel-soft eyes, and other photos in club shots: the Debate Club, the Honor Society, Amnesty International and an organization that volunteered stints at soup kitchens around the city. Apparently, there was no Future Deli Owners club at Dalton.

He flipped back to her senior portrait. Amazing eyes, he thought. Young eyes. Eyes that hadn't seen much of the world. Eyes that probably hadn't seen much of smoked fish conventions, either.

His research had told him that her grandmother wielded the real power at Bloom's. Ida Bloom was the one he really wanted to interview for his article. But he sure wouldn't mind spending a few minutes with Julia, if only to see whether her eyes had grown wise or cynical in the past ten years. They couldn't possibly be as innocent and trusting today as they'd been in that yearbook photo.

Just out of curiosity, because it was spring and he was a man, he'd like to have an up-close-and-personal look at those eyes.

Susie wasn't used to being uptown in the morning. She was usually still asleep at ten a.m., but since she wasn't sleeping with anyone at the moment, she'd figured what the hell, arisen at nine, eaten the only clementine in the fridge that didn't have blue mold staining its rind and headed to the Upper West Side.

Julia hadn't come through. God knew why—all Susie had asked was for her to take a peek at the personnel records—but several days had passed and Julia still hadn't gotten around to doing this one tiny favor. She was the president of the company—surely she could ask Deirdre to look up a simple thing for her.

But no, she hadn't done it. Susie had to take matters into her own hands.

She climbed the subway stairs, emerged from the kiosk on Seventy-Second Street and oriented herself to the angle of the sun. Broadway in the seventies was a jumble of stores—big, little, national chains and independents, pricey restaurants and Cuban-Chinese cafés, elegant boutiques and down-to-earth shops where a person could still buy a pair of jeans for less than seventy dollars. "Working man's pants," her father used to call jeans. A working man would have to be earning a heart surgeon's salary to afford most jeans nowadays.

She was wearing her favorite black jeans—for which she'd paid only forty dollars at a denim emporium above an Indian restaurant in the East Village—along with a teal T-shirt and her black denim jacket, which Caitlin and Anna had jointly given her for her twenty-fifth birthday. She'd donned hoop earrings, a silver bangle that was sort of David Yurman-ish, only a bit more industrial-looking and a lot cheaper, black leather sneakers and a touch of black eyeliner. She wasn't sure *nubile* would describe her, but she felt good about her appearance. Her haircut was truly a miracle—nearly a month old, and it still looked great.

Up ahead she saw the store, with its sign of high-kicking Bloom's-Bloom's-Bloom's extending across the top of the showcase windows. She took a couple of deep breaths to steady her pulse, shivered as the lines of her poem—which had not been deemed worthy of the two-hundred-fifty-dollar prize, damn it—flashed across her brain like the electronic headlines gliding around the skyscraper at the center of Times Square, and marched toward the store.

The familiar aromas of Bloom's wrapped around her as she stepped inside: cheese, warm bread, coffee, parsley. Honey and vanilla. Olives and onions. An indigestible stew of fragrances, yet they didn't clash. They swirled around one another in a chaotic ballet that made her hungry. That puny orange hadn't been much of a breakfast.

She'd simply have to buy a bagel.

Smiling to herself, she moved farther into the store. As always, it was crowded, but the crowd was different on a Thursday morning from what she usually found when she visited. The people meandering up and down the aisles, steering carts or carrying plastic baskets, looked not like tourists but like native New Yorkers—retirees and young mothers on outings with their toddlers. Susie was surprised by the number of cutting-edge strollers clogging the aisles. The women pushing them were trim and well made up, clad in Banana Republic and L.L. Bean and wearing blindingly large diamonds on their ring fingers. Their children were just too precious in their Baby Gap outfits, sucking on high-tech pacifiers.

The women all looked older than Susie. A good thing, since she was years away from settling down and having children—

and when she did, she wouldn't have state-of-the-art children. No, her babies would be scruffy and energetic, like her. They would refuse to sit sedately in their Mercedes strollers and Jaguar strollers, but would instead race up and down the aisles the way she used to, terrifying the clerks and making the customers either gasp or giggle. She expected to have utterly wonderful children.

She might just skip the husband part, too.

She moved as directly as she could to the bagel counter, veering around babies in unbearably cute caps and plodding elders who clogged aisles while they bickered over whether the sesame breadsticks were a better deal if they bought the fourteen-ounce package instead of the eight-ounce package. She swept past the coffee corner and the gourmet bottles of olive oil priced as if they were liquid gold, reached the bagel counter—and he wasn't there.

How dared he not be there? Had Julia fired him?

Maybe he'd quit. Maybe he'd been so terribly underpaid he'd walked out. Why hadn't Julia done something about the salaries of the bagel workers?

The older fellow who'd been working the bagel beat last time Susie was at Bloom's stood behind the counter today. Perhaps he'd been unable to quit. Perhaps he had a wife and kids and a mother crippled by arthritis, all of them crammed into a tiny two-bedroom apartment in Washington Heights, and he couldn't afford to walk away from Bloom's, even though that rotten bitch of a president, Julia Bloom, exploited her workers.

Susie would organize them. She'd bring in union representatives, and if Julia balked, she'd design rhyming picket signs for them. That would teach her sister to let a Godiva-quality employee get away.

She strode to the counter, and the exploited laborer on the other side gave her a smile. "What can I get you, sweetie?"

"Actually, I was wondering about another guy who works here sometimes." *Or used to,* she almost added.

"Another guy, huh?" He rubbed his index finger along the seam where his cheek met his bulbous nose. "Don't tell me he broke your heart. You're too pretty to let any man do that to you."

In spite of herself, she smiled. "He hasn't had a chance to break my heart yet," she explained. "I need to find out his name."

"His name." The man nodded as if this were the most ordinary request in the world. "Well, we've got a good four, five guys who work here. Couple of ladies, too, but you did specifically mention that it's a guy."

"He's got longish blondish hair, green eyes…in his twenties, I'd guess."

"Now, that sounds like about five different guys who work here," the man said.

For a moment she believed him. Then she realized he was teasing her.

"That'd be Casey," he said.

"Casey?" What a divine name. Much better than Engelhoffer—or even Studman. "Casey *What?*"

"Now, I don't know about giving you his last name. I don't think that would be right."

A white-haired woman in a garishly colored warm-up suit, the fabric of which hissed when she walked, approached the counter. Susie generously stepped aside so he could serve her. She wanted two of everything, and then she wanted to change her mind about half her selections, and then she wanted to complain about the freshness of the bagels she'd bought at Bloom's last week: "They were fresh, but not *fresh* fresh, you know what I'm saying? Make sure these are *fresh* fresh, Morty. I'm not kiddin' around."

"*Fresh* fresh," he said with a nod. He caught Susie's eye and winked, then pulled one of the raisin bagels out of the bag. "This one feels fresh, but not *fresh* fresh. I'll put in another. There, that's better," he concluded, sliding a different raisin bagel into the bag. "Will that do it for you, sweetheart?"

"Don't get fresh with me," she snapped, taking the bulky bag and dropping it into her cart. She pushed her cart away from the counter, muttering.

"Is she a regular?" Susie asked.

"She's a fine gal," he said. Susie decided she liked him—for protecting Casey's identity and for not speaking ill of a fussy customer. If she ran Bloom's, she'd make sure he got a good salary and excellent benefits.

"So…about Casey. Can you tell me his shifts?"

"He's here now," he said. "He's downstairs checking on the new batches, which—" he leaned forward conspiratorially "—will be even *fresher* fresh, once they come out of the ovens."

"I'll remember that. In the meantime," she said, feeling much better now that she knew Casey was in the building, "I'll take an egg bagel."

"You got it." He used a waxy square of tissue to protect the bagel he lifted out of the bin for her.

"Thanks." She crossed to a cashier, paid for it and left the store.

One of the outdoor basement entries was open, the heavy steel doors yawning wide against the sidewalk, the room at the bottom of the steep metal stairway bright with light. The outside entries were used by truckers delivering stock; they were equipped with both stairs and conveyor belts. Bloom's staff had access to an indoor stairway and a freight elevator, but she'd always loved the sidewalk entrance. When the steel doors were shut and flush with the sidewalk, they seemed mysterious. They rattled and echoed when stepped on; they were strangely textured and rusty-looking. She could pretend they were the portals to hell.

She knew that what was going on underneath them was not hell, but a bustling world of shelves and hand trucks and a separate kitchen area where the heat-n-eat meals, the roast meats and the salads, the knishes and the kugels were prepared, and where the breads, bagels and specialty cakes were baked so they would be *fresh* fresh when they reached the shelves upstairs. She'd rarely been allowed into the basement as a child, but every now and then she'd managed to sneak in. She'd loved wandering through the maze of shelving, counting the inventory, comparing the packaging.

She'd loved even more venturing into the kitchen, where she definitely hadn't belonged. The cooks would yell at her—it was too dangerous for a little girl to be there, what with all those hot surfaces and sharp implements. But oh, the aromas. The sight of dishes being prepared—not just the traditional Jewish foods but pasta salads, potato salads, couscous with chopped onions and peppers, rotisserie chickens. She would stand in the doorway, as quiet as she could manage, and take it all in, wondering why once she went upstairs to her family's apartment she'd find nothing as exotic as the foods being cooked here. No couscous for her family's dinner. No chopped liver and pickled herring and latkes. If Sondra was going to serve a rotisserie chicken for dinner, she'd buy it at the supermarket down the street, where it was cheaper.

Susie stared at the open doors for a moment, gnawing on her bagel as she contemplated her options. She might not be a child anymore, but she still wasn't allowed down there. The people who worked now for Bloom's probably didn't realize she was a Bloom. If she went downstairs, they might arrest her for trespassing, and then she'd have to tell them who she was, and then they'd be embarrassed and worried about their jobs.

But *he* was down there. Her deluxe chocolate. Casey.

With a shrug, she descended the stairs and ducked behind one of the towering shelves when she heard a couple of guys approaching, their conversation accompanied by a squeaking wheel on one of the hand trucks. They were discussing the Knicks in tones of great disgust, as if they believed they could have done a far superior job against the Cleveland Cavaliers last night. She waited until they'd climbed the stairs, then slipped out from behind a shelf full of dried gourmet pasta—why gourmet pasta? This was Bloom's, not Bloomicelli's—and headed for the door leading to the kitchen.

It was cracked open, and she inched it wider, until she could peek around it. Several middle-aged women wearing yellow smocks and shower caps mixed salads in huge stainless-steel bowls. Across the way the wall was filled with industrial ovens.

There he was, pulling trays of hot bagels out of one of the ovens and sliding them onto a six-foot-tall rack on wheels. Once the rack was full of trays, he would wheel it to the freight elevator and bring it upstairs so the trays could be emptied into the bins behind the bagel counter.

He didn't have to wear a shower cap, thank God. His hair was pulled back into a ponytail, and his apron was a classic style: white bib, straps tied at his waist, hem dropping to his knees. Under the apron he had on a slate-gray shirt with the sleeves rolled up and faded blue jeans.

He had the kind of legs jeans had been designed for. Seventy-dollar jeans or twenty-buck irregulars—it didn't matter. What mattered was the way the denim traced the shape of his butt.

A slow sigh escaped her.

Casey.

Smiling to herself, she tiptoed past the door and around to the elevator. She waited with barely contained patience until he emerged from the far door of the kitchen, wheeling the towering rack of bagels in front of him. He couldn't possibly see her around the rack, which was fine.

He pressed the button, and the door slid open at once. She slipped inside. He pushed the rack in, followed it into the dreary but spacious car and pressed the button to make the door close.

"Hi," she said.

Another man might have jumped. Another man might have seen her and gone ballistic, and harangued her about how many safety regulations she was breaking—to say nothing of her trespassing and, for all he knew, stealing inventory.

Casey wasn't another man, though. He stared at her for a moment, then frowned, then smiled slightly. "Do I know you?"

"You sold me a bagel two weeks ago," she said, holding up the half-eaten bagel she'd bought upstairs. "You said I was nubile. My name is Susie."

"Okay," he drawled.

"And your name is Casey."

"That's right."

"So I thought, maybe we could get to know each other." Susie was missing the shyness gene—at least, that was what her mother had always said. She herself wasn't sure it was genetic; Julia and Adam were both endowed with a share of shyness. Maybe it was a result of birth order. Being the middle child, she had always opted to go after what she wanted. Julia got attention for being the eldest, Adam for being the youngest. Whatever Susie got, she got by helping herself.

Casey contemplated her as the elevator rose. His eyes looked deceptively drowsy; she could see, beneath his half-mast lids, eyes that were sharply focused on her.

"In what way did you want to get to know me?" he asked.

The elevator bumped to a halt. "Like, we could go get a coffee and talk?" she suggested. "Or maybe catch a movie, or a poetry slam. Or," she added when none of those suggestions ignited any obvious interest in him, "you could come to my grandmother's seder."

"Your grandmother's seder."

"It's a mob scene. One more mouth to feed wouldn't matter."

He laughed. He had a great-sounding laugh, dark and husky. "I hate matzo," he told her. "It tastes like drywall."

"I wouldn't know. I've never tasted drywall."

He laughed again. She realized he was holding the Door Close button.

"When I release this button," he instructed her, "you're going to hurry down the hall to the door and outside. If anyone finds you in that hall, it's bad news."

She considered telling him her last name—proof that she would be in no more trouble lurking in the back hall now than she'd been as a child scampering around the store. But his effort to protect her from punishment, rather than report her to store Security, was kind. And promising.

"So, you just want me to leave," she said, testing him.

"You leave the building, walk around the corner to the front door and come back in. I'll be in the bagel department."

"Okay." He was still smiling, so she smiled back. "And then what?"

He released the button. The door creaked open and he motioned with his chin that she was to exit.

"Then what?" she persisted.

"We'll discuss your grandmother's seder," he promised, heaving the rack into motion and pushing it down the hall in the opposite direction.

She felt her mouth spread in a triumphant grin as she strolled down the hall to the outer door. If Casey had the balls to attend one of Grandma Ida's seders, he was definitely worthy of her undying love.

At least for a while.

7

"You look pale," Grandma Ida declared. "And what's that on your lips? You think you're going to get sunburn in my apartment?"

Julia sighed. She'd come to Grandma Ida's apartment a half hour early, just as Grandma Ida had requested. One of these days, she would learn to say no.

But Grandma Ida was eighty-eight. How could Julia say no to someone that old?

The air was heavy with the aromas of good things cooking. Lyndon had let Julia peek into the kitchen, where he and a friend—"Howard is Jewish and he's a chef, so he knows from gefilte fish, as your grandmother would say"—were orchestrating the feast the family would pray over and then devour as soon as the sun set. Although Julia would have loved to linger in the kitchen, Lyndon had sent her on her way. "She's in the living room, waiting for you," he'd said.

"How's her mood?"

"The usual."

Julia hadn't considered that a particularly useful warning. Grandma Ida's usual mood was inscrutable.

Grandma Ida was dressed for the occasion in a long gray skirt, a cotton blouse with a quaintly rounded collar and a wool cardigan that might have begun its life as lilac but had faded to an uneasy gray. Her hair was a shapeless smudge of black— clearly one of Bella's masterpiece coiffures—and she wore thick-soled leather oxfords. Gold bangles circled both wrists.

"So, why are you so pale?" she asked.

Because I'm working too hard, Julia wanted to answer. But she couldn't. Grandma Ida probably thought she wasn't working hard enough at Bloom's. Two brief visits a week did not epitomize a workaholic's schedule.

Julia sank back into the spongy cushions of the sofa, across a dark cherry wood coffee table from her grandmother, who sat with regal posture in a wingback chair. The sofa's upholstery was soft enough to drown in. And damn it, Julia felt as if she were drowning.

"It's been a stressful few weeks for me," she admitted.

"Are you having trouble running Bloom's? You're the smartest of the bunch, Julia. If you can't run it, there's something wrong with you."

The only thing wrong with her was that she had a full-time job elsewhere. And the other only thing wrong with her was that she had no training or expertise in retail merchandising, and her heart pounded with dread whenever she neared her father's office or glimpsed some new package of documents from the lawyers, and she still wasn't clear on the difference between Greek and Turkish olives, let alone Iranian and Albanian olives, and she couldn't get the bagel department numbers to add up.

Now that she considered it, there were a lot of "only things" wrong with her.

"It's just a bit much for me," she admitted.

"It's not too much. If you don't take good care of Bloom's, who will?"

"My mother," Julia said, attempting to keep her tone casual.

"Your mother is all right, up to a point. But that point is over there—" she extended her left index finger in one direction "—and Bloom's is over here." Her right index finger pointed in the other direction.

Reflexively, Julia tapped her two index fingers together, as if that might bring her mother and Bloom's into proximity.

"You need to put in more hours at the store," Grandma Ida lectured her. "Jay tells me you're invisible there, like a ghost floating in and out."

She should have known Uncle Jay would tattle on her. Didn't he realize that if Julia wasn't the figurehead president, Grandma Ida would have to align her index fingers and give the job to Sondra? Once she did, he would be in a weaker position than he was in now. Julia didn't resent him the way her mother did. She actually liked some of his ideas, and she had faith that the Internet sales would eventually become more profitable. But he didn't deserve to be president of the company—and whether or not Julia held that title was irrelevant.

Again, she realized Grandma Ida was waiting for her to speak. "You know, I can't just walk away from Griffin, Mc-Dougal. I'm in the middle of a few cases there—"

"Any civil rights cases? Anything that's going to put you in front of the Supreme Court?"

"No—and I guess once I leave them for good, I'll *never* get to argue before the Supreme Court." As if staying there and hammering out alimony arrangements would ever put Julia on the high-speed Amtrak to Washington.

"So, what are you walking away from? Something no one else in that whole *goyishe* firm can possibly do?"

"I know you think my work there isn't important—"

"I think it's not as important as what you should be doing here, for your family."

That comment was enough to detonate an explosion of guilt within Julia. She sank deeper into the cushions and bit her lip, waiting stoically as shame rained down upon her soul like radioactive dust. Of course her family was more important than the *goyishe* law firm. Of course her family was more important than anything else in her life. Of course her family was embodied by Bloom's. How could she even think of charting an independent course for herself? What kind of selfish monster was she?

The doorbell rang. It took all her willpower not to leap from the sofa and race down the hall to answer the door herself, and to drop to her knees in gratitude that someone had come to save her from this wretched one-on-one with Grandma Ida. Her appreciation waned as soon as she heard Aunt Martha's lusterless voice: "Hello, Lyndon. Do I smell borscht?"

"No, we didn't make any borscht."

"I'm sure I smell borscht."

"That woman is an idiot," Grandma Ida whispered.

Julia smiled in spite of herself. In a normal family, a son's ex-wife would not be invited to the seder. But Aunt Martha lived just downstairs, and she was Neil and Rick's mother, and so she still wound up getting invited to family affairs.

Aunt Martha made her way to the living room. Today she had on a long, fiercely embroidered vest over a white peasant shirt and baggy woolen trousers. Except for her Birkenstock sandals, she could pass as a member of a Slavic dance troupe.

"Julia," she said, a faint flicker of her brows the only sign that she was happy to be there. "Good *yontif.* Good *yontif,* Ida," she added, giving a frosty kiss to Grandma Ida.

"We're not having borscht," Grandma Ida announced.

"All I said was, it smelled like borscht. That rooty, beety smell. How are you, Julia? When am I going to get you over to the Women's Center?"

When the pope dances the *hora,* Julia thought. She smiled feebly at Martha. "That's an amazing vest," she said.

The doorbell rang again, and again. Sondra arrived with Adam, who had taken the bus down from Cornell for the holiday. Rick arrived shortly after with his brother, Neil, who had flown in from Florida and looked as though he'd slathered a golden-brown wood stain over his skin. Uncle Jay arrived with The Bimbette, who smiled and greeted Aunt Martha with such effervescent charm that Aunt Martha grew even more sullen than usual, as if The Bimbette had somehow leeched from her what little cheer she possessed. Her mouth arched downward, her eyes narrowed and her shoulders hunched under her vest.

Lyndon glided around the room, taking coats and offering drinks that no one other than Uncle Jay wanted. Julia watched Jay while he sipped his Manhattan. He ignored his ex-wife, addressed Sondra only in short, tense sentences spoken through a sneer, beamed at his bronze-god son Neil, who seemed resistant to Jay's attention, and every now and then acknowledged The Bimbette by patting her on the head as though she were a child he was congratulating on her good behavior.

Julia didn't detect any overt antagonism directed at her. He was openly antagonistic toward Sondra, but then, they'd never gotten along, even when Julia's father was alive. She couldn't exactly call his behavior toward Martha antagonistic, since he was acting as if Martha wasn't in the room. Toward his own mother he seemed ambivalent, sometimes solicitous and sometimes aloof. He would ask her if she was warm enough, then turn his back before she could answer.

"Where's your sister?" Sondra whispered to Julia. "She's late."

"It's not sunset yet," Julia whispered back, although she was also wondering where Susie might be.

"She should have been here by now. She should have gotten here before Jay's boys got here. You're here, and Adam's here. All my children should have gotten here first."

"You brought Adam with you," Julia pointed out. Although he was twenty-one, legally an adult, Adam still looked unformed to Julia. His face had a boyish softness about it, his chin a slightly indecisive curve. He possessed the Bloom metabolism, too, which endowed him with a stringy build rather than a brawny one. When he turned forty and all his contemporaries started having their first heart attacks, he'd be glad he was so thin. But ever since he'd hit puberty, his narrow shoulders and undefined musculature had irked him. Uncle Jay's boys had better physiques.

"I swear, Susie is going to age me ten years," Sondra hissed. "Where the hell could she be that's more important than getting to the seder on time? You don't futz around with Grandma Ida. She invites you to a seder, you come. You don't show up late."

"She'll be here."

"You think she forgot what day it was?"

"She'll be here," Julia repeated emphatically, hoping Susie wouldn't make a liar out of her.

"Did the sun set yet?" Grandma Ida asked. "Someone check out the window."

"It doesn't matter if the sun set," Uncle Jay corrected her. "They say in the newspaper what time the sun sets. You don't have to look out a window. You just read it in the newspaper."

"I've got a window over there," Grandma Ida retorted, pointing to the heavily draped windows along one wall of her living room. Unfortunately, it was an east-facing wall, so looking out them wouldn't prove the sun's position. "I've got a window and I don't have a newspaper. I guess we could also look up the sunset on your computer, *nu?* Isn't that what you'd do, Jay?"

"The time of sunset is scientifically determined," Jay said tightly.

The Bimbette nodded. "You should listen to him, Ida. He's so smart when it comes to scientific things."

"Lyndon!" Grandma Ida shouted above the din of voices. "Lyndon, did the sun set yet?"

Lyndon appeared in the arched doorway. "Yes, it's set," he said with such certainty that even Uncle Jay wouldn't dare to contradict him.

Next to Julia, her mother stiffened. "Okay, so the sun set. Where the hell is your sister?"

As if in answer, the doorbell rang. Sondra let out such a long breath she seemed to lose an inch in height.

"Why don't you all go into the dining room," Lyndon suggested. "Howard is pouring the wine. I'll get the door."

They milled out to the hall and into the dining room. The long table was set with heavy damask, Grandma Ida's glass seder dishes, a seder plate adorned with bowls of *charoseth, moror* and saltwater, shrubs of parsley, a charred hard-boiled egg and a bone large enough to keep a Great Dane occupied for the better part of the evening. The bone, like everything else on the seder plate, was supposed to be symbolic; it represented the *pesach,* the paschal lamb. If the bone Lyndon and Howard had come up with was from a lamb, it must have been one with a severe pituitary problem.

"We're here!" Susie proclaimed, sweeping directly into the dining room, pulling behind her a tall man who looked vaguely familiar to Julia. He wore corduroy slacks and a sweater, and his hair fell in dark-blond waves past the ribbing of the sweater's crew-neck collar. In fact, Julia realized, he was the most sanely dressed person in the room. Susie had on a long, shapeless black jumper, and Sondra was wearing one of her supposedly slimming sweaters and hostess slacks. Neil wore a white T-shirt under a white jacket, the better to show off his Key West tan, and Rick's clothes hung off him as if he'd picked them out of the Salvation Army donation box marked Extra Large. The Bimbette had on a low-cut cashmere sweater that displayed the contours of her breasts as precisely as a mammogram, and Uncle Jay wore a suit with a banded-collar shirt and beige buck shoes. Adam was decked out in a Cornell sweatshirt. Julia had dressed demurely, she thought, in a matching tunic and skirt of washable blue silk.

But that man with Susie…he looked blessedly normal, like someone she might see walking down a street, or reading a magazine in the waiting area of Griffin, McDougal, or shopping in Bloom's.

Bloom's. That was where she'd seen him before.

Oh God. The bagel man.

"Everyone, I'd like you to meet Casey Gordon," Susie declared.

Well, Julia thought, at least Susie had found out his name.

Sondra simmered. How could Susie have brought a stranger to the family seder?

Not just a stranger. A tall, blond, Aryan stranger. He looked ridiculous in the *yarmulke* Susie planted on his head. That was how Sondra could tell Jews from *shaygetzes.* On a Jew a *yarmulke* looked right; on a *shaygetz* it looked like a beanie, or maybe a misplaced diaphragm. She often could tell if a man was Jewish even when he wasn't wearing a *yarmulke.* If you looked at him and imagined him wearing a *yarmulke,* and in your imagination the *yarmulke* looked right, chances were he was Jewish.

Okay, so bad enough Susie had brought this tall blond into Ida's home for Passover. Even worse, he'd responded to The Bimbette's sugary question—"So what do you *do,* Casey?"— by saying he sold bagels at Bloom's.

Bloom's had long ago become an equal opportunity employer. Her husband, Ben, may he rest, had said it was absurd to be serving a multi-ethnic clientele in a city like New York and be worrying about whether everyone on the staff was Jewish, especially because asking people whether they were Jewish before offering them a job was against the law—although Sondra was reasonably sure it wouldn't be against the law if you were hiring someone to be, for instance, a rabbi.

There were enough places set at the long dining room table that Sondra had to assume Susie had told Ida she was bringing this lug with her. Was Sondra the last to know her daughter was seeing a bagel clerk from Bloom's? Susie was always seeing someone—even as a girl she'd been boy-crazy, and now, Sondra supposed, she was man-crazy. But honestly—a counter clerk from the store? It was humiliating! What kind of mother would raise a daughter to bring a counter clerk to a family seder?

This was going to tip the scales against Sondra, she was sure.

Ida probably had a list somewhere, the Sondra-Is-A-Bad-Mother list, and this would be added to it. She tried to console herself that two out of three had come out all right. Julia was a Wellesley graduate, N.Y.U. law school—and wasn't she the president of Bloom's these days? And Adam was a true scholar; he wanted to go on for a graduate degree in mathematics. He was going to be a doctor, a PhD doctor—the first doctor in the Bloom family. Jay hadn't raised any doctors.

She glanced down the table as the family obeyed Ida's commands about where to sit. There were her two nephews. *Schlemiel* and *Schliemazel*. She sniffed. Neil resembled a gigolo, all that deep-fried skin and that hotsy-totsy jacket. When he wasn't sailing rich tourists from key to key in Florida, he was probably searching for rich divorcées to *shtup*. How else could he afford a jacket like that? It looked like silk.

And Rick. His hair appeared not to have been near a comb in days—she hoped to hell he at least washed it and didn't have a colony of lice building a subdivision beneath all those messy curls. He was—you should pardon the expression—a film-maker. An *auteur*. The next Federico Fellini, if only he ever got around to shooting a reel of film.

So Ida had better not be thinking Jay was a better parent than Sondra was. Two out of three she'd raised perfectly, and Susie, even with her tattoo and her questionable taste in men, was vastly superior to either of Jay's sons. Sondra bet Adam could read the damn *Haggadah* better than Jay, too. Ben used to read it, but now the honor had fallen to Jay. Last year, the first Passover after Ben's death, Jay had stumbled over the Hebrew, stammered, faked it every which way. They were all Reformed Jews, so it wasn't the end of the world if Jay skipped a page here and there, but Ben had done it much better. Adam would do it better. Probably this Casey fellow from the bagel counter would do it better.

On the other hand, skipping pages would move things along.

Her gaze shifted to the tower of matzos at the center of the table. It was draped with a square of white linen, with Hebrew letters stitched onto it in pale blue, like the colors of the Israeli flag. According to family lore, Ida had sewn it. At one time, the story went, she'd been domestic, handy with a needle, skilled in the kitchen. Isaac used to say he'd married an angel when he married her. Somewhere along the line, though, the angel must have lost her wings and halo and tumbled to earth. Her flair for homemaking had vanished, replaced by ambition and stubbornness. No time for stitching Hebrew blessings onto linen when there was a business to run, to expand, to push along.

Once Ida was satisfied with the seating arrangement, she peered at Jay, whom she'd seated to her left at the head of the table. She looked less than pleased. Of course, she always looked less than pleased. She had a *farbisseneh* attitude, a well of chronic resentment that spilled over into all her dealings. Nothing was good enough for her. Not even Bloom's, which thanks to Ben's hard work—and Sondra's—was a huge success.

Sondra would continue to make it a huge success, whether or not Ida ever gave her the credit she deserved. She would do it, with Julia as her helper, her front, her puppet—her partner. They'd make Bloom's even better than Ida could have imagined in her sour little dreams. And they'd do it thanks to Susie. She might be wild, she might be lacking in dignity, she might be a poet who served pizza to people who didn't deserve the time of day from her—but she was the genius who'd come up with the scheme to keep Bloom's in Sondra's control.

Sondra was proud of her, proud of all her children. She was a good mother. If Ida had a scrap of honesty in her, she'd have to admit that. Sondra was the best mother in this room.

That Casey had agreed to attend Grandma Ida's seder amazed Susie.

She'd extended the invitation only as a joke, but he'd told her he had never been to a seder before and thought it would be interesting.

"You sell bagels for a living, and you've never been to a seder?" she'd asked.

"Not only do I sell bagels, but I design them."

"Design them? How can someone design a bagel? They're all the same shape. Some variation regarding the size of the hole, I guess—"

He'd smiled, a smile that was one part whimsy and three parts dimpled seduction. "I develop new flavors. Cinnamon-walnut bagels, tomato-pepper… Bagels are an art form. They embody an aesthetic."

Susie had been baffled. "They're food," she'd argued.

"They're a national food. Pizza isn't Italian anymore. Tacos aren't Mexican anymore. Pizza and tacos are American. So are bagels. Everything sold in this store is American—except the imported items, of course." He'd gestured toward the heat-n-eat counter. "Couscous. It's American now. Kasha—American. We've reached a moment where the melting pot really is a pot, and it's full of cross-cultural cuisine."

"Bagels are part of the melting pot?"

"If someone like me can care so much about them, yeah." He'd begun unloading the trays into bins as he spoke. "This seder thing…maybe I'll discover that those foods are part of the melting pot, too."

"I doubt it."

"So, when is the Passover party?"

"The first night of Passover."

"Sounds cool. I'm up for it."

She'd considered withdrawing the invitation but decided not to. The laws of etiquette forbade such rudeness, and besides, he hadn't seemed particularly eager to have a cup of coffee with her. The seder was the bait; once he'd spent a little time with her there, he might be more inclined to spend time with her elsewhere. Like over a cup of coffee, or in bed.

They'd exchanged phone numbers and she'd left the store. For twenty-four hours she'd kept her cell phone turned on and never more than an arm's length away, and then he'd phoned—in the evening, while she was working at Nico's.

"This is Casey Gordon," he'd said, which was how she'd found out his last name.

How he found out her last name was a little more complicated. She'd delayed mentioning it to him until they'd made arrangements to meet at the residents' entrance to the Bloom Building at five on the night of the first seder. "No kidding—your grandmother lives in the same building as Bloom's?"

"My grandmother *is* Bloom's," she'd confessed, cringing and praying he wouldn't disconnect the call. "I'm Susie Bloom. My grandparents founded the store."

"No shit?"

"No shit."

"Wow."

He'd been silent for such a long time, she'd started thinking about the rate-per-minute her cell-phone carrier charged.

"So you're Ida Bloom's granddaughter?"

"Yeah, and she's a real character. My dad was the store president until he died last year. My mom and uncle are sort of running the place. Oh, and my sister."

"What about your sister?"

"She's sort of running the place, too. I don't work there. I don't live there. I don't shop there—except for an occasional bagel. I hope you're not upset or anything."

"Upset? No. I'm just..." Another expensive-per-minute delay. "I'm just sort of blown away, a little. I mean...*Ida Bloom*. I'm actually going to meet her."

"Well, you know it's going to be a great seder. I mean, we're talking about the Blooms of Bloom's. So the food's going to be fantastic, right?" That the food would be fantastic was a tribute to Lyndon's talent. Blooms did not excel in the culinary arts, and Grandma Ida, like Sondra, rarely served food from the family store.

"All right," Casey had conceded. "I'll meet you there at five. What am I supposed to wear to this thing?"

"Clean clothes," she'd told him. "You'll need a *yarmulke,* too, but I'll bring that." She had a few lying around, black velvet with "Travis Feldman Bar Mitzvah, June 12, 2000" inscribed on the white satin lining. Travis, a cousin on her mother's side, was a twerp whose soul seemed trapped inside a whine that affected everything he did and said. His bar mitzvah had been held at the Plaza Hotel, and the entertainment had included a chamber ensemble and a low-rent metal band that played excruciating covers of Metallica. Before the cake cutting, his parents announced that in honor of Travis's bar mitzvah they'd donated twenty-five thousand dollars to Brandeis University. Travis had seemed more interested in the cake.

Susie had asked to keep Adam's souvenir *yarmulke,* as well as her father's. They both owned personal skullcaps, and Susie decided she ought to have a few on hand, just in case. She hadn't known that "just in case" would wind up being a guy like Casey Gordon accompanying her to her grandmother's seder.

He'd arrived late. She hadn't been sure whether he'd belatedly decided it was too weird to experience his first seder at the home of the family for whom he worked, or whether he just wasn't interested in Susie enough to sit through an hour of prayers and chants and songs in order to eat a meal, or whether he didn't have any clean clothes. When he finally arrived, a little past five-fifteen, she'd been so relieved she hadn't asked for an explanation. He'd provided one, anyway: "The F train stalled under the East River. We just sat there in the dark for a half hour. Definitely the pits."

The F train under the East River meant he lived in Queens. Definitely the pits was right. Queens wasn't just another borough; it was another country, another planet. Queens was where people's parents lived. It was where residents bragged that they lived on Long Island, not in New York. It was where the Mets played, for God's sake. She didn't know if she wanted to get involved with someone from Queens.

Then again, she didn't really want to get involved with Casey. She just wanted to have some fun, some friendship, some high-quality sex—and she suspected he might be able to provide at least a few of those essentials.

They'd arrived at Grandma Ida's just as everyone was gathering around the dining room table. The air was thick with the salty fragrance of chicken soup, punctuated by the zing of freshly grated horseradish. As soon as Julia saw Casey, her eyes widened. Susie's mother's eyes narrowed. Of all her female relatives, only Grandma Ida looked unfazed.

"All right, well, you'd better have him sit next to you," Grandma Ida said as soon as Susie had presented him to her family. "We're about to start, and he probably has no idea what's going on. Do you have any idea what's going on?" she asked Casey.

"None at all," he said good-naturedly.

"Then, sit next to Susie. You can be bored together. She usually gets bored when we do this. Jay, you sit at the head. Wendy, you sit here. Martha you sit over there." Grandma Ida wisely placed the length of the table between Jay's two wives.

The seder began. Uncle Jay did not read Hebrew fluently, and when he asked Rick or Neil for assistance they stared back at him blankly. Rick, seated on Susie's other side, had once confided to her that the day after his bar mitzvah, he'd forgotten every word of Hebrew he'd ever learned. She doubted Neil had much opportunity to polish his language skills while cruising around the Florida Keys in his rent-a-sloop.

Not squirming took enormous willpower. If she were younger, she could have kicked her legs back and forth and driven Grandma Ida crazy, but Grandma Ida had been nice enough about including Casey in the family gathering, so Susie forced herself to keep her legs still. She flipped pages in her *Haggadah* and studied the trite illustrations: An infant Moses floating down the river in a basket and resembling a bundle of laundry with a baby's head poking out one end. An adult Moses looking oddly like a young Bob Dylan, facing off with a pharaoh who had apparently eaten something that didn't agree with him, if his facial expression was anything to go by. A crowd of Egyptian women in some sort of marketplace, their faces frozen in agony as torrents of frogs descended from the wide African sky. The Red Sea parting as if someone had unzipped it, and Bob Dylan leading a parade of Jews through the gap. She counted the number of pages Uncle Jay would have to fumble through before she could sip some wine. She counted the number of pages before everyone could set the books aside and dig into dinner, the tantalizing aromas of which made her stomach rumble.

Every now and then she glanced up from her book. Her mother was glowering at her. Adam was fidgeting with the gold ring he'd gotten when he graduated from high school. The Bimbette kept sending her charming dinner-party-guest smile in Casey's direction. Julia slid her finger along the page, trying to follow Uncle Jay's halting recitation. Aunt Martha appeared to be dozing, but Susie knew she was only meditating on the meaning of Passover. She always closed her eyes during the seder; she claimed this enabled the story to reach her on a deeper level.

But Casey seemed to be into the whole thing. He would read the English translation on the right-hand side of the page, then study Uncle Jay, then eye the flickering candles, the tower of matzos, the Passover platter laden with all the symbolic foods…and, every once in a while, watch Susie. When she caught him gazing at her, he smiled. Not a bored smile, not an "I'll survive this ordeal and we'll go off and live our own lives and never think about this evening again" smile, but a "hey, this is kind of cool" smile.

If she were foolish enough to consider the possibility of falling in love, she'd make sure to fall in love with a man who gave her a "hey, this is kind of cool" smile.

At last, they could eat. He'd floundered three-quarters of the way through the *Haggadah*. The last part of the book had to wait until after dinner, but by then everyone would have consumed enough wine that they wouldn't all be focusing on how awkwardly he read it, compared with Ben.

Ben was dead. Jay was the senior male of the family now. And damn it, if he was going to read the *Haggadah,* he should be running Bloom's.

He stared around the table, exhausted and irritated that no one had thanked him for having plowed through all that Hebrew. Did they think it was easy? A little appreciation would be nice.

But at least they'd get to eat—and drink. He wanted another Manhattan, but bottles of a kosher rosé stood around the table, and he figured it would be too complicated to request anything else. The wine was bland, but its alcohol content, not its flavor, was what counted.

Lyndon and his buddy waltzed in and out, carrying plates of gefilte fish and bowls of steaming soup with matzo balls protruding from the broth like pale, round boulders. Everyone was talking at once. Neil was telling Julia, the famous no-show executive, about some rich European and his bosom-enhanced mistress who had chartered him to sail them from Miami to Key West. "They paid me in cash. Is that illegal? It kind of creeped me out, you know?" he asked, tapping into her legal expertise.

Now, there was an idea: send Julia down to Florida to defend his son if he got arrested for accepting cash payments. For all she was contributing to Bloom's, nobody would miss her.

That conversation was to his right. To his left, Ida was criticizing Wendy's hair—"It looks too blond," she complained.

It did, but so what? If Ida was going to criticize someone's hair, she might as well attack Rick, whose hair looked as if it had been styled with an eggbeater.

Farther down the table, Sondra and Susie were sniping at each other across steaming bowls of soup, while Adam repeatedly asked for someone to pass the horseradish. At the far end, Martha pontificated to Susie's latest boyfriend about how Judaism was a sexist religion because women weren't allowed to lead the seder. Jay took her criticism personally. She probably thought she could do a better job reading the *Haggadah* than he had, but he knew she couldn't. Just because she had taken a seminar on women and theology at the New School didn't make her an expert.

He ate his own soup. It was flavored perfectly, the matzo ball was dense, the way he liked it, and little yellow circles of chicken fat skimmed the surface of the broth like a delectable oil slick. The gefilte fish had been firm and just slightly sweet. After the soup there would be a roast. One thing about Lyndon—he sure knew how to cook. Jay wondered whether he'd be willing to give Wendy a few lessons. Maybe on Sunday, while Jay was out golfing, she could come over here, learn how to boil water and beat eggs, and work on improving her relationship with Ida. For all Jay knew, the reason he'd been cheated out of the presidency of Bloom's was that his mother hated Wendy.

Last Sunday he'd been out at Emerald View, playing a round with Stuart Pinsky, his attorney. Somewhere between the fourth and fifth hole, he'd mentioned that he was worried about his mother. "She's not as sharp as she used to be," he'd said.

"None of us is as sharp as we used to be," Stuart had pointed out.

"Yes, but we're not eighty-eight. She is. And she's making some decisions about the store that frankly worry me."

"Really?" Stuart handled Jay's private affairs—his divorce, his will, the trusts he'd set up for the boys—but he didn't work for the store. Still, he knew a lot about it. "You think it's time for you to exercise power-of-attorney over her affairs?"

"She'd disown me if I did anything that drastic. But I'm worried about the store."

"So you keep telling me."

It was true—every time he and Stuart got together, Jay wound up ranting about the store. "It's because she put my niece in charge of it, and my niece doesn't know *bupkes* when it comes to retail. Or deli. The girl probably wouldn't know what pastrami was if it bit her on the ass. But she's Ben's daughter. That's the only reason she's got the corner office."

"You sure it's got nothing to do with you?"

"Me? I'm holding the place together. But it's hard, I'll tell you. If the store's value drops, some big *macher* could come in and buy us. Then Bloom's would be just a brand name, not a place, a family's lifeblood. You see what I'm saying?"

"The store isn't publicly owned, Jay. How can you be worried about a hostile takeover?"

Jay wasn't exactly clear on how hostile takeovers worked. "Well, if we start losing money—and you know, we've been just sort of drifting for the past year since Ben died, because my mother refused to make any decisions for that whole year—and if instead of just drifting we start drifting *south,* who's to say? Bloom's is Bloom's. It goes under, a huge piece of New York culture goes under with it."

Stuart actually stopped lining up his shot and stared at Jay. "You think it's that shaky, Jay?" He sounded genuinely concerned.

"I don't know how shaky it is. I'm just saying, the store could be slipping, my mother could be slipping, and they've locked me out of the executive suite."

"Sounds like you'd better start looking for the key," Stuart advised. "You'd better find a way to get into that room and stabilize things. It would be an act of mercy, I would think. If your niece can't handle the store, you can't just stand aside and let it go under."

This was mere golf advice, nothing legal, nothing that cost six hundred an hour. But since Stuart's words had been exactly what Jay wanted to hear, he'd savored them.

He was going to find that key. It had to be somewhere. Maybe everyone else wasn't as sharp as they used to be, but damn it, Jay wasn't getting any duller.

8

This time the frantic phone call had come to her apartment the night before, rather than during the workday, when she would be up to her elbows in Griffin, McDougal business. Thank God, too. Her superiors at the law firm were growing suspicious about the increasingly frequent cell-phone calls that led to her disappearing for a few hours here and there.

"Family problems?" John Griffin himself had asked the last time. "What exactly *is* the problem? Is it something we can help you with?"

His solicitude had swamped her with guilt—as if she hadn't already felt guilty enough. "The only way you can help is to be flexible about my having to run across town," she'd told him, smiling sweetly so she wouldn't seem demanding.

He'd given her a long, pointed stare, which implied that he wasn't so much interested in helping her with her problem as he was in making her problem go away so she could once again give 150 percent of herself to Griffin, McDougal.

"Go, take care of your family problems," he'd said. "My only concern is that you're getting your work done."

Which, of course, she wasn't. She was trying to keep up. She was staying late at the office, working through the dinner hour, turning down all Heath's invitations because she didn't have time to go anywhere with him and argue about whether they should have sex. She was dragging files home and writing reports until two in the morning. But she had her limit—and she'd passed that limit well before the beginning of Passover.

Passover was done now. Someday, Julia would actually honor all eight days of the holiday. She'd skip doughnuts and eat matzo for breakfast every morning of Passover week. Maybe Lyndon would teach her how to make *matzo brei*. She'd have plenty of time to learn how to cook once Griffin, McDougal fired her.

But they weren't going to fire her today, because instead of bolting from the office during business hours, in front of witnesses, she would not be going to the office at all. She would be calling in sick. Lying seemed much more palatable than bolting.

Francine took her call. "I've been vomiting all night," Julia told her, figuring that would discourage questions. She hadn't realized she was such a smooth liar. She felt proud—and a little ashamed—that she could deceive Francine so easily.

She dressed in a below-the-knees straight skirt and matching jacket, swallowed a few handfuls of Cheerios, brushed her teeth and slicked her lips with gloss. She'd pick up some coffee at Bloom's, and she'd drink it out of a mug emblazoned with Bloom's lettering. That ought to impress the reporter.

A reporter. She couldn't believe she was going to have to meet with a reporter from *Gotham Magazine* to discuss the direction she intended to steer Bloom's now that she was behind the wheel. Her mother had explained that an article in *Gotham* would be excellent exposure for the store, a way to generate excitement for the store's new management in the new century.

"What if someone from Griffin, McDougal sees the article?" Julia asked.

"You'll tell them you're a figurehead. You'll say it's family PR. Don't worry—you'll think of something."

The sun was bright, and spring gave the air an apple-fresh scent, unusual in a neighborhood that usually smelled of bus fumes. She walked the few blocks to Broadway, concentrating on her posture and mentally rehearsing what she'd tell this reporter from *Gotham*. Would he go easy on her if she said she adored his magazine?

Journalists could be dangerous. This one might be snide and supercilious. The thrust of his piece might be that Bloom's products were guaranteed to clog one's arteries, and they weren't even kosher. Only kosher-*style*. She might have to explain the importance of kosher-style in the lives of Bloom's customers. "Kosher can be viewed as a style," she'd say. "Kind of like a lifestyle. People who want to eat a salami and Jarlsburg sandwich ought to be able to buy a kosher salami and a kosher Jarlsburg, even if piling them together between two slices of bread isn't kosher."

Too verbose. As a lawyer, she knew the value of saying the absolute minimum, answering the question but volunteering not a single extra syllable. If the reporter criticized Bloom's for being kosher-style, she'd simply smile and say, "That's the way our customers like it."

She nodded, pleased with that approach: "That's the way our customers like it." He couldn't possibly describe such a philosophy snidely.

Deirdre had set up the interview and promised to spend time with the reporter. She would be able to supply him with any business information he might want. Julia's sole function, according to her mother, was to put a human face on the president's office.

Closing her eyes, she imagined taping a yellow smiley face to her door—and locking herself inside.

She reached her desk at nine-fifteen. He was scheduled to arrive at nine-thirty. She couldn't remember his name.

She took a sip of the coffee she'd brought upstairs with her, in her nice new Bloom's mug. She'd made her purchases anonymously, paying full price. She was already thinking like a Bloom's executive, refusing to depress profits by helping herself to merchandise without paying for it. If her mother could serve food from the cheap supermarket down the street, Julia could pay her own money for a cup of Bloom's Colombian supreme.

Her door swung open and her mother bounded in, beaming like a cheerleader after a touchdown. "I've brought you some things so you'll look busy," she whispered, dumping a stack of folders on the desk. "These are the profit-loss statements for March from each of the departments, if he asks."

"Are the profits bigger than the losses?" Julia asked, opening the top folder and slamming it shut when she saw the intimidating array of numbers on the top sheet.

"I don't know. I haven't looked. Just tell the reporter our profits are growing. The store's doing great. Our customer base increases every day. The coffee department in particular is doing magnificently," Sondra added, her gaze snagging on Julia's mug and her smile fading. She was probably wondering whether Julia had paid retail for it. "On-line sales are stagnant, of course—but you don't have to tell him that. Just tell him everything's doing fantastic. He wants details, you send him to me."

"I thought Deirdre was supposed to handle the details."

Her mother pursed her lips. "Better he should come to me. Deirdre doesn't run this place."

Julia wasn't so sure of that. She also wasn't sure she wanted her mother talking to the reporter. Sondra was so eager to minimize Uncle Jay's contributions to the store that she might just say something negative—for instance, that the on-line sales were stagnant. Or she'd insinuate not only that Deirdre wasn't running the place, but that Julia, the president, wasn't, either. Julia might not know what she was doing at Bloom's, but one thing she ought to be doing was protecting the store's reputation.

Her mother left, and she thumbed through the folders, looking for the one with information on last month's Internet sales. She wondered, in particular, how well the Seder-in-a-Box sold. She'd just found that folder, stuffed between the heat-n-eat folder and the electric appliances folder, when her door opened again, this time to admit Deirdre.

One glance at the tall, red-haired woman was enough to convince Julia that Deirdre knew more about the store than all the Blooms combined. She'd been with Bloom's nearly from the first day Julia's father had become the president. First she was a secretary, then a glorified secretary, then an administrative assistant and finally assistant to the president, a more impressive title than Sondra's for sure, since Sondra didn't have a title at all.

Julia gave Deirdre her best smile. Deirdre had never commented on Julia's chronic absences. She simply did her job, put things on Julia's desk, took things off and figured out what Julia needed long before Julia realized she needed anything at all.

"These are some letters you have to sign," Deirdre informed her, setting a pile of stationery beside the heap of folders. "Oh, and Ron Joffe from *Gotham Magazine* is here. I believe he intends to speak with me first, and then I'll send him in to you. When will you be ready for him?"

Julia glanced at the stack of letters, then the thicker stack of folders. Stacks or no stacks, she would never be ready for him. "Whenever you're done with him," she said bravely.

"If it's all the same—" a man's voice floated into the office from the hallway "—I'd just as soon start with you."

The owner of the voice appeared in the doorway. He was wiry and slightly taller than Deirdre, with wavy brown hair crowning an angular face. He wore a gray tweed jacket and blue jeans, and he extended his right hand toward Julia. He marched directly to her desk. "Julia Bloom? I'm Ron Joffe."

She had no choice but to shake his hand. His grip was as firm as his gaze. His eyes were an intriguing hue, brown but with undertones of amber and copper, like autumn leaves changing color.

No, his eyes weren't intriguing, she corrected herself as she extracted her fingers from his warm clasp. They were very ordinary eyes. He was a very ordinary man. Lean and turbo charged, with a harsh jaw and a golden cast to his skin, and surprisingly wide shoulders for someone as lanky as he was.

Really, quite ordinary.

If she suddenly found getting oxygen into her lungs difficult, it was only because she was anxious about the interview. She was worried that Ron Joffe would splash across the pages of the most popular magazine in New York City that Bloom's had a do-nothing, know-nothing as its president, a woman whose only qualification to run the place was a law degree from NYU, which wasn't any sort of qualification at all.

"That coffee smells good," he said, surveying her office and opting to sit on the couch. "What do I have to do to get a cup?"

"Write a great article about us," she said pleasantly. "The coffee is from the store. Deirdre, could you send one of the secretaries downstairs to get a cup for Mr. Joffe?"

Deirdre gave the reporter a toothy smile. "Cream? Sugar?"

"Black is fine."

With a nod, Deirdre departed. Julia felt abandoned. She wished she had gone to get the coffee and Deirdre had stayed behind. She didn't want to be left all alone in her office with Ron Joffe.

She eyed him cautiously. He was digging assorted paraphernalia from his jacket pockets: a notepad, a pen, a tiny tape recorder. "You won't even notice this," he assured her, placing it on the scratched table in front of the couch and popping open a compartment to make sure it contained a tape. "It's just a backup."

She might be a know-nothing, but she knew a few things. "It's so if I say anything I shouldn't say, you'll have incontrovertible proof that I said it."

He shot her a look, then grinned. He had dimples, she noticed with some dismay. Ordinary dimples, but still...

"If you can pronounce *incontrovertible,* you won't be saying anything you shouldn't say." He pressed a button on the compact machine. "The mike's built in. Just speak in a normal voice."

She nodded.

"Okay. So, you're Julia Bloom, the new president of Bloom's. Why you?"

"Why me what?"

"Why are you the new president of Bloom's? Isn't it hard for you to replace your father, given his untimely death?"

She decided she didn't like Joffe. She didn't like anyone who used the phrase *untimely death,* even if in her father's case it was accurate. Deaths happened when they happened. What kind of death could possibly be timely?

"If you're asking whether I'm too crushed by grief to handle the job," she said, "no, I'm not. Of course I miss my father. We all do. No one can replace him. But Bloom's is more than just one person. It's family."

"Food poisoning, right?" He wrote something on his pad, then peered over the spiral binding at her. "Your father died from food poisoning?"

"Yes." She wished she could fabricate a few tears so he'd believe she really did miss her father. She was able to produce only an emotional sigh. "It's not a happy subject."

Joffe shrugged as if reluctant to move on. He studied his notepad, then asked, "What about your uncle? He started working here just a few years after your father did. How come he didn't get named president?"

"It was my grandmother's decision," Julia said carefully. "She probably believed Uncle Jay was contributing so much where he was, developing our on-line and direct-mail presence. He's doing a fantastic job there. I can't imagine we've got anyone else on staff who could have taken on that task if Uncle Jay had moved into this office."

"Oh, come on—any teenage boy can set up a Web site. Your uncle has some sons, doesn't he?"

"My cousins Neil and Rick. Neil runs a charter sailboat outfit in the Florida Keys. You probably ought to interview him. His job is much more exciting than mine." She smiled, hoping she could disarm Joffe with what he would view as charming modesty rather than the pathetic truth it was.

He smiled back at her, and the air grew precipitously thinner in the office. She didn't know why she was having trouble breathing, why her heart seemed to have the hiccups, why she was letting him get to her. She was a confident, successful woman, after all—not necessarily a successful president of Bloom's, but successful in other contexts. She was a Wellesley graduate. She was an attorney. She'd passed the bar exam on her first try. Surely she could handle this reporter.

If only his eyes weren't quite so...beautiful. If only the movement of his hand as he jotted notes on his pad wasn't quite so graceful. If only he'd close the top button of his shirt so she couldn't see so much of his neck.

"So Neil Bloom is a yachtsman," Joffe murmured.

"Not really," she argued.

Joffe flashed a skeptical smile at her, and she was once again startled by the fact that such an ordinary-looking man could look so extraordinary. He had a big nose, she observed. Straight and thick. It lent ballast to his face.

His quizzical expression prompted her to explain herself. "What I mean is that Neil works very hard, sailing rich people around the Florida Keys. It's not like he's rich himself. 'Yachtsman' makes him sound rich."

"He's a Bloom," Joffe pointed out, jotting something on his pad.

Or maybe jotting nothing. Julia knew the lawyer trick of pretending to write things down in order to panic the other side. Lawyers made grand flourishes and dramatic scribblings on their elongated yellow pads during trials, negotiations and other assorted confrontations—and frequently all they were writing was *quart of milk, peanut butter, mocha fudge ice cream.* But they seemed so energetic and intent as they scrawled words onto their pads it gave their opponents something to worry about.

She wasn't Joffe's opponent, and she shouldn't be worrying so much about what he was or wasn't scrawling. She took deep, slow breaths, trying to steady her heartbeat, and waited for him to elaborate on his comment. He didn't. He only studied her, settling deeper into the sofa and propping one leg across the other knee. On his feet were scuffed leather sneakers.

She knew she shouldn't speak, but she couldn't stand having his words linger in the air. *He's a Bloom.* What the hell was that supposed to mean? "Do you think being a Bloom means being rich?" she asked when the silence began to make her scalp itch.

"You tell me."

She forced a smile. "I don't think my family's finances are an appropriate subject for your article."

Abruptly, he leaned forward. "Your family's finances are intricately bound up in the store, aren't they?"

What was he getting at? If she could figure it out, she'd have a better idea how to deflect him. "It's complicated," she said vaguely.

"Let's uncomplicate it." He studied his pad for a moment, as if memorizing all those notes about milk and peanut butter. Before he could uncomplicate anything, Deirdre swung into the office, carrying his coffee. His came in a cardboard cup, not a Bloom's mug. Julia should have told Deirdre to bring him a mug, which he could keep as a souvenir. Maybe that would have convinced him to write a nice article about the store.

"Thanks," he said, rising at Deirdre's entrance and accepting the cup from her. She smiled, nodded and left.

He settled back onto the sofa, pried the lid off his cup, and took a sip of the steaming brew. "This is great," he said. "Better than the stuff you get at most neighborhood coffee bars."

Julia smiled; she'd have to pass his compliment along to her mother. Sondra would be ecstatic. She'd probably race across the hall to Uncle Jay's office to brag about it.

He took another sip, then lowered the cup to the table and scrutinized his notes some more. "Okay—we were discussing the Bloom family wealth."

She sighed. She didn't want to discuss the Bloom family wealth.

"Your grandparents founded Bloom's. The store supported them, it supported their sons and it's supporting their sons' families pretty nicely. The third generation—yours—all attended private school. That's not bad for a little mom-and-pop store."

"The store has done well," she conceded, then bit her lip to keep from saying anything more. She wasn't sure what to say: that discussing money was in poor taste, that the store was still doing well—not that she could prove that without going through the folders her mother had left for her—that he had a hell of a nerve and he'd damn well better tell her what his real agenda was.

She decided to say nothing.

"So, what's the problem?" he asked.

"What problem?"

"With the store."

"What problem with the store?"

"Well, it's losing money, isn't it?"

She caught herself before blurting out "It is?" The folders on her desk might answer that question. "The store is doing fine," she said, praying—for a lot of reasons—that that was close to the truth.

"What steps are you taking as the new president to make sure of that?" he asked, as casually as if he were enquiring about the location of the nearest bus stop.

Again she chewed on her lip while she willed her nervous system to settle down. What if the store wasn't doing fine? Oh God. What if it was in trouble? She was the president, and she didn't know, and this reporter *did* know. Unless he was just playing head games with her, hoping to shake a story loose.

"Bloom's sells what people want to buy," she said. "As long as our customers don't suddenly decide that bagels are repulsive, I think we'll manage to stay successful."

He laughed. It was a quiet laugh, deep in his throat, and it irked her even more. She wished he would fold his little pad shut, turn off his little tape recorder and leave. She wished all his hair would fall out—including his thick brown lashes. She wished that if he ever laughed like that again he wouldn't do it anywhere near her.

"I have more questions for you," he said, shoving away from the sofa's enveloping cushions, "but they'll have to wait. Deirdre Morrissey was supposed to be my first interview today."

"Yes. You'd better go and interview her." She hoped her gracious tone concealed her relief at his imminent departure.

"And then we'll talk some more."

"I'm not sure I'll have the time," she said, gesturing toward the pile of folders. "As you can see, I've got a lot on my desk."

His smile was slightly mocking, as if he believed the folders were full of notes along the lines of *milk, peanut butter, mocha fudge ice cream*. But he pushed himself to his feet. Julia stood, too, a lawyerly habit. Whenever a deposition or negotiation ended, everyone stood. To remain seated while the other side stood made one seem smaller or weaker.

She wasn't sure whether the past few minutes constituted a deposition or a negotiation, but she felt the need to be on her feet, if only to usher Joffe out of her office. Too bad he was so much taller than her. Her shoes didn't do much to reduce the difference. She ought to start wearing Manolo Blahniks like Deirdre.

He started to extend his hand, then hesitated. "Just one more question before I go. Why do you have two desks in your office?"

She felt her panic ebb slightly, leaving room for a glowing nostalgia. "The old desk belonged to my grandfather," she said, smiling at the stained, battered piece. "When my father became the president of Bloom's, my mother bought him this new desk." Twenty-five years old, it hardly qualified as new, but her father had taken meticulous care of it. Unlike Grandpa Isaac's old desk, her father's desk had no scratches, no dings, no water stains. No little girl had ever been allowed to complete her first-grade worksheets on its pristine surface.

"That still doesn't explain why the old desk is here." Joffe circled the coffee table and approached the desk, his gaze admiring. Did he think it was a valuable antique or a sentimental eccentricity?

Julia didn't believe she was the least bit eccentric, but she certainly felt sentimental about the desk. She crossed the office to join Joffe—to make sure he didn't leave a mark on it, although God knew one more mark wasn't going to make a difference. "My father never got around to moving the desk out," she said, deciding it was all right to talk about this. It was the sort of human-interest detail that might be effective in Joffe's article, presenting the Bloom family less as rich yacht people and more as human beings. "When I was a little girl, I used to come here after school and do my homework at this desk."

"Really?"

He gently ran a hand over the blond wood. She decided he was showing the proper reverence for it, so his touch was allowed.

"How about your sister and your brother?"

She laughed. "My sister used to go downstairs to the store and wreak havoc after school. My brother was just a baby then. He stayed upstairs with a nanny."

"Upstairs?"

"My family's apartment was upstairs. My mother still lives there."

He nodded, but his gaze remained on the desk. He wasn't taking notes. She glanced over her shoulder at his tape recorder, but she couldn't tell if the tape was still turning.

"So, what's in this desk now?" he asked, tugging on the center drawer and discovering it locked.

"It's empty."

"If it's empty, why do you keep it locked?"

She stared at him. His smile was crooked, forming a dimple where his mouth skewed higher on one side. The truth was, the desk had been locked from the day she'd first knelt on a chair beside it and traced the dotted-line letters in her alphabet workbook. She'd pulled on the center drawer, just like Joffe. It had been locked then, and every other time she'd tried to open it.

"The desk was emptied out when my father got his new desk," she said. Her father had told her this the one time she'd asked him why the drawers were locked. "And the key for the desk got lost. So if there's anything inside it, we'll never know."

"Unless you pick the lock." His smile had grown mischievous. Was this his idea of investigative journalism? Pretend to be writing a puff piece on an Upper West Side culinary landmark, and then break-and-enter an old piece of furniture? So much for his treating her grandfather's desk with the proper reverence.

"No one is going to pick the lock," she declared. "My grandfather's spirit is resting in that desk. Mess with the lock and you mess with his spirit."

Her answer seemed to surprise Joffe. It surprised her, too. It was the sort of sassy, defiant, weird thing Susie would say. Susie was more creative, more whimsical, more likely to worry about messing with dead people's spirits.

Julia would have to ask Susie if she thought their grandfather's spirit might be locked inside the desk. She herself had never considered the possibility before now.

Evidently, Joffe was impressed by her having thought of it. Impressed, or maybe just amused. "You think his spirit's in there?"

"Why not?"

"You ought to hold a séance," he suggested. "If you heard a rapping, you could assume it was the old guy inside, banging on the drawer."

"And shouting, 'Let me out of here!'" Julia added, trying to imagine her grandfather, in his rusty, accented voice, shouting such a thing. "Actually, he'd say, '*Oy, vey iz mir.* It's hot in here! I'm *shvitzing!*'"

Joffe laughed, that same dark, dangerous laugh she hated. She laughed, too. Somehow, when they both laughed together, she didn't hate his laugh so much. Which was a bad thing.

"You'd better find the key and cool the poor guy off," Joffe urged her, then turned from the desk and started toward the door. "I'll go talk to Deirdre now...get some facts and figures about the place. Will you be around later if I have more questions for you?"

"Sure." She'd be here all day. The folks at Griffin, McDougal assumed she was spending the day on her knees, hunched over her toilet; they certainly wouldn't want her to show up there.

"Great." Joffe smiled.

Julia didn't think it was great. She'd done an adequate job of answering his questions—although he apparently thought her family were a bunch of aristocrats simply because Neil ran a sailboat charter business in southern Florida. And he'd implied Bloom's was failing. If it was, no one had bothered to tell her—but someone seemed to have shared this information with him.

She didn't want him to start grilling her on Bloom's health. Nor did she want him to smile at her the way he was smiling at her right now, because it made her lungs strain and her heart stammer and her fingertips grow so icy she was afraid to shake his hand and let him find out how nervous he made her. There was no reason he should make her feel nervous, none at all.

"I'll be back," he said, so mildly it shouldn't have sounded like a threat. He paused at the coffee table to pocket his tape recorder and pick up his cup. Then he headed to the door. With a final glint of a smile, he was gone.

Julia felt herself deflate. She stumbled back to the leather chair behind her father's desk and collapsed into it. What was wrong with her? Why did she feel as if he'd tied her knee tendons into knots so she couldn't stand without feeling wobbly? He was just a magazine writer, a hack trying to stir up trouble. And she was Julia Bloom, the president of Bloom's.

Yeah, sure. He knew who she was. He could see right through her. He knew that as the president of Bloom's she was as empty as her grandfather's old desk. He'd sensed that she was a phony, and he was going to pump Deirdre for information with which to arm himself and then come back into this office and flatten her.

This was not going to be a puff piece. It was going to be a stomp-Julia-and-Bloom's-into-the-ground piece.

And she had no one but herself to blame, for accepting this position and failing to fill it. Well, she could blame Susie for coming up with the idea, and her mother for thinking it was so clever. And whoever had fed her father that salmonella-infected sturgeon. And Uncle Jay for being such a *putz* that Grandma Ida had refused to consider him for the presidency.

And Grandma Ida, too. She deserved a hell of a lot of the blame.

Yes, they were all to blame.

But Julia, most of all.

9

Jay was heading out to meet a friend for a late-morning game of squash when he spotted Sondra hovering in the hall just outside Deirdre's office. What the hell was she doing? Eavesdropping on Deirdre?

Maybe that wasn't such a bad idea. She might learn a thing or two. Everybody knew Deirdre was the brains of this outfit—right behind Jay, of course.

Spying on Sondra from his office doorway, he noticed that she'd become profoundly pear-shaped over the past few years. Her shoulders were narrow, her chest nothing to speak of, but those hips! She'd obviously spent too much of her life sitting, and gravity had caused the fat to slide down to her tush. If Wendy ever let herself go like that... Well, she wouldn't.

He'd often wondered why his brother had fallen for Sondra. She'd had a nice educational pedigree and she'd come from an affluent family, but so what? Ben hadn't married her because he'd needed her family's money or her scintillating conversation. The store had always been his primary passion.

Maybe she'd been good in bed. Jay couldn't imagine it, though. Not given her figure—or her personality.

But who was he to wonder why his brother had wound up with Sondra? He himself had married Martha, of all people.

Martha had been different back then, though. He'd been different, too—but she'd been *really* different. She used to smile a lot, tell bawdy jokes and play old folk music on the stereo all the time: Kingston Trio, Peter, Paul and Mary, corny stuff but fun. She'd wanted to raise their sons to be free, creative, adventurous and fearless, and the boys had grown up to be all those things—maybe a bit too much of some of them. At an art class Rick had taken as a kid—he'd spent most of the classes throwing clay at other kids, as Jay recalled—Martha had become friendly with some of the other mothers. Artsy types, intense, they'd all subscribed to *Ms.* and taken themselves very seriously. Martha had started reading *Ms.* and taking herself seriously, too, and eventually she'd become the new Martha, grave and grim, so sympathetic with the world's oppressed that she became a bit oppressive herself. She'd started going to meetings and attending classes. Strange newsletters regarding human rights violations in Sri Lanka and battered women in Boise had filled their mailbox. Martha had set the clock radio to National Public Radio.

She'd even flirted with vegetarianism. If Jay had had to pinpoint the exact moment their marriage disintegrated, it would probably have been the evening he'd craved a thick pastrami sandwich and all she'd had in the house were tofu and hummus.

He'd stormed out of the house that evening, gone downstairs and had one of the guys at the deli counter fix him a three-inch-thick pastrami on rye, with a spear of dill pickle. He'd brought it to his third-floor office and devoured it there, too pissed off to return to the apartment. Then he'd gone out to a movie, something with Catherine Deneuve at one of the art houses—he didn't remember the movie, but he sure as hell remembered Catherine Deneuve—and he'd gone to a neighborhood bar and downed a few beers and a hamburger, not because he was hungry but because he'd wanted meat. He'd finally gotten home around two-thirty, and he'd slept in the guest room. No way was he going to sleep with a vegetarian.

She'd started buying meat again—so much for her commitment to the idea of food as a political statement—but their marriage never improved after that.

He supposed he should be grateful that she hadn't wanted to participate in the family business. She had always viewed Bloom's with a degree of distrust. She'd never had any difficulty spending the money it brought in, but she'd often comment on the obscene indulgence of so much food when people were starving in… Where were they starving? Rwanda? Kazakhstan? As if thousands of Rwandans and Kazakhstanians were crying out for bagels and lox.

Sondra moved, drawing his attention back to the hallway. She must have sensed his eyes on her, because she spun around.

He grinned and approached her. "What?" she snapped, her voice near a whisper.

"What do you mean, what? What are you doing, hovering outside Deirdre's office?"

"She's being interviewed by a reporter from *Gotham*."

"*Gotham?*" He'd placed ads in *Gotham Magazine*. He knew the ad director there. Why hadn't he been told about this?

"The fellow wanted to talk to Deirdre. And Julia."

"About what?"

"He's doing a story on Bloom's." Sondra moved away from Deirdre's closed door, snagging Jay's elbow on the way and drawing him down the hall. "I was trying to hear what he and Deirdre were talking about. Julia told me he asked her mostly about the family. But Deirdre isn't family. He must be asking her about something else."

He might be asking her for an outsider's view of the family—and God knew what an outsider's view would be. Just because the Blooms shared a last name didn't mean they shared philosophies or personalities. Sondra was pushy, Julia out of her depth. Jay was the only one who understood how the place ought to be run.

"I'm hoping he's going to write a nice PR piece," Sondra said, her voice still barely above a hiss, "but you never know. These reporters—they all want to be the next Woodward and Bernstein. They're always looking for a scandal. Thank God we haven't got any scandals. Unless you count marrying a woman young enough to be your daughter," she added as an afterthought.

"Wendy isn't young enough to be my daughter," he retorted. No one in his family liked Wendy, but fortunately, she wasn't terribly aware of that. Thanks to her sunny disposition, her sublime naiveté and the fact that Jay treated her as if she were the jewel of the Bloom family, she just bounced along, being pleasant to everyone even though they were all jealous of her youth and beauty.

"I should talk to this reporter," he said. "I know lots of people at *Gotham*." That was a slight exaggeration; he knew one person. But that was probably one more than Sondra knew. "If he's doing an article on the store, he ought to include stuff on our Web site. It's a growing area."

"*Gotham* is a New York magazine. Its reader base is New Yorkers. Why would they be going on the Web site to buy Bloom's products when we're right here in their backyard?"

"Because Internet buying is the wave of the future," he informed her, not bothering to tamp his resentment. No one in this family recognized how important his work was, how cutting edge, how vital. If they wanted Bloom's to come across as twenty-first century, they ought to highlight the Web site in this magazine article.

"Since when has Bloom's marketed itself as a futuristic company? We're selling nostalgia here, not the Jetsons."

"The Jetsons are nostalgia," Jay argued, then let out a long breath. He wasn't going to stand in the hallway bickering with his sister-in-law. What did she know? Who was she, anyway? If she was so important, if she understood the store so damn much, Ida wouldn't have bypassed her for her own daughter for president.

He returned to his office, settled in his chair and rang Deirdre's extension. "Jay here," he said. "I want to talk to the reporter when you're done with him."

"Are you sure?" Deirdre asked.

"What, am I speaking Swahili? Sure I'm sure."

"Okay," she said, and hung up.

He hung up, too, then stared at his phone console for a minute, annoyed that Deirdre hadn't sounded more enthusiastic about his talking to the journalist. His annoyance grew as he realized he was going to have to cancel his squash date. He'd really been looking forward to that.

Damn. Well, he supposed the store was more important than squash—and getting his name prominently mentioned in the article was more important yet. Let his mother read the article and realize how essential he was to the business. She'd rethink her decision to put Julia in the top slot. One good *Gotham* article might be all it would take.

What an ass, Ron thought as he left Jay Bloom's office an hour later. What a mess. He couldn't decide which was more dysfunctional: Bloom's the store or Blooms the family.

The store was coasting and its momentum was flagging. No new products or promotions had been introduced in over a year. The store's design hadn't changed in a decade. Now that he'd met them, he could safely assume that the Blooms were the main reason the store was stagnating.

Jay Bloom was all bluster, orating about Web sales as if he'd invented the concept. And Sondra Bloom was a delicatessen version of a stage mother, alternately gloating about her daughter and presenting herself as the power behind her daughter's success. According to Deirdre Morrissey, Ben Bloom had been the only person who understood how to run the store. He'd had the brilliance, the energy, the devotion. "He lived and breathed Bloom's," the woman had said, choking up with emotion. "I ought to know—I sat at his right hand. He was the genius here. He made the place what it is, even more than Ida and Isaac did. No one else will ever be able to do for Bloom's what Ben did." She seemed to miss the late, great leader more than his own relatives did.

And then there was Julia. As slim and fragile-looking as a ballerina, yet when she smiled, when she laughed, when her dark eyes flashed in his direction, he sensed that inside her delicate body lurked one tough broad. She was a lawyer, after all. A Wellesley grad. Didn't Wellesley make their students take advanced seminars in tough-broad-ology before they received their degrees?

He wanted to find out just how tough she was, just how smart, how determined. He wanted to find out whether she was really as detached as she seemed from the workings of Bloom's, or whether she knew everything and was hiding the truth from him. He wanted to learn the truth—about her, about her store, about what was locked inside that decrepit old desk in her office. Her grandfather's spirit? Or secret documents, wads of cash, ancient records, photos of colleagues in compromising positions? Ron wondered what the courts would throw at him if he got caught sneaking into her office and picking the lock on the desk. Breaking an old drawer lock couldn't be that difficult, and he could always plead freedom of the press.

What amazed him was that he cared enough about this Upper West Side food shop to contemplate a criminal route to the truth. Christ. It was just a desk, and this was just a story about a famous delicatessen in a time of transition after the death of its longtime president. Why on earth should Ron fantasize about prying open the top drawer of a desk?

It wasn't the desk he wanted to pry open. It was Julia Bloom.

He stood at the elevator bank at the far end of the entry, mulling over whether to leave or to go back to her office. He wanted to have another look at her, but he'd run out of questions to ask her. He'd be better off returning to his own desk at

Gotham's headquarters and digging up some more stuff so he'd have a legitimate reason to come back and interview her again.

The hell with legitimate reasons. He strode down the hall, knocked on her door and heard her call from within "Deirdre?"

That was good enough for him. He swung open the door and smiled. "Not Deirdre. Can I come in?"

She gazed at him, her eyes as dark and deep as shadows at midnight. Ron knew a lot of women. He'd had his share of experiences, flings, affairs, relationships—and he definitely wanted one of each with Julia. She wasn't the world's greatest beauty; she didn't exude sexual charisma; she wasn't sending him come-hither looks or flashing a thong at him. But damn it, she turned him on.

She rose from her chair and smiled hesitantly. "Did you have anything more you wanted to ask me?"

"Not right now," he admitted, closing the door behind him. She glanced at it, then back at him, but didn't object as he approached her. He might have thought breaking into the old desk was risky, but what he was about to do was ten times riskier and he didn't give a damn.

He drew to a halt in front of her, slid one hand around her nape under a tumble of silky black hair, and kissed her. Right on the lips—a firm, dry kiss, nothing X-rated but all he'd dare when such minor issues as his professional reputation and possible charges of sexual assault were on the line.

She accepted his kiss, neither returning it nor shoving him away. When he pulled back, her eyes were round and startled, her cheeks rosy. She lifted her hand to her lips and touched them, as if to make sure he hadn't chewed them off her face.

"Sorry, but I had to do that," he said.

"I…uh…" She pressed her fingertips to her mouth again.

"I hope I didn't offend you."

"Um…no."

She wasn't smiling, though. She wasn't reaching for him, flicking the tip of her tongue, nestling up to him and letting him feel the warmth of her slim, graceful body against his. He was usually pretty good at reading signals, but if she was sending him any, they were in a language he didn't understand.

Not that it mattered. Something was going on, something he couldn't define in a few neat paragraphs for his City Business column, something that defied words and grammar. Something that made him horny just looking at this woman, whom he'd met only that morning and talked to for an absurdly short time.

"I do have more questions," he said, "but they can wait."

"I think I have some questions, too." Her voice sounded breathy. "They can wait," she added.

"I'll be in touch." He smiled, hoping she'd smile back but willing to call it a victory if she refrained from slapping him.

No smile, no slap.

He turned and left the office, once again closing the door behind him. Had he shocked her? Bowled her over? Triggered a tough-broad reflex inside her that would make any future meeting between them fraught with indignation? Had he destroyed his career?

He didn't think so. In fact, he thought that kiss had gone pretty well. The next kiss would be slower, deeper, a whole lot wetter. The next kiss wouldn't stop at a kiss.

Susie knew Julia hated coming downtown, but there she was. She'd phoned Susie and asked if she could stop by, and Susie had said, "Sure, when?" and Julia had told her she was calling from the vestibule of Susie's building, so now would be a pretty good time.

Caitlin was out; she worked as a secretary for a securities firm on Wall Street, so she actually had to wake up early enough to be at her desk by nine a.m., poor thing. Anna was home, though. She was a harpist waiting for the city schools to increase their arts budgets so she could get a job as a music teacher, and in the meantime she was registered at four temp agencies and took clerical work when the spirit and her dwindling cash supply moved her. Apparently, she wasn't broke at the moment, because she was sprawled out on the battered sofa in the living room, watching a TV talk show, the theme of which was foot fetishes.

It was eleven a.m., which meant Susie had only just finished showering and pulling on her black jeans, an olive-green T-shirt and a black sweater with a deep V down the front. At the moment her cell phone chirped, she'd been standing in front of the open refrigerator, contemplating which of the mandarin oranges on the middle shelf looked the most edible. Once she'd told Julia to come up, she selected an orange for herself and then added another scoop of coffee and another cup of water to the coffeemaker for Julia. Less than a minute passed before Julia knocked on Susie's door, which meant she'd climbed the two flights of stairs at a brisk clip. Either she'd been working out or she was *really* eager to see Susie.

Some new crisis, Susie guessed. Fine with her. She could use the distraction. Her own life was so royally fucked up, why not concentrate on her sister's life for a while?

She opened the door to let Julia in. Julia didn't seem at all winded, but her cheeks were nearly as red as her pashmina scarf, which she'd flung dramatically over her shoulder. She was wearing a plain white blouse, blue linen slacks and leather loafers. No jacket. Were her cheeks red from the cold?

What was she doing here, anyway? Why wasn't she at Griffin, McDougal running up billable hours?

"We need to talk," she announced.

"Sure." Susie led her to the microscopic kitchen but gestured with her hand that Julia should remain outside the doorway. If they both tried to squeeze in, one of them would wind up spilling coffee, or possibly breaking the other's rib with a misplaced elbow. She filled two mugs with coffee, added milk and carried the mugs out into the main room.

Anna glanced over from the sofa, smiled and waved at Julia, then turned back to the show, evidently eager to be enlightened regarding the pros and cons of toe sucking.

Susie and Julia sat at the table in the opposite corner of the room, near the window. Julia took her cup and peered into it, as if to make sure nothing was swimming in it before she sipped. Susie tucked one foot under her hips, swung the other, and used her fingernails to peel the orange.

"Okay, so how come you're not at work?" she asked.

Julia sighed. "I took a leave of absence."

Susie dropped the orange onto the heaped scraps of rind. "What?"

"I took a leave of absence from Griffin, McDougal." She unwound her scarf and gazed down into her coffee cup again. "I've got to work full-time at the store, at least for now."

"Why?"

Julia lifted her eyes to Susie again, which Susie decided meant she could stop gaping at her sister and get back to sectioning her orange. "A reporter from *Gotham Magazine* came in on Tuesday to do an interview. He's writing a story about Bloom's. Mom thinks it's going to be a promotional piece, but it's not. I think he's going to write that the store is in financial trouble."

"That's bullshit. The store isn't in any trouble," Susie argued. Julia's worried gaze made her hesitate before biting into a wedge of orange. "It *is* in trouble?" she asked, her appetite shrinking like an ice cube in the sun.

"Mom gave me a pile of folders to look at while he was in my office, so I'd appear to be working." Julia pulled a face at this, obviously not pleased with the deception. "Anyway, I studied them really closely. There are departments at the store that are losing money."

"Which departments?"

"The bagel department, for one."

Susie's appetite vanished completely, leaving room for anger. She had a vested interest in the bagel department—or, at least, in the bagel department's one-man creative department. "That can't be!" she protested, so loudly Anna tore her gaze from an analysis of ankle bracelets to glance their way.

"I'm no business expert," Julia conceded, "but I looked at the profit-loss statements and bagels aren't doing that well."

"So you're going to quit your law job and…what? Fire people?" *Not Casey,* she thought. *Please, not Casey.* Not while everything was so weird between him and her. Not when she hadn't even slept with him yet.

She couldn't understand why they hadn't gotten it on by now. She was certainly ready, willing and able. Even if he lived in Queens and was kind of quirky, and the only time they'd ever really spent together was a few minutes in an elevator and at Grandma Ida's seder more than a week ago. Since then, they'd talked on the phone—mostly about politics, Woody Allen's movies, whether raspberries belonged in bagels, and Woody Allen's sex life. But Casey worked during daylight hours, and she worked in the evening, and at the end of a long day at Bloom's he didn't want to take the train all the way downtown just to watch her serve pizza at Nico's.

She dreamed about him every night. She imagined his naked body, lean and tall and seething with desire for her. She imagined the hands that shaped circles of bagel dough in the kitchen in the store basement shaping circles around her breasts. She imagined his tongue on her, and hers on him. She'd gotten to a point where all she had to do was close her eyes and whisper his name and the temperature between her thighs shot up a good fifteen degrees.

Sooner or later, she was going to have to storm the bagel department, drag him out from behind the counter and have her way with him. He was always friendly when they talked on the phone. If he didn't like her, he wouldn't keep calling her. If they ever saw each other again, she could make a move—but she was afraid of chasing him. She'd already been the aggressor, and she was willing to give him a little more time to aggress before she took matters into her own hands again.

It did perplex her, though. What kind of man didn't want to sleep with a healthy, eager, relatively attractive woman?

A gay man, maybe? But she hadn't gotten gay vibes from him. It was something else, some reserve on his part. Maybe he was shy—although he'd held his own at Grandma Ida's.

Maybe he was involved with another woman. Maybe he was distracted by the shaky performance of the bagel department at Bloom's.

"You can't shut down the bagel department," she announced.

"I wouldn't dream of shutting down the bagel department," Julia assured her. "The thing is, trying to figure out how to improve things at the store is a full-time job. I can't do it while I'm working at Griffin, McDougal, and Mom can't do it, because if she could, she would have done it already. And Uncle Jay doesn't have the attention span for it. I wish I could get Adam to come down and help me—he's got such a good head for numbers—but there's no way he'd take time off school for this. So I've got to do it myself. I'm the president—thanks to you," she added with a scowl.

"Don't blame me. It was Grandma Ida's decision," Susie argued. She popped a section of orange into her mouth and handed a section to Julia, who bit into it. "So, when is this magazine article coming out?"

Julia's chewing slowed. She swallowed. She glanced toward the window, which would have been filled with bright spring sunshine if the surrounding buildings didn't block most of the sky. A glint of light hit some of the bars of the fire escape, where a pigeon perched, fat and iridescent green as it basked in the sliver of sun.

"I don't know," Julia finally said. She looked back at Susie. "That's one of the things I wanted to talk to you about. I think… Shit," she muttered, her cheeks regaining color. "I'm…attracted to him," she whispered, as if she was admitting to sex with corpses.

"Attracted to who?" Susie asked in a robust voice, mostly because it was fun to watch Julia blush and squirm.

"The reporter."

"From *Gotham Magazine*?"

"I'm not really," Julia corrected. "Forget I said anything."

"I'm not going to forget you said anything." Susie found this news so intriguing she didn't even swat Julia's hand away when her sister helped herself to another section of the orange. "You're attracted to him, huh? What does he look like?"

"Nothing special," Julia said. "Brown hair, brown eyes, around six feet tall. I mean, if you saw him on the street you wouldn't look twice."

"I would," Susie insisted. She looked twice at everybody. With young, reasonably attractive men, she looked three or four times. "What's his name?"

"Ron Joffe. And really, he's just a reporter. Someone who's going to stir up trouble for the store. When I think about it that way, I don't like him at all."

"You don't have to like him to be attracted to him. Ron Joffe, huh? A nice Jewish boy?"

"How the hell should I know?"

"Did you kiss him?" Susie asked.

Julia's cheeks grew darker. "No!" she said, so vehemently Anna flinched.

"You *did!*" Julia's sharp denial proved it. "You kissed him? Wow! Was he a good kisser? Did you use tongue? Did you kiss before or after you figured out he was going to do a hatchet job on the store?"

"Stop it. We didn't kiss. We just…" She slumped in her chair. "We just sort of touched lips. And it was awful."

"Why?"

"Because it shouldn't have happened. He's going to do a hatchet job on the store."

"So what? Have some hot sex with him. He might change his mind."

"I don't want to have hot sex with him. You're the hot sexy one, not me."

Not lately, Susie thought, suffering an unexpected twinge of envy. How come Julia was getting to share awful kisses with some reporter she hardly even knew, and Susie was in a torrid phone relationship with a guy who'd actually been to her family's seder, and yet she hadn't shared what she was sure would be fabulous kisses with him? It didn't seem fair.

"What about Heath?" she asked.

"What about him? I just took a leave of absence from Griffin, McDougal."

"Yeah, but that doesn't mean you have to take a leave of absence from him, too."

"Who's Heath?" Anna called over from the TV. It was broadcasting an advertisement, so she obviously felt she could join in their conversation.

"Julia's boyfriend."

"Is he a Heath Bar?" Anna asked.

Susie pondered this. She'd met Heath a couple of times, and he'd always seemed dreadfully Waspy and polished. A Heath Bar might be too exotic for him, the hard toffee too crunchy. He was probably more of a nonpareil.

"What's she talking about?" Julia asked.

Susie shook her head. Julia would never understand. She wasn't a chocoholic the way Susie was. "It's not worth explaining. So, you broke up with Heath?"

"We were never together enough to break up," Julia answered. "I never really felt…"

"What you feel with this reporter." Susie completed the thought. "Heath doesn't kiss awfully like Ron Joffe does, huh."

"No," Julia admitted, sounding rueful about it.

"This reporter turns you on," Susie said helpfully. "He makes you hot. He's going to ruin the store, and all you want is for him to ruin you."

"He's not going to ruin anything," Julia said. "But he's going to write an article that will appear in the most widely read magazine in New York, saying Bloom's is in financial straits."

"Maybe you can seduce him into changing the slant of his story," Susie suggested.

"All right, look." Julia straightened in her chair. "That's not what I came here to talk about. God knows why I'd ever want any romantic advice from you. We have such different attitudes about things like that."

"Yeah, like I'm a slut and you're a prude."

"I'm not a prude," Julia retorted.

"And I'm not a slut. So what did you come here to talk about?"

"I need you to help me with the store."

Susie reflexively shook her head. "I'm not getting sucked into the family business. No way. I've got a tattoo, remember?"

"Listen to me, Susie! If the store is failing, we've got to save it. Dad isn't here anymore. It's up to us."

"What do you mean *us?* You're the president."

"And if the store goes under, you're going to have to start supporting yourself full-time slinging pizza, because you sure as hell aren't going to make ends meet with your poetry. Bloom's is our future, Susie. Our legacy. Our trust funds. Our children's inheritance, if we ever have children. And anyway, I don't see what the big deal is. You're selling pizza—you could just as easily be selling overpriced balsamic vinegar in fancy bottles."

"Yeah, but Bloom's is uptown."

"Get over it, Susie. This is important. You've taken the subway before—you can take it again. Here's what I need you to do. Redesign the windows."

"What windows?"

"At Bloom's. You do the windows at Nico's, right? I want you to come up with a new design for the windows at Bloom's. We need to update the look of the place. It hasn't changed in a dozen years. It's got to look new without losing its good-old-days feeling. I figure you can start with the windows and then move on to the rest of the store."

"You want it to look new and old at the same time." Susie wished she were watching the foot fetish show. She wished she'd stayed in bed an extra half hour. She wished she'd told Julia she was on her way out and they would have to get together some other time. Because what Julia was asking of her was just too...tempting.

Oh God. She couldn't work at Bloom's. She couldn't commute uptown every day and work in the same building as her

mother, the building where she'd grown up, where she'd rebelled, where Grandma Ida, who had never liked her, lived. She
couldn't spend her days designing displays of kugel and knishes
and latkes.

"And you could see that guy every day," Julia added. "The
one you brought to the seder. What was his name again?"

"Casey. He works in bagels. You're probably going to lay
him off."

"No, I'm not. But maybe you can help him to revive the department. Or you can drag him off to the supply closet and
screw him during your lunch break. I don't care, Susie. I need
your creativity to give the store some spark. I haven't got a creative bone in my body. I need you."

Every day with Casey. Either he'd flee from her or he'd let
her screw him in the supply closet—she'd have to find out
where one was located—or they'd continue their strange relationship, munching on bagels and sipping coffee and arguing
whether the world would have been a better place if Woody
Allen had never heard of Ingmar Bergman.

She supposed that seeing him every day, for as long as it took
her to redesign the windows at Bloom's—because she wasn't
going to commit to anything more than that—would make
working in the family business bearable.

"Okay," she said, reaching for the last wedge of orange.
"Okay, I'll do the windows. Now, tell me some more about this
sexy reporter from *Gotham Magazine*."

10

Calling a meeting was a power thing. At Griffin, McDougal, associates never called meetings. They didn't have the clout. If they wanted a meeting, they had to ask a partner to call one. It was a rigid hierarchical process, and Julia had always resented it, even though she herself had never had any reason to call a meeting. She'd thought the rule was silly, and she'd muttered that if ever she were in charge, she'd do away with such nonsense.

But here she was, the president of Bloom's, calling a meeting. She was in charge. Authority pulsed through her, intoxicating and scary. What if everyone resented her the way she'd resented the partners who called meetings at Griffin, McDougal?

She had hoped Adam would be able to come down from Cornell for her meeting, partly because he was a math whiz— Myron Finkel still seemed to prefer his sixties-era adding machine to a calculator, so someone with a more modern approach to crunching numbers might offer a desperately needed perspective—but mostly for moral support, because he was family and Bloom's was a family matter. She'd telephoned him at his dorm over the weekend. His roommate had answered the phone, and when he'd gone to find Adam she'd heard Phish music playing in the background. This had reassured her; she associated Phish with more benign drugs than, say, Korn. She did wish bands that named themselves after foods would learn how to spell.

Adam had eventually found his way to the phone. She'd told him about her leave of absence from the law firm and her decision to become the de facto president of Bloom's, and he'd said that was cool. She'd explained that Bloom's might not be in the greatest of fiscal health, and he'd said that was cool, too. Adam wanted to be a college professor when he grew up. It was as close as he could get to spending the rest of his life living in a dorm and playing Phish—and possibly indulging in benign drugs, although Julia didn't want to explore that particular subject with him.

"So I'm going to hold a meeting. We're going to air some dirty linen," she'd told him.

"That sounds cool."

"And I thought, as one of Dad's children, you might want to be there."

"I can't, Julia. I've got midterms coming up."

She wondered if he considered midterms cool.

So all right, she would hold her meeting without Adam. She'd have Susie there, at least. And Deirdre, who wasn't anyone's blood relation. And Grandma Ida. Either Julia's meeting would be a triumph or it would be a debacle.

She considered starting her morning with two doughnuts for extra energy and a desperately needed sugar high, but then came up with a better idea. This was Bloom's, after all. People ought to have enough faith in what they were selling to eat it.

She entered the store at nine a.m. and headed straight for the bagel counter. Susie's friend was there, a natty white apron tied around his waist and his hair pulled into a ponytail. "Hey," he said, giving her a smile. "I know you, don't I?"

"I'm Susie Bloom's sister," Julia said. "Julia Bloom."

"Right!"

He wasn't movie-star material, and he didn't make her heart pound like drums along the Mohawk, but he was cute in a cheerful, gangly way.

"Julia! Hi! How's Susie?"

"She's going to be here later. You can ask her yourself. After my meeting," she added, surveying the bagels in the bins. "How fresh are these?"

"I pulled them out of the oven a half hour before opening time."

"And you have...what are those, *pesto* bagels?"

"They're a big seller."

She suppressed a shudder. How many people could possibly want to buy pesto bagels? If they were a big seller, that could explain why the bagel department numbers were weird. "Well. Here's what I want—an assortment of bagels on a platter. Do you have a platter?"

"A cardboard tray," he suggested, displaying for her a textured tray that looked like dried concrete.

"Let me see if we have something nicer," she said, then sprinted to the second floor and scoured the kitchenware department for something to serve the bagels on that would look better than dried concrete. She found a round plastic tray with a Star of David embossed at the center of it. Perhaps it would lend a certain holy flavor to her meeting.

She carried the tray downstairs to the bagel counter. "Give me a nice selection, okay, Casey? A dozen bagels in all. And can you slice them in half for me?"

"Not a problem."

"Great. Thanks."

"Should I include a couple of pestos?"

"One should be enough." More than enough, she thought. "I'll be back."

She made her way back upstairs to the kitchenware department, found an insulated coffee decanter and returned to the first floor, this time heading for the coffee department. "Please fill this up with breakfast blend," she requested.

She scooped a handful of half-and-half creamers into her shopping basket, then helped herself to several tubs of flavored cream cheese and grabbed a few wooden cream-cheese spreaders—which looked like mutant tongue depressors—from a cup near the heat-n-eat counter.

Returning to the bagel counter, she found that Casey had prepared an attractively shaped mound of bagels and wrapped the tray in clear plastic. "Excellent," she said, beaming. Had he slept with Susie yet? she wondered. Susie clearly desired him, and as a rule she threw herself at anyone she desired. Had they consummated their relationship after the seder? A little matzo, a little nookie?

She didn't have the guts to ask Susie, let alone Casey. She *was* going to ask Susie, one of these days, how she managed to treat sex so cavalierly. Not that Julia was envious, not that she intended to emulate her sister, but when a man came along who pushed one's buttons and pulled one's chain…

Julia didn't have any particular man in mind, of course.

A full seven days had passed since Ron Joffe had pressed his lips to hers. He hadn't called since then, hadn't requested a second interview, hadn't sent her a dozen red roses—which would have been a very nice gesture under the circumstances—or in any other way acknowledged that he'd kissed her in her office last week.

Shaking off the vague dismay that enveloped her whenever she thought about him, she lugged her basket to the nearest checkout line. Ahead of her stood a boxy gray-haired lady paying for a jar of sesame butter. "This stuff is supposed to increase my life span," she snarled at the cashier. "If I die, I expect a full refund."

"No problem," the cashier said, barely disguising a yawn.

The woman pocketed her credit card and stormed off. Julia

settled her basket on the counter. "I'm Julia Bloom, the president of Bloom's," she told the cashier.

The young woman's eyes widened. "*Ay!* I'm sorry I didn't answer that lady right. I know, we don't refund stuff just because someone dies."

"You handled her fine," Julia assured the young woman. "I'm going to establish an account so we can get Bloom's coffee and bagels upstairs in the offices. I'm not sure how to do that. I'll have to work it out." She was the flipping president—she could work it out any way she wanted.

"So, you want me to, like, ring this up, or you just wanna take it?"

"Ring it up." She couldn't set a precedent of having people walk out of the store with unpaid-for platters of bagels. She'd pay for the feast with her credit card and then set up an account to reimburse herself. A petty-cash account or something, so the third-floor staff could get coffee from downstairs whenever they wanted it. Clerks and cashiers ought to be able to get free coffee, too, she thought.

And she was going to run the store into bankruptcy if she wasn't careful.

She pocketed her receipt. Then, hooking the bag with the cream cheese and creamers over her wrist and balancing the decanter atop the peak of the bagel mountain, she exited through the back door to the elevator. She arrived at her office to find Susie already there, waiting for her.

"You don't have a conference room, do you," Susie said accusingly.

"I've got a couch in my office. We can drag in some chairs. You can sit on the floor." Since Susie was wearing her black denim overalls, it didn't seem like an outlandish suggestion. She handed the platter and decanter to Susie and dug her office key from the pocket of her blazer. "Casey's downstairs. He asked how you were."

"What did you tell him?" Susie sounded a touch anxious.

Shoving the door open with her hip, Julia lifted the coffee

and the bag of cream cheese from the tray. "I told him you'd run off with a lesser European prince. What do you think?"

"A *lesser* prince? Why not a top-of-the-line prince?" Susie followed Julia into the office. "How did he look?"

"He looked like he looked at Grandma Ida's seder, only with an apron on. After the meeting you can go downstairs and ogle him if you'd like. You're going to be working downstairs, anyway."

"*If* I agree to work for you," Susie warned. "I don't know anything about redesigning stores, Julia."

"You design the window at Nico's," Julia reminded her. "That's all you need to know. How big a difference can there be between Italian and Jewish windows?"

"You want original poetry in Bloom's windows?"

"I want the windows themselves to be poetry. Here comes Mom," she added in a tight voice as she shaped her mouth into a smile.

Sondra Bloom seemed disgruntled by Julia's decision to call a meeting. Julia could tell this by the clench of her mother's teeth behind her glossy lips.

"Hello, girls!" she said, spreading her arms to gather them in. Belatedly, she noticed that they were carrying brunch. "So we're going to have a meeting! This is so exciting."

She said it with the gusto one would use to describe a sinus infection. Rather than respond, Julia arranged the food on the coffee table. She pulled the plastic wrap off the bagels and stared with mild consternation at the selection Casey had chosen. One of the bagels had a pink hue to it.

"Cranberry," Susie whispered, evidently figuring out what Julia was gaping at. "Casey told me they're delicious."

Uncle Jay followed Sondra through the door, and Julia began to wonder whether maybe her office wasn't as big as she'd thought it was. Susie helpfully hoisted herself to sit on Grandpa Isaac's desk, leaving the sofa and the chairs for others. Deirdre stalked in on her porn-star high heels. Myron trudged in in his worn oxfords and immediately pounced on the bagels, grabbing the cranberry one for himself. Who would have thought he'd be so daring?

"Let's get this meeting started," Jay said brusquely. "Some of us have work to do."

"And others of us want to go play golf," Sondra murmured, shooting him a skeptical look. "I think it's very nice that my daughter prepared this spread for us. She's such a good hostess."

Julia glanced through the open door, hoping Grandma Ida would arrive. Telephoning Grandma Ida last night to ask her to attend had taken a significant amount of courage. "A meeting? You want a meeting? What for?" she'd asked.

Although she'd been far from encouraging about the meeting, she did say she would come. And finally, ten minutes past the scheduled starting time, she stepped out of the elevator at the opposite end of the hallway, her hand hooked through the bend in Lyndon's arm. Together they strode down the hall like a mismatched bride and groom, until they reached Julia's office.

"*Nu*...so everybody's here?" Grandma Ida asked, glowering at the room's occupants.

"Now that you're here, everybody's here," Julia said, her palms growing cold and slick. Oh God. She had called a meeting, and she was going to have to run it. When she'd been reveling in her power, she'd forgotten to take into account the huge responsibility that came with it. "Grandma, why don't you sit on the couch." She motioned for her mother to make room.

Lyndon helped her onto the couch. "Do you want me to stay?" he asked Julia.

"Yes," Grandma Ida answered. She turned to Julia. "If I decide I don't like it, he can get me out of here."

"I can get you out of here, too," Uncle Jay noted.

Grandma Ida ignored him. "What's with all this food?"

"It's from downstairs," Julia said, bracing for an attack. "If we're going to sell food at Bloom's, we ought to have enough faith in it to eat it ourselves."

"It's too expensive," Grandma Ida grumbled.

Julia opened her mouth to argue, but Susie gave a slight shake of her head and Julia heeded her sister's unspoken counsel. No sense arguing with Grandma Ida before the meeting had even begun. "Okay," she said, gesturing Deirdre toward one of the chairs and Lyndon toward another. Perched on the desk and swinging her legs, Susie looked more comfortable than they did. "I'm the president of Bloom's, and we have some problems."

"Why is Susie here?" Uncle Jay asked. He gave Susie a beaming proud-uncle smile that had all the authenticity of nondairy whipping cream, then glared at Julia.

"I've commissioned Susie to help redesign the store," Julia announced. "Starting with the windows," she added, but she doubted anyone heard her through all the exclamations.

"Redesigning?"

"So what's wrong with the way the store looks now?"

"Are you out of your mind?"

"Are these cranberries in this bagel?"

This was not an auspicious start to her meeting. Julia wished she had a gavel. Lacking one, she clapped her hands.

Everyone turned to her. Good. She had power, the power of the clap—and it alarmed her a little. Maybe she ought to license her hands as weapons.

"We need to make some changes here," she said.

"It didn't occur to you that Rick could redesign the store?" Uncle Jay challenged.

"He's a filmmaker," Julia said, generously stretching the truth.

"He's visual." Uncle Jay jabbed a finger toward his eye. "He thinks in visuals. Why Susie and not him?"

"Susie has experience designing windows," Julia explained, then hurried ahead. "I don't want to start by talking about design. I want to talk about the fact that Bloom's has been in a rut for a long time, and our earnings aren't what they ought to be. No one has questioned what works and what doesn't work. We've had innovations introduced by Uncle Jay," she noted, nodding in his direction. He subsided and poured himself some coffee, his mouth pinched. "But we've got departments that are stagnant. Departments that are losing money. Bloom's needs an overhaul."

"Your father," Sondra scolded, "is spinning in his grave." Deirdre indicated her agreement by sniffing sharply.

"My father was a wonderful president of Bloom's. But now I'm the president, and I think we need a face-lift and some streamlining, or we're going to be left in the dust."

"What dust?" Sondra asked.

"It's a metaphor, Mom," Susie told her.

"I've gone through these profit-loss statements on the departments." Julia reached for the pile of folders sitting on her desk. "But I want wiser, more experienced people to review each department's performance closely. Mom, I want you to review the heat-n-eat department, the meats department, the fish department and the cheese department—basically, all the protein departments. Uncle Jay, I want you to review the coffee department—"

"Wait a minute!" Sondra sent Julia a wounded look, as if she considered her daughter the worst kind of traitor. "The coffee corner is mine. It was my idea in the first place!"

"Which is why you don't have the objectivity to evaluate it. I'm going to have Myron assess our Internet mail-order businesses."

"What, are you crazy?" Uncle Jay shouted, practically leaping to his feet. He sank back into his chair and shot Myron a disconsolate look. "Nothing personal, Myron, but do you even know what the Internet is?"

"I know what it is," Myron said, nibbling delicately on his pink bagel. "This is good, Julia. Very good."

Julia felt Susie's gaze on her, communicating, *So there! Casey's a genius.* And maybe cranberry bagels *were* good. But the bagel department still worried her.

"What I want," she said, "is a one- or two-page report on each department, telling me what's selling well, what's underperforming and giving your suggestions for improving things. Deirdre, I want you to review all the reports and add your take on them. I'll need this by the end of the week."

"The end of the week?" Sondra squawked. "Like I don't have any other work to do?"

"We all have lots of work to do," Julia said. "More work than we had to do last week—because on top of what we have to do, we also have to give Bloom's a kick in the rear end."

She paced to the window and paced back. Everyone, with the possible exception of Myron and Lyndon, was staring at her as if she'd sprouted a huge pimple on her forehead. Lyndon looked amused, and Myron was busy licking cream cheese off his fingers.

"*Gotham Magazine* hasn't published anything about us yet. But I have the feeling that if they *do* publish something it's not going to be positive."

"How can you say that?" Sondra exclaimed.

Even Deirdre shook her head. "I thought we handled that reporter pretty well."

"He didn't come here to do a puff piece," Julia said, almost adding, *He came here to kiss me.* But of course he hadn't come to do that, either. His kiss had seemed like an afterthought— or perhaps an afterthoughtless—some weird impulse that had apparently startled him enough that once he'd cleared his head, he'd decided not to contact Julia again.

"What do you think he came here for?" Deirdre asked.

"He was looking for news. With most journalists, that means bad news. They want a story. Writing about how Bloom's is just sailing smoothly along isn't a story."

"But why would he come here and try to find bad news?" Deirdre pressed her.

"Because it would make a good story. In fact, he didn't just come here looking for bad news. He came here assuming he was going to find bad news."

"What makes you think that?" Sondra enquired, her voice shriller than usual. "Did he say something to you? He didn't say anything to me. In fact, he gave no indication whatsoever that he knew he was going to find something bad to write about."

"It's just a hunch." More than a hunch—it was the way Joffe had unsettled Julia, the way he'd gazed at her, the way he'd asked questions she herself ought to have been asking all along, questions she was going to ask now that she'd made a commitment to the store. "I may be new to Bloom's," she conceded, squaring her shoulders and mustering her usually subdued self-confidence, "but I'm not new to life. I've worked in a law firm for two years. I have some intelligence, and I can sense things."

"She can sense things." Uncle Jay snorted, reaching for a pumpernickel bagel and shaking his head. "Maybe she can read people's auras, too, and the lumps on their skulls. I'll tell you this, sweetheart—" he jabbed a cream-cheese applicator at Julia "—the time that reporter and I spent in my office talking about the Web site and mail-order business, there was no bad news for him. All he could see in front of him was success, success, success." He punctuated this boast by glaring at his mother. "Success," he concluded, just in case she'd missed his message.

"What's this about a reporter?" she belatedly asked, lifting dark, accusing eyes to Julia.

Julia dropped into her chair so her grandmother wouldn't have to look up at her. "A guy from *Gotham Magazine*. He approached us and said he wanted to do a story about Bloom's." Addressing the rest of the group, she continued, "He wouldn't have approached us if he didn't think there was a story here. If you want good news about yourself in the media, you have to initiate it. When they come to you, it's because they smell blood."

"She's such an expert," Sondra muttered, then sipped her coffee. "This is good," she observed, eyeing Grandma Ida over the curved edge of her cup. "Like I should be surprised. Our coffee is *so* good."

"This reporter," Grandma Ida asked, "why would he smell blood? Only thing you can smell at Bloom's is cheese and hot entrées."

"And the coffee," Sondra reminded her.

"So he comes here, what? Sniffing around?"

Julia nodded. "Exactly. Sniffing around."

"Why would he do that?"

"Because Daddy died," Susie interjected. Everyone turned to her, and she shrugged. "The man who ran Bloom's for twenty-five years is gone. This reporter dude probably thought he'd find some turmoil here."

"God knows why he'd think that," Sondra whispered, just loud enough for everyone except Grandma Ida to hear. She turned questioningly to Lyndon, who repeated Sondra's remark.

"Ben is dead," Grandma Ida declared in a ponderous tone, her hair so dark it seemed to suck in light like a black hole. "But Bloom's lives on. This reporter, who needs him?"

"I do," Julia blurted out, then felt her cheeks grow warm. "We *all* do," she went on, donning her best lawyer voice. "We need to examine just what's going on with the store. If we have areas that are bleeding—or even just oozing—we need to fix them. And we need a jolt of energy. The reporter is providing it." She resented that Joffe had been the one to jolt her—why couldn't a cup of strong coffee do the job? Why couldn't Heath? Why did she need a jolt at all?

The whys didn't matter. She did need a jolt, and whipping Bloom's into shape would give it to her, far more effectively than any guy who could sweep in, poke around in things that weren't his business, plant a kiss on her mouth and disappear. Whatever she needed, it sure as hell wasn't Ron Joffe.

"You want I should talk to this reporter?" Grandma Ida asked.

In unison, Julia, Sondra, Jay and Deirdre said, "No."

Grandma Ida absorbed their unanimous decision. "So, you're going to get all these reports," she said, pursing her lips. "What are you going to do with them?"

"Study them and figure out how to improve the store's performance."

"More than sixty years I've been with Bloom's, I never needed a report."

"You ran Bloom's differently," Julia conceded. "So did Dad. But now I'm running the place—because you named me the president." *And that was your choice, so live with it,* she wanted to add, but she was afraid she'd sound petulant and ungrateful. She'd managed to get this far with her meeting, and a sense of accomplishment spread through her. Her very first meeting, and no one had died. In fact, her mother was helping herself to an onion bagel, and Grandma Ida was pointing to a poppy-seed bagel, which Lyndon promptly smeared with cream cheese for her. Susie hopped down from the desk and grabbed an egg bagel. Skipping the cream cheese, she climbed back onto the desk, sat squaw-style and took a lusty bite.

Everyone was eating. Julia viewed this as a promising sign.

"These bagels are good," Uncle Jay said as he bit into one. "What is this? I never tasted anything like this before."

"I think that's the pesto bagel," she told him.

From the desk Susie issued a besotted grin. After this meeting was over, Julia would have to pump Susie for information on exactly what was going on between her and the bagel man.

"It's not just the flavor. It's the texture. Where'd you get these bagels, Julia?"

"Downstairs."

"These are Bloom's bagels?"

She sighed and glanced at the ceiling. What was wrong with this family, that they owned a deli and never ate its food? No wonder the store was foundering. It needed enthusiasm. It needed familiarity with the products. It needed people working for it who understood how good its merchandise was.

"I think," she said, "we should all make an effort to eat Bloom's food more often."

"It's too expensive," Sondra and Grandma Ida said simultaneously.

"Then, maybe we should reduce prices."

"No!" Myron and Uncle Jay bellowed simultaneously.

"This is really good, though," Sondra said before taking another hefty bite of her bagel. "Almost as good as the coffee."

Julia gazed at the assembled group. Deirdre plucked a plain bagel from the tray. Susie was tearing small chunks from her egg bagel and popping them into her mouth. Sondra was eyeing seconds, nudging the dwindling supply with one elegantly manicured nail to see what flavors were left. Adding cream cheese to a whole-wheat bagel, Lyndon paused and angled his head to study the Star of David, now visible as the tray emptied.

Julia cleared her throat. "If any of you have trouble getting your reviews done—"

"We won't have any problems," said Deirdre, scraping the sides of a nearly empty tub of cream cheese with a wooden applicator.

"Then, I guess we're adjourned," Julia said, smiling and feeling the tension ebb from the muscles along her spine. She'd survived the meeting. She'd emanated poise. She'd acted presidential. And now she'd like them all to leave so she could savor her triumph.

But no one left. No one even stood. They were all too busy eating.

11

Susie was not going to go to the bagel department. She wasn't even going to go near it. She was going to inspect the rest of the store, take notes, step outside to study the windows, take more notes, figure out whether the place needed a face-lift or extensive surgery—as if she had the expertise to make such a diagnosis, although she had to admit she had at least as much expertise in retail presentation as Julia had in retail management—and she was somehow going to do all this without crossing paths with Casey Gordon.

Sure. And once she'd accomplished that, she would build a car that used water for fuel, come up with a simple explanation of string theory and put an end to war.

What was the strange power Casey held over her? She wasn't used to complicated relationships—as if long, verbose telephone calls and one family seder could be called a "relationship." Her dealings with men had always been straightforward. Like with Eddie: they'd get together, they'd have some laughs, they'd have some sex. Nothing deep, nothing Byzantine. Just a man and a woman enjoying life and each other.

Why couldn't she have something like that with Casey? Just because he lived in Queens shouldn't mean he and Susie were fated to construct their entire friendship on a series of phone conversations. For God's sake, she was horny and he was gorgeous. He'd never indicated that he found her repulsive.

So what was the hang-up?

And why was she letting it bother her? There were plenty of other men in New York, men interested in laughs and sex and nothing more. Eddie, for one. Yet the last time he'd called her, she could hardly think of anything to say to him.

Unlike Casey, to whom she could always think of plenty of things to say. But she wanted more than talk. And she wanted not to be driven crazy by a man. She'd never let a man drive her crazy before, and twenty-five seemed too old for her to start.

She stood in front of the cheese display and tried to think about how the refrigerator units were set up, how clearly the prices were marked, how much the port salut smelled like sweaty gym socks—anything but the fact that just three aisles down, Casey was chatting with customers and filling bags with bagels for them. Maybe he was flirting with his female customers, telling them they were nubile. Maybe he was setting up dates with them, making plans to attend Zen festivals or Moonie mass weddings so he could continue his education in the world's religions.

Her lower abdomen ached like a menstrual cramp. She didn't have her period, so she assumed this was a psychosomatic symptom. She was out of sync with her womb, maybe. Out of touch with her womanhood. Or else nauseated by the stench of the port salut.

She moved on, ordering herself to focus on her assignment and ignore all the Casey vibes that emanated from the bagel department like a radio signal her antenna couldn't seem to avoid picking up. The sooner she devised some ideas for Julia, the sooner she could head south, back to her apartment and

Nico's, where the intrigues and tensions of her family couldn't reach her. She'd been the smartest person at the meeting that morning, but had anyone paid any attention to her? Had anyone given a shit what she might have to contribute?

Well, yes—Julia had. She'd been the other smartest person at the meeting.

Nico adored the windows Susie created for him. He adored her poems and her pizza-esque ensembles. He didn't have an ego problem, a lifetime's worth of rivalries, a love-hate relationship with everyone sharing his last name, a hunger for approval from an emotionally stingy autocrat like Grandma Ida. Susie wanted to go downtown, back to the world she knew.

But Julia needed her here.

And Casey was now only two aisles away, because Susie had abandoned the cheese aisle for the coffee corner, which smelled much better than port salut.

The store needed goosing, and it needed sprucing. Armed with a pad and pen, she pondered the shelving, seeking answers to a question she wasn't sure she understood. The wood plank floors lent the store a homey feel—if the home was, say, Ralph Lauren's vacation cabin. It felt Waspy to her, even if Ralph Lauren happened to be Jewish.

Going more modern, more sleek and streamlined, wouldn't be appropriate for Bloom's, either. The store needed to feel like…a grandmother's apartment. One containing at least as much affection as Depression glass.

She moved to the next aisle, pretending she knew what she was doing. Customers shared the aisle with her, some dawdling, some striding briskly in modified power walks, some nudging her aside to reach items on shelves. An elderly man in a V-neck cardigan and baggy green trousers shuffled past her, clutching a cylindrical tin of Danish butter cookies and mumbling to himself about the IRS being the spawn of Satan. It occurred to Susie that if the store resembled a grandmother's apartment too much, it might attract only customers like him.

She couldn't afford to do anything drastic, anyway. Julia

wanted the store goosed and spruced, but at minimal cost. The whole purpose of this project was to boost profitability so their precious trust funds wouldn't be depleted. Oh yes, and to uphold the legacy their father had bestowed upon them.

Adam ought to be here upholding the legacy, too. Julia had told Susie she'd tried to get Adam to travel down to the city for her meeting, but he had midterms. Susie loved Adam, but he really was spoiled. He always left his big sisters to cope with every crisis, while he remained sequestered in the snowy hills of Ithaca, safely removed from the tumult of being a Bloom. He believed pursuing the life of a scholar was somehow more pure than vending latkes in a deli on the Upper West Side. Go figure.

She had drawn near the bagel counter. Even before she saw Casey her pulse began to perk up. He *had* asked Julia about her. And he *did* phone her regularly, if only to discuss cranberry harvesting techniques or the subtext of the mayor's latest edict. He must like her. Maybe not enough to consider a seduction, but a little, at least.

She wasn't going to approach him like a lovesick ninny, though, some desperate chick with a demeanor that screamed, *Do with me what you will.* She was a strong, brilliant, desirable woman, a poet, a savvy survivor. If Casey didn't have the good sense to jump her bones, well, damn it, she'd find someone who did.

She turned the corner and saw him. He was handing a bag of bagels to a thin man with a retro afro, parts of which were depressed by the earphones of his Discman. Casey nodded at the man, then caught Susie's eye and smiled.

He was happy to see her. She felt ten years younger and ten pounds lighter. His smile, his sparkling eyes—she wanted to race over to him and coo, *Do with me what you will!*

Cut it out! she ordered herself. *Control yourself.* She drew in a deep breath, straightened her spine and strode to the counter, shaping her face into the most nonchalant expression she could manage under the circumstances.

God, he was magnificent. His hair begged her fingers to twine through it. His arms seemed designed for bracing himself above her, or holding her above him. His smile said, *Kiss me.*

"Hey, Susie," he greeted her. "Your sister told me I'd get to see you today."

A nice collection of sarcastic retorts filled her mouth. *I bet that must have made your day,* she almost snapped. *I hope you don't hate my sister for telling you that. I'm surprised you didn't run downstairs to the kitchen and punch in my cell-phone number so we wouldn't have to talk face-to-face.*

Exercising exemplary willpower, she said, "Well, here I am."

"You look great. Want a bagel?"

No, she didn't want a bagel. She wanted to bask in his compliment—he'd said she *looked great!*—and ask him why, if he really believed that, he wasn't suggesting they go someplace private so he could do more than gaze at her.

"We had bagels upstairs at a meeting," she told him.

"Yeah, I put that platter together for your sister. Big goings-on in the corporate sphere." His wry grin let her know what he thought of the corporate sphere.

That was all right. She didn't think much of it, either. "The accountant loved the cranberry bagel," she reported. "Julia considers the color funky."

"Pink?" He shrugged. "What's wrong with pink?"

"It's funky for a bagel," Susie clarified, suffering a twinge of apprehension. He liked pink. He wanted to talk to her, but he didn't want to *be* with her. And he was so damn good-looking. Things were starting to add up.

"Do you have a minute?" she asked impulsively.

He glanced at the older guy who shared bagel duties with him—Morty, Susie recalled. He had just finished slicing a floury bialy for a blue-haired lady who called him "dahlink," and turned to Casey, who held up five fingers. Morty's gaze shuttled to Susie and he winked and nodded.

Casey emerged from behind the counter in a long-legged

lope. He motioned with his head toward the staff door that opened to the stairway, then led the way.

They entered the stairwell, and he let the door shut behind them. Susie wondered if she should be alarmed, then remembered what she'd just figured out about him and realized she didn't have much cause for concern. He slouched lazily against the wall, digging his hands into his trouser pockets under the flap of his apron. His smile was so tender, so genuinely pleased that she wanted to weep at the tragic waste of this prime specimen of manhood.

"So, what's going on? You look like you're working," he said, aiming his chin toward her notepad.

"Julia's hired me to design new windows for the store," she told him, then moved ahead before they could detour into that subject. "Casey, I've got to ask you something."

"Sure."

"Are you gay?"

He stared at her for a minute, then shook his head. His smile never wavered. "Nope."

She ought to have been relieved; he hadn't been removed from the pool of available men. But she was even more deflated. If he wasn't gay and he wasn't hitting on her, the problem must be her. "Are you married?" she asked apprehensively.

He continued to smile, but from the cheekbones up he frowned, his brow denting and a crease forming across the bridge of his nose. "What are you really asking?"

Damn it. He was married. He'd been carrying on a telephone affair with her because he was too moral to carry on a flesh affair with her. "I'm really asking," she said, figuring she had nothing to lose, "why you don't want to have sex with me."

His smile vanished completely. With her free hand she gripped the stair railing. Despite all her courage, she needed to brace herself for his rejection. He had every right to be as blunt as she was—and if he was that blunt, his words were probably going to hurt.

"I'm not married," he said, "and I do want to have sex with you."

It took her a minute of deep breathing to assimilate his response. "You do?"

"You're beautiful. You're funny. You're smart. Why wouldn't I want to?"

Anxiety gave way to anger. What the hell was wrong with him? He wanted her, she wanted him, and they'd spent the past two weeks playing telephone. "Why haven't you done anything about it?"

He shrugged. "I'm still getting to know you," he said, as if it was the most sensible thing in the world.

Sensible? Getting to know her? What planet had he fallen to earth from?

She knew the answer to that: Queens. "What do you need to know? You want to have sex with me—you just said so. I want to have sex with you." *I've been dreaming of it. Aching for it. Hugging my pillow like a feverish teenager.*

"Well, that's good," he said, his smile returning. "But I don't sleep with women I don't know that well. I don't know you that well yet."

"We've talked on the phone a billion times."

"That many? I must have lost count." His smile expanded, taking on a teasing quality. "Look, Susie, you work nights—I work days. You live on the IRT line—I live on the IND line. Sometimes these things take time."

"I brought you to my grandmother's seder!"

"And it was a lot of fun. What was the name of that stuff again, the ground apples and walnuts with the wine mixed in?"

"Charoseth."

"Yeah. That was great. I've been thinking about whether we can make a *charoseth*-flavored bagel."

"People can't eat bagels during Passover," she reminded him. "Only unleavened bread, like matzo."

"Yeah, but for the rest of the year, if they like the flavor—"

"Casey. Pay attention. I think we should make a plan to have sex." This wasn't very romantic, but he seemed too easily distracted. She had to address the subject clearly and directly.

He mulled over her suggestion, appearing to do some calculations in his head. "How about after we've spent a minimum of twenty hours together?"

"Twenty hours?" Given how rarely they saw each other, that could take years. "Does this meeting count?"

"No. We're still working things out here."

"Where did you come up with twenty hours?"

"It's a nice round number. I like round numbers. They remind me of bagels, all that roundness."

He was nuts. Unfortunately, that made him even more appealing.

Twenty hours, like bagels. She let out a laugh. "When do we start counting hours?"

"The next time we see each other."

"Okay. Why don't you go back into the store, and then I'll come in a few minutes later and we'll start the clock then."

He gave her a slow, painfully erotic grin. "Okay," he drawled, then started toward the stairwell door. Pausing, he snagged her upper arm and pulled her away from the railing, into his arms. He bowed, covered her mouth with his and kissed her as if this was the kissing Olympics and he was going for the gold. He kissed her until her breasts burned, her stomach clenched, her toes curled and her hips nestled against his. He kissed her until the pad and pen fell from her hand and the pen rolled down several stairs, making a clicking sound as it hit each step. He kissed her until his tongue had claimed pretty much every square inch of her mouth's interior, until his hand clenched into a fist against her back, until she was absolutely certain she was in love.

Then he pulled back. He gazed at her, let out an uneven breath and said, "See you later." And strolled out of the stairwell, letting the door thump shut behind him.

"Asshole," she muttered. He shouldn't have kissed her that way, not unless he was planning to move beyond kissing as soon as possible. What was this twenty-hour rule? What kind of crap was that? He didn't know her that well? He could sure as hell get to know her better—in a lot less than twenty hours. Ten hours tops, he could know her inside and out. She wasn't that inscrutable.

Sighing, she clomped down the stairs to retrieve her pen. She scooped up her pad and shoved open the door. God, he made her angry, kissing her like that, leaving her all hot and flustered. The smug bastard.

Still, she picked up her pace as she reentered the store. The sooner she saw him, the sooner the clock would start running.

Ron Joffe studied the handwritten notes he'd just taken during a phone conversation with one Reuben Melnick, a pickle wholesaler who had enjoyed extensive dealings with Ben Bloom during the latter's decades-long tenure as the head of Bloom's.

Interesting.

"Sure, I knew Ben," Reuben had said. "Quite a guy. To know him was to know him."

"You didn't love him, then?" Ron had asked.

Reuben had chuckled. "Only person who ever loved him was that secretary of his. Don't know if you met her—tall, gawky redhead. Her name escapes me."

"Deirdre Morrissey," Ron supplied.

"That's it. Irish girl. Very devoted to him, if you catch my drift."

Ron pictured Reuben to be in his sixties and beefy, the sort of guy who would punctuate every second statement with a nudge to the ribs or a poke in the arm. Ron was glad he'd been able to do this interview over the phone.

Reuben was the third food dealer he'd spoken with; the first two had never done business with Bloom's, although one of them said he'd crossed paths with Ben Bloom a few times at coffee bean conventions and had always considered Bloom "on the chilly side."

Ron wondered whether Julia was as chilly as her father was

reputed to have been. One kiss—a rather unsatisfactory one, at that—hadn't told him much.

"The guy lived and breathed work, know what I mean?" Reuben had said. "I met his wife once—a big surprise. I hadn't known he was married."

"Because he was so close with Deirdre?"

"That, too, but mostly he seemed married to the store. He'd flirt around, you know—I figured him as someone who liked a little action to keep the juices flowing. But commitment? Till death do us part? That kind of love he saved for the store."

"What did you think of his wife?" Ron asked.

"Somewhere between gushy and pushy. She seemed to love the store, too, but I could tell it wasn't in her blood. She had more polish than he did. But she married him, you know? That pretty much meant she'd married his store, his mother, the whole shebang."

Ron's impression of Sondra Bloom matched Reuben's. This was good. It meant he could probably rely on Reuben's impressions of everyone else. "Did you ever meet his mother?" he asked.

"Ida Bloom." Reuben released a long, wheezy breath. "Met her once. She looked me up and down, told me she thought I was overcharging on the kosher dills and her husband would turn over in his grave if he knew what I was taking the store for. Ben apologized for her, said he thought my prices were fair. Which they are. My stuff has the garlic ratio perfect, and the cukes don't go limp. You want crunchy, you gotta pay. Ida didn't want to pay for anything."

Ron wished he knew more about the food business. He was an expert on Wall Street, he could hold his own in any conversation on the Federal Reserve and he could fake it when the subject was retailing. His MBA was in finance, but he'd written enough pieces on enough subjects to know a little about a lot.

Food was a whole different thing, though. Maybe Kim Pinsky should have put one of the restaurant critics on this story,

Heidi, or What's-His-Name, that chubby guy who hyperven-
tilated about wines. He could have waxed rhapsodic about the
superiority of crunchy pickles over limp.

But Ron was glad Kim hadn't put the magazine's foodies on
this story. If she had, he never would have met Julia Bloom.

How was he going to get close to her? By writing a story
that said her late father, the erstwhile head honcho of
Bloom's, had been a little too cozy with his assistant? And her
mother was manipulative and heavy-handed? And her grandmother was too cheap to pay the going rate for crunchy pickles?

Julia would surely be overcome with desire after reading such
an article.

He needed more time, more perspective, more of a chance
to figure out how to write a playful little exposé about the famous deli on Upper Broadway without alienating that famous
deli's president, who without even trying turned him on like a
halogen spotlight.

He tapped the space key on his computer to kill the screen
saver. The shape-shifting soccer ball disappeared, replaced by
the text of his regular City Business column. This week it offered a chipper little dissection of how monetary policy in
Washington wound up lining developers' pockets in the tri-state
area. Nothing profound, nothing he'd stayed up nights sweating over the way he'd stayed up nights sweating over Bloom's.

Specifically, one particular Bloom.

He e-mailed the column to Kim, then lifted his phone and
punched in her extension so he could warn her it was on its
way.

"Is it brilliant?" she asked.

"It's fine." Self-congratulation didn't suit Ron.

"And the Bloom's piece?"

"In progress." He hesitated, then asked, "Where did it
come from?"

"What do you mean?"

"One day you suddenly said, 'Ron, do a story on how

Bloom's is faring one year after the death of its president.'
Where did that come from?"

She chuckled. "You reporters aren't the only ones who have
sources, Joffe. Why?"

"Well, I'm finding stuff out, but it's nothing catastrophic.
We're talking minor tremors, not major earthquakes. No higher
than three on the Richter Scale."

"Three can start the china rattling." She had grown up in
the Bay Area. When it came to seismic activity, she knew her
Richter numbers. "If you need more time, take it. Just tell me
you're going to wind up with a worthwhile story."

"I can make it work," he promised, suspecting that she knew
more about Bloom's than she was letting on. She knew enough
to think he was going to break a few plates with his article. If
only she would share what she knew with him, it would make
his life a hell of a lot easier. "I can't figure out what angle to
take. I have no idea who pointed you in Bloom's direction, or
why. Can you help me?"

Kim didn't answer right away. She was a sharp editor, married to an equally sharp lawyer. When the two of them were
in the same room, a kind of Ninja aura filled the air. "Someone told me the company was in trouble," she finally said. "I
was stunned. I thought, this is a New York institution. If
Bloom's falls, we're going to have to question the existence of
God."

"So who told you the company was in trouble?" he
pressed her.

"Someone close to me. Someone I trust. That's all I'll say,
Joffe. Don't give me a hard time, okay? Just write the damn
story."

"I'm doing my best." He hung up, glared at his notes from
his conversation with Reuben Melnick and muttered a couple
of choice four-letter words. He had *something;* he knew that
much. He just didn't know what he had.

Other than a bad case of lust for Julia Bloom.

12

"I don't get it," Jay said.

He was seated across from Stuart in one of those intense beef restaurants that had sprung up throughout the city. This one, modeled after a clichéd gentleman's club with walnut paneling, leather chairs and inch-thick carpeting, specialized in martinis big enough to swim laps in and steaks sized by the pound. Jay had ordered a two-pound sirloin, even though he knew he'd never be able to finish it. Leaving food uneaten on his plate made him feel terribly upper class.

Stuart seemed intent on making small inroads into his twice-stuffed potato, which was the size of a bocce ball. Jay had opted for the steak fries, figuring it was hypocritical to worry about the extra fat when one was also ordering a two-pound sirloin. The steak fries were thicker than his thumbs and flavored with lots of salt and a hint of garlic.

After a lunch like this, he wouldn't want a big dinner tonight. Maybe he'd skip dinner altogether. Wendy had tickets to something for that evening—he wasn't sure what, but it had to be better than the Messiaen concert she'd taken him to a few months back: two agonizing hours of atonal music. "I'm sorry," she'd said. "I thought this was that really pretty thing they always play at Christmastime, where everybody stands and sings 'Hallelujah.'"

Unlike the excruciating noisefest they'd sat through at Alice Tully Hall, *The Messiah* had real words—in English—and tunes you could hum, even if the composition celebrated a *goyish* holiday. His father had admired classical music and played it all the time while Jay was growing up. "Handel was Jewish," the old man had insisted while they listened to Handel's grand oratorio about the birth of Christ. "Even a genius has to earn a living, no? How was he supposed to earn a living writing Jewish songs? Those English kings and queens, they were footing the bills, so Handel wrote them Christian music."

Jay could tolerate any kind of music, as long as it had a nice melody and words he could recognize. He wished he knew whether tonight's concert qualified on either of those counts. "It's for a good cause," Wendy had explained, which worried him. A benefit concert meant she'd spent a fortune on the damn tickets, and he was probably going to have to sit through a sonata for glockenspiel and tuba, or some shrill, crystal-cracking soprano who had won the job by sleeping with the maestro.

"What don't you get?" Stuart asked, apparently reaching a truce with his potato.

"My niece. She's taking the whole store thing seriously."

"Your niece who's the new president of Bloom's?"

"She's a lawyer, for chrissake. What's she doing running a delicatessen?"

"Bloom's is more than a delicatessen," Stuart pointed out. "It's an institution."

"Yeah, and the inmates are in charge." Jay took a hefty slurp from his drink. A martini this size could probably get him painlessly through tonight's cultural offering, but the effect would wear off by the time he had to suit up and straighten his bow tie. It was barely one-thirty. By five, he'd be sober.

In fact, he was sober now. No one in his family was particularly susceptible to liquor. Sondra used to say it was because all the Blooms had high metabolism; they burned everything off too fast. She always said this with a deep sigh of envy. Not only did she have more heft than any of the Blooms, but she got tipsy on a few glasses of wine. Sondra tipsy was not a pretty sight.

"So, your niece is taking the job seriously," Stuart said, gazing around the cozy midtown dining room. At least three other diners were indulging in cigars, and he pulled two out of an inner pocket of his blazer. "Cuban," he told Jay. "One of my clients gave me a box of them. Kim would give me hell if I lit one up in the house."

Kim was Stuart's wife, and Jay had met her a few times. He wouldn't wish to be on the receiving end of hell from her. Like Wendy, she was blond. Unlike Wendy, she was as tough as gristle, beautiful but hazardous. She worked as a magazine editor, and Jay had to assume she was born to the job. Barking orders at copy boys and shouting, "Stop the presses!" seemed like the sort of activity she'd excel at.

He accepted a cigar from Stuart. Not that he was any kind of a smoker, but why not? He'd already lowered his life expectancy with the well-marbled steak and the fries. How much more damage could a cigar do? He'd work it all off tomorrow at the health club.

"Can your niece handle the job?" Stuart asked once they'd both ignited their cigars and were exhaling pungent smoke at each other.

"She's driving us crazy is what she's doing," Jay complained. "Last Monday she called a meeting. Can you believe it? A meeting."

"What's wrong with calling a meeting? We do that all the time at the firm."

"Well, we *don't* do it all the time. We're a family, remember?

We get together for the High Holy Days and Pesach, and we barely survive that. Forcing us to get together on an occasion when God isn't even in the room?" He shook his head. The cigar's flavor was what he imagined elephant dung would taste like, but he still had a bit of martini left, and each cool sip rinsed off his tongue and rendered it pleasantly numb.

"And what happened at this meeting that drove you crazy?"

"She asked us to go through all the records. She's insisting she has to know what departments are making money and what departments are losing money."

"What's crazy about that?"

"It's not how we do things at Bloom's. We've never done things that way. What does she think we are, a national chain? A franchise like McDonald's? We're family. We run on trust. We each have our areas, and we take care of them. No one's counting how many bialys got sold last week, or how many jars of organic peanut butter. Things flow along."

"Last time we talked about it, you said the store was shaky," Stuart reminded him.

"So now Julia is determined to find out how shaky. Like that's going to make a difference in the grand scheme of things."

"It might."

Jay drowned his irritation in a generous gulp of martini. Why was Stuart siding with Julia? A lawyer thing, he supposed. Their brains must have been trained in law school to worship details and fuss over trivia. "She says," he told Stuart, because even if the guy was annoying he was a hell of an attorney, "we're bleeding. Not exactly hemorrhaging, but oozing." He took another draw on the cigar. Maybe he was getting used to it, because it tasted less like elephant dung and more like burned prunes, which was an improvement. "She's so interested in bleeding, she should have gone to medical school."

"Bleeding isn't good, Jay," Stuart commented. "Even if it's just oozing."

"So what do we need, a Band-Aid? She wants to be the president, let her put the Band-Aid on."

"Does she know where the cut is?"

"If she does, she hasn't told me. She's been shut up inside Ben's old office, reviewing records for days. Every now and then she tiptoes out and vanishes into Myron's office, or Deirdre's. Like she only trusts the non-Blooms."

"Do you think she's plotting against you?"

Jay hadn't actually thought it through that far. That was why Stuart was so invaluable: he thought things through. "Who knows? I can tell you she's not conferring with her mother, either. Or *my* mother. Maybe she's plotting against the whole Bloom family. Maybe she's going to figure out a way to cut us all out of the business. That would teach the old troublemaker a lesson," he muttered, punctuating his bitterness by expelling a thick cloud of smoke.

"Your niece isn't that old," Stuart reminded him.

"My mother. She puts Julia in charge and look what happens. The kid takes over and cuts us all out of the action. As my sons would say, she hasn't got a clue."

"Maybe you could win points with your mother by locating the source of the bleeding and solving the problem yourself," Stuart suggested.

Why did Stuart have to be so damn sensible? Especially after consuming profligate quantities of food and drink. This restaurant was the sort of place where privileged men came to sulk about the world beyond its doors. If Stuart were any sort of a friend, he'd indulge Jay in his sulking instead of coming up with all these clever solutions.

"My mother should have put me in charge, right from the start," he grumbled.

"You're right about that."

"We wouldn't be bleeding, then. Any blood left over from the year after Ben's death, I would have mopped it up in no time flat."

A waiter approached silently. Stuart gave a slight nod, and the man cleared away their plates. "The question is, are you going to sit around and do nothing while your niece fumbles? Are you willing to risk the store just to prove your mother was wrong to name Julia the president?"

"My mother's the one who put the place at risk." In another frame of mind, Jay would have realized that if the store was at risk, his career was at risk, too. He received a regular dividend from the Bloom Building rentals, but he pulled a hefty income from the store, and he put that hefty income to good use. Golf, racquetball, Wendy, two-pound steaks—the best things in life were not free.

But he wasn't ready to sweep in and rescue Julia. Not yet. Let her stumble a bit. Let her discover how incompetent she was when it came to managing Bloom's. Let her try to solve whatever problems she found, and let her fail. Then Ida might come to her senses and give Jay the title he deserved.

If he were president of Bloom's, the problems would have never been uncovered in the first place. What happened to a cut when you left it alone? It scabbed over and healed. As long as Julia insisted on poking at the cut, examining it, picking and probing, she was going to keep reopening it, and it was going to keep bleeding.

So let her be the one with blood on her hands, he thought, as he took a satisfyingly indignant puff on his cigar. Let Julia be the one getting blamed when the store refused to clot.

"Myron?"

For the third time in three days, Julia entered Myron's small, cluttered office and shut the door behind her.

He was seated behind his desk, slathering a cranberry bagel with strawberry-flavored cream cheese. The abundance of pink hurt her eyes.

"Look at this," he said, waving his colorful snack at her. "It's like having a bowl of fruit, except better." He took a hearty bite and grinned blissfully. Julia noticed a spot of cream cheese on his bow tie, but tactfully didn't mention it.

She was glad he'd taken her up on her policy of having employees snack on the store's food. It certainly seemed to have improved his morale. "Actually, it's bagels I want to talk to you about," she said, dropping onto the metal chair wedged into the corner of his room. In her hands she carried a folder. She'd been examining its contents, running the numbers through her calculator over and over. "I've been worried about our bagel department since I first saw the figures last week. This should be our strongest department, right? I mean, bagels. What could be more Bloom's than bagels?"

"Knishes," he suggested.

She shook her head. "Knishes are a delicacy. Bagels are a staple. We're selling tons of them, according to all the figures I've seen. More accurately, we're turning over tons of inventory."

"But?"

"But the income isn't matching the number of bagels we're selling. By my calculation, more than a hundred bagels are disappearing every week."

He wiped his fingers on a paper napkin and gestured for her to pass him her folder. "How much more than a hundred?"

"It varies. Maybe a dozen dozen. What's that called?"

"A gross." He opened the folder, took another bite of his bagel and chewed as he read. "One gross a week? What are we talking?" He blotted his fingers with the crumpled napkin, then set them loose on his adding machine, flicking on its motor and hitting the keys so rapidly his fingertips scarcely touched the buttons. "A little more than a hundred dollars a week. Not a catastrophic loss, sweetie."

Julia let the endearment go unchallenged. Myron had known her since her training-pants days. As long as he didn't pinch her cheek, she'd cut him some slack. "In dollars and cents it's not much. But it bothers me that it's happening every week. I think someone's stealing from the department."

"What, one of the bagel guys? You've got Morty Sugarman there—he's been with Bloom's for ages. The man's solid as a rock."

"Maybe he's a rock who filches spare bagels."

"Or maybe it's the younger one—what's his name?"

"Casey Gordon," Julia muttered. Wouldn't it be just swell if she had to inform her sister that the man she had a crush on was a bagel thief? "He's the guy who introduced the cranberry bagels," she told Myron. "He comes up with all the weird flavors."

Myron looked stricken. He gazed adoringly at his pink bagel. "I hope he's not your problem."

"It's more than just bagels, Myron. A few other departments are showing small but regular losses, too. The coffee department, the pastry department—everything's selling, selling, selling, but the income isn't matching up with the units sold. I'm guessing the reason no one has noticed this is that the sales numbers are so good. Nobody bothered to check and see whether the money coming in made sense."

"So." Myron popped the remainder of his bagel in his mouth, swallowed and patted his lips with his napkin. "What are you going to do about it?"

"I was hoping you could give me some ideas."

"What am I, Scotland Yard? I'm an accountant, bubby. You got theft, you need to find out who's stealing. Simple as that."

Julia snorted. As simple as *what?* Hiring an army of rent-a-cops to patrol the store? Installing hidden cameras like the ones they used in convenience stores and banks? This was Bloom's they were talking about. Bloom's had an aura, a style—and that style did not accommodate mechanisms for spying on shoplifters.

Unfortunately, she doubted the problem was shoplifters. Shoplifters wouldn't be moving merchandise out of the store so regularly, in such constant quantities. This was something else, something organized, something premeditated.

Myron patted the folder as affectionately as he would have patted the hand of a loved one. "The store's breaking even, right? It's been breaking even for a while. So it's not growing. This is not the end of the world. I stopped growing when I was fourteen, and I've lived another fifty years so far without any ill effects."

She was kind enough not to point out that he might not

have looked quite so wretched in his plaid blazers and tacky bow ties if he'd kept growing into his late teens and wound up a few inches taller. Myron's height wasn't the issue. The store's future was.

At least she could talk to him. She couldn't talk to her mother or Uncle Jay because she suspected they were part of the problem. Not that they were filching bagels from the bins. Her mother always bought frozen bagels from the cheap supermarket down the block when she wasn't on one of her diets and swearing off bagels altogether. If she desired the superior quality of Bloom's bagels, she could easily afford them. Julia had learned her mother was being paid one hundred seventy-five thousand dollars from the store.

Uncle Jay was drawing two hundred thousand dollars, which Julia felt was unfair. Her mother ought to be earning as much from the store as Uncle Jay. She certainly worked hard enough. But everything in the Bloom's corporate structure operated with all the rigor and precision of a Florida election. "It's family," Grandma Ida told Julia when she'd telephoned her to question the haphazard system. "All the money's going into the same pot."

Julia had tried to argue that Uncle Jay's pot was not the same as Sondra's pot. She'd asserted that if a person was working, that person ought to know what her job was and what salary that job paid. The cashiers and clerks had titles and pay levels. Why not the Blooms?

What made the salary thing even more of a mystery was that Julia's mother was supposed to be receiving the same amount of money the store would have been paying her father if he were alive. The store accounts showed her earning twenty-five thousand dollars less. But when she'd discussed the shortfall with her mother, Sondra had said she was in fact receiving the full two hundred thousand a year. The difference was coming out of the Bloom Building income. "It's to preserve your uncle's fragile ego," Sondra had explained. "It would kill him to know I was making the same amount as him."

Creative bookkeeping bothered Julia. So did the family dynamics polluting Bloom's management.

The fact was, she earned less than anyone on the third floor but Deirdre, whose salary equaled hers. Evidently, Grandma Ida thought Julia was experienced enough to be the company's president, but too young and green to pull down the kind of money her mother and uncle made. Julia didn't mind too much, though. She'd feel peculiar earning more than her mother—and besides, she wasn't going to be working at Bloom's forever. She hadn't resigned from Griffin, McDougal; she'd just taken a leave of absence. Sooner or later, she would be returning to the firm, where when people threw hissy fits or played ego games it didn't affect her personally because she wasn't related to any of them.

One reason she was troubled by her mother's and uncle's generous salaries was that the store wasn't making a profit. It should be. It was *Bloom's,* for God's sake—the finest delicatessen in New York City if not the world. The aisles were always crowded, the cash registers always humming. Clusters of visitors speaking French or German or Japanese held their Bloom's tote bags high and posed for photographs in front of the main entrance. People stranded in Nigeria or Fiji could enjoy a Passover meal catered by Bloom's, as long as they had access to a phone line and an international delivery service.

How could the place not be showing huge profits?

She wished she knew someone with an up-to-date business degree. Myron had graduated from City College sometime during the Kennedy administration, and as far as she knew he hadn't contemplated business theory since then. Heath would probably know some business experts, but if she called him, he'd tell her to haul her ass out of the delicatessen and return to the work she was born to do—trying to keep estranged spouses from killing each other—and while she was at it, she should also sleep with him.

"Thanks for your time, Myron," she said, pushing to her feet and gathering her folder from his desk.

In a spasm of paternal courtliness, he stood, reached across the desk and squeezed her shoulder. "Everything's going to be fine. Don't let the numbers worry you. That's my job—the numbers."

She wanted to point out that if he were doing his job, *he'd* be worrying about the numbers, too. But he was from the old world of Bloom's, her grandmother's world, her parents' and uncle's world. She was an interloper, a snippy little upstart who didn't know *bupkes* about how to run a food store.

Bupkes. Look at her. She'd been the official president of Bloom's less than two months, and already she was thinking in Yiddish.

She left Myron's office and hesitated outside Deirdre's door, thinking she could pester her for the insights Myron had failed to supply. Then she heard Susie calling through the open door of her own office: "Hey, Julia?"

She'd rather talk to her sister than Deirdre any day.

She found Susie lounging on Grandpa Isaac's desk, which had apparently become her favorite seat in the room. She was fondling the coleus, stroking the leaves and adjusting a few that were tangled with the stems.

"This thing needs food," she said. "If you don't want to feed a plant, get a cactus."

"I water it," Julia told her.

"Did I say it was thirsty? It's hungry. Feed it."

Julia was too frazzled to argue, and too relieved by Susie's presence to resent her bossiness. After closing the door, Julia flopped down onto the sofa and groaned.

Susie seemed oblivious to her mood. "I've been working on concepts for the windows. I've got some ideas I wanted to run by you before I start making changes."

"Just tell me—are these changes going to cost a lot of money?"

"No. I'll be using what we've already got." She abandoned the plant, lifted a notepad and hopped down from the desk. "I said concepts, and that's the operative word. We're going to con-ceptualize the windows."

Julia gazed warily at her. "How do you conceptualize a window?"

"Unify it. Make it be about something other than 'Look at all the crap we sell.' Let it talk to the browser, the passerby. Let it say, 'If you come in here, you will leave happier than you felt when you entered.'"

"Happier? You really think buying a chunk of goat cheese is going to make people happier?"

"If it doesn't make them happier, they're not going to buy it. So here's what I'm thinking." She plunked herself on the sofa, forcing Julia to shift to make more room. Susie flipped open her pad to show Julia a pencil sketch. "Here's my first concept. Grandma's home. It's warm. It's inviting. It's a place where you went when you needed great food and unconditional love."

"That doesn't sound like any grandmother I know."

"Myths, Julia. Don't be literal. We're exploring the myth of the ideal grandma."

"Do you want to fill the windows with Depression glass?"

"That would work. I was thinking more of overstuffed chairs with faded antimacassars on them, and a decanter of schnapps and a bunch of those long-stemmed crystal glasses that always seemed to survive the journey from the Old Country. On the table, a plate of rugelach and a glass dish piled high with fruit and chocolates. That would be one window—dessert at Grandma's. And the next window would be brunch at Grandma's—a plate of lox, a bowl of bagels. They're served in linen-lined baskets nowadays, but mythical grandmothers never served bagels in wicker. So it would be a bowl of bagels, with one bagel out, sitting on a cutting board with a sharp knife next to it. And a crystal dish of cream cheese, garnished with a black olive—"

"Turkish or Greek?"

"Whatever. These would all be fake. You don't put real food in windows. It spoils."

"This all sounds very expensive," Julia reminded her.

"Yeah, I know." Susie sighed. "I just wanted you to see this brilliant concept before you rejected it."

"So now I've seen it and I'm rejecting it."

Susie flipped the page. "Here's the next concept. Food is fun."

Julia stared at the drawing. It appeared to be a lot of bagels levitating.

"We hang them on threads. They float through the air. It's like a dream. A bagel dream."

"You said we can't use real food in windows."

"I think we can use bagels. We'd spray them with a low-gloss polyurethane or something to preserve them. We'd have some floating in the air, and others doing other things. Like this one is hooked over the spout of a teapot. And we could stack a few of them up and prop utensils inside—a whisk, a stirring spoon, a garlic press, whatever. Eye-catching juxtapositions. We could even seat a Barbie doll inside one of the bagels, like it's a tire swing. Then in the next window, we do the same thing with bread sticks. And in the next one, we do it with boxed and bottled goods—hanging by fish wire from the ceiling, stacked in interesting configurations on the ground, jars of pickles placed here and there for emphasis. All very whimsical."

"Pickles for emphasis?" Julia scowled. "It would remind people less of the ideal grandma than of some nightmare preschool."

Susie rolled her eyes at Julia's lack of whimsy. "Okay. My third concept—" she flipped a page again "—also involves bagels. The theme is 'Bagels are lifesavers.'"

"Lifesavers."

"Like on cruise ships. The shape is perfect. We can even use Barbie again—dressed in a swimsuit, with a bagel around her waist."

"Our bagels are much too big for her skinny little waist."

"We could work it out. Maybe we could stuff Ken into the bagel with her. We could even have him tugging on the bra of her bikini… Just joking," she added, obviously sensing Julia's disapproval. "We could have bagels lined up like life preservers along a railing, with 'Bloom's' stenciled on them instead of, say, *S.S. Titanic.* Maybe Neil could give us some ideas."

Julia shook her head.

"You're a pain in the ass, you know that? Okay, here's my last concept, and if you don't like it I'm going back to Nico's, where I'm appreciated."

"I'm sure I'll love it," Julia said, praying that she would. She couldn't afford not to. If she wanted changes in Bloom's earnings, she was going to have to make changes in the store. The windows seemed to her the least dangerous thing to change. If new displays didn't destroy Bloom's, she could move on to bigger changes.

"The theme is 'Eat your bagels.' We'd have little signs scattered through the windows with bagel sayings on them—'Eat your bagels.' 'Bagels are the eighth wonder of the world.' 'A bagel a day keeps hunger away.' 'The best bagels are born, not made.'"

"You want to imply we're hatching bagels instead of baking them?"

Susie gave her a withering look, then continued with her bagel signs: "'Real men eat bagels.' 'I was a teenage bagel.' 'My kingdom for a bagel.' 'Lox, stock and bagels.' Of course, we'd have lots of bagels scattered around the windows, too—and maybe a few nonperishables. The concept is to get people laughing, to make them believe Bloom's is a fun place."

"It's great," Julia said.

"You think it's stupid. You think it implies we're hatching bagels."

"I was only kidding when I said that," Julia assured her, angling her head to scrutinize Susie's sketch. The signs dangled on threads like the bagels in the earlier concept, and some bagels dangled, too. It gave a surreal impression—but also a playful, inviting one. And it could be done cheaply.

"So you think we should emphasize bagels in the windows."

Susie shrugged. "A kosher-style deli. Bagels. What else would you emphasize, a bacon cheeseburger?"

"I'm only asking whether your concepts were maybe influenced by Casey."

"Absolutely not," Susie retorted. "I came up with some non-bagel concepts, too."

One non-bagel concept, and it was too expensive. Julia studied the "Eat your bagels" window, wondering if decorating the display windows like that would use up a gross of bagels a week.

"What?" Susie must have sensed her thoughts had taken a turn.

"Nothing." Julia put down the pad. "The last one is good. Are you sure this polyurethane thing will work?"

"I'll grab a couple of bagels and experiment with them," Susie said, folding up her pad. "Maybe I can work downstairs in the kitchen. They've got those long tables down there."

"You're not going to spray polyurethane in a place where food preparation is going on," Julia argued. "You can work in here, if you want. Use Grandpa Isaac's desk."

"I'd rather work downstairs," Susie said, eyeing the desk.

"You can't spray where there's food!"

"Yeah, but I've got to accumulate hours."

"What hours? I'm paying you a flat fee for this job."

Susie shook her head. "Hours with Casey. It's this deal we've got. The more hours I spend with him, the better."

"Better for what?" As soon as the words were out, Julia regretted them. She didn't want to know what Susie was up to with Casey. She already had too much on her mind; she couldn't waste time contemplating an hourly romance between her sister and a possible in-house bagel robber. "Susie, this is a crazy thing to ask you, of all people, but do you know any business experts?"

"Me?" Susie laughed. "Yeah, like I hang out with the Wharton crowd. Maybe Rick would know some. He's always hitting up businesspeople for money to invest in his movie."

And all those businesspeople said no, which, Julia considered, meant they might have some intelligence. "Maybe Adam's business professor up at Cornell," she said.

"He'd never go within ten miles of a business professor," Susie pointed out. "He's so afraid if he had any expertise at all, someone might make him come to New York and work for Bloom's."

"He *should* work for Bloom's. You and I are working for Bloom's."

"I'm only doing it because you'd kill me if I didn't." Susie pushed away from the couch and tucked her pad under her arm. "I'm going downstairs for some bagels. I can get in a few minutes before I start spraying them."

"Whatever you say." Julia held up her hand, warding off any explanation of why Susie wanted to accumulate hours with Casey. Let Susie accumulate as much time as she wanted with him. Maybe, if Susie got close enough to him, she'd be able to find out if he was stealing a gross of bagels a week from the store.

She pondered asking Susie to spy on him, then decided against it. If Julia implied anything negative about him, Susie would be so indignant she might not do the windows. Right now, Julia needed Susie as an ally even more than she needed to figure out how all those bagels wandered out of the store every week. "If you get any other ideas about someone with a business degree, call me."

"Don't hold your breath," Susie said cheerfully as she headed for the door.

The phone rang. Susie twisted the doorknob, and Julia waved to her as she crossed to her father's desk to answer. "Hello?"

"Julia," one of the receptionists said, "that reporter from *Gotham Magazine* wants to talk to you. Ron Joffe."

She gave Susie a frantic smile and another wave, waited until her sister had departed from the office and then lowered herself into her chair. Joffe. The reporter. The shark who had smelled blood in the waters around Bloom's before Julia had even been aware of seepage. The jerk who had kissed her once and then disappeared from her life without any explanation.

He was a business expert, wasn't he?

The worst one she could possibly turn to. She wasn't going to ask him for any recommendations. She was simply going to be pleasant and upbeat and give him whatever he needed to write a puff piece on Bloom's for his magazine.

And she'd never let him kiss her again.

"Okay," she said. "Put him on."

13

He saw her waiting for him outside the restaurant, dressed in a pale-gray top and a matching skirt that revealed a satisfying amount of leg. It wasn't a micromini, but from where he stood on the corner of Eighth Avenue, he could see her calves, her knees and a hint of thigh.

Her legs were actually on the thin side, but it didn't matter. His body temperature notched up a few degrees from the mere sight of her. Not because of her knees, not because of the rest of her—which was also on the thin side—but because if you touched two live wires together, you could fry your circuitry, cause an explosion, ignite a fire, black out an entire region. When it came to Julia Bloom, Ron became not just a live wire but an exposed one, stripped of insulation. He saw her and automatically started shooting sparks.

He kept walking toward her, reminding himself of the reason he'd asked her to meet him at his favorite Italian place on Restaurant Row instead of at her office. The last time he'd been in her office, he'd closed the door, and he still considered it something of a miracle that nothing more than a single kiss had occurred between them. If he wound up behind a closed door with her again, there would be more than a kiss. A lot more. Short circuits, blackouts, a minor apocalypse.

The sky stretched pink above the towering buildings. He'd arranged to meet her at seven, figuring that by then most of the theater crowd would be finishing up their meals and heading out to catch their shows. The restaurant would empty, and he and Julia would be able to linger over dessert—although she didn't look as if she ate dessert very often. He'd talk her into something—a pastry, a cordial, whatever it took to prolong the evening. Just because this was a working dinner didn't mean they couldn't make it last.

She spotted him and smiled—and immediately stopped smiling, as if she didn't want him to think she was happy to see him. That fleeting smile stuck in his mind like a gnat on flypaper. She *was* happy to see him, and knowing that caused his body temperature to hike another degree.

He might just as well have been fourteen years old again, a lowly freshman at Stuyvesant High School catching his first glimpse of Heather Fenster, a statuesque junior with plump lips and a shimmying stride whom he and just about every other boy in the school had lusted after. Julia Bloom looked nothing like Heather Fenster; she wasn't statuesque and her lips didn't shape a sultry pout. Her modest proportions in no way reminded Ron of Heather Fenster's abundant bosom. But his reaction to her was just as physical, just as adolescent and just as instantaneous.

"Hi," she said once he was close enough for them to speak. Her voice was ordinary, neither husky nor kittenish, but it made his skin tingle.

He held open the door for her and let her precede him into the restaurant. Inside, the din of street noise was replaced by the cushioning sound of muted voices and silverware clinking elegantly against china. He gave his name to the host, who led them past the bar to a cozy table for two.

"I hope you don't mind meeting me here," Ron said, her silence compelling him to fill the space between them with words. "I thought it would be easier for us to talk if we got away from all the interruptions at work." *And you're safer around me if we're someplace public, surrounded by witnesses,* he almost added.

"This is fine." She shook out her napkin and spread it across her lap.

A waiter approached their table, bearing bread and water. Julia surprised Ron by ordering portobello mushrooms and polenta, a large salad and a glass of Chianti. Given her slender build, he would have guessed her to be one of those women who ordered only salads—dressing on the side—and then picked at them, leaving half the serving untouched.

The thought of Julia eating heartily turned him on even more than seeing her had. Women didn't seem to realize how incredibly sexy they could be when they were eating.

He ordered something Milanese—swordfish or scallops, whatever—and a salad, and suggested they split a bottle of Chianti. The waiter departed, and Ron tried to study Julia without staring. Maybe it was her eyes, as dark as espresso, or the way the corners of her mouth tilted up even when she wasn't smiling. Damn it, there had to be *some* reason for his hormonal reaction to her.

"*Gotham Magazine* hasn't published your article on Bloom's," she said.

He wasn't sure whether to be grateful or pissed off that she wanted to talk business. He thought about it while the waiter went through the whole wine rigmarole, displaying the label for Ron as if he cared what it said, then popping the cork, sniffing it, snapping his corkscrew shut and pocketing it, and splashing some wine into a glass. Ron sipped it, nodded like an expert and gestured for the waiter to fill Julia's glass. A little wine might loosen her up, make her more willing to discuss things that weren't business—or to discuss business in such a way that he could tie his story up in a neat ribbon and drop it on Kim's desk.

"I'm still working on it," he told her.

She sipped her wine, her gaze remaining on him above the rim of her glass. "It's not going to be a puff piece, is it."

"You were expecting a puff piece?"

"I wouldn't have agreed to be interviewed if I'd thought it was going to be anything else."

He reminded himself that she was a lawyer. Her pale skin, her elegant posture and his raging hormones had nothing to do with the fact that she was one sharp lady, intellectually well exercised and protective of the store she'd been selected to run. As a lawyer, she probably knew as well as he did how to pose questions and elicit information. He mustn't let his attraction to her cause him to let down his guard.

He considered suggesting they drink more wine before they started debating what his article would or wouldn't be, but then remembered that this was supposed to be a working dinner. She had a right to introduce the subject of the article, and if he possessed half an ounce of sense—which seemed to be a pretty close estimate of his supply at the moment—he'd follow her lead.

"Bloom's is in trouble," he said.

Her already round eyes grew rounder, and her cheeks picked up some color, although that might have been a reflection of the red wine in the glass she held just below her chin. "What makes you think that?"

"I have a source."

"What source? Bloom's is a privately held company. My family and a few trusted employees are the only people who know just how well the store is doing. And I know those employees would never say anything bad about the store behind my back. Especially since it's not true," she added—a bit desperately, he thought.

"My source says Bloom's is bleeding."

The flash of color in her cheeks had nothing to do with the wine. He'd scored a direct hit with that particular choice of words—words Kim had shared with him, words she must have gotten from someone in the Blooms' inner circle.

Julia lowered her glass, sat back in her seat and regarded him as if he'd just descended from the hatch of a flying saucer at the center of a crop circle. "I'd be very curious to know who told you that," she said.

"I'm sure you would." He helped himself to a thick slice of bread, smeared butter on it and took a bite. He liked watching her squirm, on a whole lot of levels.

"Let me guess," she murmured. "When you were fifteen, you read *All the President's Men* and decided you were going to be an investigative reporter. Somehow you wound up writing fluff for *Gotham Magazine,* but the old muckraker inside you refuses to give up the dream."

He laughed. "Actually, no. I decided I was going to be a reporter because my eleventh-grade English teacher made me join the school newspaper staff as a punishment for mouthing off in class, and it turned out to be a lot of fun. And I don't write fluff for *Gotham Magazine.* I'm the magazine's business and economics reporter. I've got an MBA and I write the weekly City Business column. Occasionally I do business-related feature stories on topics the readers might enjoy. Everyone in New York knows and loves Bloom's. When I got a tip that the store might be struggling, it was right up my alley."

"You have an MBA," she repeated.

He hadn't mentioned that to impress her. Well, yeah, he had—given her fancy schooling and her law degree, he thought he ought to reinforce for her that he wasn't just some hack with half-baked fantasies about uncovering the next presidential scandal.

"So I know a thing or two about business," he assured her. "Is Bloom's in trouble?"

"No."

He weighed the sound of that single syllable, trying to decide how convincing she sounded. Not very. If he were a boxer, he'd go for her midsection with a flurry of jabs and have her down on the canvas before the bell rang. But the waiter was delivering their salads, and by the time he'd finished grinding fresh pepper all over the weedy-looking greens, she no longer appeared quite so vulnerable.

Ron decided to back off a little. "Have you unlocked your grandfather's desk yet?" he asked.

She smiled—another flash that staggered him more effectively than a boxer's right hook. "Why are you so curious about that desk?"

"It comes with being a journalist," he explained. "You see something locked, you want to unlock it."

She shook her head. "I asked Deirdre about it. Deirdre Morrissey," she clarified, and he nodded to indicate that he knew whom she was talking about. "She said she has no idea where the key is anymore, but she's sure the desk is empty."

"You didn't run our theory by her—about your grandfather's spirit being locked inside?"

Julia chuckled and shook her head. "If I told her that, she'd think I was nuts."

"So, you're finding your place at the store? They don't really think you're nuts, do they?"

"Who, Deirdre and the others?" She shrugged and munched on her salad. He liked watching her jaw when she chewed. Her chin moved in an almost circular path as she ground the leaves and stems down into swallowable form. "I do things a little differently from the way they used to be done. I guess everybody's still adjusting—including me. If that's the so-called trouble you've heard about Bloom's—"

"No, I definitely heard the place was bleeding."

All traces of humor vanished from her face. "It's not," she said coolly.

Maybe he should come at her from a different angle. "Do you miss your law firm?" he asked.

"Not as much as I'd expected." She ate some more salad, apparently enjoying it. He'd ordered a salad because he figured it was healthy, but she actually seemed to be savoring it. "Most of the cases I was involved with were divorce cases. It was pretty depressing."

"I'll bet."

His parents had split when he was ten. Neither of them had had the bucks to hire a law firm like the white-shoe outfit Julia had been working for—he had her firm's name in his notes back at the office, and he remembered thinking it was just the sort of place a Wellesley grad who wanted to make a lot of money might end up hanging her shingle. When his parents had decided to call it quits, his father had used his sister Ruth's husband, Louie, who was a real estate lawyer in Jersey, and his mother had gone with a neighbor, Ellen Weintraub, whom she'd met at a tenants' meeting a year earlier. Ron and his brother had never been clear on what function the attorneys served in the divorce. All they'd known was that their parents had spent a lot of time screaming at each other and referring to each other in the third person when they were in the same room. And then they'd gotten divorced and seemed twice as miserable apart as they'd been together.

He'd rather run a deli than be a divorce lawyer any day.

"And the hours were awful," Julia was saying. "I was an associate there. We worked very long days."

"Were you in line for a partnership?"

"I think so. I'd been there only two-and-a-half years, but no one ever told me I wasn't on the partnership track."

"So you gave up a lot to go to Bloom's."

She shrugged, then took a piece of bread and dabbed it into the puddle of herbed oil and vinegar on her salad plate. "What's a lot? I'm still a lawyer."

"But you aren't practicing."

"Who knows? If you publish a bunch of lies about Bloom's, I might put my law degree to use suing you for libel." She gave him a sly smile.

"I would never publish lies about Bloom's," he assured her, smiling back. To be sharing a smile over a threatened libel action may have been odd for them, but he felt as if they were connecting on some other level.

Neither spoke as they finished their salads. The waiter

brought their entrées, topped off their wineglasses and vanished. Julia immediately dug into her food.

"You like to eat," Ron observed. He'd meant it as a compliment, but her scathing glare told him she wasn't flattered. "I think that's great," he hastened to add.

"What's great? That I'm a pig?"

"You're not a pig. Did I say you were a pig? Did you hear me say anything remotely like that?"

She lowered her fork and stared hard at him. "You said I liked to eat."

"Which, in my book, is a good thing."

She seemed to wrestle with her response, then surrendered to the tantalizing meal on her plate and tasted a forkful of polenta. Her sigh of delight proved his point. "This is delicious."

"That was all I meant," he insisted. "You appreciate good food." He tried his seafood and nodded. This restaurant had never let him down. "It must have been great growing up with all that Bloom's food around."

She grinned. "We hardly ever ate Bloom's food when I was growing up."

"You're kidding. All that amazing food at your fingertips, and you didn't eat it?"

"No." She sliced a wedge of mushroom, tasted it and sighed again. He could get a permanent hard-on just listening to her sigh like that.

Shifting in his chair, he focused on the conversation. "Why not?"

"The family operated under the theory that Bloom's merchandise was for customers, not for us. It was to be sold. It was profit centers, not family indulgences. Every now and then— as a big treat—my father would bring home a babka or maybe some knishes from the store. This was only on special occasions, someone's birthday or something. And maybe once a year we'd have a big Sunday brunch with Bloom's bagels and lox. But for the most part, my mother shopped at the grocery store down the street. She said the prices were cheaper."

"She's crazy," he blurted out, then smiled apologetically. "I know that grocery store. I live on West Seventy-Sixth."

"Really? I live on—"

She cut herself off. She looked the way she'd looked outside the restaurant, right after she'd stopped smiling when she saw him, as if she was happy and didn't want him to know. "Where do you live?"

"West Seventy-Fourth."

"So we're neighbors."

"It would seem." She attacked her food with singular determination.

He successfully suppressed his own smile. But while he worked on his dinner he kept his gaze on her, trying to read her expression. Some tension in there, a hint of panic but a sort of fizziness, too, like bubbles in a bottle of soda someone had shaken. Just one twist of the screw cap, and they'd come squirting out.

He decided not to dwell on how terrific it was that they were neighbors. "Number one," he said, "that grocery store isn't cheap. And number two, Bloom's is less expensive than it could be. Besides, you'd have gotten the food wholesale."

"But then the store wouldn't have made its profit." She tilted her head slightly, and her sleek black hair brushed against her shoulder. "I hope you won't put any of this in your article. I know my family is a little eccentric, but it would be cruel for you to make us look ridiculous in your magazine."

"I have no interest in making you look ridiculous." *Colorful* and *interesting* would be more accurate.

"I've been encouraging employees to use our merchandise. I couldn't believe that people working for us would stop in at the McDonald's to buy a cup of coffee to bring to work with them. It's absurd. They should be using and enjoying the products they're selling to others."

"And they didn't do this before you came along?"

"Apparently not. They probably think I'm some kind of crazy radical, turning the place upside down."

He mentally stored her words. He'd try not to embarrass her family, but a lot of this stuff belonged in his article. She hadn't said any of it was off the record, so he could use it if he wanted. "Are you turning Bloom's upside down?"

"Maybe just sideways," she said with a smile. "We're re-designing our display windows, and if that's successful, we'll think about updating the interior a bit."

"That doesn't sound so radical."

"*I* don't think it's radical. It's just a little different from the way things have been done for the past sixty years."

"What else are you doing to turn the place sideways?"

"We have meetings. I gather that before I took over, no one on the third floor had meetings. They just kept their office doors open and shouted back and forth a lot."

"Do they like doing it your way?"

"I'm not sure. But I try to have a platter of Bloom's bagels for them to nosh on during the meetings. I'm sure that helps." Another smile, this one ironic. "I'm trying to upgrade the way we do business in general. My father ran the store brilliantly, but he did a lot of it by instinct. I lack his instincts, so I have to do things more step-by-step."

Her father. The cold one who'd been so close with Deirdre Morrissey. Did Julia know about that special relationship? Did she know her father was a philandering schmuck?

"Because he did so much by instinct, there aren't a lot of paper trails and road maps. So I'm still feeling my way along. But I'm getting there. I'm figuring things out."

"Are you putting in the kind of hours he put in?"

She arched an eyebrow. "What do you know about his hours?"

"Julia, I've been talking to people—both in and out of Bloom's. I'm a journalist. It's my job to find things out." He drank some wine. "Everybody I talked to told me your father worked twelve-hour days and seven-day weeks. He was always at the office, always doing Bloom business. That's what people say."

"I suppose that's a fairly accurate description. He loved the store."

"He spent more time there than with you."

"Well, he—" Again she cut herself off. Again her cheeks darkened. "He worked very hard," she admitted.

"Did you and your family resent that?"

"Of course not! My mother worked there, too. Even when we kids were young, she'd put in four or five hours a day on the third floor. We'd hang out at the store and get in the way. It was fun. Not too many kids get the run of a famous delicatessen like Bloom's."

"Where they aren't even allowed to eat all that great food because it could be sold for a profit."

She set her fork down on her plate with a staccato clatter. "I think we're done."

"No." He reached across the table and covered her hand with his. "I'm sorry, okay?" he said, trying to ignore the smooth warmth of her knuckles against his palm, the jarring realization that he was touching her. "It's a family business, and I want to get a sense of the family dynamic. That's all."

"You're saying my father ignored his family."

"I never said that."

"He worked hard to honor the legacy his parents had created, and to make sure it was an even better legacy when it was passed along to my generation. He worked hard because running a delicatessen on the scale of Bloom's isn't easy. I'm learning that. It's a monumental responsibility, and he lived up to it. When I was a kid, I didn't care about eating food from Bloom's. I never felt deprived."

She was lying. He could tell by the darkness in her eyes, by the way she didn't quite look at him, by the cooling of her hand beneath his. She'd felt deprived, and she didn't need Ron to tell her her father was a schmuck. She knew it.

"Okay," he relented, letting go of her. She flexed her hand a couple of times, then studied it as if she expected to find that he'd left a mark on it.

His own hand felt empty without hers. "I'm trying to get a sense of things, that's all," he said—another apology. "It's what reporters do."

"Right." She sighed, and when her eyes met his she no longer looked resentful. "You're just doing your job."

"The more interesting stuff I include about your family and the history of Bloom's, the better the publicity for the store. Trust me on this. Customers will pour into the place if they've learned a little of the background story."

"Do you think so?"

"I'm sure of it." He wasn't just saying that to mollify her. People who read in *Gotham* that Ida Bloom was the iron-fisted queen, that her son Ben spent more time at the deli than in his home, that his children had the run of the place while eating inferior bagels from the supermarket down the street—this was the kind of color that lured the curious. They'd flock to the store just to see what it was all about. "I'm not writing a puff piece, but what I write is going to mean a lot more traffic for you at Bloom's. I don't want to inflict damage on the store. I just want to write an interesting story. Trust me."

She stared at him for a moment. He held her gaze, hoping he looked suitably trustworthy. Finally, reluctantly, she smiled and took a final bite of portobello.

"I'm stuffed," she said.

She'd made a respectable dent in the large portion, but there was still a bit left over. "Would you like some dessert?"

"No, thanks. Will they wrap the leftovers for me?"

He struggled not to laugh. Not only did Julia eat enthusiastically, but she had no qualms about requesting a doggie bag. Most women behaved as if they didn't want men to realize they actually ate. Julia was uninhibited about eating.

Damn. Contemplating her lack of inhibition caused that short circuit inside him to start shooting sparks again.

"When is the article going to be published?" she asked.

"When I'm done writing it."

"Will you need to interview me again?"

A million times. Every day. Every night. "I don't know."

She sipped her wine and watched him. He couldn't read her mind, and that bothered him. He considered being able to figure out what people were thinking one of his most essential skills as a journalist. And he'd figured Julia out pretty well throughout most of their meal. But not now.

He signaled for the waiter, told him to wrap up her leftovers and asked for the check.

As he pocketed his receipt, she said, "There's something I need to ask you."

He stood and circled the table to pull out her chair, but she was on her feet before he could take her hand. "Fire away," he invited her.

She started toward the front door, then halted and turned, nearly causing him to bump into her. "Why did you kiss me?"

All right. She was going to force him to address the constant arousal he felt around her. It attacked like a low-grade virus, an incurable malady that left him functional but vaguely feverish. Surely she felt it, too. Surely it was as vivid to her as to him, as visceral, an invisible power plant pumping heat into the air around them and infecting them with its fumes.

He touched his hand to her shoulder and steered her out of the restaurant. Outside, the street was relatively calm—all the theatergoers were probably just returning to their seats after intermissions at the various playhouses in the neighborhood. The sky was dark, the air nippy.

On the sidewalk she stopped and turned to him again. Her eyes were wide, questioning, slightly impatient.

He would answer her question. She deserved that much. He'd apologize for the kiss he'd given her at her office, tell her it had been a reckless impulse, explain that he was a professional and didn't behave that way, that he knew better, that he must have momentarily lost his mind that day. He'd describe faulty wiring to her, short circuits and the way they could cause fires and breakdowns and other problems.

She gazed up at him with those big brown eyes and that enigmatic smile, and he knew there was only one answer, one explanation, one way to get past that first kiss.

14

They stopped kissing only long enough to climb into a cab. Then they started again—deep, luscious kisses, wet kisses, gentle kisses, greedy kisses. It was all one big kiss, actually, like a pasta salad that contained different shapes and colors of pasta, each of them distinct yet all of them combining to be ultimately about one single thing: pasta.

All his kisses were about one single thing: kissing.

She was scarcely aware of the cab's movement, its aggressive swerves through the traffic as it carried them uptown. Her consciousness zeroed in on Joffe's mouth covering hers, his tongue tasting of wine, his hand warm against her cheek, his fingers wandering under her hair to stroke her nape and a heaviness inside her, settling between her legs, making her want to rub up against him like a cat. The meter ticked like a time bomb.

When the ticking stopped, she came up for air. The cab had halted in the middle of West Seventy-Sixth Street, blocking the road. She swallowed, flexed her lips to see if they still worked and found her gaze drawn to Joffe's hip when he pulled out his wallet.

His hip. Oh God. What was she doing?

She knew what she was doing: going to his apartment to have sex with him. She, Julia Bloom, who generally avoided sex because she'd never found it to be particularly enthralling, was about to get naked with a man she hardly knew. She was doing this because his kisses turned her on enough to convince her that anything—even a halfway decent sexual experience—was possible. She was on the verge of going all the way with a reporter who might wind up humiliating her and her family in the pages of the most popular magazine in New York City, for no other reason than that she wanted to.

It was just the sort of thing Susie would do. That thought scared the hell out of her.

Joffe took her hand and helped her from the cab. Only after it sped down the street did she remember that her doggie bag was still sitting on the seat.

No big deal. If she was hungry now, it wasn't for polenta.

He continued to hold her hand as he led her past a spindly tree surrounded by a knee-high fence and into one of the charming, well-maintained brownstones on the block. He unlocked the inner door and ushered her up the stairs. His hand enveloped hers, his fingers thick and warm between hers.

When they reached the third floor, he unlocked a door, pushed it open, tossed his keys onto a table just inside and drew her over the threshold. Kicking the door shut, he hauled her back into his arms.

The kissing began again, and she reveled in it. If this was what Susie went through when she was with men, no wonder she spent so much time with them. If Julia had known kissing could be this magnificent, she'd have been collecting lovers the way a philatelist collected stamps. She'd have had entire albums of them, licked and laid out.

It wasn't kissing that was so magnificent. It was kissing Joffe.

She'd known there was something about him the first time she'd seen him, the morning at her office when they'd laughed about Grandpa Isaac's desk and he'd kissed her before leaving the building—a kiss that had as much in common with tonight's kisses as a raw potato had with a crisp, steaming latke. Unlike that kiss, these kisses were hot, moist, a little spicy and incomparably delicious.

He cupped her face in his hands and kissed her. Slid his hands down to her waist and kissed her. Slid them lower, to her bottom, and pressed her against him the way she'd wanted to press herself against him in the cab…and kissed her again. He kissed her so insistently that she might have stopped breathing, except that if she had she would have passed out, and she wanted to stay conscious, aware of every sensation, every touch. Every kiss.

Still kissing her, he tugged on the buttons of her top. His tongue playing with hers, he shrugged off his jacket and let it fall to the floor. He combed his fingers through her hair until they reached her shoulders, then eased her shirt down her arms and off. And kissed her some more.

They still hadn't moved from the dark entry of his apartment. At another time, in another, saner life, she would have wanted to turn on a few lights and inspect the place, to make sure it was at least moderately tidy and to get an idea of his taste in decor. Instead, she pressed her flattened hands to his chest and let his warmth seep through his cotton shirt to bathe her palms.

He walked forward, forcing her to walk backward. She nearly tripped on a rug, and he swung her into his arms with all the panache of Rhett Butler carrying off a resistant Scarlett O'Hara. Julia was hardly resistant, and she'd never considered Rhett Butler much of a bargain, with his macho swagger and that all-knowing smirk. Thank God Joffe didn't look all-knowing. Forcing her eyes open, she saw that he looked as bewildered as she felt, as crazed, as ravenous. The erstwhile sane Julia would have peeked past him to check out the room he was carrying her through, but the current, intoxicated Julia couldn't shift her gaze from his lean, handsome face.

They entered another room and he lowered her onto a bed. She suffered a moment's apprehension. At some point, if this thing kept going, he was going to find out that her talents did not include lovemaking. She'd do something awkward, something wrong, something that would cause the moment to fizzle like a campfire in a downpour.

She might as well enjoy this until the clouds opened up, she thought with a fatalistic sigh—and pulled him down into her arms so they could get back to kissing.

Articles of clothing disappeared—her skirt, his shirt, her shoes wrested from her feet and her panty hose peeled away. In rare moments of lucidity, she found herself astonished to be in bed with a man as hunky as Joffe. Once her eyes adjusted to the gloom, she was able to make out the dimensions of his chest. His physique didn't imply that he worked out obsessively, but his torso was shaped by genuine muscle, sleek and athletic. A nice patch of hair spread across his upper chest—nothing that put her in mind of Sasquatch or shag rugs, just a modest wedge that made him look even hunkier, and that made her breasts perk up when his chest brushed against them.

Her breasts. Somehow he'd gotten her bra off, and her panties, and the rest of his clothing. She was stripped bare, in bed with a man who could do her store and her family enormous damage, and who probably hadn't believed her when she'd insisted Bloom's was in excellent financial health. She was nude, and he had stopped kissing her mouth to graze her throat. He continued downward until he reached her breasts. This man she neither knew nor trusted was nibbling her nipples.

She trusted him here, though, with this. She trusted his caresses, and the teasing flicks of his tongue. She trusted his weight on her, the way the muscles in his back flexed when she ran her hands down from his shoulders to his waist, the way his breath caught when she ventured as low as his rock-hard buttocks.

That one faint gasp was the only sound he made. He rose higher on her and she brought her hand forward, thinking that if she touched him more intimately he might believe she knew what she was doing. When her fingertips skimmed his penis, it gave a little jump for joy.

She wanted to laugh, but he was kissing her again, sliding his hand between her legs and readying her for him. This was the point at which things were likely to go downhill, but she gamely let him keep at it because the stroke of his fingers felt much better than it should have, much better than anything had ever felt in bed before.

He leaned away from her, fumbled in his night table drawer and pulled out a condom, which he donned one-handed, with a deftness that alerted her to the fact that he'd perfected the technique through regular practice. That didn't bother her—this wasn't a love affair, after all, anything involving their pasts or their futures. Her only concern that she was a lot less experienced than he was, and any minute now he was going to discover just how inexperienced she was.

He surged into her, and it felt so much better than she'd expected that she writhed, forcing him deeper. He gasped again, and that reminded her to keep breathing.

But it was hard to breathe when she'd rather submerge herself, give herself up to the dark, wet tide, drown in it. He kept moving, stroking her body with his, and she kept feeling the pressure, the pull, the fluid pulse of it. One final kiss from him and she slipped under for good. Incredibly good, indescribably good.

His chest pumped against hers, hard, ragged breaths as he settled on top of her. Maybe she hadn't drowned after all, because she felt blessedly, resplendently alive.

Okay. She might just be getting the hang of this whole sex thing.

Or else she simply might have found the right guy. Of course, she couldn't imagine how Ron Joffe, of all people, could be the right guy.

"Julia," he murmured, then grazed her shoulder with his mouth.

"What?" Her voice came out hoarse and cracking.

"Would you do me a favor?"

Anything, she wanted to promise. "Depends on what it is," she said, clinging to the few shreds of rationality she had left.

"Say my name."

"Hmm?"

"I don't think I've ever heard you say my name."

"Joffe," she obliged. He propped himself up on his arms and she peered into his face. He wasn't smiling. "Ron," she added, and got a glint of a grin out of him.

"I just wanted to make sure you knew who you were with."

"Oh, I knew. I know." She reached up and traced the lines of his face, his long, sharp nose, his angular chin. "It's probably too late for me to warn you that I'm not very good at this."

"At what? Saying my name?"

"No, *this.*" She wiggled her hips slightly. He was still inside her, and the billowing warmth caused by her movement made them both groan.

He laughed. "Right. You're not good at *this* at all. Mediocre at best. Maybe not even that."

She regretted her candor. "Don't make fun of me."

"There are a lot of things I'd like to do with you—and most of them are fun." His smile faded. "Why on earth would you think you're not good at this? Just from one time, I'd say you've leapfrogged right past the opening heats to qualify for the championship round."

"Well, I usually…" She sighed. Discussing her previous failures in bed didn't seem romantic, but it was her own fault for raising the subject. "Let's say I usually don't break the tape." She usually didn't even *reach* the tape, but she wasn't going to admit to that.

"Julia. Sweetheart." He touched his mouth lightly to hers. "I would say we didn't just break the tape here—we incinerated it. We pulverized it. It has been obliterated."

"Can tape be obliterated?"

"Were you here in bed with me?" At her nod, he said, "Then you've got your answer."

She considered. Yes, tape could be obliterated. "It's just…the whole thing is so bizarre. You're a perfect stranger."

"Perfect, yes. Stranger, no."

She laughed. "Actually, what you are is a stuck-up ass. Remind me never to confess anything of a personal nature to you again."

"I'll remind you every chance I get," he vowed, then kissed her, which was far too effective a method of quelling her indignation. "But only if you say my name."

"Ron Joffe," she sighed, then pressed her lips to his. "Ron Joffe." He touched his lips to hers. "Ron Joffe," she whispered, and the next kiss didn't end for a long, long time.

Something was going on with the girls. Sondra couldn't figure it out, and it was driving her crazy.

They'd come over for Sunday brunch, and Susie had dragged Rick along with her, insisting that he needed to be fed. He didn't look undernourished to Sondra, but he was her nephew and she couldn't very well turn him away. She supposed she ought to be happy her daughters were close to their cousins. She *would* be happy, if only those cousins didn't have to be Jay's sons.

She'd been hoping she and the girls would have brunch together, just the three of them, to discuss Bloom's, among other things. Susie was going to start revamping the windows next week—this was a big project, and Sondra wanted to make sure she knew what she was doing. If she came up with some design that was too TriBeCa or SoHo or East Village, all funky and tattooed, it would scare the store's regular customers away. Julia had assured her the new concept for the windows was going to be great, but that could have simply been Julia sticking up for her sister.

And then there was the financial stuff. Julia was turning the third floor upside down with her Sturm und Drang about the numbers not adding up. She hadn't been in business long enough to know that numbers *never* added up. No one sweated it. It was just like balancing a checkbook. If you came close, you rounded off the numbers and called it a day.

It wasn't as if Bloom's was under attack by thieves. If it were, they would have to be the most dull-witted thieves this side of Hoboken. The discrepancies amounted to pennies—maybe nickels—but the thing was, no one was talking organized crime here. A hundred bagels a week? Probably that gangly *shaygetz* Susie had the hots for was snacking on the job. Someone should talk to him—Julia, since she was the goddamn president. She should tell him to stop consuming the profits.

There. Problem solved. If Sondra were president, the whole mess would have been dispensed with by now.

Rick was eating everything within reach, despite Julia's ir-ritation that the food hadn't come from Bloom's. "I've ex-plained this, Mom—how can we sell food we don't even buy for ourselves? It's a matter of knowing and supporting what we sell, of being so in love with our merchandise that we choose to use it ourselves."

"They were having a sale on bagels down the street," Sondra explained, not wanting to go through this silly argument again.

"It's all delicious, Aunt Sondra," Rick said, and Sondra couldn't help leaning over to give his cheek a loving pat just above that scraggly little tuft of hair he called a beard. It looked like a cobweb clinging to the tip of his chin, but she was sure he considered his appearance quite sophisticated.

Susie and Julia picked at their food and didn't say it was de-licious. Sondra would be the first to admit the bagels weren't as chewy as at Bloom's—they tasted more like doughnut-shaped bread—but some habits were hard to break. For all her adult life, she had shopped down the street because she viewed Bloom's food as profit generators, not nourishment. Every bagel was worth a certain number of pennies on the bottom line. Every cup of coffee meant X amount of income for the store, and that income had paid her husband's salary and now paid Julia's salary, and Susie's fee for doing the windows.

You didn't eat profits, period.

The girls weren't eating profits or anything else. Julia had accepted Sondra's offer of a screwdriver, but Susie was drinking her orange juice straight, which was odd. Usually Julia was the teetotaler, while Susie indulged. Susie looked kind of pale, too, and Julia had color in her cheeks. It wouldn't have shocked Sondra to lift up their pant legs and discover that Susie's butterfly had flown over to Julia's ankle.

What was going on with them?

"I mean it, this food is really great," Rick said as he stabbed another slice of red onion and added it to his bagel. "I always loved eating here, Aunt Sondra. Even when we were kids, remember? I'd always come down the hall to eat here."

"I remember," Sondra said, feeling her lips purse. *Kina hora,* Jay's boys used to eat. Neil every now and then, but Rick all the time because he and Susie had been such buddies. Downstairs, upstairs, back and forth in the hall, they'd been two mischief makers, a coed, Jewish Tom Sawyer and Huck Finn. But when it was time for a snack they had inevitably wound up in her kitchen.

"You always had, like, cookies, you know? My mother never had cookies in her kitchen. She used to say refined sugar made men violent."

"That sounds like her." Martha was full of odd theories like that. Just the other day, Sondra had run into her in the compactor room and gotten stuck agreeing to have a cup of tea with her. They'd sat in Martha's Zen-temple kitchen, with weird masks of goddesses and totems hanging on the walls, and Martha had rambled for the better part of an hour about the relationship between destiny and penmanship, something to do with handwriting analysis and brain waves. Sondra hadn't really followed her—and the tea had tasted like dead grass.

"So I met the coolest guy yesterday." Rick was regaling the girls. "He used to work for CBS. Now he's an independent producer."

"Producer of what?" Sondra asked skeptically.

"Game shows," he told her, giving her such a sweet smile that she felt guilty for having questioned him. "He was involved with some of their reality programming, too, although I'm not exactly sure what he did there. So anyway, he's gone independent. He doesn't want to be stuck in some faceless bureaucracy anymore, you know?"

"In other words, they laid him off," Sondra guessed.

"No, he really wanted to leave. It was his choice. He's looking for projects to develop. We had a really good talk. I'm in his Rolodex now."

"That's great," Susie said, sipping daintily from her orange juice.

"What does that mean, you're in his Rolodex?" Sondra asked. "He's going to phone you on a regular basis?"

"It's just an expression, Aunt Sondra," Rick explained as he reached for his fourth bagel—she was counting. "He doesn't really have a Rolodex. He's got a PalmPilot."

"And you're in it?"

Rick nodded jubilantly. "Once I get a few more details put together on my film, he said he wants to see what I've got."

"That's great," Julia said, prodding the chunks of honeydew on her plate, arranging them in a lopsided circle.

"I was thinking, maybe we could celebrate some evening this week," Rick suggested. "Have you got an evening you aren't working, Susie? Maybe we could get together. You could bring Anna or Caitlin."

Susie laughed. Sondra wondered what Rick wanted with Susie's roommates. Then she figured out what Rick wanted with them, and her skepticism returned in full force. Well, they were all young and single—and Anna and Caitlin were kind of on the wild side, as far as Sondra knew. Thank God her own daughter wasn't promiscuous that way.

"Of course you could come, too, Julia. I'm just thinking, being a lawyer and an executive and all, you're probably pretty busy these days."

"Isn't that the truth," Julia said mildly. "I'm booked solid for the rest of the decade."

"You're being facetious, aren't you?" Sondra asked, annoyed by the fact that she wasn't sure. What would Julia be booked solid with? It wasn't as if she was still working at that law firm, where, if she was fortunate to have a few spare minutes when her bosses hadn't dumped more assignments on her, she was futzing around with that colleague of hers who looked like a member of the Protestant Hall of Fame. Heath, that was his name. Julia hadn't mentioned him since she'd temporarily stepped off the ladder of success at Griffin, McDougal.

It *was* temporary. Sondra understood that Julia had had to take occupancy of the corner office on the third floor for a while, to satisfy Ida and keep Jay from plugging his computer into a socket in Ben's old office. But once Ida backed off, satisfied that the store had truly survived Ben's passing, Julia would return to Griffin, McDougal and Sondra would take over Bloom's. Maybe she wouldn't relocate to Ben's office—not immediately, not as long as Ida still kept poking her nose into the business—but in time, in the not-too-distant future, they would all wind up where they were supposed to be. Julia would forget her regimen of meetings and inventory checks. Susie would do whatever god-awful thing she was going to do to the windows and then go back to her arty life downtown, writing poetry and slinging pizza until, God willing, she met a nice boy and settled down.

Sondra loved her daughters. It wasn't that she wanted to deprive them of the chance to run the family business. But neither of them had ever taken much of an interest in Bloom's. They had their own dreams, their own goals—for Julia, a partnership with a solid law firm, and for Susie, heaven only knew, but Sondra prayed it would include a healthy, handsome husband who earned enough money that Susie could stay home and write poetry and stop dressing in black all the time, as if every day was a funeral for her.

The person destined to run Bloom's was not Susie or Julia—or even Adam, although he could handle it if he wished. He didn't wish. It wasn't his dream, either.

It was *her* dream, Sondra's. Just because she was a middle-aged widow, a doting mother carrying a few extra pounds on her hips, didn't mean she wasn't entitled to have dreams. Bloom's was in her blood every bit as much as it was in the blood of people who were born into the name. She could do a better job of running the business than Julia ever could, and unlike Julia, she wouldn't always be *noodging* everyone about scheduling a meeting, locating a missing bagel or shopping at Bloom's instead of the bargain place down the block. That grocery store doubled coupons, for Chrissake. Bloom's didn't. Why should she shop at Bloom's when so many extravagant people who didn't care about double coupons were happy to spend the extra money there?

Her dream would come true soon. Julia would leave and everything would resolve itself, and maybe her daughters would truly bless her by giving her grandchildren. After they got married, of course.

It was only a matter of time before Sondra took over. And she'd do just as good a job as Ben, if not better.

"The trouble with meetings," her mother said, "is that they force us all to be in the same room. That's not such a good idea, sweetie. We all work better when we've got some distance among us."

"You're always shouting back and forth between offices," Julia argued. "With meetings, we spare everyone's vocal cords."

"I don't know that anyone needs their vocal cords spared. I've been shouting across the hall for twenty years and my cords are still vocal."

True enough. Julia wondered whether the shouting might in fact strengthen everyone's vocal cords, tempering them through constant exercise. All her relatives seemed quite adept at top-volume bellowing. "It's not like we have a meeting every day. What have we had, three? And the real reason for them," she explained, "is that it's useful to make eye contact with the person you're talking to—and listening to. It's important to view the body language, the facial expressions, and to go face-to-face with a person you might be criticizing."

"Who criticizes?" Sondra shrugged and sipped her coffee. "I never criticize. None of us does."

Julia swallowed some coffee to keep from guffawing.

Rick had left for his mother's apartment and Susie had gone to the bathroom, stranding Julia to talk shop with her mother. More accurately, to listen while her mother talked shop. Sondra clearly felt compelled to criticize her leadership style—well, no, not criticize; no one at Bloom's criticized. If asked, she'd probably say she was merely offering recommendations.

"Jay doesn't like the meetings, either. Deirdre—who the hell knows what she likes? Myron probably liked them until he realized he didn't have to sit through a meeting to get one of those pink bagels. Ida misses most of them, anyway. So what's the point?"

"The point is, there are problems at Bloom's, and they're better addressed when we're all in a room concentrating on them than if we're separated and thinking about different things."

"The only problem at Bloom's is, you think there's a problem. So a few items disappear each week. It happens in every store. Shoplifters, carelessness, lazy clerks who forget to ring up a sale—it all gets absorbed."

"This isn't just carelessness and lazy clerks, Mom. It's a hundred brunches walking out of the store every week."

"Don't be silly. Brunches can't walk."

The phone rang, rescuing Julia from a conversation she didn't want to have. As soon as her mother went to answer it, Julia rose from the table and headed down the hall. Susie was exiting the bathroom, and Julia grabbed her arm and steered her into the guest room so they could talk without Sondra present.

The guest room had once been Julia's bedroom, but when she'd left for college her mother had denuded the room more efficiently than Agent Orange. Julia had already taken her stereo system and a significant portion of her wardrobe with her to

Wellesley. That had left little for her mother to purge: Julia's stuffed animals, her collection of Far Side anthologies, her Sting poster and the lopsided throw pillow she'd sewn in a consumer studies class in seventh grade.

The room looked as characterless today as it had the day Julia had come home for Thanksgiving that first year of college. But she no longer cared. Then, she'd wept and raged and accused her parents of expunging her very existence from their home. Now, this apartment was no longer her home and Sting no longer did much for her, so she couldn't get upset about the room's bland, impersonal feel.

She peered out into the hall and heard her mother chattering on the phone—to Aunt Martha, evidently, since Sondra was providing a description of everything Rick had eaten at brunch. Aunt Martha would keep Sondra occupied for a while.

Satisfied, Julia closed the door and turned to Susie, who had flopped down across the brown futon that extended along the wall where Julia's bed once stood.

"I need your advice," Julia said.

Susie's face brightened a bit. She'd been looking rather dreary and hungover. Usually Susie sparkled, but today the shiniest thing about her was her hair. To have her big sister ask for advice seemed to pump her up.

"About the store?"

"God, no. I get all the advice I need on that from Mom." Julia sank into the canvas director's chair that faced the futon. It was, she realized, one of the least comfortable pieces of furniture in her mother's apartment. "It's about—well, men."

"Men?" Susie laughed sourly. "Like I'm such an expert."

"Compared with me, you are."

"I used to think I was. Now I'm thinking maybe I was just an idiot savant. I could dazzle people, but the truth is, I don't know nothin'."

"Which is more than I can say." Julia leaned forward. She found it easy to talk to Susie about most things, but not about men. Partly it was jealousy, partly sheer awkwardness, partly the discomfort of being the older sister and having so much less experience and wisdom than someone who'd entered the world three years after her. "I need advice about sex, actually," she said.

"You're pregnant?" Susie exclaimed, her eyes widening with what appeared to be a combination of horror and glee.

"No, of course I'm not pregnant. For God's sake, I know what a condom is."

"Okay." Susie grinned wickedly. "I'm glad I don't have to explain contraception to you. So, who's the lucky condom wearer? Big blond Heath?"

"No." Julia's neck seemed to be burning up. She expected steam to start rising from her skin any second. "It's not Heath. It's not anyone I—well, *know.*"

"Wait a minute." Susie sat upright, her eyes growing impossibly wider. "You had sex with a stranger?"

"Not a complete stranger." A *perfect stranger,* she thought, recalling the way Joffe had claimed he was perfect but not a stranger. "We'd met a couple of times, and then I just…"

"You just what?" Susie asked breathlessly.

"I went back to his place."

Susie subsided. What had seemed perilously out of character and high-risk to Julia didn't excite her jaded sister. "Okay. It's not the end of the world."

"Well, we had sex more than once."

"Uh-huh."

"Several times." Julia sighed. "More than several."

"How many?"

"A lot."

"When did this happen?"

"Friday night."

"And what happened Saturday?"

"We had sex again. More than several times."

Susie let out a hushed cheer. "Way to go, Julia! This guy must be hot. Is he good-looking?"

"Of course he is!" Did Susie think Julia would have gone to bed with someone she didn't find attractive?

"And he's good in bed?"

"That's the thing, Susie. I just..." A thin film of sweat formed under her chin. "I'm not used to having this much sex."

"With a nearly complete stranger." Susie assessed the situation, shook her head and chuckled. "He's that good, huh?"

"He was very good."

"So what do you need my advice for? Sounds like you're doing a hell of a lot better than I am."

Julia hardly thought so. What had occurred Friday night and well into Saturday with Joffe was what she imagined occurred to Susie all the time, and Susie undoubtedly handled it with a lot more savoir faire. "The thing is, I don't know how I feel about the whole thing. I guess that's where I need advice. How am I supposed to feel about this?"

"Replete?" Susie suggested. "Fulfilled? Fucked?"

"Stop." Julia felt the heat rise into her cheeks.

"If he were chocolate, what would he be?"

"Chocolate? What are you talking about?"

"Never mind." Susie jiggled her foot and fingered one of her silver hoop earrings. "Enjoy it, Julia. Don't get all hung up. Have fun. You're allowed. You and Mr. Condom should screw yourselves silly. Why not?"

"I don't...I don't love him," Julia struggled to explain. "I mean—maybe someday I could love him. He's very lovable. He's got a good job, and he's literate, and he's age-appropriate—"

"Age-appropriate?" Susie struggled against a laugh. "So he isn't some teenage stud you picked up?"

"No."

"Or a silver-haired sugar daddy?"

"I think he's around thirty. We never got that specific."

"Okay. So you're getting off on him, and maybe someday you'll fall in love with him. Where's the problem?"

"I'm not in love with him now."

Susie shook her head again. "Who cares? I've slept with guys I wasn't in love with, and it hasn't made my hair fall out or my soul turn black like Madame Bovary's. In fact, I've gotten a lot of good poetry out of those relationships."

"I'm not a poet."

"Then, you'll get some prose out of it. Maybe a limerick or two. 'There once was a fellow named Condom, And sex with him was kind of *rahn*dom…'"

"Stop!" Julia giggled. "His name isn't Condom."

"What's his name?"

"Ron Joffe."

"The reporter from *Gotham*?" At Julia's nod, Susie hooted, "Way to go! All right. There once was a fellow named Joffe, Who was more stimulating than coffee…"

"I don't want to hear the rest."

"You'll have to," Susie declared. "I'm on a roll." She pondered for a moment, then resumed: "He made Julia climax, Like clockwork, a Timex, And instead of chocolate, he was toffee."

"Why do you keep mentioning chocolate?" Julia asked.

"Because I'm chocolate deprived." Susie sighed dolefully. "Look at me. Do I look like I've lost weight?"

"No, but you do look like shit. Are you coming down with something?"

"Terminal horniness. I'm living like a nun, Julia. It's horrible. A Jewish nun, can you imagine?"

"I live like a nun most of the time. It's not so horrible," Julia argued—although now that she'd had a taste of the non-nun's life, she wondered if she would find celibacy debilitating. After all of one night—and most of the next day—had she become a sex addict? Was it like heroin or cocaine, where one hit was enough to hook a woman for life?

What if the more she got to know of Joffe, the less she liked him? What if she found out he was a jerk? What if he published nasty things about the Bloom family in *Gotham*? What if he hadn't asked her to call him as soon as she got home from her mother's, so they could make arrangements to spend Sunday night together? What if a day came when he vanished from her life?

She'd survive. She was sure she didn't love him. But now that she'd had a taste of really, really good sex… More than a taste—she'd been a glutton. What would she do if her supply of Joffe dried up and she could never indulge like this again? Would she end up as dreary and glum as Susie was now?

"I thought you were seeing What's-His-Name, the bagel guy. Casey."

"I am seeing him," Susie said. "One minute at a time. Don't ask, Julia—it's really pathetic."

Julia conceded with a shrug. But mentioning Casey pulled her mind in another direction. "You see Casey every now and then?"

"Not often enough. I'm working on your damn windows and putting in my hours at Nico's. We've been taking breaks together when I'm at the store, but still, it's been frustrating."

"Well, listen." Julia sat forward again, wondering if what she was about to ask Susie would be even harder to articulate than her questions about sex. "We're missing bagels."

"What bagels?"

"At the store. Nearly a hundred and fifty bagels disappear from Bloom's every week. And some other things, too—cream cheese, coffee, brunch foods in general. Mom thinks I'm making a big deal about nothing. Myron has gone over the books and can't figure it out. No one seems to care about this but me."

"And…? You think Casey should care about it?"

"I haven't discussed it with him," Julia admitted. "I don't know him, and I don't want to come across as the demanding boss lady when I've been in the job less than two months. I thought, since you know him better than I do, maybe you could see if he's had anything to do with the disappearing bagels. I'm not saying you should accuse him or anything—"

"Accuse him? You think he's stealing a hundred and fifty bagels a week?" Susie bristled with righteous anger.

"I have no idea who's doing what. But he works in the bagel department. Maybe he knows something. Do you think you could maybe feel him out about it? Casually."

"Oh, sure. I could casually say, 'Casey, where the fuck are all the bagels?'"

"You could use a nicer vocabulary."

Susie scowled. She swung her foot and gazed toward the window, which was filled with the murky light of an overcast noon. "Maybe I could talk to him," she finally said. "Only because it would add a few more minutes."

"A few more minutes to what?"

Susie pushed away from the soft cushion of the futon. "You wouldn't understand," she said as she crossed to the door and swung it open. "You're getting sex."

Julia watched her sister depart but remained in the director's chair. From down the hall she heard the lilt of her mother's voice; Sondra was still on the phone. She closed her eyes and reviewed her conversation with Susie: the limerick, the reassurances, the bagel stuff, the chocolate references.

A lot of it didn't make sense—but then, Julia rarely turned to her sister when she wanted things to make sense.

Susie made sense about one thing, anyway. Julia was getting sex.

15

Susie dared to be hopeful. Today was Monday, and she'd convinced Casey that they should spend next Saturday together. She would trek out to Forest Hills, where he lived, and kill some time with him there, and then they'd ride the subway—at least a half hour together in transit, probably closer to forty-five minutes—to her downtown neighborhood for dinner and a movie. She had in mind a midnight flick, because that would mean a whole bunch more hours in each other's company. By the time the movie ended, it would be too late for him to travel all the way back to Queens alone, so she would insist that he spend the night at her place. He wouldn't be able to accuse her of plotting a seduction, since Anna and Caitlin would be around. But hours were hours. If she and Casey both slept in the living room, it ought to count toward the final tally.

By her calculation, they'd spent at least five hours together so far. Every day she had come to Bloom's to contemplate the windows and the store's general appearance, she'd shared a lunch break with him, shadowed him to the basement kitchen when he went downstairs to restock the inventory, ridden the elevator with him and talked. Those minutes added up—excruciatingly slowly, but tick by tick, tock by tock, the time was accumulating.

He hadn't kissed her again, thank God. He'd already established himself as a heterosexual, and given how they'd both responded to that one kiss, she knew another kiss would either lead to something more or, more likely, leave her hating him because the kiss *hadn't* led to something more. That he'd kissed her once and then walked away had infuriated her. If he did it again, she'd hate him.

Maybe she already hated him. She wasn't sure. She could easily hate him for putting her off. No man had ever strung her along like this before. She'd had men say no to her, and she'd handled rejection without tears or trauma. But Casey *hadn't* rejected her. He wanted her, maybe even as much as she wanted him, which made his refusal to let them do what they both wanted incredibly frustrating.

But also intriguing. What kind of guy said no when he wanted to say yes? What kind of guy would put both the woman and himself through this kind of torture? As much as she might hate Casey, she had to admit he fascinated her. And she still wanted to screw him senseless.

To her amazement, she also wanted to spend time with him. Twenty hours was a ridiculously arbitrary goal, but in the meantime, she was getting to know him. All those minutes they'd spent together not having sex, they'd wound up talking. In the elevator or sipping coffee from steaming cardboard cups in the tiny staff lounge on the second floor, Susie had chattered to keep from jumping him. She'd peppered him with questions, and he'd answered every one. He'd told her about his father, an electrician, and his mother, a school bus driver, and his sister, a dog groomer. He'd told her he'd attended the Culinary Institute of America for a year because he enjoyed working with food, but then he'd decided becoming a chef or running a restaurant would mean wretched working hours and too much stress, so he'd transferred to St. John's University and taken a degree in English. English! He liked poetry, even if his first love was food.

He was funny. He knew dozens of jokes that began "A man walks into a bar." He was a regular in a neighborhood basketball game on Thursday nights. The other regulars were all friends of his from high school. He listened to Pearl Jam, Frank Zappa and late Beatles albums, when the group had gone druggy-experimental. Art museums bored him, he was a terrible dancer and he preferred the sports reporter on channel four to the one on channel two. Oh, and he thought that *charoseth* stuff he'd eaten at Grandma Ida's seder was incredible and it was a shame that Jews ate it only during Passover and not throughout the year.

Susie couldn't believe she'd learned so much about him and they hadn't even seen each other naked. Sometimes he would touch her—a pat on the arm, a brush of his hand against hers—and she'd react all out of proportion, her body sizzling as if he'd lit a fuse inside her. When their twenty hours were finally up and they tore off their clothes, she'd probably explode.

In the meantime, she loathed him. But sooner or later, maybe Sunday morning after their Saturday marathon, she and Casey were going to take this thing to the explosion level.

She tried not to think about him as she stood, armed with several bags full of polyurethaned bagels and a pile of signs containing clever sayings, in the newly empty showcase window facing Broadway. She'd decided each window would focus on a different product. The first would have the theme "Eat Your Bagels." The second would have the theme "A Life Without Gadgets Is Not Worth Living." The third would be "Coffee: Nectar of the Gods"; the fourth, "Staff of Life, Stuff of Dreams." Only the first window had been emptied out so far. The rest remained jammed with Bloom's clutter, a multitude of products jumbled together without any organizing principle. A kosher garage sale.

She'd get them worked out soon. Today bagels, tomorrow the world.

Pedestrians on Broadway paused to watch her through the glass. She could feel their eyes on her even when she had her back to the street. Down at Nico's, whenever she changed the windows, she attracted an audience of neighborhood folks— guys with nose rings, girls with green hair, the usual. At Bloom's, the onlookers were Upper West Side types—well- toned intellectuals clad in Banana Republic and Birkenstocks, carrying PBS and Lincoln Center tote bags. The afternoon was sunny and Broadway was teeming with pedestrians.

Susie ignored them.

Sitting cross-legged on the floor, she sorted through her signs. She'd picked them up from the printer that morning and shown them to Casey while they'd eaten lunch in the lounge— a chunk of Havarti and a box of stoned wheat crackers which he'd purchased using the employee discount that Julia had in- stituted to encourage Bloom's workers to partake of the food they sold. "You're the bagel expert," she'd asserted after he stud- ied all the signs. "What do you think?"

"Some are funnier than others," he'd said. "I like this one— 'A bagel saved is a bagel earned.' It's just the right amount silly."

"I was going to print one that said 'It's better to steal a bagel than to waste one,' but I thought people might see that as an invitation to rob Bloom's."

"We wouldn't want that," Casey had agreed solemnly, al- though his eyes were full of laughter. Such beautiful eyes, she'd thought. Hershey's Kisses eyes, only green. "Of course, it would be hard to steal the bagels, given that they're all in bins behind glass. Whoever is behind the counter has to get the bagels for the customer. They can't just help themselves."

"They could still steal a bagel. You could give them one, and they could hide it in their pocket and walk out without pay- ing for it."

"Yeah, I guess. But they can't just lift one without me or Morty noticing."

"Is there much theft in the store?" she'd asked casually. She hadn't wanted to pump him for information, but Julia was hung up about the missing bagels, and Susie was a good sister. If she could solve the mystery, she'd be the heroine of the Bloom family, and Julia could move on to other obsessions.

Casey had shrugged. "All I know is the bagel department. And I don't do the final tallies. Morty does that. I'm more of the quality control guy. He's the quantity control guy."

Susie had abandoned the subject. Casey wasn't stealing the bagels. He didn't even seem aware that they were being stolen— if, in fact, they were. It was always possible someone was making the wrong calculations on all those printouts Julia pored over. Maybe Morty couldn't count. Maybe when a bagel fell it rolled away like a tire, and there were hundreds of forgotten, petrified bagels lying in some dark corner under a shelf, like one of those tire dumps that occasionally caught on fire, causing stinky black smoke to plume into the air and making Susie wonder why piles of old tires wound up in segregated dumps rather than being mixed up with other garbage in more ecumenical dumps.

She lifted the first sign, the one Casey had judged just the right amount silly, and strung fish line through the hole at the top. Then she stood, looped the clear plastic string over one of the metal beams in the center of the window alcove and tied the string in a knot. The sign would remain readable even if it rotated, because she'd had the slogans printed on both sides.

Threading another sign, she felt someone staring through the glass at her—not just pausing to watch her for a minute but really staring, as if transfixed. She glanced over her shoulder and saw him. Dark brown hair, an angular face, a lopsided smile, a lean body. Neat blue jeans, a white shirt and an old, out-of-shape tweed blazer. Battered leather sneakers, no tie.

Not bad. Not Casey, but not bad.

Shrugging, she strung up the second sign, adjusting the fish line to alter the height. "A bagel a day keeps the doctor away," it read. Once she had all eight signs hung, she'd spread the polyurethaned bagels all around the showcase. She hadn't worked out the arrangement yet; she was a word person, not a visual person. But she hoped inspiration would strike her when it came time to do something with the bagels.

Bending to lift a third sign, she glimpsed the dark-haired man still outside the window, still watching her, his posture relaxed and his hands in the front pockets of his jeans. How long was he planning to stand out there ogling her? Sure, he was cute and she was flattered, but five minutes was way longer than any sane person should waste observing her while she did this. His presence on the other side of the glass was beginning to get creepy.

She wished she could ignore him. But he was only a couple of feet away from her, and his unwavering gaze was like a spotlight—even if she couldn't see it, she could feel its heat between her shoulder blades. Maybe she ought to ask Casey to go outside and have a few words with the guy. Not only was Casey taller than him, but going to the bagel department to tell Casey about the guy would add a few more minutes to the time-o-meter.

Pestering him about a curious pedestrian just to bulk up her time with him didn't seem fair, though. Besides, Casey was working, and boss Julia could get pissed if Susie pulled him away from his job only so she could move a little closer to having sex with him. Sooner or later, the weirdo outside the window would grow bored and go away. She ought to pretend he wasn't there.

She hung the fourth sign, the fifth, the last three. Each was at a different height, some closer to the glass and some farther from it, to give a staggered appearance. Before she started with the bagels, she needed to see how they looked from the street.

After climbing down from the window into the store, she stretched her limbs, then jogged past the cashiers and out the main door. The traffic noises and the slightly sour scent of the outside air wrapped around her and filtered through her brain, refreshing her.

She moved down the sidewalk to the window—and the weirdo was still there, staring at the signs and chuckling. As she neared him, he turned to her and smiled.

She could run, she could scream, she could kick his shins black and blue—but he looked pretty harmless, even without the barrier of glass to protect her. "You must be Susie," he said, which simultaneously reassured and alarmed her. Either he knew her somehow or he was a stalker. If he recited her social security number, she'd definitely start kicking.

"I'm Ron Joffe," he said, extending his right hand. "I write for *Gotham Magazine*. Julia told me she'd hired you to redo the windows."

The reporter. The guy Julia was sleeping with. Okay.

She shook his hand and nodded, resisting the impulse to wink and smirk. "When is that article coming out, anyway? Everybody's dying to read it."

"Soon," he said vaguely. He really was kind of cute. Not her type—he had to be at least thirty, which as far as she was concerned was too old to be age-appropriate, as Julia would put it—but not bad.

She pivoted to look at the window. The signs were readable, although she'd have to check in the morning, when the sun hit the windows, to make sure the glare on the glass didn't obscure them.

He pivoted to study the window, too. "They're funny, but the window looks pretty barren."

"It's not finished," she told him, wondering whether this conversation, held against the buffeting noise of cars and buses and the jostling of passersby, was going to wind up in *Gotham Magazine*. "Don't judge it until it's done."

"Well," he said. His hands were back in his pockets, giving his shoulders an amiably slouchy shape. "I've got to see your sister. I'm glad we had a chance to meet."

That was it? Her grand interview? Her moment in the media spotlight? Big whoop. She'd be lucky to merit a subordinate clause in his article.

The signs in the window looked all right, at least. Maybe she should go inside and drag Casey out to the sidewalk to get his input. She'd told the magazine reporter it wasn't fair to judge the window until she'd finished with it, but if she fetched Casey and brought him outside, it would chip a few more minutes off the twenty-hour block.

Grinning, she headed into the store to find him.

Ron actually did have business to discuss with Julia. He'd brought her a tear sheet of his rough draft so she could review it. The story wasn't done yet—that morning, he'd talked to a chatty teller at the bank that handled most of Bloom's business, and he hadn't yet incorporated information from that conversation into the piece. And he'd sure as hell like to hear more from Julia about whether she thought her business was hemorrhaging or just trickling blood.

The weekend they'd spent together had complicated matters. He hadn't actually believed that screwing Julia would bring him closer to his story—but even if he had, he discovered that he possessed too much integrity to exploit their intimacy. One of the systems that Julia had succeeded in short-circuiting inside him was the one that said, "The story is the only thing that matters."

Julia mattered. The way she moved, breathed, laughed and came mattered. Last night they'd made love on the living room floor and in the shower, and then she'd tried going down on him. It had been clear she'd never done that before, but her ineptitude had excited him more than any skilled female mouth might have. He'd returned the favor, with a bit more proficiency, and by the time she was done moaning, she seemed so exposed, so vulnerable, he couldn't possibly say afterward, "So, Julia, can you give me a ballpark figure on how much money Bloom's is losing per annum?"

But he did have to talk to her today. He probably should have phoned her to talk, and faxed her the tear sheet, but he was enough of a fool to grab any opportunity to see her. He'd keep his hands in his pockets and his tongue inside his mouth, and maybe they'd get through a conversation without locking lips or bodies.

He waited until her sister, Susie, had gone back into the store, then strolled around the corner to the Bloom Building entrance and took the elevator up to the third floor.

Emerging into the broad hallway that connected the offices, he saw Jay Bloom practicing his putts on the carpet. The Bloom's executive lined up his putter, wiggled one elbow and tapped the ball, which rolled smoothly across the floor and into a tumbler lying on its side. Jay punched the air triumphantly, crossed to the glass to retrieve his ball, and turned to see Ron looming at the end of the hallway.

Jay had the good grace to appear abashed. "Hi," he said, straightening up and adjusting the collar of his shirt. "You're..."

"Ron Joffe. *Gotham Magazine,*" Ron prompted him.

"Right. I knew you looked familiar." He grinned and bent again to pick up the glass. "Just loosening up a little. Spend too much time slaving over a computer, and you can get pretty stiff."

"Isn't that the truth," Ron said, recalling that his initial impression of Julia's uncle Jay was that he was a boob. The past two minutes had done nothing to change Ron's opinion. But he viewed the man with gratitude. Boobs were often the best sources for a story. They didn't have enough sense to comprehend how much they were giving a reporter.

Ron was aware Julia was behind the door at the other end of the hall. His emotional radar sensed her nearness, beeping and blipping like a screen in the control tower at LaGuardia. But once he saw her, he wasn't going to want to talk to Uncle Jay or anyone else for the rest of the day.

Better to pump the uncle first, see what he could find out, then invade her office and test the limits of his self-control. "Have you got a few minutes?" he asked Jay. "Maybe we could talk."

"Sure," Jay replied, adjusting his posture in a preening way.

When he beckoned Ron to follow him into his office, Ron smiled, reached for his notepad and felt his journalist juices start to flow.

Julia stared at the man before her and decided she would have to institute a new policy: no visitors without appointments. "What are you doing here?" she asked, trying to keep her tone free of the vexation she felt at his invasion of her office.

He flicked a lock of hair off his forehead and grinned. "Just wanted to see what was so enticing about this place that you'd give up your life at Griffin, McDougal to sell sauerkraut."

"I don't sell sauerkraut," she explained steadily, her gaze circling the office. Granted, most company presidents had more elegant surroundings. They featured plusher carpets, cleaner windows, fancier sofas and no abandoned old furniture occupying valuable square footage. But her office at Bloom's was an infinite improvement over the glorified cubicle she'd been assigned at the law firm, and Heath's imperious smile irked her.

He propped one hip on the corner of her desk and peered down at her as if she were his underling. "I had to visit a client at the Dakota and I thought, since I was in the neighborhood, hey, why not stop by and see how Jules is doing?"

"I'm doing fine," she told him, again struggling to remain cordial. She used to date him, after all. She used to watch him eat sushi. She owed him courtesy, at the very least.

But he seemed like an alien to her, a relic from a life she could scarcely remember. In his Armani suit and his Bally tasseled loafers, with his burnished blue-blood features, he didn't fit into the world of Bloom's. Sure, he'd fit in downstairs, where the clientele included everyone from Fortune 500 CEOs to recent parolees from Sing Sing. But Heath was terribly out of place on the third floor, where the majority of Bloom's executives were Blooms, and screaming at one another from office to office was the preferred mode of communication.

"Your desk is still empty at Griffin, McDougal," he reported, which flattered her until he continued. "Obviously, they're waiting to find a replacement until May, when they'll have a new crop of law school graduates to choose from." In other words, she was replaceable by someone fresh out of law school.

Perhaps she was. Only someone fresh out of school, as she'd been when the firm had hired her, would be willing to put up with their draconian hours and demands—which, she had to admit, weren't so different from the hours she put in at Bloom's or the demands of her family. But the store needed her attention right now, and her family would be bugging her whether or not she worked at Bloom's.

"I'm happy here," she said, startling herself. It was the first time she'd actually expressed such a sentiment. She wasn't even sure it was true. As her mother might say, what was to be happy? She had to mediate between her mother and Uncle Jay, with their thwarted ambitions and unthwarted jealousies, and chisel away at Deirdre, who did everything she was supposed to but never revealed a hint of feeling, let alone an opinion, and jostle Myron, who had grown so addicted to cranberry bagels she expected to barge into his office one day and find him sniffing pink crumbs through a rolled-up hundred-dollar bill. Her mother hated Susie's window concepts, Jay bristled at Deirdre's unearthly efficiency, Myron criticized Jay's long lunches, Susie sulked about Grandma Ida's disapproval of her and everyone despised Julia for some reason or other.

How could she possibly be happy?

Yet she was, in some perverse, indefinable way. For the first time in months, she actually awakened before her alarm buzzed. More often than not, she had a Bloom's bialy for breakfast, instead of a stale doughnut, and she wore outfits she chose because they were comfortable, not because they made her look like partner material. She filled her Bloom's mug with Bloom's coffee each morning before coming upstairs to her office, where she spent her days engaged in trying to figure out how to beef up some departments and perk up others, how to maintain peace among the warring Blooms and how to improve the anemic bottom line. It wasn't what she'd been trained to do, what her entire education had been geared toward, what she'd dreamed of when she'd lain in bed at night, thinking, *Just because I'm a Bloom doesn't mean I'm doomed to give my life to the store, the way my parents and my uncle and my grandmother did.*

"Yes," she said, astonishment coloring her voice. "I'm happy here."

Heath appeared nonplussed. "I browsed through your deli, and—I mean, Jules, it's food. Ethnic food. A lot of it is the sort of stuff your people came over here to escape."

"I think my people came over here to escape the pogroms and Hitler, not to escape the food."

"You know what I mean."

Unfortunately, she did. She stared up at him, still seated proprietarily on her desk, and wondered what his attraction had been. He was bright, he was handsome, he was accomplished and he wore an Armani suit very well—none of which explained his appeal. What she'd seen in him was that he'd been the anti-Bloom. At one time, she'd thought escaping the insidious bonds of the family was more important than anything else. Neil had escaped by fleeing to Florida; Susie by tattooing her ankle; Adam by hiding out at Cornell, listening to Phish and fantasizing about becoming a math professor; Rick by making himself endearingly useless.

She'd tried to do it by becoming a lawyer and dating a colleague whom she'd never wanted to have sex with because she felt no charge in his company, no zing, nothing but anti-Bloom-ness.

Scrutinizing Heath, she realized that she could not picture him eating heat-n-eat blintzes or kasha varnishkes from the hot food counter downstairs. She couldn't even imagine him attending a seder at Grandma Ida's. She'd witnessed him eating sushi, Thai cuisine, stir-fry, quesadillas, coq au vin, paella, moussaka and sauerbraten. But she'd never seen him eat a bagel and lox. And she never would. That had once been his greatest attraction. Now it was his greatest shortcoming.

And there was that other thing, too, she acknowledged

when, all of a sudden, thanks to the absence of a policy banning unannounced visitors, she heard a tap on her open office door and turned to find Ron Joffe standing on the threshold.

Passion. Yearning. Plain old guilty lust. Memories of everything they'd done to each other during the past few days caused heat to rise to her cheeks. Oh God—had she really used her mouth on him *there?*

Not only had she, but she'd do it again, in an instant, just to feel him shudder with the kind of helplessness she felt whenever he touched her. Right here, in her office, if he wanted, she'd do it. He obviously had the power to turn her brain as well as her knees to jelly.

She struggled to keep from sighing. The sound of Heath clearing his throat prompted her to impersonate a sane, composed adult. She pushed her chair away from her desk and rose. "Hi," she greeted Joffe in an artificially calm voice. "What are you doing here?"

Joffe eyed Heath, who reluctantly stood, as well. After a minute, Joffe steered his dark eyes back to her. "I've got something to show you—but you're busy right now. I should have called."

"No, that's all right. Come in." What did he want to show her? Would it require her to shut and lock the office door? She hoped so.

Heath cleared his throat again.

Shaking her head to dispel the steamy thoughts Joffe's mere presence stirred up, she said, "Ron Joffe, this is a former colleague of mine, Heath Blodgett. Heath, this is…Ron Joffe." She wasn't sure how to introduce him. A reporter? A lover? A man poised to humiliate her family in the pages of *Gotham Magazine?* A guy who did things with his tongue that she really shouldn't be remembering at a time like this?

Joffe and Heath shook hands in a show of macho camaraderie. Then they sized each other up, all traces of camaraderie gone. Heath had an inch or two on Joffe, but Joffe's nose and chin were better defined. Heath's apparel was probably worth ten times what Joffe's had cost. Joffe's shoulders were broader. Heath ate raw squid. Joffe was born to love pastrami on rye.

Julia had never wanted to have sex with Heath. Just looking at Joffe caused her to overdose on her own hormones. "Heath was just leaving," she announced.

He shot her a glare, then acquiesced with a bitter smile. "Your office at Griffin, McDougal isn't going to stay empty forever," he reminded her.

"I know."

"Think long and hard, Jules. Mid-May the hordes descend. Push is coming to shove."

"I know. It's so thoughtful of you to warn me."

"Nice meeting you," Joffe said helpfully. When his gaze intersected with hers, he flashed her a conspiratorial grin. She pressed her lips together to keep from smiling back.

Heath looked uncharacteristically uncertain. He planted a hesitant kiss on her cheek, mumbled something about being in touch and left the office, far more tentative than anyone in Armani should be.

Joffe watched through the open doorway for a minute, as if checking to make sure Heath didn't change his mind and return, and then he shut the door.

Good. Maybe he was going to show her something obscene. She couldn't believe she was thinking that way.

It didn't matter. She *was* thinking that way, and she circled her desk and approached Joffe with one thing on her mind.

He had something else on his mind. "A boyfriend?" he asked, angling his head toward the door.

"A lawyer I used to work with at Griffin, McDougal."

He eyed her skeptically. "None of my business, right?"

"He was almost a boyfriend," she conceded. "He never quite made it all the way." In any sense, she added silently.

"It's none of my business," Joffe repeated, as she rose on tiptoe to kiss him.

He moved his lips against hers briefly, then drew back. "Don't," he whispered. "I came to your office so we could talk."

"But you closed the door."

"I'm ambivalent." He covered her mouth with his, nipped at her lower lip, then pulled away. "You free tonight?"

"Probably."

"Okay." One more kiss, and he took a step backward. "I brought you a tear sheet of the article. I thought you could check it for spellings and stuff."

"What, do I look like a secretary?" She wasn't even sure what a tear sheet was, but she'd be damned if she was going to proof-read his article for spelling errors. "Doesn't your computer have a spell-check function?"

"People's names don't get picked up by spell-check."

"Like Bloom is such a difficult name to spell." She laughed to take the edge off her words. She was actually thrilled to have a chance to read his article before it went into print. If it was embarrassing, she could persuade him to tone things down. If it implied Bloom's was financially shaky, she could beg him to concentrate on Bloom's being a New York fixture, indispensable to the city's sense of itself. She could remind him of how often tour buses stopped at its front door so people from all over the world could browse and shop. She could make sure he emphasized how superior their merchandise was. Even if it wasn't a puff piece, she could convince him to puff it up a little.

He pulled a folded sheaf of papers from an inner pocket of his jacket and handed them to her. "Here it is. Have a look."

She carried them to her grandfather's old desk. For some reason, the new desk seemed tainted, now that Heath had sat on it. She didn't want to go near it until any molecules Heath left behind had dissipated.

She hoisted herself onto the desk, the way Susie always sat on it, and started to read the computer printout of the article: "Bloom's is to New York City what the Louvre is to Paris or Beefeaters are to London: not just a symbol but a distillation of a city's essence. When we think of New York, we think of the generations of immigrants who brought their culture here and made it their home, who built this city and continue to build it today. We think of food—not just tasty, nourishing food but food that represents the values those waves of immigrants brought with them when they settled here. Bloom's is a place filled with your grandmother's food and her values, the recipes she carried in her heart when she landed at Ellis Island."

"Wow." Julia's eyes clouded with tears. She glanced up to find Joffe at the window, viewing the Broadway traffic through the dingy glass. He turned at the sound of her voice. "This is beautiful."

He chuckled. "It gets worse."

"I don't care. It starts out great."

"You're not crying, are you?" He frowned.

"No." A fat tear skittered down her cheek, making a liar out of her.

He crossed to the desk. "Hey, if it's going to get you all upset—"

"I'm a big girl, Joffe. Let me read it." She lowered her gaze to the papers, but another tear slid down her cheek and dropped off her chin, hitting the top page and creating a blot.

He pulled the article from her hand, used his thumb to tilt her face up and peered into her watery eyes. "I'm not that good a writer, Julia. What's the problem? PMS?"

"Why do men always assume that if a woman gets emotional she's got PMS?"

"Because nine times out of ten, we're right."

"You're an ass."

"Yeah." He grinned. His hand was still tucked under her chin and his face was so close it seemed like a waste not to kiss him. This time he didn't pull away. He returned the kiss, deepened it, stood between her legs and lifted them around his hips. Her body shimmered and tensed. He was working his magic again, and she welcomed it. She didn't have PMS, but her emotions were raw, right on the surface. She'd just experienced an epiphany about her life and her future. She didn't want to go back to practicing law. She wanted to stay at Bloom's. There were things more important than escaping her destiny, and one of them was embracing her destiny.

For the moment, Joffe seemed to be part of her destiny. She'd cried in front of him—well, not really cried, just shed a couple of tears—and he'd accepted those tears. He'd teased her about them, but he was kissing her, wasn't he? Comforting her and stroking her back and moving his hips against her crotch in such a way that she not only didn't forget why she'd been crying but recognized him as part of the reason. He'd captured Bloom's in his article. He understood it. And he was so wonderfully sexy, and he made her feel sexy even when she'd never thought of herself as sexy before, and she knew she looked shitty right now because she always looked shitty when she cried, and he understood.

The desk vibrated beneath her as he leaned his weight into it, as he rocked his body against hers. He lifted his leg, using his knee to rub her inner thigh, and she moaned softly. She wanted him. The door was closed, and he'd written beautiful, brilliant things about Bloom's, and she wanted him.

He moved his knee against her thigh again, and his foot banged against one of the drawers. "Ow," he muttered against her mouth.

"Are you okay?" she whispered.

"Um...no." He leaned back and wavered slightly, balanced on his left foot. "My shoe is stuck."

She unwrapped her legs from around him, smoothed her bunched up skirt across her lap and peeked over the edge of the desk. The toe of his sneaker was jammed into the handle of one of the side drawers. She laughed.

"It's not funny." He wobbled and gripped the desk to keep from falling. "Get my foot out of the sneaker, would you? It's hurting my ankle."

Stifling her giggles, she reached over the edge of the desk and tugged on the sneaker's laces. They came undone and she loosened them. He wiggled his foot back and forth to free it, and she heard a rattling noise.

"There's something inside," he said, tossing his sneaker to the floor. "Did you hear it?"

Julia nodded. She almost wished she hadn't. She wanted to go back to kissing him, or reading his article, or pondering her revelation about being happy working here.

"Don't you want to find out what it is?" he pressed her.

"If it's my grandfather's bones, no."

"Come on—where's your spirit of adventure?"

"It was busy kissing you," she said, watching with misgivings as he shoved his foot back into his sneaker and then dug in his pocket. He pulled out a pocketknife and pried loose the awl. "What are you going to do?"

"Pick the lock," he said.

"What if I tell you not to?"

Frowning, he stared at her. "Don't you want to open it?"

"I—I don't know." One minute ago she'd felt daring, liberated, ready to plunge into an unknowable future. But now... Now she was apprehensive, and she didn't know why.

"How about if you leave the room while I pick the lock? If there are any bones in it, I'll shut it and lock it again so you won't have to see them."

"Those weren't bones," she said, attempting a smile and failing. Whatever was in there had sounded small and light. It was probably something no more sinister than an old chewing gum wrapper. But it had been in there for so long. No one had used the desk since her father died. Maybe even since long before he died.

Joffe was already poking at the lock on the center drawer with his pocketknife. Julia took a deep breath. She wanted to be strong and tough and mature. She wanted to be a leader, a president, the person who'd catapult Bloom's into the twenty-first century. Surely she could handle the contents of the old desk.

"Easy," he cautioned himself, maneuvering the awl attachment deftly, sliding it in and out of the keyhole in a way that struck Julia as erotic. She climbed down from the desk and took more deep breaths, trying hard to regain her equilibrium. "Okay…okay… There it is." She heard a click, and he pulled out the center drawer.

It was empty. She sighed, far more relieved than she should have been.

"No bones," he announced, reaching for the top right-hand drawer and opening it. It contained a pencil stub and an old pink eraser. "There are your bones."

Her heartbeat returned to normal. Her body heat subsided to a healthy range. "A pencil."

"And an eraser." He pulled out the items, felt inside the drawer to see if there was anything else, then shut it. Then he pulled out the second drawer. "Empty," he reported.

Her cheeks relaxed into a natural smile. Emboldened, she hunkered down and yanked open the bottom drawer—and let out a yelp. "Oh!"

"What?" He knelt beside her and peered.

There, lying inside the otherwise empty drawer, was a box of condoms.

16

Ron was all in favor of getting at the truth—hell, he wouldn't be much of a journalist if he didn't believe in searching for facts in the darkest corners and turning a bright light on them. While he'd decided that the facts of Ben Bloom's sex life didn't belong in an article in *Gotham Magazine,* he believed that, in general, most people were better off knowing the truth about things.

But finding a box of rubbers in the bottom drawer of a desk in her late father's office was probably not a good way for Julia to learn that her father had spent time in his office doing the horizontal tango with someone who wasn't her mother.

She lifted the box out of the drawer, tilted it and read the tiny print on the side flap. Was she trying to figure out when the box had been purchased, based on the expiration date? He'd never had a package of condoms lying around unused long enough to find out what happened after they were a year old, but that was another story.

Mere minutes ago, she'd been reduced to tears by the opening paragraph of his article. That guy in her office when he himself had arrived had cranked up her emotions, too. And the hot bout of kissing they'd just engaged in couldn't have had a calming effect on her. So she probably wasn't in the right mood right now—as if there was ever a right mood to be in when you stumbled onto evidence of your father's hanky-panky.

Still holding the box, she moved to the sofa and sank onto it. He scrambled to figure out what his role in this scene was supposed to be. Providing comfort, he guessed. Hugging, but not kissing. A gentle arm around her, a shoulder to lean on, an ear to absorb her furious ranting.

He doubted that telling her about his chat that afternoon with her uncle Jay would improve her spirits. The guy had babbled like one of those New Age tabletop fountains on high speed. Bloom's wasn't in major trouble, according to Jay, but it was in minor trouble, and the reason was that its current leader, Jay's precious and beloved niece, for whom Jay had all the respect in the world, was so hung up on the trees that she was unable to see the forest. This was Bloom's basic problem, according to Jay: the company needed a president who could see the big picture. Ben had been a big-picture guy, but he had passed on, and no one but Jay possessed that same panoramic vision, the same reach, the same global perspective on how to sell delicatessen delicacies to the masses. According to Jay, Julia was plagued by bagel counts when there were entire worlds to conquer. Jay knew how to conquer them, thanks to his Internet-savvy approach to marketing and promotion. Julia thought like a lawyer, he'd explained, which meant she was always looking for the tiny mistake that could turn an argument inside out. None of which was to say he didn't adore his niece and think she was wonderful....

With uncles like that, who needed enemies? Ron had thought as he'd departed from Jay Bloom's office at the far end of the hall. He would have pitied Julia for being stuck in such a dysfunctional family, except that his own family was just as dysfunctional and nowhere near as rich. If anyone was going to be feeling sorry for anyone, he was just as deserving as she was.

But she was the one who needed comfort right now—an arm around her shoulders and a compassionate ear. And no cracks about PMS.

He lowered himself onto the sofa next to her and slid his arm along the back cushions. She immediately hunched forward, her body language screaming that she didn't want him to touch her.

Damn. Was she going to decide, based on her father's misbehavior, that all men were scum? He'd dated a woman like that once. Her previous boyfriend had done something awful. As Ron recalled, it had had something to do with refusing to attend a couples-sensitivity weekend because the Giants were in a play-off game. Once Ron had entered her life, she'd always been watching him, just waiting for him to choose football over sensitivity, and blowing up at him if he so much as hinted that televised sports appealed to him. "You men are all alike!" she would rail. "You'd rather watch overpaid athletes throw a funny ball around a field than connect with a real woman."

He'd choose sex over televised football any day. He might even choose sex over fifty-yard-line tickets at Giants Stadium for a play-off game—probably, if he got to pick the woman involved. But he'd choose a diet of liver and broccoli over a couples-sensitivity weekend. There were connections, and there were connections.

Julia clearly didn't want to connect with him right now. She only wanted to stare at the expired box of prophylactics.

"Hey," he murmured, trying to jar her out of her trance.

"What?" She whipped her head around to face him. He saw anger and embarrassment and distress in her glistening brown eyes.

"Why don't you think of it as kind of a first-aid kit? Something a person keeps on hand but hopes he'll never need."

If that sounded as inane to her as it did to him, she would

have laughed. He'd discovered over the weekend that Julia laughed a lot. She'd laughed at his attempt to make grilled cheese sandwiches in the microwave, at the Monty Python poster in his bathroom and at the story—one-hundred-percent true—he'd told her about how he'd gotten a scar on his butt during a Little League game. His baseball pants had been loose around the waist and he'd forgotten to wear his belt. The pants had started sagging while he was running the bases on a triple, and when he'd slid into third base the pants had drooped a couple of inches too far down and his ass had smacked against the sand and pebbles in the base path.

Finding condoms in her father's old desk apparently wasn't as hilarious as hearing about how in sixth grade, Ron had sacrificed his tush for the sake of his team.

"My father was having an affair," she declared.

"That would be my guess, too," he said in his most placating voice. Should he tell her what Reuben Melnick had insinuated about her father and Deirdre Morrissey? Of course not. He was supposed to be offering comfort, not pouring acid into the wound. This whole situation was his fault because he'd insisted on picking the lock on the damn desk. He sure wasn't going to make it worse by suggesting whom the condoms had been purchased for.

"Right here, in the office. In the heart of Bloom's."

"These things happen, Julia."

"They don't just *happen*. You make it sound like a quirk of fate or something. People trip over potholes. People catch pneumonia. People have affairs in their offices."

"Well, they do." He might have pointed out that given the way she'd kissed him just minutes ago, she and Ron had been heading full-speed toward condom use in this very office, in the heart of Bloom's. But of course, it was different when one of the parties was your father. Your *married* father.

She ran her fingers obsessively along the edges of the box. It was still sealed in clear plastic, which had to count for something.

"He never used them," Ron said hopefully. "Didn't you tell me you had a younger brother? Maybe your dad bought them for him."

"My father would never buy condoms for Adam."

Unfamiliar with the dynamics of their father-son relationship, Ron didn't argue. "The thing is," he said quietly, "people do stupid things. No one's perfect. You can't judge someone based on the one stupid thing he might have done."

Eyeing the box, she muttered, "This would have enabled him to do twelve stupid things." She tossed the box onto the table in front of her and scowled. When Ron leaned toward her, she turned away. "Why are you defending him? My father…my father…" She obviously couldn't get the rest out.

"I'm not defending him. I'm trying to make you feel better. Tell me what you want me to do." It occurred to him that making Julia feel better was the only goal of any importance to him at that moment. It astounded him to realize he cared that much about her, but he did.

He risked touching her shoulder, and she sighed. "He was my idol," she muttered, her gaze straying back to the box. "He was like a king in our house, one level above us ordinary folk. He worked so hard, he spent so many late nights at the office, and I always felt kind of bad for him—and in awe of him, too, because of the way he knocked himself out to make Bloom's successful. And all that time, instead of working, he was burning through condoms with someone. Who? Who could he have been having an affair with?"

"Does it matter?" Ron asked, hoping to steer her in another direction.

"I'm trying to think of everyone who came to his funeral. The chapel was packed. Dozens of people I'd never met before were there—they all knew him from work. His coffee broker. His honey supplier. Some guy who sold the store the plastic tubs they put potato salad and cole slaw in. He had a wart on his hand. I didn't want to shake it but I had to."

Ron nodded sympathetically.

"There were women, too," she continued, "but I don't re-member who they were. None of them had warts." She sighed again. "What if it's someone I know? Someone here at the store—one of the clerks, maybe? A lot of them have been with us for years." She shook her head. "I can't imagine my father with any of them, though. I can't imagine him with anyone other than my mother. Actually, I can't imagine him with her, either."

"Not a very romantic guy, huh."

"Apparently, there was a side of him I never saw." At last she leaned back and let Ron loop his arm around her. "You must think this is so tawdry. It would make a good headline for your article, wouldn't it—'Benjamin Bloom Left a Bustling Store and a Box of Contraceptives When He Died....'"

"None of this is going in my article," he assured her.

She gazed into his face, not in gratitude as he would have hoped but in curiosity that quickly evolved into suspicion. "You knew."

"I knew what?"

"You knew my father was screwing around. You knew be-fore this." She gestured toward the box.

"How could I have known?" Ron wasn't good at pretend-ing to be ignorant, but he gave it his best shot.

"You're a reporter, Joffe. You've been researching this store for a month. You probably talked to everyone I met at the fu-neral, even the guy with the wart on his hand."

"I might have talked to them, Julia. I talked to a lot of peo-ple. I didn't see their hands. I did most of the interviews over the phone."

"Did you talk to any women?"

Evasion was one thing, dishonesty another. He wasn't going to lie to her. "I spoke to a few," he said vaguely. "And no, none of them volunteered that she was fooling around with your fa-ther. But what difference does it make? Your father had his strengths and his weaknesses, and now he's dead."

"So why aren't you putting this in your article?" Again she waved at the condoms. "I bet it would sell magazines."

He wasn't putting it in his article because he didn't want to hurt Julia. Because as much as he loved magazine work, as much as he treasured his integrity, as much as he got a rush from beaming bright lights into dark corners, he couldn't bring himself to humiliate her family by publicizing Ben Bloom's zipper problem. "It's not relevant to the story," he said. "Bloom's is a delicatessen, not a brothel. If it were a brothel, I'd write a different kind of story."

"You know who he was screwing," she accused, her eyes narrowing.

He remembered that she was a lawyer, that she'd had experience interrogating witnesses and taking depositions. Her shit detector had been fine-tuned in her previous career.

"Don't do this, Julia. Forget the condoms. Let's pretend all we found in the desk was Grandpa's spirit."

"My grandfather did not have a Trojan spirit. Tell me who it is, Joffe."

Her voice was steely. He sensed none of the weepiness she'd exhibited earlier, none of the emotional spillover. She was a tough prosecutor now, demanding the truth.

If he told her, could she handle it?

He respected her enough not to patronize her. "All I know is what people have hinted to me," he warned.

"And they've hinted…?"

"Deirdre Morrissey." *Don't fire her, Julia,* he wanted to add. *Don't kick her skinny ass out of here. You need her at Bloom's. She's got more sense than your mother and uncle combined. Get past this if you can.*

Julia took a deep breath and let it out. Another one. He heard the air hissing through her teeth. She wasn't going to cry, and he felt a surge of pride and admiration sweep through him. He much preferred women who wept over nonsense than those who wept over real crises and heartaches, the challenges a person had to face with strength and courage. Julia was strong and courageous.

"My parents split up when I was a kid," he told her. "It

sucked. Sometimes it's better if parents stay together. You had both parents. Maybe that was worth a little deception on your father's part."

"It wasn't little. Deirdre," she murmured, shaking her head. "His office wife. What a cliché."

"We can't all be original."

"What am I going to say to her?"

"Why say anything at all? She works here. She does good work. Judging by my interviews with everybody, she's holding this place together and keeping it running. And she's probably grieving for your father, too. Leave her alone."

"She had an affair with a married man."

"And he had an affair with her. It's history now."

"Only because my father pigged out on funky sturgeon in St. Petersburg." She didn't pull away when he took her hand. Her fingers were cold and he sandwiched them between his palms, trying to warm them. "What will I tell my mother?"

"Nothing."

"How can I lie to her?"

"Don't lie. Don't say anything at all. What's the point of telling her about it at this late date? It would only hurt her."

"Maybe you're right." The sigh she let out this time was so deep it seemed to have originated on the first floor. "Oh, Joffe... I don't know what to do."

"Don't do anything." He pulled her against him and wrapped his arms around her. "There's nothing for you to do. This isn't a problem you can fix. Just leave it alone."

He felt her head move against his chest as she nodded. She fell silent, and he kept his arms around her, thinking that for a clueless guy who'd just paddled a canoe over Niagara Falls, he'd done a pretty good job. He hadn't capsized, hadn't drowned, hadn't lost Julia to the treacherous current. Maybe he'd even kept her dry. Knowing he'd been able to navigate her safely through all that demonic white-water filled him with a sense of accomplishment he'd never felt from writing an article that moved readers, or exposing some son of a bitch in print. He felt accomplishment…and wonder. He'd gotten Julia through what might be the worst thing ever to happen to her, and she hadn't drowned.

He still would choose the Giants over a couples-sensitivity weekend, but…yeah, he'd done all right.

If she hadn't been distracted by thoughts of her father—her father and *Deirdre,* for God's sake!—she would have marveled at the realization that Joffe was holding her without sex being a part of it. His arms felt wonderful around her, as wonderful as every other time he had embraced her. But she didn't even want to kiss him. She just wanted to feel his warm, firm chest against her, and his hand moving soothingly along her upper arm.

Her father and Deirdre.

Shit.

She sorted through her thoughts and admitted that shock wasn't among them. Disgust, distrust, indignation that on a scale of one to ten, hovered somewhere in the vicinity of seventeen. But not shock. Not even all that much surprise.

Deirdre Morrissey was too tall to be considered mousy; in her stilt-like high heels, she'd stood taller than Julia's father. Yet the way she did her job, quiet and capable, unnoticed half the time, had a kind of rodentlike efficiency. Or maybe it was just her buck teeth that made Julia think of gnawing mammals.

How could her father have kissed a woman with such an egregious overbite?

Julia didn't want to think about Ben Bloom and Deirdre Morrissey knocking teeth. She didn't want to think about whether her father had a fetish involving three-inch spike heels on women, or whether what had really turned him on was Deirdre's passionate grasp of inventory management.

Why had her father been so careless as to have left condoms in Grandpa Isaac's desk? Obviously, he'd assumed he would be returning alive from Russia. He'd kept the condoms in Grandpa Isaac's desk because no one ever opened its drawers, so no one knew what he kept in it. Except, apparently, half the world—the half Joffe had interviewed for his article.

"Who told you about my father?" she asked.

"A few people implied things. No one came right out and said anything. They couldn't. How could they know for sure?"

"They could know if my father told them." But that wasn't likely. Her father hadn't discussed personal matters with his family. Why would he discuss them with herring merchants?

"I suspect it was more that people picked up on the vibes," Joffe said, tracing lazy figure eights on her arm with his fingertips. "Look, Julia, it's not my business, and you can tell me to back off—"

"Don't back off," she said, nestling closer to him. At that moment, she was sure she loved him, which was really rather odd, since learning that her father was a philandering bastard ought to have turned her off the idea of love. But what Joffe had given her over the past weekend was nothing compared with what he was giving her now: solace. For all her life, it seemed, she'd been the one to offer solace to everyone else, making sure her loved ones were happy, knocking herself out to satisfy Grandma Ida's demands, her mother's and her siblings' needs, her father's expectations. Susie had rebelled and riled the family, but Julia had been the one to calm things down and smooth things out.

She wasn't sure whether things ought to be calm and smooth right now, but if they weren't, Joffe would handle it. This man she'd known such a short time, who could turn her on and fire her up like a gas grill, could also cool her off. If that didn't make him deserving of her, she didn't know what did.

"All I'm thinking," he continued, "is that I've talked to a lot of people about Bloom's—including the people who work here—and Deirdre seems to be pretty essential to the functioning of the place. I know she's not family…"

"Maybe she was angling to be. Maybe she thought sleeping with my father made her family." Julia at last pushed herself to sit up straight. Her heart was no longer thundering in her chest, and the tension that had fisted around her brain was beginning to relax its grip. "Maybe she was only screwing him because she thought it was the quickest route to power."

"If she wanted power, do you think she would have hung her fate on a family-owned delicatessen?"

"This isn't just a family-owned delicatessen. It's Bloom's. It's the kind of institution a magazine like *Gotham* writes stories about." She let out a long breath. "Maybe she thought that if she serviced my father, he'd move up to chairman when Grandma Ida died and he'd name Deirdre president. That sure would have pissed my mother and Uncle Jay off." Shaking her head, she laughed sadly. "Everyone wants to be president of this place—except me."

"That could be why your grandmother chose you." He wove his fingers through hers. "The thing is, if you do something precipitous about Deirdre, it's not going to be good for Bloom's, especially when the store is bleeding."

"It's not like the store is gushing blood," she retorted. "It's just not thriving the way it should be." His hand was so much bigger than hers. Her fingers looked skinny and pale intertwined with his, and she hadn't done anything with her nails except trim them since the fateful day Grandma Ida had told her she was going to be the store's new president. They were short and unpolished; she'd had no time to take care of them. "I'm not going to give Deirdre the boot. Whatever she and my father were doing, they aren't doing it anymore. And it can't be undone."

"Are you going to tell your mother?"

"I don't know." If she did, maybe her mother would stop playing the loyal widow and start socializing, if only out of spite. Julia and Susie desperately wanted Sondra to find someone to fill her off hours with, so she wouldn't fill them with her daughters.

But Julia wasn't sure she wanted to deal with her mother's rage. Sondra would be hurt, possibly awash in despair—and Julia would wind up having to make her feel better. God, what if Sondra started phoning in the middle of the night and wailing about how Ben had betrayed her?

On the other hand, how could she keep such a significant piece of information a secret from her mother?

"I'll have to talk to Susie about it," she said. Susie was smarter than Julia, who'd achieved what she had simply because she was more dogged. Susie was the most undogged person Julia knew, which was why she earned her living serving pizza and draft beer to downtown folks. But she was brilliant. If the store's showcase windows turned out well, Julia would have Susie progress to the interior. It could almost be like a real, full-time job. Perhaps Julia could come up with a title for her: director of presentation. A fancy title and a real salary might lure her out of the pizzeria and into the family firm.

Julia shook her head in amazement. She'd just learned her father was an adulterer, and she was plotting ideas for managing Bloom's. Where were her priorities?

Where were her tears? Where was her outrage?

Her father was a schmuck. End of story.

"You okay?" Joffe asked her.

"Who knows?" A small, weary laugh escaped her. She rotated her hand, twisting Joffe's, as well, and glanced at her watch. Nearly five. "How long have I been sitting here in a catatonic trance?"

"A while."

"Was your editor expecting you back at your desk?"

He grinned. "My editor expects me to submit my column on time. Other than that, she doesn't make demands."

"She demanded that you write about Bloom's."

"She requested it. She thought there might be a story."

"What a story—money and sex. Why doesn't it seem more glamorous?"

"Probably because the windows in this office are caked with soot. For real glamour, you'd need clean windows. And thicker carpet. And an uncle who doesn't play golf in the hallway with a drinking glass."

"Uncle Jay was playing golf in the hallway?" She rolled her eyes. "They're all crazy. All of them. Do you think that if I got enough transfusions I could rid myself of Bloom blood?"

"If you wanted to get rid of it, you'd probably need a vampire to suck you dry." He stretched, bringing her hand with him so that when he pulled his arms up over his head, her bottom lifted off the cushions. "What do you say we get some dinner?"

"I've got to talk to my sister." Freeing her hand, she crossed to the new desk, the safe desk, the desk whose drawers held no surprises. She lifted the phone receiver and punched in Susie's cell-phone number.

"Isn't she just downstairs?" Joffe asked, remaining near the couch. She appreciated that he didn't hover over her as if he expected her to collapse. She was okay, and she liked the fact that he knew it.

She shook her head and listened as Susie's phone went unanswered. "She's probably on the subway, heading downtown to Nico's. Her cell phone can't pick up calls on the subway."

"Who's Nico?"

"Nico's. Her other job." Julia gazed at the papers spread across her desk and decided she didn't give a damn if Rabinowitz Incorporated had nearly doubled their price on onions and radishes over what they'd charged last year. Not long ago, she'd cared. Not long ago, she'd been about to put in a call to Ari Rabinowitz and tell him that if he didn't keep his prices steady she was going to start buying from cheaper wholesalers. A radish was a radish, and most of the radishes they used were cut up into little magenta-and-white flower shapes and used for garnish in the cold cuts and salad cases, so if they weren't the freshest radishes in the world, it wasn't a big thing.

But Rabinowitz's prices were not central to her well-being. Her mind was crowded by the realization that her father was a stupid putz who'd had an affair that his professional colleagues knew about, and who'd used Grandpa Isaac's heirloom desk to store his contraceptives. It occurred to her that Bloom's stagnation might be due to her late father's vindictive lover sabotaging the place. Who knew? Maybe Deirdre was sneaking in after hours—she had a key—and stealing bagels.

If she was, at least she'd be stealing stale bagels. New batches were baked fresh every morning.

"So, where is this Nico's?" Joffe asked.

She eyed him, his long legs slightly parted, his expression intent. That he'd known about her father's infidelity before she did irked her, but he was a nosy journalist poking around a story, and he had sources. Someone had told him about her father, just as someone had told him Bloom's was bleeding. Her exact word, *bleeding*.

"Deirdre," she guessed. "Deirdre told you Bloom's is bleeding."

"No."

"She's getting back at us by talking to you behind our backs."

"Why would she want to get back at you? And even if she did, why would she do it by talking to me? She's got lots of better ways to take revenge, if that was what she wanted to do. Which I don't think is the case."

"Somebody told you Bloom's was bleeding. Someone used that word."

He opened his mouth and then shut it. "It's a secondhand source," he confessed.

"What do you mean?"

"Someone told someone who told me."

"And you wrote about it?"

"I didn't use the word *bleeding*. Someone told someone who told me, and I investigated. Everyone in this place had something to tell me, okay? Your mother, your uncle, Deirdre, that little accountant with the bow tie—"

"Myron."

"That's the guy." He nodded. "Everybody talked to me, Julia. Even you."

"You haven't talked to Grandma Ida."

"Not for lack of trying. Can you arrange for her and me to—"

"No."

"Why not?"

"She's an old woman. I don't want you badgering her with

questions. She's old, she's retired and she's earned the right not to have to deal with magazine reporters."

"She could give me great background," Joffe pointed out. "I had to piece together the store's history from what other people told me. If I could talk to her—"

"You'd ask whatever you needed to make your story better, even if it was about her son's infidelities. No, Joffe. Leave my grandmother alone."

Scowling, he crossed to Grandpa Isaac's desk and gathered up the draft of his article for her. "You think I have it in for your family? This thing brought tears to your eyes, don't forget. It isn't the final draft, but go ahead and read it."

"I'm almost afraid to," she muttered, scanning the pages in the hope that anything incriminating would leap out at her. God knew what other dirty secrets he'd learned about Bloom's and the Blooms.

She couldn't concentrate on reading it right now. She needed to see Susie so they could figure out what to do about their mother and Deirdre and everything else in her chaotic life. "I've got to go downtown and talk to my sister," she said, letting the pages lie unread in her lap.

"I'll come with you."

She almost blurted out a no. But when she saw him standing before her, she felt a rush of warmth. Not heat, not the rabid, breathless yearning she usually felt when he was nearby, but something softer, something that nudged rather than shoved. Something that told her seeing Susie would be easier if Joffe was by her side.

She didn't like that feeling at all. She much preferred the fiery, passionate hunger she usually felt around him, the desire that was still such a novelty for her. It was scary and fun and it didn't force her to think. The spreading warmth she felt now did.

She didn't want to think. She just wanted to go back to where she'd been when she'd read his first paragraph and kissed him. But it was too late.

"Okay," she relented. She stuffed the article into her briefcase, along with Rabinowitz's radish and onion figures. Surveying the office, she paused when her gaze captured the box on the coffee table. She grabbed it, carried it to Grandpa Isaac's desk and dropped it into the bottom drawer, which she kicked shut. "Okay," she said again. "Let's go."

17

Jay had visions of Wendy dancing through his head—specifi-cally, lap-dancing—as he shut off his computer, stashed his golf club behind the door and fished his keys from his pocket. He had visions of climbing into the Z3, putting down the top and cruising through Central Park to the East Side, where Wendy would be waiting for him without fund-raiser tickets, without plans and, hopefully, without underwear.

It had been an excellent day. He'd started laying groundwork for a new mail-order program in small appliances, he'd prac-ticed his putts and he'd finessed the *Gotham Magazine* reporter. He was feeling fine.

His phone rang just as his hand touched the doorknob. He wished he could swing the door open and stroll out of the of-fice, but he lacked the discipline to walk away from a ringing phone. He grabbed the receiver and pressed it to his ear. "Jay Bloom here."

"It's Lyndon," his mother's majordomo announced. "Your mother would like to see you."

So much for his excellent day. In his mind, Wendy slid off his lap and put on some panties. "About what?" he asked, not caring if Lyndon heard him sigh.

"I don't know. She'd like you to stop by at the apartment before you leave for home."

It was almost five o'clock. He should have taken off early; if he had, he would have missed Lyndon's call. But a day this good couldn't U-turn and go bad. He was on a roll; maybe he'd finesse his mother, too. "Sure. I'll be right up," he said.

The elevator carried him to the twenty-fifth floor. He still experienced a twinge of dread when the floor indicator lit up with "24," as if the doors would slide open on that floor and he'd find himself in a time warp, once again married to Martha, once again returning home to that drearily earnest apartment, spending his evenings listening to her pontificate on the cultural morass of professional wrestling or the fate of the sperm whale.

But the elevator kept going, the light changed to "25" and the doors opened. Releasing a pent-up breath, he strode down the hall to Ida's apartment. Lyndon let him in. "You really don't know what this is about?" Jay whispered.

"I really don't," Lyndon answered in a normal voice, "except that she's having tea and she'd like for you to join her in a cup. I'm brewing it now."

Jay hated tea. "I'd prefer coffee, if she's offering."

"She's not," Lyndon said, his voice so silky Jay wanted to slug him. Instead, he resigned himself to the prospect of forcing down a few sips of tea. Hell, he'd drink piss-water if that was what it took to get his mother to give him more power in running the store. Most tea tasted like piss-water, anyway.

"She's in the living room," Lyndon directed him, turning back toward the kitchen. "I'll be right in with the tea."

"Take your time," Jay muttered, ambling down the hall to the living room. Ida sat in one of the wingback chairs, her posture straight, her hair settled on the top of her head like an unusually dark storm cloud, her wrists circled in clinking gold bracelets. "Hello, Mom," he said, dutifully leaning over to kiss her cheek before he lowered himself onto the sofa across from her.

"Jay." She eyed him up and down. "For a man who spends his life shut up in an office, you look not so bad."

Was that her way of saying she knew he didn't spend his life shut up in an office? So what if it was? He was getting his job done; golf, squash and his other activities didn't keep him from meeting his responsibilities.

"How are you feeling, Mom?" he asked. "Everything okay?"

"At my age, how should I feel?"

Eighty-eight. In two years she'd be ninety, if she didn't die. One good look at her made it clear she was nowhere close to dying.

Lyndon appeared in the doorway carrying a tray laden with a teapot and two cups. There was no escape. Jay would have to drink some.

He pretended patience while Lyndon set the tray on the coffee table, filled a cup with the steaming brew and placed it on the side table near Ida's elbow, then filled the other cup and handed it to Jay, who had to thank Lyndon even though he wasn't the least bit grateful. When Lyndon left the room, Jay glanced at his mother and found her watching him. Trying not to grimace, he took a sip.

That seemed to satisfy her. Without drinking any of her own tea—she probably knew how wretched it tasted—she folded her hands in her lap and said, "What's with the reporter?"

"Who? The guy from *Gotham*?"

"Lyndon bought this week's copy of the magazine. There's no article in it. He bought last week's copy, too. Same thing, no article. So? It's not being written? What?"

"It's being written," Jay assured her. "The reporter was just in today. He wanted to interview me one more time." A slight exaggeration; Joffe hadn't come to the office to interview Jay. Although maybe he had. Jay wasn't exactly sure why he'd come.

"Sondra tells me it's going to be nice and schmaltzy, all about how wonderful Bloom's is," Ida said.

"Sondra has no idea what she's talking about." He adjusted his tone to imply that it pained him greatly to admit this.

"It's not going to be schmaltzy?"

"I think he's digging a little deeper, getting into the nitty-gritty. He asked me about how the store is run, how responsibilities are divvied up. And of course, how Bloom's has remained synonymous with the best delicatessen food in New York all these years. I've explained to him how I've spread the Bloom's brand far and wide through mail order and the Internet. It's that kind of fame that brings the crowds in, and I wanted to make sure he included that in his article."

"What about Julia? What does she think of this article?"

"Why don't you ask her?" Jay retorted, then sipped some more of the vile tea to atone for having spoken sharply to his mother about her favorite grandchild. Why she preferred Julia to the others he couldn't guess. But if he drank enough tea, maybe his mother would stop shoving Julia in his face. "If you want to know the truth," he said in a gentler voice, "Julia gets tripped up on trivia, on *mishegaas* that's not worth the effort she puts into it. I love Julia, you know I do—but she's shortsighted." He'd said as much to the reporter, carefully couching his opinions in euphemism. He might as well express his opinions to his mother, too. She needed to know what was going on at her beloved store.

"What *mishegaas?*"

"Well...for instance, the inventory. She reviews the numbers again and again. She *shvitzes* when a single knish is unaccounted for. And her meetings—they waste everybody's time. We can talk to one another without meetings."

"I liked that one meeting I went to," his mother said. "Having everybody all together in one place—it was like a party."

His mother obviously didn't go to too many good parties. "Look, Mom—I know Julia is trying hard, and she's smart. Maybe in time she'll get the hang of it. But right now she's struggling. She doesn't do things the way we've always done things at Bloom's."

"And is that such a bad thing?" At last his mother drank some tea. "I want you to tell me when this magazine story comes out. I want to see if it has things I don't like in it. Who's writing it?"

"A guy named Ronald Joffe. He writes the magazine's weekly business column, and he seems smart. He listens very closely to what people tell him. I think he's going to portray Bloom's fairly." *And he's going to report that I'm the brains of the outfit, the one with vision.*

"Maybe I should talk to him."

"No," Jay said quickly. "He's only talking to the people actively involved in the store." In fact, Joffe had asked Jay if it would be possible to interview Ida, and Jay had thought it best to keep Joffe away from her. God only knew what she might say in an interview. Given the opportunity, she might go off on a tangent about her beloved hairdresser, Bella, or she might declare that her dear husband, Isaac, may he rest, didn't know *bupkes* about running a store. Ida often said things that made her sound unhinged or unpleasant. Bloom's didn't need that kind of exposure. Jay was sure the rest of the folks on the third floor would agree.

"So, Julia is concerned with the inventory?" Ida asked.

"Petty stuff, Mom. Nothing you should worry about."

"I'll decide what I want to worry about."

She pursed her lips in that forbidding way of hers and searched his face with her hard, clear eyes. Why couldn't she get cataracts like a typical woman her age? Why couldn't she require trifocals as thick as thermopanes? What magic elixir did Lyndon feed her to keep her from falling apart like a normal person? Something he brewed into the tea, maybe?

Jay had his own magic elixir to keep him young: a wife like Wendy, sexy and compliant and never too much of a strain, combined with adequate amounts of recreation to keep him physically fit and mentally relaxed. Jay didn't think his mother

viewed Lyndon as sexy or compliant—the idea was so outrageous Jay had to stifle a laugh.

He sipped some tea and concluded it didn't taste too ghastly.
If it really contained anti-aging properties, they ought to be
selling it at Bloom's.

"All right, then," his mother said, dismissing him. "You want
to leave, I can tell. You've got that bouncy wife waiting for you
at home."

"She's not bouncy," Jay argued, although in truth she was.

"Go home. But promise me you'll let me know when that
magazine article comes out."

"I promise."

"And if Julia's having problems, help her. That's part of your
job, Jay. It's important, for the store."

If she thought his job was to help Julia reap all the glory, he
obviously hadn't been as successful at presenting himself as the
mastermind of Bloom's with his mother as he'd been with Joffe.
"Listen, Mom," he said, "the thing about Julia getting caught
up in *mishegaas*… She's a great kid, but she's coming at the job
from a lawyer's perspective. I think she's terrific, but I wonder
if she has retailing in her blood."

"She's got Bloom blood, no? That's all the blood she needs,"
Ida declared.

"I'm just saying, a little guidance, maybe a little power sharing—"

Ida peered up at him, her eyes as clear and sharp as crystal
shards. "You think you could do a better job?"

He hadn't expected her to be so direct, but what the hell.
She'd asked; he would answer. "As a matter of fact, yes."

Ida sniffed. She didn't laugh, didn't shake her head, didn't call
him a fool—but she also didn't say he could take over the store.
Just that single sniff, like someone with hay fever, too lazy to
get a tissue and blow her nose.

He would win her over. He'd get the edition of *Gotham
Magazine* with the Bloom's article in it as soon as it hit the
stands, and he'd bring her a copy. Two copies, one for read-

ing and one for safekeeping. He'd have Lyndon prepare her a cup of tea to drink while she read the article. In it she would read that Jay was the de facto leader of the company, the visionary, the genius who could accomplish more in a six-hour day than Julia could in a twelve-hour day, because she was so busy fussing over the number of bagels the store sold in a given week.

His mother would see that she'd made a mistake in naming Julia the president. She'd see her error, and she'd correct it— and Jay would get what he deserved.

"This pizza isn't so good," Joffe grumbled.

Nico's wasn't packed, but it was bustling enough to deny Susie the chance to sit for a minute and talk. Julia didn't know why she'd thought to come downtown tonight, except that sisters needed each other in times of trauma. And while Julia was managing to maintain a calm facade about her father's infidelity, inside she felt traumatized.

She picked at her own pizza, a slice of Sicilian with mushrooms. Joffe had ordered two slices with meatballs for himself, along with a beer, and although he was complaining about the food's quality, he was close to polishing off the first slice. She'd witnessed this male idiosyncrasy before: a woman tried something, didn't like it and set it aside, while a man tried something, didn't like it and proceeded to wolf it down.

"We should have picked up some takeout from Bloom's," he said after popping the last of the crust from his first slice into his mouth.

She shrugged. "I wanted to see my sister."

"We could have eaten in the cab on the ride down." He'd insisted on taking a cab. No way was he going to dangle from a subway strap all the way down to SoHo at rush hour. "What's it called? Heat-n-eat. Those hot meals are great. You ever have the stuffed cabbage? It's fantastic. Of course you've had it," he corrected himself before lifting his other slice and catching a wad of melted cheese that threatened to slide off the crust.

Actually, she'd never had Bloom's stuffed cabbage. She made a mental note to try all the heat-n-eat entrées.

Susie hustled past them, carrying a tray laden with plates of manicotti. She flashed them a smile but didn't break her stride. "It must be tough for her, doing your store windows all day and then waiting on tables here at night."

"The windows are just a temporary job," Julia explained. Speaking the words deflated a mood that hadn't had much air in it to begin with. She wished Susie would leave Nico's—as she herself had left Griffin, McDougal—and devote herself full-time to Bloom's. Julia could use her there for moral support and aesthetic perspective. "Susie's so smart," she said, surprising herself by giving voice to her thoughts.

Joffe followed Susie around the room with his gaze while he sipped some beer. "If she's so smart, what's she doing waiting on tables in a pizzeria?"

"She's a poet," Julia answered.

He nodded as if that explained everything. "So—assuming she can spare five minutes sometime before midnight, what are you going to tell her?"

Before Julia could answer, the door swung open and in walked Rick. She cursed under her breath.

"What?" Joffe twisted in his chair to see what had caught her attention. Rick was heading straight for their table, his face breaking into a smile. Joffe turned back to her. "Who's that?"

"My cousin." Her lips strained at the effort to return Rick's smile. Encouraged, he dragged a chair over to their table and flopped down into it. "Hey, Rick," she said. "Should I ask you to join us?"

He laughed. "What brings you down here to the netherworld?"

"I was dying for some pizza." She glanced at her scarcely touched slice and forced another feeble smile. "Rick, this is a friend of mine, Ron Joffe. Ron, my cousin Rick."

"You must be one of Jay Bloom's sons," Joffe guessed.

Rick's eyebrows vanished behind the hank of hair that fell across his forehead. "How'd you know that?"

"I've told him a little about the family," Julia said quickly. She didn't want Rick to learn that Joffe was a reporter. If he did, he'd start badgering Joffe in the hope of gaining connections or money for his filmmaking ventures. And Joffe would interview Rick to learn more about the Bloom family for his article.

She had the rough draft in her briefcase, which was wedged between her feet under the table. She ought to have skipped this trip downtown, gone home and read the damn thing. She was never going to have a chance to talk to Susie, especially not now that Rick was present, and she was stuck eating pizza when she should have been eating Bloom's stuffed cabbage, and her father was a two-timing bastard—a dead one, but still—and her head hurt.

She brought her attention back to the two men at her table and realized that her caution in introducing Joffe had been for naught. Rick was describing the plot of his movie—not so much a plot, actually, as a string of concepts: "There's a car chase, of course—gotta have a car chase—and sex and anomie. You know what anomie is? I think any flick that's going to be taken seriously these days has to have some anomie in it."

"Who's producing it?" Joffe asked.

Bad move, but it was too late. Rick happily launched into a soliloquy concerning his financing woes. Julia nudged her plate toward Rick, figuring he must have come to Nico's because he was hungry, and excused herself to use the ladies' room.

On her way to the back hall where the rest rooms were located, she spotted Susie behind the counter, handing an order to one of the chefs on the kitchen side of the pass-through window. When Susie turned away, Julia grabbed her hand and dragged her down the hall.

"I'm working," Susie reminded her, although she didn't put up much resistance.

Julia nudged her into the one-seater ladies' room, followed her in and locked the door. "We have to talk."

Susie crossed to the mirror above the sink and fussed with her hair. "About what? You like the bagel showcase? I'm not done with it yet, but—"

"Susie. Listen to me. Dad was having an affair with Deirdre Morrissey."

Susie spun around so fast she banged the paper towel dispenser with her elbow. "Ow! My funny bone," she wailed, rubbing her arm.

"Did you hear what I said?"

"Daddy and Deirdre Morrissey." Susie twisted her arm in an attempt to view her wound.

"Doesn't that shock you?"

Susie regarded Julia enigmatically, then shrugged. "You want to know the truth? I always figured he was screwing around with someone. He was never home, for God's sake. If the only thing keeping him from us was Bloom's, I mean, that would be pretty pitiful." She rubbed her elbow and ruminated. "Deirdre? I don't know. She's not exactly hot stuff."

"Damn it, Susie! You're supposed to be shocked. *I* was shocked." In truth, Julia wasn't sure about that. At least she was conscious of the fact that she *should* have been shocked.

"I mean, Deirdre." Susie shook her head. "She's so skinny, and those teeth of hers. I figured, if Dad was screwing around, it would have been with someone like The Bimbette."

"The Bimbette?" Julia wasn't sure which image nauseated her more: her father with Deirdre or her father with a woman like Uncle Jay's Wendy, all twinkly and buxom. "I thought he was having an affair with the store."

"The store was his one true love," Susie agreed. "The rest was just getting his rocks off."

"Why aren't you upset? You should be. *I'm* upset." Merely saying the words forced Julia to acknowledge that she wasn't as upset as she wanted to be. "Don't you even feel bad for Mom?"

Susie hoisted herself to sit on the sink counter. She swung her feet and twisted her arm again, searching her elbow for a bruise. "I feel bad for Mom that Dad was never around, and the only way she could spend time with him was when they were both at the store together. I feel bad that she thought she could get his attention by pretending to love the store as much as he did."

"You don't think she loves the store?"

"Are you kidding? She loves the money, she loves the power, she loves getting in Uncle Jay's face. But she doesn't even love the food. She's always on a diet." Susie gave up on her elbow and propped her chin in her cupped hands. "A woman who wears a two-carat tennis bracelet doesn't belong on the payroll of a delicatessen."

"It's not just a delicatessen. It's Bloom's."

"You're a Bloom. So am I. Mom's a Feldman. It's not the same thing."

"Susie." Julia felt drained, and stupid. How could her sister have psyched out their father while she herself had been clueless all these years? "If you knew Dad was having an affair, why didn't you tell me?"

"I didn't *know.* I just sort of sensed it. And I didn't tell you because I figured you'd be shocked."

Julia sighed. "What do you think I should do?"

"Keep it out of *Gotham Magazine,*" Susie suggested, then smiled gently. "Leave it alone, Julia. What *can* you do? It's history. He's dead."

"But—but he betrayed Mom. He broke his wedding vows. He had sex with his assistant. In his office. I found a box of condoms."

"Condoms? What a good boy." Susie snorted. "Imagine if he hadn't been careful. We might have had another baby brother."

"One brother is enough." Julia closed her eyes and drew in a deep breath. "What'll we tell Adam?"

"Nothing. Why tell anyone anything, Julia? What's the point?"

"The point is, our father was a shithead."

"Like, this is news?" Susie slid off the counter and enfolded Julia in a hug. "I gotta go." She yawned. "Juggling two jobs isn't good for me."

"Quit Nico's. I'll hire you full time."

"I make a lot here with tips."

"I'll give you tips. Come work at Bloom's, Susie. I need you." For a lot more than what she could contribute to the store, but Julia didn't say that.

"Yeah, right." Susie released her and unlocked the door. "Go take that cute little reporter boy home and have your way with him."

"I might do that," Julia said, following her sister out of the rest room and acknowledging that while the thought of sex right now excited her about as much as the thought of eating the cooling, congealing slice of pizza she'd left on the table, she couldn't come up with a better idea.

"I could put your cousin in touch with some people," Joffe said.

Julia sat naked in his bed, the sheet pulled up to her waist, a box of graham crackers by her side and the rough-draft pages of his article spread across her lap. She'd had her way with her reporter boy, found the act had distracted her quite nicely, and when they were done she'd realized that she was famished. He'd offered to race over to Bloom's to pick up a stuffed cabbage for her, but the store closed at ten. "Maybe we should stay open later," she'd remarked, when he brought her the graham crackers. "We could attract a younger, hipper clientele. Maybe we could have singles' nights at Bloom's. From nine to eleven, only singles would be allowed. It would be an improvement over most singles' bars. Better lighting, better nutrition. What do you think?"

"Great idea," Joffe had said, sprawling across the foot of the bed. He'd donned a pair of navy-blue sweatpants, which paradoxically made him look sexier than he'd looked naked. She kept glimpsing the waistband where it clung to his abdomen just below his navel, and thinking about what was underneath that dark-blue fleece. "If you really want to institute something like that, let me know. I can put it in the article and see what kind of interest it generates."

The article. For some odd reason, she hadn't given it a thought while Joffe had been lying under her, his hands clamped around her hips as he guided her up and down in a devastatingly effective rhythm. Nor had it entered her mind after she collapsed sweaty and panting on him and assured herself that she was nothing like her father, even though she'd discovered, to her amazement, that she liked sex. But once she'd regained a degree of lucidity that enabled her to nibble on graham crackers and shape coherent sentences, his comment had reminded her that the tear sheet was still in her bag, awaiting her attention.

It was wonderful. Not a puff piece but close, with lots of juicy descriptions of the different departments, the cluttered counters and packed shelves, the blended aromas of cheese and coffee, warm bread and hot entrées, the clatter of voices and footsteps and churning cash registers. In the article, Uncle Jay was depicted as rather lightweight, Deirdre as rather grim, Sondra as a yenta and Myron as having the personality of library paste, although Joffe put it a bit more tactfully. Julia herself came across as overwhelmed but learning on the job, which was true. At least he hadn't made her sound like a ditz.

She'd just finished reading the article, when Joffe mentioned her cousin. "I know lots of people looking for projects to invest in."

"If they're your enemies, send them to Rick," Julia suggested.

"You don't like him?"

"I love him. But I don't think he's ever going to make a movie."

"Probably not. The thing is, I know investors who've got money to burn and like to think of themselves as artistic. They buy paintings that are never going to appreciate. They invest in Broadway shows—which is about as sound an investment as buying lottery tickets. Some of them might like to get in on the ground floor of an independent movie—even if it never leaves the ground floor."

"How do you know people like that?" she asked.

He grinned. "I'm a financial writer, remember? I hobnob with Wall Street types."

"You've got an MBA."

"That, too."

She stacked the pages of his article and set them aside, then helped herself to another cracker and munched on it thoughtfully. "Joffe, I need your help."

She must have sounded pretty somber, because he straightened up and stared at her. "With what?"

Everyone she'd discussed the bagel situation with at Bloom's had laughed at her, and perhaps he would, too. But after reading his article, she felt she could trust him. He respected Bloom's, and she couldn't figure out the damn bagel problem on her own. Maybe he could help. "It's such a small thing, it probably isn't worth thinking about," she admitted. "The store is losing nearly a hundred and fifty bagels a week."

"Losing them?" He frowned.

"They just disappear. There's no record of them. They aren't bought. They aren't thrown out at the end of the day. They just disappear."

"You've talked to the bagel department?"

"Susie talked to one of the guys in the department. He didn't know anything—although she's hot for him, so who knows how the conversation went."

"You're hot for me, and this conversation is going fine," Joffe said with just enough arrogance to make her want to throw a pillow at his head. "Maybe I should talk to the guys in the department."

"No," she said hastily. "We need to keep it in the family. Anyway, it's not just bagels. There are other unaccountable losses. Cream cheese. Sometimes a little lox or smoked whitefish. A pound of coffee here and there, or tea."

"Shoplifting," Joffe told her. "Every store has problems with it, Julia. The losses are built into the pricing structure. If these thefts are causing Bloom's to falter—"

"It's not shoplifting," she explained. "This is organized. There's a consistency in the amount of stuff vanishing each week. I can't go around accusing my employees of stealing stuff, but something's going on. I don't know how to investigate it."

He ruminated. "My specialty is finance, not retail," he conceded. "But maybe if I inspected your books—"

"I've inspected the books. Myron has inspected the books. You're not going to find anything in them that we haven't already found."

"Then you're going to have to start talking to your employees. You don't have to accuse them, just question them."

"Oh God." She shuddered. She was still so new at running the store. To rage at the personnel, giving them the fifth degree over missing bagels… It would resemble that awful scene from *The Caine Mutiny,* when Humphrey Bogart accused the crew of stealing his strawberries and everyone realized he was crazy. If she started interrogating people at Bloom's about the missing bagels, they'd think she was crazy, too.

"Your other option is to write off the loss and forget about it," Joffe said.

"That's what my mother and Uncle Jay want me to do." She sighed, tossed the box of crackers onto the night table and sank into the pillows. Tears of dejection and fatigue threatened her eyes. "I wonder if it was going on while my father was still alive. I wonder what he would have done about it. Screwed Deirdre, probably."

"I guess you don't want to discuss this bagel problem with her," Joffe surmised.

"I don't want to discuss anything with her ever." She sighed. "Do you think I should discuss it with her?"

"She seems to know what's going on, a lot more than other people who work at Bloom's do. And if you want to keep working with her, Julia, you're going to have to talk to her."

"I doubt I can even look her in the face."

"So talk to her over the phone. Or else forget about the

whole thing. It doesn't sound like something that's going to drive the store into bankruptcy."

"I can't forget about it. Bloom's should be doing better than it is. It's like a tire with a slow leak in it—it's holding up okay, and you can drive on it as long as you remember to add a little air once a week. But you know in your heart that leak is there, and sooner or later you're going to have to patch the damn tire."

"Then patch it. You're the boss. If you want to fix the tire instead of refilling it with air all the time, you're the one who's going to have to patch it."

Julia decided Joffe was a pain in the ass. She wanted him to tell her, *Here's why you're losing bagels. You're miscounting your inventory. You forgot to factor in the X formula. They teach this in business school—you multiply, take ninety percent, work out the square root and calculate the secant. Once you do that, you'll see that all those bagels are accounted for.*

He didn't say that, though. He said, "I don't know what you want me to do. Hold your hand? Write out questions you can ask your people? Serve on bagel patrol? Give me a hint."

I want you to make everything better, she longed to whine. *I want you to make all my problems go away.* She couldn't ask him to do the impossible, so she only said, "Hold my hand."

He held all of her, wrapping his body around hers and tucking her head against his shoulder. Beyond exhaustion, she felt a deep, throbbing sorrow. She supposed that if she'd thought long and hard about it, she would have reached the same conclusion Susie had reached long ago about their father. But Julia had always believed the best of him. She believed the best of everyone. She believed the best of the employees she didn't want to interrogate, and her mother and uncle, and her sister, and her grandmother. She even believed the best of Deirdre, who knew everything and kept her mouth shut.

And Joffe. Except for the fact that he couldn't perform miracles and renew her ability to believe the best of everyone, she believed the best of him.

She'd figure out what to do about the bagels, and Deirdre, and her memory of her father, tomorrow. If Joffe couldn't help her, she'd work it out on her own.

In the meantime, she'd take comfort in the fact that he was holding her.

18

"All right," Ron wheedled. "You don't have to tell me who your source is. Just blink twice if I guess right."

Kim Pinsky snorted and flicked her ash-blond mane behind her shoulders. "What I'd like to know is, when the hell am I going to see this damn article?"

"It's not like I could work on the thing full-time. I have to write my weekly column, too," he said with abundant indignation. No matter what they argued about, he knew she would win. She always did. The best he could hope for was to pick up a few points by defending his honor.

"Spare me," Kim said.

"I'll have the Bloom's story done by next week," he promised. "I had it all written up, but then I had another chat with Jay Bloom and I need to tweak some stuff. It'll be on your desk Monday morning." He said Jay Bloom's name in an even tone, but observed his boss's expression. He was convinced Uncle Jay was Kim's source. It had to be a third-floor denizen, someone who would have been familiar with Julia's use of the term *bleeding* to describe the store's condition. Of all the third-floor folks, Jay seemed most eager to cause Julia headaches.

Kim's eyes didn't flicker, let alone blink.

"It wasn't Jay?" he asked, stumped. Who else would have wanted to stir up trouble? Julia's mother? Not given the pride she took in her daughter's ascension to company president. Deirdre? Not enough personality. Myron? Not enough gray matter.

"You want to know the truth?" Kim tapped an elegantly polished fingernail against her lower lip. "It was no one at Bloom's. And that's all I'm telling you."

"You assigned me this article on a secondhand tip?"

"A very reliable secondhand tip. You've gotten something good out of it, haven't you?"

"Not what I expected." He'd gotten a tawdry little family scandal he didn't want to write about and a financial struggle that wasn't particularly dire. Missing bagels, big deal. He'd gotten a story about a bottom line that was seeping but not hemorrhaging, about a stagnant company trying to jump-start itself.

And Julia. He'd gotten her.

"If it's going to be a good story, the source doesn't matter." Kim held her hand out as if expecting him to place the pages of his draft into it. "If it's good enough, we'll put it on the cover. But I need to see it."

"Next Monday," he swore, backing out of her office.

Once he'd returned to his own, much punier, much drabber office, he slouched in his chair and called up the article on his computer. He was aware that although it had a nice, warm undertone—all that nostalgia stuff, the paean to traditional foods and so on—it was thin and watery. He didn't want to strengthen it enough to hurt Julia, but he knew that if he submitted it in its current form to Kim, she would stuff it down the toilet. Better to crank it up before he showed it to her.

If only she'd confirmed for him that Jay was her source. The guy's preening and posturing irked Ron, and most of the revisions were going to be at his expense. But Ron would feel more gleeful about targeting Jay if he knew Jay was the one who'd instigated the article in the first place. The jerk would be hoisted by his own petard—whatever the fuck a petard was.

And let brother Ben hoist himself, too, Ron thought. If Julia's father had kept his pants on, Ron might have been willing to tread lightly on the guy's memory. He wasn't going to humiliate the Bloom family by writing about Ben's peccadilloes, but he could nail the SOB on other issues—his being detached and driven, for instance. While Julia and the rest of the family hadn't criticized him for devoting himself to the store above all else, enough people outside the family had described him as a cold bastard. Ben Bloom wasn't going to emerge from the article qualifying for sainthood.

It bothered Ron that he would even consider exercising restraint in his reporting. But damn it, he didn't want Julia injured by what the magazine published. She deserved to have someone on her side. She couldn't count on her mother or her doofus uncle. Probably not even her sister, who seemed far too content working at that low-rent pizza palace downtown. If Ron turned out to be the only person standing between Julia and the big ugly world...well, it was a hell of a place for him to be standing, given his job, but he wasn't going to move.

He scrolled down the first page of the article, remembering how Julia's eyes had welled with tears as she'd read it. It wasn't *that* good, but it pulled the right strings and pushed the right buttons. Ron was a professional. He knew what he was doing when he pounded the keyboard.

His phone rang. His eyes still on his monitor, he lifted the receiver. "Ron Joffe here."

"Mr. Joffe?" a honey-smooth male voice coursed over the line. "My name is Lyndon Rollins. I'm calling for Ida Bloom."

Ida. The one Bloom he'd been denied access to. He sat straighter. "Yes, Mr. Rollins. What can I do for you?"

"Mrs. Bloom heard that you were putting together an article about Bloom's for *Gotham Magazine*. She would like to meet with you."

"Great!" Ron grabbed a pencil and notepad. "How about now? I could come right over—"

"She'd prefer to come to you," Lyndon Rollins said.

"She wants to come here? I know she's…well, what I mean is that if traveling is difficult for her, I could—"

"She's eighty-eight," Lyndon declared, barreling past Ron's attempts at tact. "But she isn't housebound. We can be at your office in an hour."

"One hour is fine." One hour barely gave Ron time to review all his notes and formulate some questions, but he could do it. He gave Lyndon the magazine's address, thanked him and hung up.

Ida Bloom. The grand dame, the queen of the realm, the delicatessen Hera descending from Mount Olympus to talk to him. He wondered why, then decided he didn't care.

He spent the next hour scrolling through his computer files and plowing through his notes. Five minutes before her scheduled arrival, he ducked into the bathroom, combed his hair and popped a breath mint—approximately the same last-minute grooming he underwent before seeing Julia. He had a tie in his desk drawer, but it featured a pattern of dancing Daffy Ducks, so he decided to leave it off. Returning to his office, he cleared his throat a few times, stared at the telephone and waited for the receptionist to announce Ida Bloom's arrival.

Ten minutes later, his phone still hadn't rung. Damn. If he'd known Ida was going to stand him up, he would have guzzled a cup of coffee rather than sucking on a Tic-Tac.

He took a deep breath. He'd dealt with difficult interviewees plenty of times, tardy ones, imperious ones. He'd never before dealt with an interviewee who was the grandmother of the woman he was sleeping with—but things were good with him and Julia, and really, the fact that they'd set the world on fire a few times over the past week had no bearing on what he and Ida would talk about.

Why did she want to talk to him, anyway? Why would she *say* she wanted to talk to him and then not show up? Why was he feeling even edgier than he had the evening he'd met Julia for dinner at the Italian place on Restaurant Row? That had turned out all right—much better than all right. He assured himself that this would turn out all right, too.

It occurred to him that Ida Bloom must be problematic. After all, she'd tossed Julia into the presidency and left her to fend for herself. And of the two sons she'd raised, one was an asshole and the other was a dead asshole. Hera or not, old Ida had some explaining to do.

The phone rang. He flinched, then took another deep breath, tasted the residual mintiness on his tongue and answered to hear the receptionist announce that Ida Bloom had indeed arrived.

He strolled down the hall to the reception area to greet her. He was startled by her size, or lack thereof. She couldn't be more than five feet tall, although her puffy, artificially black blob of hair added an inch or two to her height. Her shoulders were narrow, her body slim and erect in a plain navy-blue skirt, a pink blouse, a maroon cardigan and flat leather oxfords with ridged antislip soles. Not that he was any judge of geriatrics, but she didn't look eighty-eight years old. He would have guessed seventy, at most.

She was accompanied by a slender, dark-skinned young man with a fringe of braids framing his face and a smile as big as the Staten Island ferry. "Mr. Joffe?" he said. "I'm Lyndon Rollins, and this is Ida Bloom."

Ron shook Lyndon's hand, but Ida's stern expression didn't invite a handshake. She was of a prefeminist generation where men and women didn't shake hands, but he knew she wasn't some delicate blossom who required gentle handling. His research into the history of Bloom's informed him that she'd been a powerhouse during the business's early years, putting in as much time and labor as her husband while they built their shop into the institution it was today. Still, one look told him she didn't want a handshake.

He led her and Rollins down the hall to his office and inside. She gazed around and sniffed. "This is your office?" she asked, obviously underwhelmed.

He didn't think it was so bad. In fact, he thought it was better than Julia's office on the third floor of the Bloom Building. True, it was smaller, and its solitary window overlooked an air shaft, but the carpeting was newer. He lacked a leather sofa, but his chairs were ergonomically designed. Ida Bloom settled into one, folded her hands primly in her lap and studied his animal posters, her gaze lingering on the picture of an orangutan, which had always seemed somehow obscene to Ron, though he wasn't sure why. Something about the beast's wide, flaccid lips, maybe.

He sat at his desk and gave her his best smile. "I'm really glad you came, Mrs. Bloom. I've wanted to talk to you. I hope you don't mind if I tape our conversation."

"Tape?" she asked suspiciously. "What do you mean, tape?"

He pulled his tape recorder from a desk drawer and set it up. "The microphone is built in. If you speak in a normal voice, it'll record you. Pretend it isn't there."

"Why do you want to tape me?"

"I can't take notes fast enough," he explained. "If I relied on my written notes, I might miss something important. Using the tape recorder means I won't miss anything. Okay?"

She eyed the machine dubiously, then lifted her gaze to him. "So, tape." Her incongruously dark hair seemed plastered in place. It didn't move when she did.

"Thanks." He pressed the button to turn on the machine.

She craned her neck to view the tape as it moved from spool to spool. "It's working now?"

"It certainly is."

"It's too small. I never knew from such a small tape recorder."

"Well, this one fits in my pocket, which can be handy. Shall we get started?"

"You want to start? So start. What's with this article, anyway?"

What kind of question was that? How was he supposed to

answer? "It's a good article," he assured her. "Julia saw an early draft and was pleased."

"So, you showed Julia." She sniffed again. Her nostrils pinched together when she inhaled. "What did she tell you?"

For now, he decided to let Ida ask the questions—although he wished she would phrase them to offer clues about what she was getting at. "If you mean what did Julia tell me about Bloom's, mostly she discussed the store's worldwide fame and the variety of its merchandise. The article isn't going to be an ad for Bloom's, though. It will deal with the dynamics of a family running a tightly integrated business."

"We have no dynamics," Ida declared firmly.

Ron exchanged a glance with Lyndon Rollins, whose face gave nothing away. His smile was placidly neutral.

"We're a very ordinary family, Mr. Joffe," Ida insisted. "Except maybe my granddaughter Susie. You've met Susie?"

"Yes, I have."

"What did you think of her?"

He'd thought she seemed pleasant enough. "She's got some funny ideas for updating the display windows."

"What do you mean, funny? Funny ha-ha, or funny like mayonnaise goes funny if it's kept out of the refrigerator?"

"Funny ha-ha."

"So you've met both my granddaughters." Ida nodded and tapped her fingers together. They were slightly bent and swollen with arthritis, but her nails were painted a pearly pink. "Sondra—you met her?"

He nodded. "Your daughter-in-law."

"She told me about you. She said, maybe Susie would like you. Julia I don't worry about. She's got that boyfriend, the *goyishe* lawyer, I don't know what's going on with them. At least he's a lawyer. But Susie! With the tattoo and the hippie life— I know, it's the wrong decade for hippies, no? The wrong century. But you know what I'm talking about. She's a poet."

"The world needs poets," Ron murmured, making a mental note to ask Julia about this *goyishe* lawyer boyfriend. Was that the blond guy she'd kicked out of her office the day they'd found the condoms in the old desk? Or was there some other *goyishe* lawyer? She'd gone to NYU law school and joined a law firm while the ink was still wet on her diploma. She probably knew hundreds of *goyishe* lawyers. Thousands. They definitely had to discuss this.

He realized Ida was chattering away, and forced himself to pay attention. "Susie needs a nice boy in her life. Someone like you. Stable. You work at a desk. You work with computers. She's been friendly with someone in the store's bagel department—not Morty, the other one. What's his name?" she asked Lyndon.

Her companion shrugged. "I don't remember."

"She brought him to the seder."

"I remember that. His name escapes me."

"A big boy, very tall." Ida turned back to Ron. "All right, so his name is not important. But you—you work at a desk. That's a very stable thing to do."

He wondered if Ida Bloom had come all the way to his office to make a match between him and Julia's sister. The absurdity almost made him laugh out loud. "Susie strikes me as the sort of woman who knows what she wants and doesn't need her loved ones interfering," he said.

"You're such an expert? You think my family has dynamics. What do you know about Susie?"

"Just that I don't think she and I would be…compatible."

"Forget compatible. Sondra said…" Ida sighed and peered at Lyndon. "Why do I listen to Sondra? She's always trying to stir up trouble. She should keep her nose out of other people's business. Her nose is too small, anyway, am I right?" At Lyndon's helpful nod, she turned back to Ron. "So. You're not interested in Susie."

He didn't have the nerve to say no flat out. "I doubt Susie would be interested in me," he said, instead. "What I'm interested in is, why did you put Julia in charge of Bloom's? Why did you skip over Jay and Sondra and name Julia the president?"

"Why?" Ida seemed surprised by the question. "Because Julia is just like me, of course."

He stared at the old woman. Her lips curved in an unremitting scowl, her gaze pierced, her chin jutted. Julia was nothing like her.

"Julia thinks the company is bleeding," he said.

Ida Bloom pursed her lips and narrowed her eyes. "Bleeding what?"

"It's not growing. Profits aren't what they should be. You've got a bustling business, yet it's not making money the way it should be. This is the mystery at the heart of your store, Mrs. Bloom. Can you explain it?"

"What are you talking? It's doing fine." She fiddled with one of several gold bangles ringing her bony wrists. "There are ups and downs in a retail business, always. When my parents were selling knishes from a pushcart on the sidewalk, there were ups and downs. You think lots of people want to buy hot knishes in August? So there were downs. Then it got cold and there were ups. You're not in retail, what do you know?"

"I do know a fair amount about business, Mrs. Bloom." He eyed the tape recorder to make sure the tape was moving. "I have an MBA and I write a weekly column on business and finance for the magazine." He leaned forward slightly. "Is Bloom's in trouble, Mrs. Bloom? Shouldn't the store be earning greater profits?"

"Don't be silly," she scoffed. "Bleeding? I never heard from such a thing."

"Have you talked to your accountant about the store's performance?"

"Myron?" She issued a disdainful grunt. "Look, you want to write a story? Don't write a story about Myron. He's a *schlemiel*. A good man, but not worth a story. Here's the story you should write—the story of Isaac Bloom."

Ron lifted a pen as if waiting for her to tell that story.

"Isaac was my husband. He came over after Krystallnacht. You know Krystallnacht? He was just a young man, and he came steerage to America. We met, we married, we took over the knishes cart and we turned it into Bloom's. Hard work. *Oy,* such work we did! But here was the magic of Isaac. He could schmooze. You know what schmoozing is?"

Ron nodded.

"Isaac, he could schmooze anyone into buying anything. A woman would come into the store thinking she wanted to buy only a quart of borscht, he'd say, 'Mrs. Zaretsky, what a lovely scarf. So how's your son? He still has that cough? Hot, wet cloths on his chest, that'll break up the phlegm. What do the doctors know? Hot, wet cloths, I'm telling you.' And the next thing, Mrs. Zaretsky is buying a challah, some pickles, a pound pastrami. That was the way Isaac was. He used to say it didn't matter what you sold, as long as you were paying attention to who you were selling it to."

"The people I've talked to imply that *you* were the brains behind the store."

"I was," Ida agreed. "But Isaac was the heart. You can't sell if you don't have heart." She ruminated for a minute, her bullet-hard eyes aiming at him. "So, you think the heart of my store is bleeding?"

"You tell me, Mrs. Bloom."

"My son says Julia worries too much, she fusses over details. You know so much about business, what do you think?"

Ron paused to consider his answer. "What you've got, Mrs. Bloom, is a very insular company. You've got family running the place, along with a couple of outsiders so close they might as well be family, too. There's no objectivity at work in the way Bloom's is run."

"Julia's the objectivity."

"She's trying to figure out why the store isn't doing better."

"She told you to put that in the article?" Ida waved at his pad, as if there were any question which article he might put it in.

"Actually, no. She told me to keep it out of the article. And I hope I can, Mrs. Bloom. But—"

"What kind of article is this, anyway? You want to write bad things about Bloom's, am I right? Like those silly magazines that always have bad things about perfectly nice actors and actresses, that they're on drugs, they're breaking up their marriages, they cheat on their taxes, their titties are falling out of their dresses, all kinds of bad things. You're going to put in your magazine that we're insular. What is that, anyway? I thought it was something to do with diabetes."

Explaining insulin wasn't worth the effort. "It could be that the family is sparing you," he suggested. "According to Jay and Sondra, you're not all that involved in the running of the store anymore—"

"I'm the CEO," she announced. "What does that stand for again, Lyndon?"

"Chief executive officer," he supplied.

"That's right," she agreed, nodding resolutely. "Chairman of the board. If the store is bleeding, someone's supposed to tell me. Certainly they should tell me before they tell you, some reporter who wants to write bad things about my family."

"I don't want to write bad things," he insisted. It wasn't his fault that bad things sold more magazines than good things. "I don't understand why Bloom's isn't earning profits hand over fist. The store is always full of shoppers. The quality of the merchandise is excellent. Do you think someone is skimming?" he asked. "Myron, maybe?"

"Myron doesn't know from skimming. No one is skimming."

"Deirdre? Do you suppose she might have a reason to want revenge?"

"Everybody's got a reason," Ida said flatly.

If she knew Deirdre had been her son's paramour, she gave no indication.

"I came here to make sure you wrote a nice story and put in something about my Isaac, may he rest. I didn't come here so you should write bad things about insular and skimming."

Ron didn't remind her that she'd come to try to sell him on Susie. "I'll include everything you said about Isaac," he assured her. "But in the meantime, Julia says merchandise is disappearing."

Ida suddenly sat forward, reached across the desk and clamped a surprisingly strong hand over Ron's. "My granddaughter will suffer if you write bad things."

Her protectiveness toward Julia appealed to him. "I intend to write the truth, Mrs. Bloom," he told her. "I don't want to do anything to make Julia suffer."

"Then don't put in anything about this—the bleeding, the diabetes, all that stuff." She released his hand and settled back in her chair. "You know so much about business, you think the store should make more money? Tell me how. New windows? Susie's doing new windows. Computer? Jay does computer. Low fat? Sondra thinks we need more low-fat foods. She's always on a diet. So fine, introduce low-fat foods into the inventory. But you can't make a low-fat bagel, I'll tell you. Bagels already have no fat." Her gaze met Ron's, steady and challenging. "You're such an expert, you tell me. Nobody ever skimmed from my store. So what else would make these problems you think we've got?"

"I haven't reviewed your store's finances, Mrs. Bloom. I can't begin—"

"You talked to everyone. You know." Her eyes hardened, almost accusing. "You think Julia doesn't know how to run the store? She doesn't have the heart, she doesn't have the brain, is that what you're saying?"

"Of course not." But how could he know for sure?

"So, you'll come," Ida was saying.

"I'll come where?" Once again he had to scramble to catch up to her.

"You'll come and figure out why Julia thinks the store is bleeding."

She nodded to Rollins, and he rose and helped her to her feet. Ron sprang to his feet, as well.

"Do you think that's a good idea?"

"My store could be bleeding, and you're worried about

ideas? Come and tell me what's wrong, Mr. Hoo-ha Business Expert. If the store has a problem, someone has to tell me what it is. Jay won't. Sondra won't. Julia doesn't know. So you'll come."

If she was serious about letting him investigate Bloom's finances, he could write the truth about Bloom's—and help Julia, too. He had one week to get the piece finished and on Kim's desk. Why not review the store's records and turn the article into what his editor wanted it to be?

"You find a problem," Ida challenged him, "and I'll nominate you for that prize, what's it called? The Plotzer Prize."

"The Pulitzer," he corrected her.

"That's the one. Let's go, Lyndon. I need to get back to the store and find out if it's bleeding. You come with us," she ordered Ron.

"I can't. I've got...work," he said vaguely, because the only work he had was the Bloom's article.

"So you'll get your work done later. Come." She hooked her hand around his elbow and pulled him away from his desk. If she looked no older than seventy, her grip felt no older than a twenty-five-year-old's. "First we'll fix Bloom's, and then you'll write your story. And maybe you could talk to Susie a little, see how things go. Not that I'm pushing, but it wouldn't kill you to talk to her."

There was a crisis in the deli-meats cooler. A trucker whose first language was Latvian had dumped a delivery of Camembert and Roquefort in with the meats. Bloom's wasn't strictly kosher, but sensitivity to the laws of kashruth meant not tossing cheeses in with the meats.

As president, Julia had overseen the removal of the cheeses. She'd calmed down a few fretful elderly customers, including one wizened man who shouted at her that if only he were dead he could be rolling over in his grave right now.

Julia was not going to discard the cheeses or the meats—or, for that matter, the cooler. She assured the man who wished he were dead that she'd have a rabbi come in to say a prayer over the meats, and that mollified him. He didn't move from the bin, though. Evidently he intended to remain in place until the rabbi arrived.

She had no idea how to summon a rabbi on such short notice. Returning to the third floor, she called through Deirdre's open door, "Do you know a rabbi?"

The minute the words escaped her, she clapped her hand to her mouth. Why would Deirdre, of all people, know a rabbi? And why was Julia hollering through open office doors? Had the culture of Bloom's permeated her that thoroughly?

Deirdre slipped her feet into her spike-heeled shoes and stood, straightening each long limb until she loomed over Julia. "I have a variety of rabbis in my files," she said. "You want Orthodox, Reformed, Hasidic or Zionist rabble-rouser?"

Julia gazed up at her and experienced a soul-deep shudder of understanding. No wonder her father had fallen for Deirdre: not because of her gangly appearance, her toothy smile, her wispy red hair and her eyes the color of unripe crabapples. Not because he'd wanted an illicit thrill, or because he'd experienced an uncontrollable urge to liberate himself from the constraints of his marriage, but because Deirdre had a variety of rabbis in her files. For that alone, Julia was half in love with the woman.

"We need a blessing said over the meat in the deli-meats refrigerator," Julia told her.

"Reformed," Deirdre decided, flipping through the wheel of phone numbers on her desk. "I'll take care of it."

With a weary sigh, Julia nodded, thanked her and continued to her own office. She slumped in her chair and shook her head. If she ever confronted Deirdre about her affair with Julia's father, Julia would lose her. And if Julia lost her, Bloom's would collapse.

Her father and Deirdre had had what they'd had. Maybe it had been nothing more than lust, maybe the result of boredom or too much time spent in proximity. It had been wrong, it had been dishonest, but it was over. Nothing Julia did today could change what her father and Deirdre had done years ago. But what she did today could affect what happened tomorrow.

She needed Deirdre, if only for those catastrophic times when Baltic-native deliverymen dumped cheese into the meat bin.

The sound of footsteps, barely muffled by the paper-thin carpeting, alerted her to someone's approach. She glanced toward her door in time to see Joffe, and her spirits rose like a helium-filled balloon. "Hey! What are you doing here?" she asked, leaping out of her chair and crossing to the door.

He closed the door and opened his arms. She settled into them and met his lips with a sweet, warm kiss. It still amazed her that being kissed by him was like getting hit by a wrecking ball, only less painful. She felt shattered inside, shaky, on the verge of collapse. She wouldn't mind collapsing, as long as when she did collapse and wound up on the floor he'd be down there with her, still kissing her.

But he ended the kiss before they could get to the down-on-the-floor part. "What are you doing here?" she asked again.

"Your grandmother brought me," he said.

"What?" She fell back a step and gaped at him. "Grandma Ida?"

"I think she wants to set me up with your sister."

"You're kidding." Julia didn't know whether to laugh or curse. She opted for laughter. Susie and Joffe together made about as much sense as liverwurst and Camembert.

"I did my best to discourage her," he said, moving farther into the room. "She's a stubborn woman, though."

"When did you see her?"

"Today. She wanted input into the article."

Julia pursed her lips, less than thrilled. Grandma Ida had her own agenda, and no one—probably including Grandma Ida herself—knew what it was. "So you interviewed her?"

"She came all the way to my office to see me. She was insistent."

Julia had never been to his office. To think her grandmother had been there miffed her. "Did she tell you anything you can use in your article?" she asked cautiously.

"Some interesting stuff about your grandfather." He ran his hands gently over Julia's shoulders. "In the course of our conversation, it came out that I have some business expertise, and she asked me to figure out why Bloom's is bleeding."

Julia took a moment to absorb his words. She herself had asked him to help her investigate the mystery of the missing merchandise. But she'd asked him when they were in bed together, a woman requesting a favor of her lover. And she'd been asking his help only in trying to discover where the bagels were disappearing to. And he'd pretty much brushed her off.

This was different. This was her grandmother going behind her back to ask a reporter to find out why the store wasn't as profitable as it ought to be. It was her boss inviting an outsider in to do the job Julia had so far been unable to do.

She felt shaky again, shattered inside—but suddenly as cold as the Hudson River in January. She took another step backward, and another, until she reached the sofa and sank onto the cushions. "Why would she ask you to do that?"

To his credit, Joffe seemed sensitive to her dismay. "I don't know. A whim, I guess."

"You told her no, of course."

"I'm here, aren't I?"

He'd told her yes. Julia drew in a deep breath and struggled to compose herself. "You came here to humor her."

"Partly."

"And to see me."

"Of course."

"And now you're going to leave, go back to your office and write for your magazine."

He shook his head. "I'm going to review the store's records over the past couple of years."

"I've already reviewed them, Joffe. There's nothing there."

"Then, I'll find nothing. Your grandmother asked me to do this—"

"Oh, please. You're not doing this because my grandmother

asked you to. You're doing it because you're a reporter. You're looking for dirt to put into your article."

"I'm not," he said, sounding far from persuasive. "Julia, you yourself asked me to do this."

"I asked you to help me figure out why the bagels were unaccounted for. I never asked you to review the store's records!"

"Well, your grandmother did ask me."

"Did you promise her you wouldn't write up what you found?"

"She didn't ask for that promise."

"Suppose I asked for it. Would you give it to me?"

He gazed at her from where he stood near the door, his eyes much too clear, too beautiful. She knew before he spoke what his answer would be.

"No."

"Then, you can't see the records."

"Your grandmother—"

"My grandmother is eighty-eight years old."

"And sharper than some recent presidents. Julia, she opened the company's books to me. I'm going to look at them. In return, I hope I'll be able to make some suggestions that will strengthen the company. Okay?"

"No." She felt stronger now, strong enough to shove herself to her feet and glare at him. "It's not okay. You're going to publish in your magazine that the store is teetering, it's poorly run, the new president doesn't know her ass from her elbow—"

"Sure, you're the new president. You're learning on the job. I'll put all that into the article, Julia. Do you honestly think I'd write an article that would make you look bad?"

What she honestly thought was that he'd write an article that would make him look good. If doing so meant making her look bad—publishing a hard-hitting exposé about mismanagement and family strife in the delicatessen business—he'd do it without qualms.

Even worse than the comprehension that Joffe would smear Bloom's was the realization that he was doing it at her grandmother's invitation. Grandma Ida, who'd ignored Julia's objections and put her in charge, had just given her a vote of no-confidence. She'd asked in an outside consultant—none other than a business reporter for a splashy, glossy, top-circulation magazine—to fix things Julia had been unable to fix. It was one thing for Julia to ask Joffe for help, and quite another for Grandma Ida to go behind Julia's back and ask him for help.

All she'd ever wanted to do was make Grandma Ida happy. She hadn't requested this job, hadn't positioned herself for it, hadn't been grateful when it was forced upon her. But once she'd committed to it, she'd worked hard and tried her best. Everyone had told her to shut up and forget about the missing bagels, but she hadn't—and now her perseverance had caused her grandmother to undercut her.

It was enough to make her wish she'd never quit her job researching divorce settlements at Griffin, McDougal.

In fact, it was enough to make her want to divorce her whole family. And Joffe, too, even though she wasn't his wife. Just for the satisfaction of causing him grief, she wanted to marry him—so she could drag him through the ugliest, nastiest divorce New York had ever seen.

19

Three windows down, one to go, and Susie was hungry. Carrying two plastic forks and her purchase from the heat-n-eat counter, she climbed the back stairs to the third floor, shouted a greeting to her mother through the open doorway to her office and knocked on Julia's door before entering. Julia had asked her to come up for lunch. "We need to talk," she'd said ominously.

Something was going on with Julia—something bad, Susie suspected. Julia had been mopey all week, dressing in shades of gray that reminded Susie of chilly rain. Julia's gloominess had lasted too long to be hormonal—besides which, she never had hormonal mood swings. She was always so dogged and earnest, so determined not to be a slave to her cycles. Susie often wondered whether mood-and-hormone immunity was something they taught in law school. It sure hadn't been part of the curriculum at Bennington. Among her classmates, it had seemed that those with steady temperaments and chaste love lives were ostracized. "Don't hang out with *her*," someone might warn. "She's so, like, pleasant."

Julia was almost always pleasant—except for recently.

She'd taken the news of their father's infidelity pretty hard. Maybe Susie should have taken it hard, too, but she'd never thought as highly of their father as Julia had, so discovering he was a schmuck hadn't flattened her. She'd deduced long ago that there could be only two possibilities when it came to him: either he was screwing around or he was celibate. He simply hadn't been home often enough to have a tight relationship with his wife. And Sondra was always inundating her children with her love—either because Ben wasn't around to receive any of it or because she didn't love him that much in the first place.

Who knew? Susie was no expert when it came to love. Sex she understood. Love… Love was so damn *intimate.* It meant sharing more than climaxes. She loved Julia and at least some of her other relatives, but men? To love a guy meant knowing his tastes, knowing his dreams and goals, knowing red licorice was his favorite comfort food and scouring the tub was his least favorite chore, and he thought T.S. Eliot was overrated, and his best shot was a three-pointer from slightly to the left of the top of the key. It meant knowing that to him bagels were a medium, not an end in themselves, and that when he was eight he'd wanted to be Beast from X-Men when he grew up, and that not having sex with him was like being deprived of chocolate for a month. Sheer torture.

Not that she was in love with Casey Gordon.

But it was Friday afternoon, and her marathon with him would begin tomorrow morning, when she ventured into that foreign land known as Queens, New York. By Sunday morning, they would have completed their twenty hours, and Susie had every intention of bingeing. Who was it who'd nicknamed orgasms *petit morts?* Small deaths. Susie was anticipating death-by-chocolate.

Julia was seated at her desk in one of her overcast-sky outfits. She'd set up a computer on one corner of the desk—their father had never installed one in his office, claiming Jay could take care of the computer end of the business. Now that Julia was in charge, however, a computer had invaded the late Ben Bloom's inner sanctum. From where Susie stood, just inside the doorway, she could see that the monitor was filled with some sort of graphics program.

Julia spun in her chair and faked a smile. "Hi, come on in."

"What are you working on?" Susie enquired, closing the door and then crossing to the desk. She put down the plastic tray holding their lunch and dragged over a chair from near the sofa so she could sit close to Julia.

"I'll tell you in a minute. What did you bring?" Julia eyed the container.

"Stuffed cabbage. I hope that's okay. It looked good and smelled even better."

Julia's cheeks went almost as gray as her sweater set. "Wonderful," she muttered.

"You wanted something else? You should have told me."

"No, stuffed cabbage is fine. I've heard the way they make it downstairs is delicious." She sounded about as enthusiastic as a death row inmate being offered a tour of the gas chamber. She picked up a plastic fork, tapped the tines idly against her blotter and turned her gaze back to her monitor. "All right, you want to know what I'm working on? The *Bloom's Bulletin.*"

Susie shifted in her chair so she had a better view of the monitor. The image on the screen resembled a newspaper page, with rectangles outlined to hold articles and *Bloom's Bulletin* typed in a large Old English font across the top. "What's that?"

"It's a newsletter we're going to start publishing. It'll advertise our weekly specials, of course, but it'll also contain recipes, employee news, anecdotes and stories about the products we sell—you know, like maybe an article explaining the difference between Turkish and Greek olives."

"I know that mystery's been keeping me up nights," Susie joked as she pried the lid off the container. A puff of tangy fragrance wafted into her nostrils: sour cabbage and sweet tomato sauce and earthy beef and rice all mixed together to jolt her stomach awake.

"It'll also announce our singles' night."

"Singles' night?"

"I'm going to institute a singles' night at Bloom's. Thursday night, probably, from eight to ten. Maybe we'll have cheese tastings or something."

"Eeeuw. Eating cheese is going to give everyone bad breath."

"Well, something else, then. Cracker tastings."

"Coffee tastings."

"Right!" Julia's smile actually looked genuine for a second. "Or we can get experts in to give talks."

"What kind of talks?"

"I don't know. An olive expert can explain the difference between Turkish and Greek olives. Who cares, as long as the customers mix and mingle."

"And if some married person appears at the door suffering from a craving for Turkish olives, you're not going to let him in?"

"Of course we'll let him in. But the thing is, it'll be a social evening. Folks will linger, they'll flirt…and they'll buy stuff. What do you think?"

"I think it's a terrific idea." Susie herself could not imagine spending an evening at Bloom's, trying to pick up anyone—other than the tall, sexy guy behind the bagel counter, perhaps. But it sounded like a reasonable way to bring people with shared interests together, in this case their shared interests revolving around garlicky salami and dill pickles. It could be the Upper West Side version of a poetry slam—an excellent idea, if you wanted to meet Upper West Side–type people. Maybe singles could even recite poetry. "'A man who preferred olives Greek, Went to Bloom's, a new lover to seek…'" she began.

"Oh, that's great! God, Susie, you're so brilliant. We could put your poetry in the *Bloom's Bulletin,* starting with that limerick."

"I haven't written the rest yet," Susie protested, but she was so glad to see Julia smiling that she completed the rhyme. "'The ladies were rallyin' for olives Italian! They decided the man was a geek.'"

"Never mind," Julia said with a laugh. "We'll leave that one out of the bulletin."

Pleased with herself for having wrung a bit of laughter out of her sister, Susie broke off a chunk of one of the stuffed cabbages, bit into it and sighed happily. It was delicious, just like grandma used to make—if one's grandmother ever did much cooking, which neither of Susie's grandmothers did. "Try this—it's good," she said, nudging the plastic tray toward Julia.

Julia dropped the plastic fork as if to keep herself from eating. "Maybe later. Listen, Susie—here's my thought. I want you to edit the *Bloom's Bulletin*."

"Me?"

"Like I said, it would come out once a week. We'd have stacks throughout the store for browsers to pick up, and maybe we'll do a mailing. I've looked into the cost of bulk mailing versus inserting it in the Sunday paper, but I think people would be more likely to read it if it wasn't stuffed in with all the other Sunday circulars. So we'd do a bulk mailing. It'll put Bloom's on the map with a younger clientele. It would be witty, fun to read."

"How do you know that?"

"Because you'd be the publisher."

"Wait. I'm the editor *and* the publisher?"

"Probably the author, too—although you could get other people to write some of the articles for it. Like reminiscences about how their grandmother always skinned her knuckles while grating horseradish by hand, or how their grandfather was afraid to eat tomatoes when he first came to this country, he thought they were poison or something. You'd be in charge. You could solicit stories."

"Why me?"

"You're a poet."

"Yeah, and I could write limericks about grating horserad-ish." Actually, Susie thought it might be fun putting together a weekly newsletter, but she couldn't just say yes. Writing the newsletter would mean working for Bloom's—which she was already doing with the windows, but only on a contract basis. The newsletter thing would be ongoing. She'd be an actual employee, on a salary. She'd see her mother every day. If she worked full-time for Bloom's, the family might think she'd gone straight or something.

"What about Nico's?" she asked.

"What about it?"

"I've got a job there."

"You can quit."

"Quit Nico's?" Susie did her best to appear outraged by the mere suggestion. She speared another chunk of cabbage, chewed and found herself hoping Julia would continue to ignore the food so Susie could eat the whole thing. "Nico needs me."

"He needs you to change his window once a month, and you could still do that. He sure as hell doesn't need you to serve pizza. Anyone can serve pizza."

"You think?" Susie snorted. "It's a highly skilled position. It takes strength and patience."

Julia laughed. Not a hearty laugh, more like a smile mixed with heavy breathing.

"Okay, so maybe I'm not the strongest, most patient person in the world," Susie conceded. "Nico loves me."

"I love you, too. And I'll pay you more than he pays you."

The offer suddenly became more tempting. "I make a lot in tips, don't forget."

"I'll take that into account."

"So how much would you pay me to write this newsletter?"

Julia broke Susie's heart by using the edge of her fork to cut a small chunk of stuffed cabbage. "We'll have to figure that out when—" She faltered, then covered by popping the food into her mouth.

"Figure it out when what?"

Julia swallowed and swiped a hand through her hair, shoving it back behind her ears. "When they're done reviewing the records," she muttered.

"They? Who's they? Mom? Myron? Does he still wear a bow tie every day? That's so creepy."

"Yes, he still wears a bow tie, and *they* are an outsider Grandma Ida brought in to figure out why the store isn't making more money."

"Grandma Ida brought in an outsider?" This was breaking news. If the *Bloom's Bulletin* were a real newspaper, the fact that an outsider had been brought in would deserve a banner headline. Bloom's was family, Grandma Ida always said. No outsiders need apply. "Why did she do that?"

"She wants to ruin my life," Julia moaned.

"I thought she ruined it when she named you the president."

"It must have been so much fun the first time, she decided to ruin it again. Being a serial life ruiner probably brings her a perverse thrill."

"So, who'd she bring in? One of those slick, expensive consulting guys wearing a Rolex who's going to tell you to lay everyone off?"

Julia shook her head. "It's not just any outsider she brought in. It's Joffe."

"Joffe? The magazine reporter? The *stud?*"

Julia forked another chunk of stuffed cabbage into her mouth and chomped hard on it. "He's not a stud," she mumbled through a mouthful of cabbage, ground beef and sauce. "He's a prick."

"Yeah, well, same thing. You're not letting this get in your way, are you? Relationship-wise, I mean." Susie wasn't sure why she'd asked; she already knew the answer. Julia had been sulking all week for a reason, and now Susie knew what that reason was. "Forget it, Julia. Forget what he's doing at Bloom's. You can have sex with him without dragging your jobs and personalities and everything into it."

She wasn't sure why she'd said that, either. She didn't actually believe it. A month ago she might have. But then she'd met Casey, and she'd gotten to know him, and if and when she ever had sex with him—Sunday was still D-Day, if her calculations for the weekend proved accurate—it would be about more than sex. She knew too much about him. By the time they got it on, it would be like a three-course dinner, with wine and something from every food group in the pyramid. Chocolate dessert, maybe, but all those other flavors, too.

"I can't sleep with him—not knowing he's had full access to our records," Julia explained. "I went through all our records, and I couldn't find anything wrong. So Grandma Ida asked him to go through them—to check up on me. To catch my mistakes. To find out how incompetent I am. And the worst part is, he's going to take what he learns and stick it in his article."

"How do you know that?"

"He refused to promise he wouldn't. Which means he will."

"Shit." Susie twisted the handle of her fork between her thumb and index finger. She wished she could think of something optimistic to say.

"It gets worse," Julia said, pulling the tray closer to her and digging into the stuffed cabbage. "Grandma Ida wanted to fix Joffe up with you."

"Me? Nothing personal, but he's not my type."

"He's not my type, either. He's a sleazy scumbag who's plowing through our store's financials in search of dirty secrets."

"Yeah, but I mean, he's not my type. And I don't need fixing up."

"Grandma Ida thinks you do."

"Grandma Ida is a dangerous woman. What did you call her? A serial life ruiner."

"Well, she didn't ruin your life. She's ruined mine twice."

"That's because you're her favorite granddaughter." Since Julia didn't seem inclined to nudge the tray toward Susie, she reached for it and pulled it out of Julia's hands. "Don't eat it all."

"I don't want to be Grandma Ida's favorite granddaughter.

I don't want to be here. I don't want to sit in this office knowing Joffe is going to figure out what's wrong with this company and splash it all over the pages of *Gotham Magazine.*"

"And you want to get back to having sex with him."

"No," Julia said resolutely. "He's called me a bunch of times.
I told him I didn't want to see him. He betrayed me, Susie. How
can I have sex with him?"

"Because he's good in the sack?" Susie suggested.

"It was a rhetorical question." Julia pulled the tray back to
herself and speared the last piece of stuffed cabbage.

"Is he here now?"

"No. He spent an afternoon downloading data onto disks
and took them with him."

"He took disks with him?" Susie's voice rose to a near shriek.
She was no business genius, but even she knew this was bad. A
reporter with computer disks filled with all the financial data
on the store that was the subject of a feature article he was writing… This was really bad. "Why did you let him do that?"

"I didn't. Grandma Ida did."

"Why didn't you stop her?"

"Because she's Grandma Ida. Have you ever tried to stop
her from doing anything she wanted to do?" Julia flopped back
in her chair. It was so big her head landed several inches below
the headrest. "Anyway, I didn't know he was copying everything onto disks until he appeared in my doorway and told me
he was all done and ready to leave. He'd been here less than
two hours. I couldn't believe he'd finished reviewing everything in so little time, and he told me he was taking all the information home with him so he could work on it when he
had a free minute. I went ballistic, but he didn't care. He just
shrugged and left."

"And phoned you a bunch of times."

"I'm not going to sleep with him. Not when he's in posses-
sion of disks because our idiot grandmother told him he could
take whatever he wanted."

"I can't believe she did that."

"She likes him." Julia paused, then added with emphasis, "She likes him for *you*."

"She's crazy. Maybe the time has come to put her in a facility." Susie didn't really believe that. Even if Grandma Ida was deteriorating, she'd be better off in Lyndon's hands than in the fanciest nursing home in the city. And Susie didn't believe Grandma Ida was deteriorating, either. "You know, Julia, if you sleep with him, he might give you the disks back."

"Oh, right. That's a swell idea. Maybe he'll throw in a little cash to sweeten the deal." Julia's glare was as blinding as a solar eclipse.

"Well, okay. What's done is done. Forget him. Find someone else. How's old Heath Bar doing?"

"Heath? He's out of the picture."

"So put someone else in the picture. There are lots of men out there, Julia. And who needs men, anyway? They're mostly pains in the ass."

"You're right about that."

"Look. Let's have dinner together tonight, okay? We can get more stuffed cabbage—and some salad. What kinds of salad do they sell downstairs?"

"I don't know—deli kinds of salad. Red Bliss potato salad. Pasta salad. Cole slaw. Carrot salad. Sauerkraut."

"The red kind? I love the red kind. And some carrot salad, too—as long as it doesn't have too many raisins in it. We'll go to your place because it's closer."

"This has to be one of the most exciting dinner invitations I've ever received," Julia grumbled. "Takeout at my own place."

"And we'll rent a movie. Something with a revenge plot. *Attack of the One-Breasted Amazon Warrior Bitches.* Or *Thelma and Louise.*"

"It's a date," Julia said. "Is that a real movie? Not *Thelma and Louise.* The other one."

"I don't know," Susie admitted. "But if it isn't, it should be."

★ ★ ★

Sondra wondered when Julia was ever going to start leaving her door open. It was the way things were done on the third floor. Open doors welcomed an ebb and flow, a give and take, lines perpetually open for communication. Plus, with the doors open, it was possible to keep tabs on how many hours a day Jay actually spent in his office.

Very few, in fact. Sondra paid attention.

She was going to have to figure out a way to mention Jay's chronic disappearances to Julia. If by chance she wasn't aware of what a sluggard her uncle was because she never kept her door open, Sondra would sneak the information into a chat. Given that Julia was the president of Bloom's, she ought to make sure she was getting a full day's work from her underlings.

That Jay was Julia's underling was a source of great satisfaction to Sondra. It was so satisfying, it almost made up for the fact that she herself was also Julia's underling.

It wasn't supposed to happen this way. Here they were in May already, and Julia seemed further than ever from returning to her job at Griffin, McDougal. Sondra was going to have to figure out a way to finagle that into a discussion, too. She needed to know where she stood at Bloom's, and how long she'd have to stand there.

Nothing was going as she'd planned. That good-looking reporter? He'd come and gone, and she'd be damned if he'd exchanged more than three words with Susie, who still seemed to be mooning over the bagel clerk. For God's sake, he was so inappropriate! Why couldn't Susie find a nice Jewish boy? Or at least someone with an education and a real job. What had Sondra and Ben invested all that money in private schools and Bennington for, if Susie was just going to throw herself away on some behind-the-counter *shlub* from the store? Was it a class thing, Susie rejecting the affluence she'd grown up in? Was it the exotic appeal of the forbidden? Sondra wasn't forbidding anything. All she wanted was for her daughter to give a nice boy like that Ron Joffe a chance. She'd wanted it so much, she even mentioned it to Ida. The woman was such a master of manipulation Sondra thought maybe she could manipulate Susie into his arms.

Julia didn't seem to think the writer from *Gotham* was nice. Mention his name and she started snarling like a dog at the end of its leash. Who would have thought she'd respond so badly to the pressures of being president? Especially after working in a big, high-power law firm for two years. You wouldn't think the mere mention of a magazine reporter would throw her into such a state.

The girls were talking. Hovering right outside Julia's closed door, Sondra could hear their muffled voices but she couldn't make out the words. Were they plotting something? Or gossiping, maybe? Giggling over Sondra's thwarted desire to match her daughters up with suitable suitors? Julia had that lawyer, at least. Not Jewish, but his being a lawyer compensated for that. For all Sondra knew, though, the girls were talking about her, complaining. Shutting her out.

Julia never came to her own mother with ideas and questions about the store. She bounced all her ideas off Susie—who didn't even officially work here. And she bounced all her questions off Deirdre, who undoubtedly knew everything but wasn't a Bloom.

When Ben died, Sondra had felt closer to her daughters. But now that Julia was filling her father's chair, she didn't seem to want that closeness anymore. Suddenly she had ideas of her own. She wasn't interested in Sondra's ideas. She wasn't interested in *any* ideas. All she cared about were teeny-tiny discrepancies in the inventory numbers. She nitpicked over the bagel count, while Jay was off having marathon lunches or playing racquetball during business hours.

Why didn't Julia pay attention? Why wasn't she making sure her employees were getting their jobs done? That was her role; she always made sure everything was all right, and if it wasn't, she'd fix it. She'd been such a sweetie.

Not anymore. She'd had a taste of power and she'd changed. Now she let everything hang out—good moods, bad moods, annoyance, frustration.

It must be Susie's fault. Susie had always let it all out. Now, instead of Susie becoming more like Julia, Julia was becoming more like Susie. This wasn't the way it was supposed to be.

Only two more weeks and Adam would be home from college. Sondra hoped he was still a sweetheart, at least. She used to feel as close to her daughters as peanut butter to jelly, but now...now she felt as close as pasta to mustard. They didn't go together anymore. They didn't even belong on the same plate.

At least she had a son, and thank God for that.

20

"Women!" he grunted.

God, what a cliché. Every heterosexual man in the western world, and probably a few gay men, too, at one time or another must have sprawled out across a sofa with a beer in one hand and the remote in the other and grunted "Women!" in the same tone of voice he might use upon discovering the dog had pooped on the carpet or the IRS planned to audit him. *Women!*

Really, what else was there to say?

Plenty, if the guys announcing the basketball game would quit babbling long enough for Ron's brain to fill with his own words. Words about *women*. About how generally useless they were, how stupid, how they threw their little hissy fits and refused your calls because, gee whiz, it was so much more fun to be pissed off than to get off your chest whatever was on it. If only Julia had accepted his calls, they could have worked this thing out. He would have said, *I don't know why you've got a bug up your butt about my helping your grandmother. So shake it off, get your ass over here and let's have sex.*

Yeah. A calm, rational discussion between adults, a meeting of the minds. They could have gotten back on track in no time.

If only she'd answer her damn phone.

He had tried her at work and at home. He'd developed a special relationship with her answering machine as well as with one of the secretaries at Bloom's. There were things he wanted to tell Julia, important information about what he'd learned after poring over the past few years of Bloom's financial records. Information she might actually want to hear.

Beyond being able to discuss Bloom's with her, he wanted her in his bed. Hard to believe they'd only just gotten together so recently. It seemed as if they'd never *not* been together. The inevitability and certainty of it had nothing to do with love, with eternity or till-death-do-us-part, but damn it, he and Julia were good together, and not being together was turning out to be really bad.

So why wouldn't she take his calls? Maybe she was out tonight with the *goyishe* lawyer her grandmother had mentioned. Maybe she hated her grandmother so much that she had cut Ron dead just because he'd thought the old lady was a hoot and he'd agreed to do a favor for her.

All right—a favor for himself, too. That was what Julia was really upset about: that Ron would use what he'd learned from the company records in his article.

Of course he would. What did she think, he was an idiot? He had a job to do, he was damn good at it, and if Her Majesty Ida Bloom, Queen of the Deli, supplied him with material that enabled him to do his job better, he sure as hell wasn't going to seal that material inside a box and ship it back to the sender unused. If Julia was looking for a guy that moronic, a guy who took that little pride in his profession—well, who needed her?

He drank some more beer and pressed the Scan button on the remote. The screen flipped through an absorbing array of offerings: an SUV ad, professional wrestlers in tiger-striped latex yanking on each other's hair, a *Saturday Night Live* repeat, a bombastic report on the Battle of the Bulge, an ad for jock-itch ointment, a dazzling cubic zirconium pendant for sale, a preternaturally attractive duo squaring off to the accompaniment of hysterical canned laughter, another SUV ad and a commercial for *Greatest Songs of the Seventies.* Ron couldn't think of any great songs of the seventies, let alone *greatest* songs. Perhaps the *Greatest Songs of the Seventies* CD would turn out to be blank.

He wished Julia were with him so he could have shared his ironic observation with her. She would have laughed. Maybe she would have snatched the remote from him, turned off the TV and then loosened the drawstring at the waistband of his sweatpants and slid her hand inside, as if he needed any help getting in the mood for her.

But she wasn't with him. She was doing the hissy-fit thing and leaving him to the mercies of her answering machine. And he was working on his third beer and grunting "Women!"

Queens was weird.

Well, okay, that wasn't fair. It had a lot more sky than Manhattan, more air, more space. The park Casey took her to for a picnic lunch might well have been smaller than Central Park, but it seemed larger because it wasn't hemmed in on all sides by skyscrapers.

"Is it really called Flushing Meadows?" she asked, trying not to curl her nose. "That sounds like the name you'd give a sewage treatment center."

As parks went, Flushing Meadows was adequate: grass, trees, artificial ponds, a few odd buildings left over from the 1964 World's Fair and lots of broad paved paths filled with kids on scooters, skateboards and in-line skates, cyclists, parents with babies in strollers, parents with toddlers who raced off in assorted directions until the parents hollered, "Get back here this instant!" and dog walkers. And a few couples like Susie and Casey.

Her second favorite thing about Flushing Meadows was that, although Queens residents obviously enjoyed their little patch of green, the place wasn't clogged with crowds the way Central Park would be on a balmy Saturday like today. Her favorite thing, though, was that she and Casey were a couple.

Neither of them had to say it. It was just there, as if they were wearing invisible matching jackets. When they observed the people around them, analyzing the technique of a skater or chuckling over the rainbow-hued Mohawk sported by a heavily tattooed guy walking a dachshund, when they swapped sandwich halves so they could each have half a turkey on rye, and half a tomato, Swiss and Dijon mustard on whole grain, when they debated whether the rap blaring from someone's boom box was truly street poetry or just a lot of noise, they were a couple. Something connected them, something they didn't have to see or feel to know.

It was almost like sex, that connection.

Before going to the park, they had spent a little time at his apartment, which impressed her mostly for being three times the size of the apartment she shared with Anna and Caitlin in the East Village—and Casey didn't even have to share it because the rent was actually affordable. She had no idea what Bloom's paid him, but she'd bet it was a decent salary. Plus, he told her, he occasionally did freelance gigs for a caterer he'd gotten to know at the Culinary Institute. He felt Bloom's ought to be pushing their catering service more. Susie told him to recommend that to Julia. She wanted him to get the credit for a useful suggestion, and she wanted her family to admit that he was clever, with valid ideas to contribute.

She'd never before cared what her family thought of the men she knew. She'd never bothered to introduce most of them to her family. And while she hadn't cared much what the Bloom clan would think when she'd brought Casey to Grandma Ida's seder, she cared now. She didn't want Grandma Ida setting her up with Julia's magazine guy. If Grandma Ida ever spent five minutes talking to Casey, she would recognize his quality.

They left Queens around five, rode the subway into Manhattan and downtown, and ate pizza at Nico's. She'd arranged to have the night off, and it was fun to be waited on by the people with whom she usually worked side by side. Casey thought the current window—which featured a bicycle with two fake pizzas where the wheels were supposed to be, and information about Nico's delivery service—was catchy, but he wasn't overwhelmed by the pizza itself. "Not enough texture to the crust," he critiqued it.

After dinner they went to a Jackie Chan double feature, which let out around eleven. Then to a café for espresso and cannolis, and then back to her apartment.

Fourteen hours they'd spent together so far. And now they were going to sleep in the same room, which she was prepared to argue should count toward the final hour tally if he gave her a difficult time about it. A part of her was edgy with excitement, but another part of her was totally calm. *Of course,* that part of her seemed to say, *this is what's supposed to happen. You spend a day together. You spend a night together. Sex or no sex, you're connected.*

Unfortunately, Anna and Caitlin were both without plans that evening. Anna told Susie she'd gone out earlier for Thai with Rick, but even though he'd invited her she'd wound up having to pay for most of it because he'd had only eight dollars on him. "Your cousin is a great guy, but he's a turd, you know?" Anna said.

"That about sums it up," Susie agreed.

Apparently, there were no hockey teams in town, so Caitlin was home, too. She and Anna retired to the bedroom, and Susie told Casey they would both sleep in the living room. No way was she going to use her bed in the other room while he slept in the living room. If she did, it wouldn't count toward their total hours together.

Although, as she thought about it, the whole hours thing didn't seem to matter anymore. She just wanted to be in the same room with him. He insisted that she take the couch, and she dragged out her old sleeping bag—which at one time had been her cousin Neil's, although she wasn't really sure how she'd wound up with it. She had a vague memory of Aunt Martha's having pressed it upon her when she was packing for Bennington. "Perhaps up in Vermont you'll become one with nature," Aunt Martha had predicted. Susie had become one with a few boys at Bennington, but nature hadn't done much for her.

She gave Casey the pillow from her bed, spread a sheet and blanket for herself over the lumpy sofa cushions, and wondered what would happen next. She didn't want to sleep clothed, but what was she supposed to do, strip down to her undies in front of him? She'd greatly prefer for him to strip her himself, but that wasn't going to happen when they still had at least five hours left.

He excused himself to use the bathroom. While he was gone, she shed her black jeans and V-neck, leaving on her kelly-green camisole and panties. She slipped under the blanket and tried to find a comfortable position on the cushions.

Lumps or no lumps, she'd be more comfortable in Casey's arms. She'd be more comfortable if he just held her, let her use his shoulder for a pillow—even if it was a pretty bony shoulder—and allowed the quiet, steady thump of his heartbeat to lull her to sleep.

He returned from the bathroom wearing only his cargo pants. She tried not to ogle his naked chest, but the whole warm, connected, sex-doesn't-matter concept was hard to hang on to when she was confronted with the sight of Casey stripped to the waist. His blond hair hung loose against his shoulders, his eyes were radiant despite the late hour, his torso was sleek and golden—and he barely spared her a glance.

"Where's the light switch?" he asked.

All right, so she didn't tempt him the way he tempted her. He'd kissed her once in the stairwell at the Bloom Building, decided she wasn't worth pursuing beyond that one kiss and opted to play with her head for a whole bunch of hours. There she was, clad in the closest apparel to lingerie that she owned, and he was going to spend what was left of the night no more than five feet away from her, and he didn't even consider her deserving of a good-night peck on the cheek.

Twenty hours she'd invested in this guy! Twenty hours with him and untold hours dreaming about him, puzzling over him, trying to psyche him out and convincing herself that the effort, however futile, was great fun. And tomorrow she was going to wake up to find him gone, or laughing at her. "Suckered you, didn't I?" he'd snicker. "Do you honestly think I would have wasted all those hours talking to you if I wanted to get it on with you? Think it through, Susie! Does that make sense?"

No, it didn't make sense—and the sudden realization caused her nose to clog as tears filled her eyes and backed into her sinuses. The couch was uncomfortable—parts of the upholstery were soft enough to swallow her, and other parts jutted into her as if the cushions had baseballs and burrs embedded in them. She'd sacrificed her pillow to Casey, and her head banged against the couch's arm. The light was off and she couldn't see him, but she could hear his steady breathing, she could smell his Ivory-soap scent, and she hated him for having made a fool out of her.

It was well past one-thirty, however, and she'd put in a long day traipsing all over Flushing Meadows with him, and she would be able to hate him more effectively after she'd enjoyed a good night's rest. Closing her eyes, she mouthed a blasphemy in his general direction and glided into a surprisingly deep sleep.

"Susie."

She'd barely drifted off, and now someone was rousing her with a sibilant whisper. She resisted, but the voice hissed into her ear again. "Susie?"

Irked, she squinted one eye open. Anna was hunkered down beside the couch. The living room was bathed in murky light that seeped through the window shades. "What?" she grunted, not quite awake enough to remember that she was supposed to be full of resentment about something.

About *someone*. Casey. She hated him; it was coming back to her. She hated him for toying with her for twenty hours and not even feeling enough attraction to her to kiss her goodnight.

"Caitlin and I are going out for brunch," Anna informed her. "We'll be back at noon, okay? That gives you two-and-a-half hours."

In two-and-a-half hours, she could stab Casey through the heart, dismember him and shove his body parts down the compactor chute.

She attempted a smile. Anna and Caitlin thought they were doing her a huge favor, clearing out of the apartment so she and Casey could have two-and-a-half hours alone, but she didn't feel grateful. What could happen between them in those two-and-a-half hours? Besides bloodshed. They could have a nasty argument. She could kick him out. She could phone Julia and ask her to fire Casey—except she'd never do that, because his inventiveness with bagels was too valuable to the store.

Shit. She hadn't even officially accepted the job as editor of the *Bloom's Bulletin,* and already she was thinking about what would be best for the store. If Casey's talent was required by Bloom's, Susie was just going to have to let him live.

What was happening to her? Why did she care about what was best for Bloom's? Had she turned into a pod person?

The door closed with a *thud,* and then silence settled into the room. She closed her eyes in the hope of falling back to sleep. Maybe Casey would leave while she was dozing. Maybe he'd sneak out like a coward. If he knew she was contemplating stuffing pieces of him down the compactor chute, sneaking out would be a wise move.

She heard him stir in the sleeping bag, and squeezed her eyes so she wouldn't be tempted to open them. He shifted some more, and the sleeping bag's zipper opened with a rasp. She breathed deeply, focused her vision on the nothingness on the inside of her eyelids and prayed for sleep to steal her away.

He touched her foot, and she nearly leaped off the cushions in surprise. "Is this the ankle with the butterfly?" he asked, sounding absurdly lucid.

Damn. He was awake. He had obviously heard Anna and Caitlin leave. He probably thought Susie had schemed with them ahead of time to remove them from the premises in the futile hope that Casey would want to do something with her that required privacy.

But his hand was warm on her ankle, massaging her instep, and instead of screaming at him that he should have kissed her last night, she said, "No, it's the other one."

She felt a chill as he pushed the blanket off her, and then she decided it was silly to keep her eyes closed. She opened them in time to see him bow over her legs and brush her tattoo with a kiss.

All right, so she maybe didn't hate him.

He lifted his head and gazed at her, and what she saw in his eyes—hunger, yearning, lust, a single emotion refracted a million different ways—made her hate him even less. She pushed herself to sit as he reached for her shoulders, and then she tumbled off the couch and onto the floor, into his arms.

His mouth met hers and it was like that time in the stairwell, only much, much better because this time they were horizontal and all he had on was a pair of silk boxers and all she had on was her camisole and panties, which he promptly removed. His hands felt delightful on her skin, large and warm and possessive. She imagined his hands kneading dough, rolling it and shaping it into bagels. She imagined them twining through her hair, and in less than a minute she didn't have to imagine that anymore because his hands were stroking her hair back from her face, caressing behind her ears, cupping her cheeks while he kissed her.

She sensed the connection between them again, just like yesterday in Flushing Meadows. Unspoken, unseen, yet as powerful as a force of physics, magnetism or electricity or one of those things. She'd never excelled in science, but right now she was thinking chemistry. The chemistry between her and Casey was incredible.

She touched his chest, stroked his sides, eased back to look at him. He was smiling, that same wonderful smile she'd fallen in love with nearly two months ago, when he'd selected an egg bagel for her because he thought she was nubile. She felt nubile now, as if her insides were swelling and softening for him.

"Why are you smiling?" she asked.

"I'm happy. Why are *you* smiling?"

She hadn't realized she was until he mentioned it, and then she felt the ache of her smile in her temples. "I'm just wondering whether we would be doing this if we'd only spent, like, eighteen hours together."

"I'd give us a discount on those last two hours," he murmured, running his hands up and down her back, tracing the roundness of her bottom and then drawing them forward, up over her ribs to explore her breasts. "I think we're ready for this, don't you?"

She'd been ready since that first day with the egg bagel. But no—he was right. Then it would have been sex. Now it was more. They were talking too much for it to be just sex. "Frankly," she said, "I don't know how you managed to resist me for so long."

"It wasn't easy," he admitted, then sighed as she slid her hands down to the waist of his shorts and pushed them down his legs. "I guess I'm just tough."

"How tough?"

"Tough enough." He sighed again when she stroked his erection. "Almost," he added with a laugh.

She joined his laughter. God, this was good. Better than good. They were talking, laughing, touching, kissing again, moving against each other, kissing some more, pulling back to catch their breaths and laughing again. He eased her onto her back on the sleeping bag, then reached under the coffee table for his trousers and pulled open the Velcro flap on one of the pockets. He removed a condom.

He'd come for this. He'd been counting the hours as obsessively as she had, and he'd known today would be the day. That thought made her smile, and he smiled, too, and kissed her breasts, kissed her crotch, kissed her lips and fused himself to her.

Atop Neil's old sleeping bag, Susie became one with Casey, and it was as natural as nature itself. She closed her eyes and thought about all kinds of things she never thought about during sex: the length of his fingers, the shimmer in his gaze, his critique of Jackie Chan's foot movements during the second movie last night. His description of his best shot, the three-pointer that people thought was so hard but was pretty much instinctive to him. "It's just the way I'm used to moving," he'd told her. "I don't even slam it. I hardly even aim. It just happens."

That was how this was: just happening, instinctively, his aim perfect. She came, and he kept moving inside her until she came again, gasping and clinging to him and feeling his climax as keenly as her own. They sank onto the sleeping bag, holding each other tight, breathing hard.

Moments passed, and she relaxed her arms enough for him to lean back. His hair was disheveled, his face damp with sweat. Fudge, she decided. The richest, densest fudge in the world. She had been well and truly fudged, and she felt fat and sated.

"I think I'm in love," she murmured.

He grinned. "Let me know when you're sure."

His body softened and he slid out of her. She wanted him inside her again, as soon as possible. "How many condoms did you bring with you?"

His grin widened. "Eight."

"All right. I'm sure I'm in love," she announced.

He laughed.

She joined his laughter for a moment, then grew pensive. "Why did you make us wait so long for this?" she asked.

"I didn't make us wait," he told her. "We were heading in this direction all along. I just thought a little foreplay would make it better."

"Twenty hours of foreplay?"

"Exactly."

She considered his words. Maybe sex wouldn't have been so spectacular if they hadn't waited, if they hadn't explicated Jackie Chan and T.S. Eliot, if they hadn't discussed traditional Passover dishes or shared so many lunches in the tiny second-floor lounge at the store. She couldn't prove that the twenty hours had made all the difference, but who was she to argue with success?

"Do we have to wait twenty hours to do it again?" she asked.

His first answer was "We can't do that. Your roommates are going to be back at noon." His second was to place his hand between her legs and make mischief with his fingers, until she startled herself by coming again. She moaned, pleased and embarrassed.

He smiled down at her. "I think you're amazing."

"Let me know when you're sure," she said, once she got her breath back.

"Okay. I'm sure." He kissed her, a long, wet kiss that nearly caused her to come yet again. "I'm sure."

Through the mist her brain had dissolved into, she heard a vaguely familiar chirping sound. She didn't have a pet bird, and the chirping sounded more technological than avian. When Casey finally slid his mouth from hers, her mind cleared enough to recognize the noise.

"My cell phone," she muttered.

"Ignore it."

"It's my family." She pushed herself up to sit, and experienced another bout of embarrassment when she noticed the damp spots on Neil's old sleeping bag. "Only my family calls me on my cell phone."

"All the more reason to ignore it," he joked, but he rolled off her so she could stand.

Her legs felt rubbery as she picked her way around their underwear and the coffee table to reach her bag, which she'd left on the table near the window. She dug out her phone, flipped it open and gazed across the room at Casey. He was sitting on the sleeping bag, long and lean, reminding her of a Rodin sculpture. She wasn't sure which one. Whichever was Rodin's sexiest, that was the one Casey resembled.

"Hello?" She spoke into the phone.

"Susie?" Her mother. "You've got to come to the store."

"It's Sunday."

"So, the store isn't open Sunday?"

"I meant, it's *Sunday*. My day off."

"It's everybody's day off. As if that matters. Your sister is holding a meeting."

"On a Sunday?"

"She just phoned me. She said we have to meet on the third floor at twelve o'clock. Her and her *meshugena* meetings! I thought, maybe we should all refuse to show up, but then I realized Jay might show up, and if I wasn't there it would make him look good. Not like I think he's going to show up. He's out on the island, golfing."

"How do you know that?"

"He's always out on the island golfing. So he'll miss the meeting and I'll be there, and maybe Julia will fire him, which is what he deserves."

"Okay. Sure. Why did you call me, Mom?"

"Because you need to come to the meeting."

"Does Julia want me there?" She hadn't officially become the editor-publisher of the *Bloom's Bulletin,* which didn't even exist yet. Susie wasn't sure why she should attend Julia's meeting, unless it was to lend moral support to her sister.

"Julia asked me to call you and tell you to come. But listen to me. I'm worried about your sister. I think maybe the stress is too much for her. To insist on a meeting on a Sunday—it's crazy. She's been working so hard, in over her head with this business, and the nonsense about the bookkeeping, the details, missing bagels… And you're her sister, Susie, you tell me—hasn't she been acting particularly uptight lately? Very grouchy, very—pardon my French—bitchy. I'm afraid she's going to snap. She wants this meeting, so she'll have this meeting. But even if she hadn't wanted you there, I'd want you there. Just in case."

Susie hated to agree with her mother about anything, but the temptation was strong. Julia *had* been stressed out, grouchy, upset. Sondra probably didn't know that the main source of her stress was her lover's collusion with Grandma Ida. But it was not beyond reason to fear she was ready to snap.

And if she snapped, Susie definitely ought to be there to gather up the pieces and glue them back together. No one else loved Julia the way Susie did.

Her gaze returned to Casey, still seated across the small room. He watched her, obviously aware that the call wasn't good news. But he didn't crowd her, didn't rush to her side and take over. He just watched, his expression concerned but trusting.

She would much rather spend the rest of the morning making love with him, over and over and over. Twenty hours of foreplay had left her so primed that merely looking at him caused her womb to tighten and her thighs to clench. But her sister needed her.

And Casey wasn't going to disappear. She knew that in her soul. It was all part of that connection between them.

She turned back to the phone. "All right," she promised. "I'll be there."

21

The intercom buzzer sounded like a bumblebee on steroids.

Julia glared at the clock built into her oven. Nine on a Sunday morning was too early for someone to be visiting. But the buzzer kept sounding. Whoever was downstairs in the building lobby really, really wanted to see her.

Tightening the sash of her bathrobe, she set the box of Cheerios on the counter and pressed the button to speak through the intercom. Before she could say a word, Joffe's voice came through the speaker, sounding tinny and adenoidal. "Julia? I need to see you. It's important."

She wasn't sure she'd ever told him her exact address. But he was a reporter. He knew how to find things out.

"Julia, are you there?"

"I'm here." She sighed.

"I've got breakfast with me. From Bloom's. I've got four bagels, a tub of cream cheese and a quarter pound of smoked Nova. And two large coffees. Let me come up."

Her gaze wandered to the Cheerios. Joffe had lox. If she had eggs, she could make lox and eggs. It wouldn't taste as good as Lyndon's, and she hadn't bought eggs in months, so if she had any they weren't going to be fresh.

Still, she could warm the bagels, and he had hot coffee. She hadn't even inserted a filter in her Mr. Coffee yet.

"Julia, are you still there?"

The food sounded so appetizing. She felt her stomach clutch, pleading with her to release the locked inner door for Joffe. She felt another clutch lower, between her legs. A response to the prospect of breakfast from Bloom's, she assured herself. It had nothing to do with Joffe.

"If you don't let me upstairs," he threatened, "I'm going to hit every other button down here until some idiot releases the inner door for me."

"All right." She pressed the button to admit him, then leaned against the wall and groaned.

He'd said he needed to see her, it was important. Well, food was important. Maybe what he'd meant was that he had too much food to eat all by himself.

Hell. He needed to see her because he was a man with an ego and he couldn't bear the idea that she'd shut him out of her life. She'd been ignoring his phone messages—well, no, not ignoring them; she hadn't been able to put them out of her mind, but she hadn't returned his calls—so he was going to force her to acknowledge his existence by appearing before her in the flesh, bearing bagels. Men couldn't stand being ignored.

She shouldn't have let him upstairs. He was going to barge in and see her in her ratty old bathrobe with her hair tangled after a night of tossing and turning, and he was going to view his invasion of her apartment as some sort of triumph. *Ha, you've acknowledged me!* he would crow. *Now, stop being such a ninny about the fact that I conned your grandmother into letting me walk out of the Bloom Building armed with financial data I'm going to use in my magazine article. Wanna mess around?*

She didn't want to mess around.

Well, yes, she did. But not with Joffe. Not while he had the power to humiliate her store and her family in New York City's most popular magazine.

Her doorbell sounded. She tucked the cereal box back onto a cabinet shelf, raked one hand through her hair while the other drew the lapels of her bathrobe closer together and crossed to the door. Through the peephole, she saw Joffe's face, distorted by the fish-eye lens. He held up a bag, and the upward-sloping Bloom's logo swelled toward her.

She unlatched the chain and opened the door.

He stepped inside, and she swallowed hard. He'd brought with him not just food but warm, pulsing energy. His presence made her aware of how anemic her existence had been in the days since she'd banished him from her life. For one crazed moment, she fought the urge to fling herself into his arms and plead with him to make her feel all the things he'd made her feel before, things she'd never even sensed a glimmer of with other men.

She diverted that impulse by grabbing the bag and carrying it into the kitchen.

"Yeah, hi," he said conversationally, remaining by the door. "Great to see you, too. You're looking terrific. That bathrobe is *you*."

"If I'd known you were coming, I would have gotten dressed," she shouted out from the kitchen.

"Please don't ever get dressed on my account." He entered the kitchen, which seemed crowded enough with one person in it, but induced claustrophobia with more than one. Especially when the other person was Joffe. His blazer smelled of wet wool and his hair sparkled with raindrops. His gaze latched on to her, hot and inviting, and she fought another of those urges.

He'd come here in the rain. He'd gone to Bloom's, bought food and come here, without a word of complaint about the weather, because it was important.

"I've missed you," he said.

She turned away. She didn't want to feel kindly toward him,

grateful for his having gone to so much trouble on a drizzly Sunday morning. She didn't want him to say he missed her, because that would remind her of how much she missed him. She had missed him so much, it took some effort for her to remember why she'd been furious with him.

"What are you going to put in your article?" she asked, trying but failing to keep her tone neutral as she pulled the bagels out of the bag and sliced them.

"You read the rough draft."

"Have you changed that draft since plowing through all the intimate details of the company's bookkeeping?"

He swore softly. She peered over her shoulder at him. "Of course I've changed it. What am I, a moron?"

"That would be one possibility." She finished slicing the last bagel and arranged all the halves on a baking sheet, which she slid into the oven. "How bad is it going to be?"

"If it brings tears to your eyes, they'll be tears of nostalgia."

"I'm too young for nostalgia."

"Then you probably won't cry."

"But you're going to use the financial information my grandmother gave you in your story."

"The financials weren't as bad as I thought they'd be. That's why I wanted to talk to you, Julia. If you hadn't acted like such a jerk—"

"Excuse me?"

"Refusing my calls, hiding from me... I mean, come on! What would you call that?"

"I'd call it feeling betrayed because you obviously agreed with my grandmother that I was unable to handle things at the store, so she had to bring an outsider in."

"Your grandmother *does* believe you're able to handle things. Why else do you think she named you the president?"

"Because she's a jerk. How should I know? She should have named my mother."

"You're joking, right?" He approached the counter, carefully leaving some space between them as he reached into the bag and lifted out the coffees. He pried the lid off one cup and took a sip. "Your mother would have been a disaster as president of Bloom's."

Julia should have objected but she was too intrigued. "What makes you say that?"

"She lacks the commitment."

"What? She's worked hard at that store all these years—"

"She worked hard because she thought that made her a good wife. She did it without pay because she thought maybe your father and Ida would love her for it. Do you really think she gives a flying fuck about the store? She doesn't even eat Bloom's food. She buys all her food at the supermarket down the street. She told me that the first time I interviewed her."

"Okay. My mother works at Bloom's because she wants to be loved. I see. And when did you say you got your degree in psychology?" Indignation still didn't come easily to Julia. What Joffe said made too much sense.

"And your uncle Jay is the court jester. The man has the smarts but he's too lazy. He loves working at Bloom's as long as he can put in four-hour days and doesn't have to sweat." Joffe took another sip of coffee and rested his hips against the counter. "I didn't need access to the store's files to figure all this out. I talked to people. Lots of them. It's clear you were the best pick to replace your father. Your grandmother knows what she's doing."

"I'm sure that's why she wants to match you up with my sister." The fragrance of her coffee was so strong she felt a caffeine rush just from inhaling the scent.

"All right, look. Do you want to hear what I found? Yes, you do," he answered himself. "Where do you keep your plates?" He flung open a cabinet door, stared in apparent dismay at the sparse contents—a tub of uncooked oatmeal, a few cans of tomato soup, a jar of cinnamon and an unopened pack of sugarless gum. He shuddered, shut the door and opened another. That cabinet was filled with enough lidded plastic containers to open a Tupperware franchise—but all of them were empty.

Her mother was always bestowing plastic containers on Julia, no doubt thinking that someday she would have leftovers. Perhaps someday she would.

She opened the cabinet with the plates and handed him two. He carried them to the table in the nook off the living room that served as her dining area. She pulled the bagels out of the oven, arranged them on a third plate and opened the waxed paper wrapping of the lox. If only Lyndon were here, along with a carton of farm-fresh eggs... But this would have to do. Compared with dry cereal—in fact, compared with just about anything except Lyndon's cooking—this was a gourmet feast.

They settled at the table. Joffe pulled a notepad from an inner pocket of his blazer, placed it next to his plate and busied himself smearing cream cheese on a bagel half. "Okay, here's what's going on." He glanced at his notes. "You're grossing around a hundred-fifty thousand a week. That's not bad. It could be better, but it's not bad. Your payroll could go on a diet—not that you should fire anyone, but you're paying way above minimum wage, even for your cashiers."

"Most of them have been with Bloom's for a few years," Julia explained, forcing herself to overcome her irritation at the fact that he knew these figures.

"Okay, so they've been with Bloom's for a few years. You're paying them good wages, which makes them want to stay, which means you'll keep giving them raises and you'll never get out of this high-payroll situation."

"You're saying you think I'd be better off paying lousy wages and seeing lots of turnover?"

"No. I'm just explaining to you where your money is going. You want to pay good wages, fine. We're just adding up the numbers." He spread a layer of smoked salmon across the creamy surface of his bagel and took a bite. "This is great," he commented on the food before resuming his calculations. "You've got some sort of creative deal going with your rent. The store is occupying prime real estate, but it pays rent to the Bloom Building, which is owned by your family. So you catch a real break there."

"You could put it that way," she said, forking some lox onto her own bagel. "Or you could say the Bloom Building is taking a major hit."

"It's all in the family. You can work it any way you want."

She nodded, bit into her bagel and sighed. "You're right. This *is* great."

"'Thank you, Ron, for bringing this feast,'" he coached her.

She hadn't wanted to smile, but she couldn't help herself. "Thank you, Ron."

He smiled back. "You're welcome. Now..." He flipped a page on his pad and skimmed what he'd scribbled there. "Your losses due to theft and spoilage are smaller than average. Spoilage is always a problem in the food business, but you aren't doing too bad there. You could probably tweak your prices up a bit to increase your profits. Not a huge price hike, but a nickel here, a dime there. It would add up."

"You don't think it would alienate shoppers?"

"They're used to rising prices. The prices on most items in your store haven't risen since before your father died—and yet you're giving all your personnel annual raises. It's time to adjust the prices."

She nodded. In all her scrutiny of the financials, the possibility of raising prices had never occurred to her. She ought to thank Joffe for suggesting that.

"So, that's it, then? We should just raise the prices?"

"There's one other thing," he said, then popped the last of his bagel into his mouth and washed it down with a slug of coffee. She waited until he was done chewing. "You're losing three hundred dollars in merchandise every week."

The missing bagels. Everyone on the third floor acted as if she was crazy to care about those bagels, but if Joffe had noticed the problem, she wasn't crazy. He could tell them she wasn't. He could explain to her mother and uncle and accountant and assistant that three hundred a week in unaccounted-for bagels was worth noting.

"What do you think?" she asked cautiously. "Any ideas why

we might be losing this amount of merchandise on a weekly basis?"

He eyed her over his cardboard coffee cup. "It's pretty much the same items vanishing every week. A lot of bagels. Some cream cheese. Coffee. And then a few variants...rugelach one week—have you ever tasted the Bloom's rugelach, by the way? They're incredible."

"Yes. I've also tasted the stuffed cabbage," she confessed.

"Yeah?" His eyes glowed. "What did you think?"

"Incredible."

"Okay. So sometimes rugelach are missing. Sometimes mandelbrod."

"Did you ever notice how mandelbrod resembles biscotti?"

"Yeah, except our grandparents called it mandelbrod and didn't realize you could charge an arm and a leg for stale, funny-shaped cookies. Anyway—" he reached for another bagel half "—it's as if someone was catering a brunch every week for a hundred of his nearest and dearest friends. It's the same basic menu each week. Brunch food."

"What do you think it going on?"

"I think someone is hosting a big weekly brunch," Joffe said.

"Get serious."

"I *am* serious. This is too organized to be random theft. Someone is doing something specific here." He folded his pad shut and stuffed it back into his pocket.

"Are you going to put this in your article?"

"Put what? That someone is systematically stealing three hundred dollars' worth of brunch from Bloom's every week? Why would I do that? Next thing, you'd have police crawling all over the place, trying to find a culprit."

"If someone's hosting a weekly brunch... Uncle Jay," she guessed, rolling her eyes. "I bet he's doing something at his country club. He's out there every Sunday, some ritzy place on Long Island. Maybe he's showing off to all the rich snobs he golfs with, treating them all to some *real* food, proving to them you can run a New York deli and still be a big shot, you know?

The club probably serves cucumber sandwiches and watercress, so he brings bagels to show the boys how a genuine brunch is supposed to go. I bet that's it."

She waited for Joffe to sneer at her idea, the way everyone on the third floor might, but he didn't. "That sounds like a real possibility," he agreed.

"I'd like to drive out to that country club of his right now and see what kind of breakfast buffet they've got," she said, so enthusiastic she grabbed a second bagel and bit into it without bothering to add cream cheese or lox. "If only I had a car. I wonder if I could rent one and get out there before he finished his eighteen holes."

"Not likely. It's Sunday morning. People reserve rental cars way in advance for the weekends."

She sighed. "You're right." Aware of how dry the naked bagel was, she tossed it on her plate and stared at Joffe. "How did you get to be so smart?"

"I was born that way," he said, then grinned, a sizzling, seductive grin that made her wish he hadn't pumped her full of insights into the store's economic situation. A grin like his deserved a response—and that particular grin told her explicitly what response he wanted—but she couldn't think about sex when she had so many other things to work through: Uncle Jay's regular food thefts, the deli's pricing policy and her decision to forgive Joffe.

She wasn't sure when she'd made that decision, or even if she consciously had. She just knew that before he'd used bagels and lox to bribe his way into her apartment she'd resented the hell out of him, and now she no longer did. Now when she looked at him she saw an ally, someone who confirmed her suspicions. Someone who didn't think she was obsessed or insane or too detail oriented for her own good.

She saw someone whose mind was in alignment with hers.

"What we need to do," she declared, "is—"

"Take a tour of your bedroom," he finished for her. "I missed you, Julia. I'm horny as hell. We could have spent the whole weekend trying out new positions, and instead, you were locking me out. We need to make up for lost time."

She laughed, even as she felt her cheeks grow hot. "One thing you stink at is sweet talk. Suggesting a tour of the bedroom and trying out new positions is not a good way to soften a woman up."

"You're already softened up," he said, his arrogance just this side of bearable. "You missed me, too."

"Not for an instant," she lied.

This time he laughed. "How about it? You need to get dressed, anyway. You may as well get undressed, first."

"Joffe. You've just convinced me that I'm not deranged when it comes to the missing bagels. I can't think about sex now."

"I can think about sex all the time."

"That's because men's brains have much more rudimentary wiring. Just one basic circuit—sex, food, sleep, sex," she said, tracing a loop in the air. "Women are a bit more sophisticated. They actually have room in their brains for other things."

"Like missing bagels."

"Exactly. What we need to do," she declared, "is have a meeting."

"In the bedroom?" he asked hopefully.

"A Bloom's meeting. Today. Right now, in fact. Uncle Jay would have to drive back to the city. My mother would have to wake up. I've got to show them not only that I am not crazy, but that I'm the best damn president Bloom's could possibly have. Are you going to help me?"

"Will you have sex with me if I do?"

She threw her bagel at him. He caught it and grinned again, that irresistible grin. "Probably," she said.

22

Jay carried his cell phone with him when he golfed so he could make calls. Not so he could receive calls. He'd never given the number out to anyone other than Wendy, and she knew better than to phone him while he was playing.

But Julia had tracked him down. "I called your home, and your wife gave me this number," she'd explained.

Jay was going to have to have a serious talk with Wendy about that. The cell phone was for *his* convenience, not for anyone else's.

Julia's call came as he was lining up for a putt on the eleventh hole. The sudden *beep* shot his concentration to hell. And for what? For what great purpose had Wendy shared his cell phone number with his niece? For what profound reason had Julia interrupted his game?

She wanted to have a meeting. On a Sunday, for God's sake.

He consoled himself by admitting that it was a lousy Sunday for golf. The sky leaked a steady drizzle, his golf shoes were wet and grass stained and he was going to have to shell out a whopper of a tip for the caddy because holding an umbrella over the player's head demanded extra reimbursement. Muttering his apologies to Stuart, Jay bogeyed the eleventh hole, stuffed thirty bucks into the caddy's outstretched hand and sloshed through the damp, spongy grass to the clubhouse, where he bought a can of cola to drink on the drive back to the city.

He supposed he could have told Julia to stuff her meeting where the sun don't shine—but the sun wasn't shining on New York City today, so her meeting was already stuffed there. Besides, he didn't think it would be wise to miss a meeting. If everyone showed up but him, they'd all talk about him behind his back, and he wouldn't be there to defend himself. Given the lousy weather, what the hell. He hadn't been having a good game, anyway.

He emerged from the Lincoln Tunnel into the heart of a soggy Manhattan at a quarter to twelve. Julia could have scheduled the meeting a little later, to accommodate traffic problems, but he hadn't been about to point that out to her. She'd sounded almost tyrannical on the phone. "This meeting is important, Uncle Jay. It's not open to discussion. I've asked Mom to call Susie, and Deirdre to call Myron. Everyone is going to be there."

"What about your grandmother?"

"I'll be calling her after I call you. I'll see you in my office at noon, Uncle Jay."

The nerve of her, handing out orders as if she were his boss or something.

Which she was, but he hated thinking about it.

To make it across town, uptown to the store and into the back alley it took him fourteen-and-a-half minutes. He spent a few more minutes covering the car with its canvas tarp. Julia could cool her heels for a few minutes while he protected his beloved vehicle.

He hoped she would have food at this meeting. He was hungry. Wendy had bought some crullers at a chic Belgian bakery that had opened recently in their neighborhood, but he'd eaten only one before departing to meet Stuart out on Long Island. If not for Julia, he'd be finishing the eighteenth hole right about now, after which he'd be returning to the clubhouse with Stuart for martinis and roast beef sandwiches. The sandwiches at the club were a world apart from what was sold at Bloom's— roast beef at the club was served *au jus* on toasted French bread, with a side of fried potatoes shaped like round waffles. They didn't understand rye bread at the club. He'd once tried a sandwich on what they called rye. The bread had tasted like cardboard, only blander.

The hot roast beef sandwiches at the club seemed appropriate for the setting, but if he was going to be at a Bloom's meeting, he might as well have good food. A roast beef sandwich—or, better yet, a Reuben—from downstairs would be ideal, but he'd settle for bagels if that was all Julia had thought to provide.

He stalked down the hallway to her office. The door was open a crack and voices bubbled out. Sondra was ranting about how NASA was spending billions of dollars to send *nudniks* into space, while the schools in New York were crumbling. Susie laughed, presumably not about NASA's budget, and Julia asked someone to bring more chairs into the room. As Jay reached to push open the door it swung inward, and Ron Joffe, his buddy from *Gotham Magazine,* filled the doorway.

What was he doing here?

Apparently, moving furniture was what he was doing.

"Hi, Jay," he said. "I've got to get some chairs, so…"

He waited for Jay to step out of his way, then entered the open secretarial area and wheeled two desk chairs over. Jay might have offered his assistance, but why should he? Joffe was at least twenty years younger, and as far as Jay knew, he hadn't just raced to the Upper West Side from a golf course.

Jay's sour mood galvanized when he saw no food in Julia's office. Just the usual gang—Myron, Deirdre, Sondra and Julia— augmented by Susie and that tall blond guy she'd brought with her to the seder. He looked vaguely familiar, not from the seder but from somewhere else. Jay wasn't sure where.

"Good," Julia said, beckoning him inside. "We're all here."

"What about my mother?" he asked, commandeering one of the chairs Joffe had wheeled in. There was no room on the sofa. Myron was tucked between Sondra and Deirdre and looked dismayed about it. Jay realized it was the first time he'd ever seen Myron without a bow tie. Even when he'd viewed Myron outside of work—at his sons' bar mitzvahs, for instance—Myron had worn a bow tie, as if his neck were some thrilling gift that deserved to be adorned with a bow. Today, however, he wore a plaid shirt—buttoned tightly over his throat—starchy khaki trousers and no tie at all.

Sunday was clearly dress-down day at Bloom's. Sondra wore a denim skirt with a long, textured blouse over it that emphasized the expanse of her butt rather than downplaying it. Deirdre wore tight designer jeans that would have looked suitable at a late-seventies disco—and didn't look bad today, either, especially paired with the high-heeled open-toed shoes she had on. Julia was in a crimson blouse and jeans that, unlike Deirdre's, did not appear to have been painted onto her legs. Susie, as usual, was dressed for a funeral.

"I talked to Lyndon," Julia told him. "He said he wasn't sure if Grandma Ida would be able to join us."

"She's got such a busy schedule," Jay muttered sarcastically.

"It's Sunday and she's an old woman," Sondra intervened, obviously positioning herself as the reasonable, compassionate one. "If she doesn't want to come, is it the end of the world?"

Jay hadn't wanted to come, and here he was. But maybe the meeting would be easier without Ida present. If he wanted to score points with his mother, he could do so later, one on one.

"So, where are the bagels?" Myron asked. Jay silently cheered him on.

"That's a good question," Julia replied cryptically. Then she added, "I'm sorry, I didn't have time to pick up any for this meeting."

She dragged her own chair out from behind the desk, but instead of sitting, she stood behind it, resting her hands on the edge of the high leather back as if it were a lectern. Susie and the familiar blond guy sat on the old desk, side by side, every now and then exchanging a look Jay could easily interpret. Every time their gazes met, the room's temperature seemed to rise a few degrees. Julia must have dragged them away from something even more satisfying than golf.

"I wanted a bagel," Myron grumbled.

"Let's get started," Julia said, her voice sounding more forceful than usual. She must know she'd annoyed everyone in the room just by calling this meeting, and annoying people was the last thing Julia ever wanted to do. She was the conciliator of the family, the facilitator, the smoother-outer. The only reason Ida could have named Julia president of Bloom's was that Ida figured Julia would never alienate anyone.

She didn't sound conciliatory today. She stood straight, visible only from the bosom up because Ben's old chair was so big. Her hair was held off her face with simple silver barrettes, which made her eyes look larger than usual.

"The reason I called this meeting is that I've been vindicated," she orated from behind the chair. "Grandma Ida asked Mr. Joffe here to review our finances. He has an MBA, and he was able to assess our records with the kind of skill and training I lack."

"You're a lawyer, dear," Sondra interjected. "Don't belittle yourself."

Julia smiled faintly. "I'm not belittling myself, Mom. I'm just saying Grandma Ida asked Joffe to look at our records, and he did."

"I'm trained," Myron remarked, clearly disgruntled about the absence of food. He usually said nothing at these meetings.

"Mr. Joffe brought a fresh eye to the records. A fresh—and desperately needed—perspective."

Joffe rolled his fresh eyes as if being the topic of conversation embarrassed him.

"And he found that, yes, we are missing bagels."

"Oh God—not with the missing bagels again," Sondra moaned.

For once, Jay was in complete agreement with her.

"Show some respect, Mom," Susie called from her perch on the desk. "Julia wouldn't have dragged us all here if this wasn't important."

"The hell with respect. I've had it with the missing bagels. Julia—" Sondra twisted to view her older daughter, a movement that caused something of a tidal reaction along the sofa, with Myron and Deirdre rocking in her wake "—you have a store to run. A business. You're fussing over a few missing bagels a week like Lady Macbeth with invisible bloodstains on your hands. It's enough already."

Jay suppressed a snort. Leave it to Sondra to drag Shakespeare into it.

Julia stood taller, as if leaning into a stiff wind. "Mr. Joffe found the same discrepancy I found in the records. It's not a small thing. It's three hundred dollars' worth of food systematically disappearing from the store every week. About a hundred and fifty bagels, a few gallons of coffee, cream cheese and the occasional dessert. We're talking about brunch for a hundred. Every week. This is not some accidental misplacement of food. It's not spoilage or shoplifting. It's a real problem." She turned until her dark eyes were homing in on Jay.

What was she staring at him for? What had he done? He wasn't the one calling her Lady Macbeth.

"Three hundred dollars a week adds up over time. Beyond that, it's a mystery that needs solving." That she was staring at Jay was so obvious, the other people in the room turned to stare at him, too.

"What?" He threw his hands in the air. "What are you all looking at?"

"I've thought about it and thought about it, Uncle Jay," Julia explained. "I was trying to figure out who among us would be most likely to host a brunch for a hundred people every week."

Judith Arnold

"Not me! I hate entertaining. Ask Wendy. Ask Martha, too." He'd hated entertaining in both marriages. Of course, with Martha, entertaining had involved drinking fruit brandy that tasted like cough medicine and discussing philosophy with boring people she met on picket lines or in classes at the New School. Sometimes, when she got dangerously creative, she'd prepare stuffed grape leaves or chicken steamed in green tea. At least when Wendy entertained, they served regular booze and had the food catered by that fancy French place on Madison Avenue.

"Every week, you go to your country club to play golf," Julia pointed out. "That's where you were when I called you today, right?"

"So I golf on Sundays. Since when is that a crime?"

"And do you eat after you golf?"

"As a matter of fact, I do. *Goyishe* food, too—forgive me, Deirdre and…" He glanced toward Susie's boyfriend but the name didn't come to him. "Anyway, the food isn't to write home about. But it's better than what you put out for this meeting. I happen to be hungry right now."

"So if the food at your golf place isn't good," Julia intoned, leaning over the back of the chair, "it would make sense if you brought food with you, wouldn't it? Enough to share with the other members of the club?"

"What, you think I bring bagels to the country club? What are you, crazy? It's a *goyishe* club. What would they want with bagels?"

"Even non-Jews have taste buds," Deirdre remarked. "I'm Irish and I eat bagels."

"Because you work here. You've seen the light." Jay shook his head. If Julia truly believed he would tote a hundred-fifty bagels out to Long Island every week to share with the guys at the club, all those Wallaces and Pierponts and Van Der Horns, she was crazier than Lady Macbeth. "Julia, *bubeleh*. Use your head. A country club like that, they'd probably kick me out if I brought them bagels. They only let me join because Stuart Pinsky nominated me and he's less ethnic than I am."

"You know Stuart Pinsky?" Ron Joffe asked.

"He's my lawyer—and my friend," Jay said. "How do you know him?"

"His wife is my boss."

"That's right. She's a magazine editor. Small world." Jay smiled, although his brain suddenly felt overloaded. That Joffe had out of the blue decided to write about Bloom's—did Stuart's wife have anything to do with it? Jay had certainly told Stuart plenty about Bloom's. But everything he said to Stuart was lawyer-client, wasn't it? Confidential.

Not if they were having lunch together or playing golf. They weren't a lawyer and a client then. They were just friends.

What had he said to Stuart? If the magazine article was full of criticisms and insults, would anyone trace them back to Jay? For God's sake, he'd only been unloading on a friend. It wasn't as if he was a bagel thief or anything.

At last Julia released him from her stare. She peered at Joffe, who raised his eyebrows and nodded. What did he know? Jay wondered. Whatever it was, had he found it out through some slip of Jay's tongue? Was Jay's indiscretion—and Stuart's, the son of a bitch!—going to cause Bloom's to go under?

"Okay," Julia said, sounding a touch less sure of herself. "I'll accept Uncle Jay's statement for now—"

"Statement? What statement?" he erupted. "This isn't a courtroom, sweetie. You're not a lawyer in here. What exactly are you implying?"

"I'm implying that for now I'll assume you're not the one taking three hundred dollars' worth of brunch out of the store each week." She circled the room with her gaze, as if in search of culprits. "Who could it be? It's got to be someone in the store. Do you think it could be one of the clerks?"

"Why don't you accuse your mother?" Jay asked. "She loves food."

"I don't eat Bloom's food. It's too expensive. And too fattening," Sondra shot back. "She knows better than to ask me because she's eaten in my home for twenty-eight years. If I was going to steal three hundred dollars' worth of food a week, it would be cheese crackers from the grocery store down the block."

"This is true," Susie confirmed.

"Then, what about Deirdre? You just said you're Irish but you eat bagels."

"Not a hundred-fifty a week," Deirdre retorted. "Jay, you're the obvious one because you get together with a hundred people every week—on a Sunday morning when people would want to have brunch."

"She—" he pointed at Julia "—just said she considered me innocent."

"And I'm saying, maybe we've got a hung jury here," Deirdre argued.

"You sound pretty defensive," Jay retorted.

Deirdre's smile was bitter, and way too toothy. "The best defense is a good offense, huh?"

"Okay, okay!" Julia held up her hands like Gandhi trying to quell the rioting Indians. She glanced at Joffe again, silently questioning.

He shrugged. "It's your family."

"What's that supposed to mean?" Sondra asked. "Why are you even here, anyway? You're supposed to be writing a nice article about what a great place Bloom's is. The beauty of a family-owned establishment—"

"Yeah, it's a real beautiful thing." Joffe cut her off. "I'm here because at Ida Bloom's behest, I examined the books. And your daughter—your *president*—is right. There's something going on with this three hundred dollars' worth of brunch leaving the store every week, unaccounted for. You're all executives here. You're supposed to deal with things like this."

"I'm not an executive," Susie declared. "Just family."

Jay looked toward the desk, but he didn't sense so much heat between Susie and her boyfriend now. The guy looked...bored, maybe, and bemused about why he was there. Jay could have explained to him one of the immutable facts of life: sometimes a man had to sit through a lot of crap if he wanted to get laid.

Julia addressed Deirdre. "Did my father ever discuss a hundred brunches a week with you?"

"Why are you asking her?" Sondra blurted out. "Why don't you ask me? I was his wife."

Julia seemed momentarily rattled. "I asked Deirdre because it's a business matter, and she was the person he discussed business with."

"He discussed business with me," Sondra asserted.

"Okay. So did he ever mention a hundred brunches a week to you?"

"Of course not."

"He mentioned lots of things to me," Deirdre said archly.

Jesus. Things were getting weird. Jay couldn't believe he'd been dragged off the golf course for this—except that if he hadn't come it would have been worse. They would have assumed he'd failed to show because he was busy hosting some weekly Bloom's buffet at Emerald View Country Club.

"What, you think I don't know you and he were close?" Sondra leaned over Myron's lap to address Deirdre. Myron shrank back into the sofa cushions, looking as if he wished he could disappear like a hundred and fifty bagels. "You think I'm an idiot? You think I don't know you and Ben worked *very* closely?"

"I'd kill for a cup of coffee," Jay said, partly because he wanted to cut Sondra off before she flipped and partly because killing someone suddenly seemed like an appealing idea. He wasn't sure who the victim ought to be, but given the tension level in the room, a murder wouldn't be out of place. Even the lovebirds on the desk didn't look so loving anymore. Susie had propped her feet on the desk and bent her legs so she could hug her arms around her shins and rest her chin on her knees. She was all tied up into a little ball. And Loverboy looked as if he had a mouth full of sawdust. Julia was paler than usual—which was pretty damn pale—and the reporter was taking it all in. God help them if he was going to put any of this in his *Gotham* article.

"Mom," Julia said in an ameliorating voice. "Let's not go there."

"I'm not going anywhere," Sondra said, settling back into her side of the sofa. Myron looked measurably relieved. "All I want to say is, I was Ben's wife. The only wife he ever had, and the mother of his children. And he never mentioned anything about missing bagels to me."

"Nor to me," Deirdre muttered through clenched lips.

"Okay," Julia said with all the enthusiasm of a cheerleader whose team was down by a thousand points. "Is it possible someone downstairs might be filching three hundred dollars' worth of brunch every week? One of the cooks or clerks?"

"Anything's possible," Myron offered. A big help he was.

"You know," Susie said, her head bobbing with each word because she kept her chin pressed to her knees, "I can't believe the bagel department hasn't noticed anything strange. I mean, Casey, you and Morty run that department. I know you told me you didn't know anything about missing bagels, but how could you not notice? You keep track of what's being baked and what's being sold, don't you?"

Loverboy shifted, putting another inch between him and Susie. "We keep track," he confirmed. "But I don't know anything."

"Casey." Susie lifted her head so she could peer into his eyes. "You wouldn't lie to me, would you?"

He glanced away. "Look," he said quietly. "Okay? I've been sworn to secrecy."

"You *do* know?" Susie appeared shocked.

Julia moved in front of her chair. "You know, Casey? You see? I'm not a crackpot! I'm not crazy!"

"Who says you're not?" Myron retorted. "This guy's your character witness, and he's not talking."

"Please tell us, Casey," Julia implored.

Susie took another tack; she socked him in the arm, nearly

knocking him over. "You lied to me! I asked you about this weeks ago, and you said you had no idea."

"Because I was sworn to secrecy."

Julia stepped forward. "I'm the president of Bloom's, Casey. We're all family here—even Deirdre and Myron, in a way."

"He's not family," Jay observed, pointing to Joffe.

"He's my character witness," Julia declared, shooting the reporter a quick smile that raised the air's temperature again.

What was with Sondra's daughters? Both of them were in heat all of a sudden?

Julia turned back to Susie's boyfriend. "Do you want me to empty the room out? Do you want to tell just me?"

"That sounds like a plan," Jay said, starting to rise. Sondra sent him a scathing stare, and he sank back into his seat.

"I made a promise," Casey said. "Someone's taking the brunch food every week, and that person doesn't want anyone to know about it, so Morty and I have been covering."

"But we all do know about it," Julia argued. "Whoever this person is, he's stealing from Bloom's."

"No."

"He is. He's taking three hundred dollars' worth of food and not paying for it. That's theft."

"It's your grandmother," Casey said, then looked stricken. He leaped from the desk and stalked to the door. "Excuse me," he muttered, then stormed out, shutting the door behind him with a quiet click.

The silence he left in his wake was broken by Susie's springing down from the desk and racing after him, slamming the door on her way out.

More silence. "She's sleeping with him," Jay commented to Sondra. Saying that was a poor substitute for killing someone, and it wouldn't result in his getting a cup of coffee. But he was tired, it had been a long morning, he'd had a lousy, rainy eleven holes, and now this: his mother was stealing bagels. He decided he was no longer responsible for anything he said.

"What am I, an idiot?" Sondra grimaced. "What am I, blind?

You think I don't know what's going on in my family?" She gave the reporter an accusatory look. "It would have broken your heart to ask her out so she'd stop throwing herself away on a bagel man?"

"He's sleeping with me," Julia announced.

More silence. Jay gazed upon his niece with newfound respect. She had guts. He'd never realized that before. Maybe she'd never had them before. But now, after this whole *farkakteh* meeting, she was showing what she had, and he was impressed.

Sondra was obviously too stunned to speak, but Deirdre didn't have that problem. "Does this mean," she asked Joffe, "that you'll write a nice article about the store for your magazine?"

"I'll write a good article," he promised. "I don't do 'nice.'"

"Why do you suppose Grandma Ida has been stealing bagels from the store?" Julia wondered aloud.

"You'd better ask her," Joffe said.

They gazed at each other long enough for the room's temperature to fluctuate like a woman in the throes of menopause. Jay had been through that with Martha, and he hoped he never had to go through it again—although he supposed that if he stayed married to Wendy long enough, he would have to.

"I've got to go talk to Grandma Ida," Julia said. "This meeting is adjourned."

Joffe came upstairs with her, for which she was grateful. He'd already met Grandma Ida, he knew her, she trusted him for some reason, and anyway, Julia didn't think she could get through the experience of accusing her grandmother of stealing from the store without having someone by her side. Preferably someone smart, someone strong and someone who wasn't a Bloom.

Lyndon answered the door. "I'm sorry she missed your meeting," he said, exchanging an air kiss with Julia and then offering one of his patented sunbeam smiles. "Hello, Mr. Joffe!" He turned back to Julia. "She slept late today. She's only just finishing her breakfast now." He checked his watch and winced. "Lunch, I guess."

"Do you have any leftovers?" Julia asked, knowing the answer. She could smell the velvety aroma of coffee, the mellow fragrance of toasted breakfast pastries.

"A couple of bialys and a little herring in cream sauce. Are you hungry?"

Julia was tempted, but she had to take care of business first. She was the president of Bloom's, and she had to get through this confrontation. "Maybe we'll have a snack later. Let me talk to my grandmother."

"Lyndon, who is it?" Grandma Ida's voice drifted in from the dining room. "Not those people with the Chinese-restaurant menus again, is it?"

"It's your granddaughter," Lyndon shouted back, waving Julia and Joffe inside. Joffe brushed his hand against the small of Julia's back, a tiny touch, just enough to remind her that he was with her, supporting her.

Drawing in a breath, Julia headed for the dining room, Joffe and Lyndon behind her. Her grandmother sat at the head of the long table, her hair arranged in inky waves around her face, her eyes dark but clear.

"Julia," she said, as Julia circled the table and kissed her cheek. "Lyndon was just telling me you were having one of your meetings today. I slept terribly last night, though—I stayed up to watch an old Alfred Hitchcock movie. Hello, Mr. Joffe," she added. "Do you like Alfred Hitchcock?"

"Some of his movies. I thought *Psycho* was silly."

"Very silly, that dead lady in the rocking chair. With Anthony Perkins's voice, no less. A dead lady wouldn't have a man's voice, even if he talked all squeaky. What I saw last night was *Vertigo,* and it kept me up half the night. So Lyndon let me sleep until noon." She lifted her cup of coffee to her lips, then paused. "You're not hungry, are you? If you had one of your meetings, you must have had food."

"We didn't have time for food," Julia said. "But that's all right. Joffe and I had a nice breakfast."

"I'll get you some coffee," Lyndon offered.

Julia declined with a wave of her hand. "No, that's all right. Grandma, we need to talk."

"*Nu?* Sit down." She pointed to a chair.

Julia sat. Joffe sat next to her. His nearness helped. His nearness and her own sense of—not power but *rightness.* She was the president of Bloom's. The store was no longer just the legacy she'd inherited; it was the legacy she would leave to her heirs. It was hers to lead, to nurture, to build into something even more wonderful than it already was.

"Grandma. Tell me about the bagels you're stealing."

"Bagels? Stealing?"

"Your secret is out, Grandma. You've been stealing bagels, coffee and cream cheese from the store every week, to the tune of three hundred dollars."

"Who told you such a thing?"

"Someone from the bagel department—and he's very upset that I made him reveal your secret. Don't be angry with him, Grandma. *You* were the one who was stealing."

"*Oy,* what are you talking? I don't steal. I own the store. How can I steal what I own?"

"You've taken things without accounting for them. You do this every week, and all we have are numbers that don't add up. Why?"

"Why? You want to know why? I'll tell you why." Her eyes tightened as if they were screwing themselves deeper into her face. "It's none of your business, that's why."

"It *is* my business, Grandma. You made me the president of Bloom's. That makes it my business."

"What are you talking? I'm still the chairman."

"So what are you doing with all this stuff you're stealing every week?"

"Lyndon!" Grandma Ida hollered, the strength of her voice belying her age. "Lyndon, bring them some coffee. They need to eat. They need to fill their mouths with food."

"So we won't be able to talk?" Julia laughed. As recently as a couple of months ago, she would have been cowed by her grandmother's indignation, but now she wasn't. Nor was she angry. She was amused. Grandma Ida was actually pretty funny. "Grandma, tell me. I'm not going to get mad. I'm not going to fire you. I'm so glad we're not getting ripped off by some outsider, or by my mother or Uncle Jay——"

"You don't mind getting ripped off by your grandmother? Not that I'm doing that. Ripping off. I don't even know what it means."

"Tell me about the bagels, Grandma."

She sighed. She tapped her fingertips together. Her bracelets clattered. "There are people in this city," she said. "Old people. They aren't sick, they don't live in homes, in——what's the word, facilities? They live by themselves, they get by, they don't like to complain. But it's hard for them. Day to day, they get the pension check, the Social Security, but there's no money for anything special." Her grandmother tapped her fingers together again.

"I'm sure the city is filled with people like that," Julia murmured, since Grandmother Ida seemed to want her to say something.

"So, this agency comes to me and says, 'These people could enjoy a brunch from Bloom's once a week. You supply, we'll deliver.'"

"Grandma, that's lovely! Why on earth would you keep it a secret?"

"Why? You think I want every *schnorrer* in town looking to me for a handout? First it's the old people, then it's the new people. Then it's this group, it's that group, and the next thing, we're giving the whole store away."

"But why would you hide it from *us?* We're your family. Why keep it a secret from us?"

"You think there aren't any *schnorrers* in the family? Every time I see your cousin Ricky, he's asking me to invest in his film. What film? When he starts making films like Alfred Hitchcock I'll think about it. And your mother, wheedling her way into a job on your father's coattails. And Adam, your brother——

he doesn't dare to come right out and ask for money, but he writes me letters from college, telling me about the great concerts on campus, the Cornell jacket he wants to buy—too bad he hasn't got any money for these things. They're all *schnorrers,* Julia. The world is full of *schnorrers,* and the Bloom family is part of the world."

"But these people you provide a weekly brunch for, they're not *schnorrers?*"

"They're old," Grandma Ida said. "Not like me—they're *old.*"

Maybe giving old people free brunches made Grandma Ida feel superior to them. Maybe it made her feel younger. Or maybe she just felt a kinship with them, as strong as any kinship she felt toward her own flesh and blood.

"Grandma, I think it's beautiful that you're doing this. I only wish you had told me, so I wouldn't have spent the past few weeks having my family believe I'm insane because I kept insisting that bagels were disappearing from the store." She reached across the table to cover her grandmother's hand with her own. She couldn't remember ever squeezing Grandma Ida's hand that way before, but it was either squeeze her hand or burst into tears, and Grandma Ida had no patience for tears. "Tell me more. What's the name of the organization you work with? Where do the people who get the brunches live?"

Grandma Ida told her. The people lived all over the city, many of them alone. Some of them were shut-ins, others had nurses and companions during the week but were on their own during the weekends—which meant they didn't always eat right. The organization checked up on them, delivered Bloom's brunches to them, helped them out. Grandma Ida had been donating bagels for four years. Julia's father never knew about it. Neither did Deirdre. The only people who knew were the managers of the bagel and coffee departments. They were discreet. Nobody had caught on.

Until now. Until Julia had paid attention to the numbers, the inventory, the details. "Everyone thinks you fuss too much over the little things," Grandma Ida informed her. "Your mother, your uncle, Myron, everyone. What do you think?"

"I think the little things are important. What do *you* think? Do you regret having named me president?"

"Sometimes," Grandma Ida admitted somberly. "There are always regrets. You live to my age, you learn to put them aside and move on." She stared disapprovingly at Julia's hand covering hers, and Julia pulled it back. Then Grandma Ida peered past her at Joffe. "So, you're not going to get together with my granddaughter Susie, are you."

"I'm afraid not," he said, giving Julia's shoulder a caress.

"She's got a tattoo, that Susie. On her ankle." Grandma Ida clicked her tongue in disgust.

"Then, I guess I'll stick with the sister I have."

"You don't *have* me," Julia remarked sharply. "What do you think, I'm something you can *have?* Like—like a bagel? Or indigestion?"

"More like indigestion," he said. "Listen, I've got to go. I've got to do some more revisions on that damn article. My editor expects it on her desk first thing Monday."

"You're not going to write about this, are you?" Julia whispered, indicating Grandma Ida with a roll of her eyes.

"I'm a reporter, Julia. Trust me—the article is going to be great."

"She doesn't want anyone to know."

"She just told the whole story in front of a reporter. Isn't that right, Ida?" He gave her a suspiciously charming smile.

"I haven't decided if I like you yet," Grandma Ida warned him.

"You haven't decided if you like *me* yet," Julia commented.

Grandma Ida dismissed Joffe with a flutter of her hand. "You want to write an article? Go. Write. No one's going to read it, anyway."

"That's probably true," Joffe said, pushing himself to his feet. "I really should leave. Julia?"

"I think I'll stay a while." She glanced at Grandma Ida, half expecting the woman to suggest that she depart with Joffe. But Grandma Ida said nothing.

Joffe seemed to understand. "Will I see you later?" he asked.

"Maybe. If you're suitably contrite and you bring me stuffed cabbage."

He planted a kiss on her lips, light but full of promise.

Julia heard his muffled exchange of farewells with Lyndon and then the front door closing after him. She turned back to her grandmother, wanting to laugh, wanting to weep, wanting to squeeze her hand again. "I don't know why you think I'm anything like you," she murmured.

"It's the nose. Whatever you do, don't ever change your nose the way your mother did."

"Okay."

"You love that boy?" She gestured at Joffe's empty chair.

"I'm afraid so."

Grandma Ida sniffed. "Well, he's probably no worse than that lawyer you were seeing."

"He's better, Grandma. Much better."

"Even if he puts all my secrets in his magazine for all the world to see?"

"I love you, Grandma." It was the first time Julia had ever uttered those words. But this was the first time she'd ever glimpsed the kindness inside Grandma Ida, so carefully hidden beneath layers of brusqueness. "It wouldn't be such a terrible thing if all the world found out that you were nice."

"You don't know what you're talking." Grandma Ida sniffed and settled back in her chair. "You hungry? Lyndon could fix you a little something. We've got maybe some stollen, you want a piece?"

"Stollen? From the store?"

"From where else? Lyndon," Grandma Ida bellowed. "Bring Julia some stollen. She needs to eat."

Julia smiled. There were so many things she used to need that she now had in ample supply: confidence, backbone, hot sex with a man she could count on, even if he exasperated the hell out of her sometimes…and her grandmother. She had her grandmother now.

But she always needed to eat. And she certainly wasn't about to say no to a piece of stollen from Bloom's.

Epilogue

"Come here often?" a warm, male voice murmured behind Julia.

Smiling, she turned to find Joffe sidling up to her. He looked weary but triumphant, as well he should. Making his way from the cheese department to the olive oil department in this crowd must have been a challenge on the order of scaling Annapurna.

Julia had not anticipated that Bloom's first singles' night would be such a hit. True, Susie's write-up in the *Bloom's Bulletin* had been enticing. And the Upper West Side teemed with singles the way a landfill teemed with flies. The new look Susie had been gradually imposing on the store helped, too. After her success with the display windows, Julia had bestowed upon her sister the title of creative director and set her to work on the store's interior. "Don't make it hip," Julia had instructed. "Just make it hipp*er.*"

"Gotcha," Susie had said, and in the month since she'd begun simplifying the shelf displays and reducing the clutter, the store did look hipper. Not hip. Never hip. Bloom's needed an aura of nostalgia to work, an Old World, immigrant-grandparent feel. Immigrant grandparents might be cool, but they weren't hip.

Susie deserved an enormous amount of credit for making Bloom's first singles' night a success. So did Joffe. His cover story in *Gotham Magazine,* which had appeared just a week ago, had attracted far more interest in the store than Julia would have expected. In fact, when she'd read it, her heart had twinged with dread. Joffe had put nearly everything into the damn piece.

Nearly everything. He hadn't mentioned her father's adultery. He did mention, though, that the late Ben Bloom had a reputation as a cold, aloof man whose passion was channeled into his store. Not the nicest thing anyone had ever said about Julia's father. But, as Susie had commented, "What did you expect Joffe to do, lie?"

He hadn't lied. He'd described Julia as earnest and hardworking, which made her sound like a drone, but he'd also said she had beautiful eyes and a great sense of humor, and that she'd turned Bloom's not upside down but sideways, which were her own words and pretty accurate. He'd treated her mother and Uncle Jay more gently than he'd had to, and he'd written so many nice things about Susie's whimsical taste and forward-thinking ideas that Sondra commented that she thought he might just be a little sweet on her.

"Yeah," Joffe had assured Julia when she'd questioned him about that. "I think she'd make a sweet sister-in-law."

"Are you asking me to marry you?"

"I said, *I think*. I'm thinking about it."

"Well, let me know when you're done thinking."

Susie did not think Joffe would make a sweet brother-in-law. "He's a lot of things, Julia, but I wouldn't put *sweet* on the list of adjectives. He's brainy, he's pushy, he's kind of arrogant—"

"He's gorgeous," Julia had supplied.

"Nice body," Susie had agreed. "Awfully verbal."

"He's a writer. Verbs are his business."

"He invests his money wisely."

"It's that MBA," Julia had explained. "He's very sharp about finances."

"And according to you, he's good in bed," Susie had summed up. "Go for it, Julia. He's great. But he's not sweet. Not the way Casey is."

She was behind the bagel counter with Casey right now. Morty had opted to leave at his usual time—five o'clock—claiming he was too old for singles' night, as well as too married. Casey had insisted he could handle the bagel counter solo, but Susie had decided to don an apron and help him anyway. She just wanted to be with him, she told Julia. "Isn't it weird? It's like, I want to be with him even when he's dressed."

From where Julia stood, near platters of babka and carrot cake and chocolate halvah cut into bite-size chunks, she could see Susie and Casey. He towered over her sister, his hair was longer than hers, he was pale and Waspy—"He's a lapsed Catholic, not a WASP," Susie had told her—and she was petite and dark and had the pronounced Bloom nose. But they looked good together. Very good.

Music hummed through the air, a tape Susie had put together with input from cousin Rick and Deirdre, of all people, in a meeting outside Julia's office. She'd taken to leaving the door open on occasion, because there were advantages to knowing what everyone was talking about. With the music, Susie had originally recommended that they play only klezmer music. Deirdre had worried that it would be too ethnic. "We don't want people thinking they're at a bar mitzvah," she'd said.

"Klezmer is so cheerful, though," Susie had argued. "You'll get people dancing in the aisles."

"Klezmer is fun, but it's not romantic," Deirdre had maintained. "A little goes a long way."

"If you want people dancing," Rick had suggested, "I could make a tape of some good dance cuts. I know this guy who's a deejay downtown. He could help me put something together."

"Go with Harry Connick Jr.," Deirdre had declared.

"Harry Connick Jr.? Are you kidding?"

Rick had cast his vote with Deirdre. "I think she's right. He's got lively numbers and moody numbers. I once seduced this seriously cute chick with a little help from Harry."

So tonight Harry Connick Jr. was crooning in the background, audible but not loud enough to compete with the din of conversation in the crowded store, and Rick cruised the crowds, presumably hoping Harry would bring him more luck with a seriously cute chick. Julia had heard him ask Susie several times if either of her roommates was planning to show up at Bloom's tonight, and she'd insisted neither was coming. "You'll have to set your sights on someone new," she'd told him.

Rick wasn't the only one cruising, of course. Hundreds of people wandered up and down the aisles, nibbling on cheese, crackers, bagels and pastries, sipping nonalcoholic wine from tiny plastic cups, chatting and flirting and eyeing one another with expressions ranging from icy disdain to fiery lust. Julia would estimate the average age of the evening's participants to be early thirties, but she also noticed people younger and older. The elderly man who always got into arguments with his wife about whether to buy the economy-size breadstick package was there—without his wife. He was chatting up the kvetchy woman who liked her bagels superfresh.

Julia grinned, even though the lawyer inside her wondered whether Bloom's would be named as a co-respondent in any divorces that might result from singles' night.

She spotted a couple of new arrivals, one older and one younger than the median age. They were both single, and she was delighted to see them. "Look, there're my mother and brother," she said, nudging Joffe and pointing to Sondra and Adam as they meandered through the milling crowd. "You should meet Adam. He'd make a very sweet brother-in-law."

Joffe laughed and dropped a light kiss on her lips. "Okay, let's go meet Adam."

They eased their way among the pastry-devouring hordes,

and they got briefly tangled up with a group of three men playing a social version of musical chairs with two women, the men
all competing to avoid being the odd one out. But eventually
Julia and Joffe made it past that little interaction, past the pickle
display and over to the coffee department, where Sondra was
explaining to Adam the different beans, as if she were an expert. "Arabica," she said to him. "Great stuff. Have you ever had
Arabica?"

"I really don't know," he confessed, looking sheepish. He always looked sheepish, a little bewildered, a little panicked. His
boyish face seemed chronically frozen in an expression that said,
How did I get here? Can I leave now?

He didn't seem to want to bolt, though. He nodded obedi-
ently as Sondra moved from Arabica to Sumatra. He'd just finished taking his finals at Cornell. Maybe he was still in study
mode, boning up in case his mother decided to surprise him
tomorrow with a pop quiz on roasts and blends.

"Hey, stranger," Julia greeted him. She hadn't seen him since
Passover. He'd only arrived home from Ithaca yesterday
evening, and according to her mother, he'd intended to sleep
all day today, so Julia thought it best not to ride the elevator
upstairs during her lunch break to say hello to him.

He spun around and grinned. "Hey! What's up?"

"Welcome to singles' night. You want to pick someone up?"

"Yeah, sure." He laughed. "Mom dragged me here."

"I didn't drag you," Sondra protested. "I simply said you
ought to come and have a look."

"I'm looking. This is great, Julia."

"I want you to meet Ron Joffe. He's thinking about marrying me, but he's afraid of having a bunch of Blooms as his
in-laws."

"I don't blame you," Adam murmured, shaking Joffe's hand.

"So where's your grandmother?" Sondra asked. "Is she coming tonight?"

"Lyndon said he'd try to bring her," Julia said. "You know
she's not crazy about crowds, though."

"Let me go call upstairs," Sondra said, weaving a narrow path through the crowd to the head cashier's counter, which boasted a phone.

Adam leaned in toward Julia. "You and Susie have really done some cool things with this place."

"Cool but not hip. That's our motto," Julia joked.

"Well, I'm thinking…like, maybe you're hiring for summer jobs?"

"Do you want to work here?"

"I don't know." He shrugged. "Ithaca's kind of dead in the summer, and that girl I was seeing is spending the summer in Seattle, so I was thinking maybe I could hang out here, stock shelves or something."

Julia impulsively flung her arms around him. "Welcome to the business, brother. Of course you can stock shelves."

"Hey, if you're gonna be that way…" He backed off and blushed. "I mean, I'm not joining the business, okay? All I said was, just for the summer."

"Of course." Given that he'd spent most of his life swearing he never wanted to get absorbed by Bloom's, the prospect of his joining the payroll, even if only for a summer job stocking shelves, represented a significant change of heart. Julia savored the moment but refrained from hugging him again. She didn't want to scare him away.

"I guess I should go say hi to Susie," he said.

Glancing toward the bagel counter, Julia noticed a cute young woman with a prominent chest purchasing a pumpernickel bagel. She grinned and gave him a nudge. "Definitely. Go say hi to Susie."

Alone with Joffe at the coffee counter, she let out a breath. "Do you think my grandmother will come?"

"Why not? She's single."

"She's pissed at you."

Joffe looked affronted. "Why?"

"Because of what you wrote about her in your article." He'd written that Ida Bloom was crusty and bossy and mule-headed, and that she didn't want anyone to know about her donation of a hundred brunches of Bloom's food each week to needy elders around the city because it would ruin her reputation. "She said you misrepresented her. The only reason she didn't want anyone to know about her generosity was that she didn't want to get taken advantage of."

"Bullshit," Joffe retorted, although he was still smiling. "No one has ever taken advantage of her, and no one ever will. She just doesn't want anyone to realize she has a soft side."

"She doesn't," Julia insisted. "She's very tough."

Joffe's smile evolved into a laugh. "Oh, yeah, she's tough. Just like you."

"I'm very tough," Julia insisted. "I'm exactly like her. She tells me that all the time."

He shut her up with a kiss deep enough to remind her that she did indeed have a soft side. She'd always worried that she was too soft, actually, too eager to fix everything and make everyone happy. Not anymore. She'd gotten tougher. More like Grandma Ida, tough and soft combined.

"Looks like at least one happy couple is going to come out of this singles' night," someone in the crowd that swarmed around the coffee department remarked.

Yes, thought Julia as she returned Joffe's kiss, it certainly looked that way.

*Judith Arnold invites you to read more about the Bloom family—
especially Susie Bloom—in her upcoming novel*
Blooming All Over.

*Available from MIRA Books
July 2004*

Prologue

Bloom's Bulletin
Written and edited by
Susie Bloom

*A fellow addicted to knishes
Found at Bloom's all his favorite dishes.
   He bought bagels, a blintz
   And some stuffed cabbage, since
Bloom's cuisine fulfills all his wishes!*

Welcome to the May 14 edition of *Bloom's Bulletin,* which is jam-packed with tasty tidbits, recipes and—of course!—news about sales and specials throughout the store. Bloom's has become the most famous kosher-style food emporium not just on Manhattan's Upper West Side but all over the world by fulfilling our customers' wishes.

All over the world? Believe it. Jay Bloom is the director of Bloom's Internet and Mail-Order Services, which

Judith Arnold

distributes Bloom's Seder-in-a-Box, a package containing matzo, gefilte fish, horseradish, *charoset,* chicken soup with matzo balls, salt and Haggadahs—just add eggs, wine and an entrée for a complete seder. According to Jay, by mid-April, the store had filled Seder-in-a-Box orders from thirty-seven states and fifteen foreign countries, among them Finland, Japan, South Africa, New Zealand, Bolivia and…are you ready?…the research station at the South Pole! Yes, Bloom's has extended its reach into Antarctica. When an order arrived from the McMurdo Station on Ross Island, Bloom's was able to get four Seder-in-a-Boxes prepared and ready for delivery by the New York Air National Guard, which serves the U.S. Antarctic Program. The seders arrived in time for the holiday, along with two complimentary bottles of Passover wine, Bloom's gift to the intrepid researchers who live and work at the South Pole. Good *yontif!*

Feeling bleu?

French cheeses are specially priced all this week at Bloom's. Camembert, Port Salut, Brie, Roquefort—come on in, buy some cheese and keep the change!

Did you know…

The word *schmaltz,* which is used to describe music or a story that's overly sentimental, is derived from the Yiddish word *schmaltz,* which means congealed fat. In Ida Bloom's day, chicken *schmaltz* spread on a slice of dark pumpernickel was considered a gourmet treat. These days, the mere thought of it is enough to give most people heartburn. If you're in the mood for *schmaltz,* listening to Rachmaninoff is a whole lot healthier.

Employee profile:

Who's that tall-blond-and-handsome fellow standing behind the bagel counter? None other than Casey Gordon, comanager of the bagels department. Casey studied at the Culinary Institute of America before transferring to St. John's University, where he earned a degree in English. Ask nicely, and he might just recite a little Shakespeare while he counts a dozen sesame-seed bagels into a bag for you.

Since joining the Bloom's staff three years ago, Casey has put his culinary-school experience to work by designing a variety of new flavors of bagels. Thanks to him, Bloom's sells pesto bagels, cranberry bagels, apple-cinnamon bagels and sour-yogurt bagels, along with the standard plain, egg, garlic and poppy-seed varieties. "Some flavors rotate in and out," Casey says. "Some are interesting experiments that just don't click. Others become very popular, so we make them a permanent addition to our inventory." Among those that didn't "click" he mentioned curry bagels and banana-cream bagels. His most recent surprise hit? Dill pickle bagels, which customers seem to love.

When he's not dreaming up sensational new bagel flavors, Casey says he likes to play basketball, analyze movies and spend time with his girlfriend. What's her favorite kind of bagel? "Egg," Casey reports. "But she's adventurous. She'll try anything."

Wise words from Bloom's founder, Ida Bloom:

"There's a reason for everything, but some reasons are stupid."

On sale this week:

Pita crisps, all varieties of blintzes, smoked sable and more.